6/93

WAR REPORTS FROM
BATTLESTATION

Transmitted by . . .

David Drake
FACING THE ENEMY

The mission:
Capture an alien monster—and become one!

Mike Resnick and Barbara Delaplace
TRADING UP

Interstellar war is bad for business—or is it?

Steve Perry
BLIND SPOT

On a warship with a crew of thousands,
murder is inevitable. So are detectives.

AND MANY OTHERS!

BATTLESTATION

BOOK ONE

EDITED BY **DAVID DRAKE** AND **BILL FAWCETT**

ACE BOOKS, NEW YORK

Prologue and Interludes copyright © 1992 by Bill Fawcett & Associates.
"Facing the Enemy" copyright © 1992 by David Drake.
"Trading Up" copyright © 1992 by Mike Resnick and Barbara Delaplace.
"Globin's Children" copyright © 1992 by Christopher Stasheff.
"The Eyes of Texas" copyright © 1992 by S. N. Lewitt.
"Starlight" copyright © 1992 by Jody Lynn Nye.
"Comrades" copyright © 1992 by S. M. Stirling.
"Gung Ho" copyright © 1992 by Judith R. Conly.
"Blind Spot" copyright © 1992 by Steve Perry.
"The Stand on Luminos" copyright © 1992 by Robert Sheckley.
"Killer Cure" copyright © 1992 by Diane Duane.
"A Transmigration of Soul" copyright © 1992 by Paradise Productions.

This book is an Ace original edition, and has never
been previously published.

BATTLESTATION

An Ace Book / published by arrangement with
Bill Fawcett & Associates

PRINTING HISTORY
Ace edition / July 1992

All rights reserved.
Copyright © 1992 by Bill Fawcett & Associates.
Cover art by Bob Eggleton.
This book may not be reproduced in whole or
in part, by mimeograph or any other means, without
permission. For information address: The Berkley Publishing Group,
200 Madison Avenue, New York, New York 10016.

ISBN: 0-441-04878-1

Ace Books are published by The Berkley Publishing Group,
200 Madison Avenue, New York, New York 10016.
The name "ACE" and the "A" logo are trademarks
belonging to Charter Communications, Inc.

PRINTED IN THE UNITED STATES OF AMERICA

10 9 8 7 6 5 4 3 2 1

SC
BAT

for Peter Heck
      Welcome Aboard

for Brendan
      Another Survivor

CONTENTS

BATTLESTATION

PROLOGUE

"HAVEN'T THOSE GUYS ever heard about noise pollution?" grumbled the tech, reaching up to adjust the volume on his monitors. The sound of the intruder's warp drive lowered from a deafening howl to a merely unbearable screech.

"Well, at least we know they aren't trying to sneak up on us," said the ensign, peering over his shoulder.

They still hadn't managed to pinpoint the origin of the approaching ship, but this didn't bother either of the two men on bridge watch on the Fleet Cruiser *Peter the Great*. Schlein Epsilon was technically a frontier world, but there hadn't been any combat within parsecs since the end of the Family war, decades earlier. Very few of their stellar neighbors were brave or foolish enough to challenge the two thousand worlds of the Alliance. Whoever was responsible for building the mistuned warp drive, odds were they hadn't come looking for trouble.

Three minutes later, the still-unidentified ship had dropped into normal space and was entering the system at a large fraction of the speed of light.

"They'd better brake soon," said the tech. The ship's course would take it directly into this system's star. Almost as if it had heard him, the intruder began to slow. The dials and visual displays of the control panel changed to reflect the new type of energy the intruding ship emitted as its magnetic drive attempted to reduce its velocity.

"*Merde alors!*" exclaimed the ensign, reverting to his native

1

language. He pointed to a readout. "Does that mean what I think it does?"

"Yeah, their sublight drive just died," confirmed the tech. His fingers moved in a blur, adjusting the readings from one dial to another. Suddenly he stopped and turned toward the younger man who was his superior officer. "We have maybe three minutes to start moving for an intercept, or we don't need to bother."

The young ensign thought quickly. It would take at least two minutes to get the *Peter*'s own magnetic drive operating. More likely longer, since there was only a skeleton watch on duty in Engineering. There wasn't even time to ask the captain. If he misjudged this one, it was bye-bye to his career. Maybe he'd get lucky and find out that the unknown was some Alliance senator's private yacht.

"Get us moving," he ordered, trying to sound confident. "And sound general quarters." That would bring the captain at a run. As they moved to save the unknown ship, the ensign kept trying to match its energy profile and appearance to any known design. He kept coming up with blanks. After the successful, nearly routine interception and rescue, the reason why became obvious: the intruder was a type of ship no human had ever seen before, not even in the age of the last Great Empire.

The ship turned out to have come from virtually the center of the galaxy, from the thick "donut" of tightly packed stars surrounding the massive black hole at the galactic center. This area, known as Star Central, had hundreds of races on as many planets, many of them separated by only fractions of a light-year. Despite the closeness of civilized worlds, there was neither a united government nor any real military tradition: the few more aggressive races had either emigrated or killed one another off ages ago. Nor, with the stars so closely packed, had there been any need to develop an efficient warp drive. So when three races embarked on a desperate mission out along the spiral arm in which the Alliance was located, they had to rely upon an experimental drive that no Fleet mechanic would have allowed out of the shop. It was the highest achievement of their technology.

When scientists finally established communications with the three races of aliens aboard their unarmed ship, the reason for their nearly suicidal mission became clear. A race known as the Ichtons had recently emerged from another spiral arm and begun attacking the Central worlds. Little was known of these invaders, except that once they conquered a world they stripped it of every possible resource—including every living creature. One of fifty ships sent out from the beleaguered Gerrond home world, the ship had brought with it hundreds of hours of records and tapes of ravaged worlds to bolster their plea for assistance. Originally, they had hoped to find help closer to Star Central. But as they made their way up the spiral arm, they found the Ichtons had been there before them, pillaging and leaving whole worlds wasted in their wake. In desperation, the mixed crew had continued outward in hopes of finding anyone that might stand against the Ichtons. And thus they came to the Alliance—and the Fleet.

They were met with a mixed reaction. It had been almost fifty years since the Family war, but citizens of the Alliance worlds still paid its cost through their taxes. The defeated Family worlds had been absorbed, as well, so the war debts for both sides had to be paid. Now these strange aliens were asking the Fleet to take on an even greater enemy, one that was not yet a danger to any Alliance world. The ensuing political debate was heated and divisive.

One side argued that the Ichtons would not be a threat for centuries to come, if ever. Their opponents pointed out that each new conquest would increase the Ichtons' strength. With the resources of the densely populated galactic core, Star Central, at their command, they would be unbeatable when the confrontation finally came. And, of course, a few politicians suspected a trap, and openly doubted whether there were any Ichtons at all.

Inevitably, the final decision was a compromise. A number of ships were sent on the months-long journey to Star Central, using charts provided by the aliens. As always, the Fleet's task began with the gathering of needed intelligence.

FACING
THE ENEMY
by David Drake

1.

OVAL MEMBRANES ALONG the Ichton's lateral lines throbbed as the creature writhed against the table restraints. Two audio speakers flanked the observation screen that Sergeant Dresser watched in the room above. One speaker keened at the edge of ultrasound, while a roll of low static cracked through the other.

"What's the squeaking?" Dresser asked tensely.

"Just noise," said Tech 4 Rodriges, looking up from his monitor. "Moaning, I guess you'd say. Nothing for the translation program"—he nodded toward the hissing second speaker—"to translate."

He hoped Dresser wasn't going to nut, because the fella didn't have any business being here. That was how the brass would think, anyway. So long as the Ichton was alone, Rodriges's job was to flood it with knock-out gas if something went wrong. That didn't seem real likely; but if the creature damaged its *so*-valuable body, there'd be hell to pay.

Dresser's lips were dry, but he wiped his palms on the thighs of his fresh utilities. The uniform felt light compared to the one he'd worn during the most recent mission on *SB 781*. The scout boat's recycling system had cleaned away sweat and body oils after every watch, but there wasn't anything machines could do about the fear that the cloth absorbed just as surely. . . .

That was thinking crazy. Had to stop that *now*.

4

"Don't worry," he said aloud. "I'm fine."

"Sure an ugly bastard," Rodriges commented in a neutral voice.

Upright, the Ichton would be the better part of three meters tall. The creature's gray body was thin, with a waxy glow over the exoskeleton beneath. By contrast, the six limbs springing from the thorax had a fleshy, ropy texture, though they were stiffened internally by tubes of chitin. Now they twitched against invisible restraints.

"First good look I really had of him," Dresser said softly. "Of it."

He wasn't sure how he felt. He wiped his hands again.

"Huh?" said Rodriges in amazement. "But—it was you caught him, right? I mean—you know, the real one. Wasn't . . . ?"

Light winked from the Ichton's faceted eyes as the creature turned its head mindlessly from one side to the other.

"Hey, no sweat," Dresser said. A grin quirked a corner of his mouth. The first thing that had struck him funny for—

From since they'd made landfall a month and a half ago. Rodriges thought the Ichton *looked* ugly, but he hadn't seen what the creatures did. . . .

The Ichton on the screen relaxed. One speaker squealed plaintively; the other asked in an emotionless voice, "Where . . . ? Where am I?"

"Sure, that was us," Dresser said. "*SB 781,* not just me; but my boat, my crew, you bet. Only you don't . . . I didn't really look at it, you know? Bundled it up and slung it into a stasis field before we bugged out. Scout boats don't have what you'd call great passenger accommodations."

A separate chirping punctuated the sounds the Ichton made. In a voice identical to that provided for the prisoner, the translator said, "Please relax. The restraints are simply to prevent you from injuring yourself upon waking. When you relax, we will loosen them."

"That's Admiral Horwarth, the project head," Rodriges said knowingly. "Don't know jack shit about medicine or biochem, but she sure can make a team of prima donna medicos get on with the program."

Dresser was lost in memory. He said, "When we landed, I was watching on my screen, and there was this city, a Gerson city it turned out. . . ."

Thomson was at the center console, watching the ground swing toward *SB 781* with the leisured assurance of a thrown medicine ball. Occasionally her fingers scissored over the controls without touching them.

The approach was nerve-wrackingly slow, but that was the way it had to be. Staying out of Ichton warning sensors was the only way the scout boat was going to survive. The turbulence and friction heat of a fast approach would have pointed a glowing finger straight toward them.

"Lookit that sucker!" muttered Codrus.

Dresser and Codrus didn't bother to back up Thomson, but the chance that she would have to take over from the boat's artificial intelligence was a million to one—and the chance that a human could do any good if the AI failed was a lot worse than that.

Codrus was watching the nearest Ichton colony, a vast pimple of blue light projecting kilometers into the stratosphere. Ichton strongholds began as hemispheres of magnetic force. The flux was concentrated enough to sunder the molecular bonds of projectiles and absorb the full fury of energy weapons. As each colony grew, the height of its shield decreased in relation to the diameter.

This colony was already a hundred kilometers across. It would not stop growing until its magnetic walls bulged against those of other Ichton fortresses.

Lookit that sucker.

The scout boat quivered and bobbed as the AI subtly mimicked the patterns of clear air turbulence, but the computer-enhanced view on Dresser's screen remained rock solid. It had been a city of moderate size—perhaps fifteen thousand inhabitants if human density patterns were applicable.

The buildings tended to rounded surfaces rather than planes. The palette was of earth tones, brightened by street paving of brilliant yellow. From a distance, the soft lines and engaging ambiance of the city as it originally stood would have suggested a field of edible mushrooms.

The tallest of the surviving structures rose about ten meters. The ragged edges in which the tower now ended were the result of Ichton weapons.

A column of Ichtons had passed through the community. The invaders' weapons, derivatives of their defensive shields, had blasted a track across the center of the inhabited area and gnawed apart most of the rest of the city as well.

"Hang on," warned Thomson.

"What gets me," said Dresser, "is they didn't attack the place. It was just there, and they went through it rather than going around."

"They took out major urban centers with antimatter bombs," Codrus said. "Musta had a scale of what they blitzed and what they ignored unless it got in the way. Of course—"

"Touchdown!" Thomson said.

SB 781 fluffed her landing jets—hard twice, while there were still twenty meters of air beneath the boat's belly, then a softer, steady pulse that disturbed the soil as little as possible. No point in inserting stealthily through a hundred kilometers of atmosphere and then kick up a plume of dirt like a locating flag.

"—sooner or later, they cover the whole land surface, so I don't guess they worry about when they get around t' this piece or that."

The scout boat shuddered to a halt that flung Dresser against his gel restraints. His display continued to glow at him with images of the wrecked city, enhanced to a crispness greater than what his eyes would have showed him at the site.

Ichton weapons fired beads the size of matchheads that generated expanding globes of force. Individual weapons had a range of only three hundred meters or so, but their effect was devastating—particularly near the muzzle, where the density of the magnetic flux was high. The force globes acted as atomic shears, wrenching apart the molecules of whatever they touched. Even at maximum range, when the flux formed an iridescent ball a meter in diameter, it could blast the fluff off the bodies of this planet's furry natives.

Dresser was sure of that, because some of the Ichtons' victims still lay in the ruins like scorched teddy bears.

"They're Gersons," Dresser said to his crew. "The natives here. One of the races that asked the Alliance for help."

"Too late for that," Codrus muttered. His slim, pale hands played over the controls, rotating the image of the Ichton fortress on his display. From any angle, the blue glare was as perfect and terrible as the heart of a supernova. "Best we get our asses back to the *Hawking* and report."

This was Dresser's first mission on *SB 781*; the previous team leader had wangled a commission and a job in Operations. Thomson and Codrus came with the boat . . . and they were an item, which sometimes worked and sometimes didn't.

It didn't work on *SB 781*. Both partners were too worried about what might happen to the other to get on with the mission.

"Not till we've done our jobs," Dresser said softly. He raised the probes, hair-thin optical guides that reeled out to the height of twenty meters above *SB 781*'s camouflaged hull. His display immediately defaulted to real-time images of a wind-sculpted waste.

The immediate terrain hadn't been affected by the Ichton invasion—yet. Eventually it too would be roofed by flux generators so powerful that they bent light and excluded the blue and shorter wavelengths entirely. Within their impregnable armor, the Ichtons would extract ores—the rock had a high content of lead and zinc—and perhaps the silicon itself. The planet the invaders left would be reduced to slag and ash.

Thomson tried to stretch in the narrow confines of her seat. Her hands trembled, though that might have been reaction to the tension of waiting above the flight controls against the chance that she'd have to take over. "No job we can do here," she said. "This place is gone. *Gone*. It's not like we've got room t' take back refugees."

Dresser modified his display. The upper half remained a real-time panorama. The glow of an Ichton colony stained the eastern quadrant in a sickly blue counterfeit of the dawn that was still hours away. The lower portion of the display became a map created from data *SB 781*'s sensors gathered during insertion.

"Command didn't send us for refugees," he said. He tried to keep his voice calm, so that his mind would become calm as well. "They said to bring back a live prisoner."

"We *can't* get a prisoner!" Codrus said, maybe louder than he'd meant. "Anything that'd bust open these screens—"

He gestured toward the Ichton fortress on his display. His knuckles vanished within the holographic ambiance, then reappeared like the head of a bobbing duck.

"—'d rip the whole planet down to the core and let *that* out. The place is fucked, and we need to get away!"

"They're still sending out colonies," Dresser said.

His fingers raised the probes ten meters higher and shrank the image area to five degrees instead of a full panorama. The upper display shuddered. The blue glow filled most of its horizon.

Five Ichton vehicles crawled across terrain less barren than that in which the scout boat hid. Trees grew in serpentine lines along the boundaries of what must once have been cultivated fields. For the most part, the land was now overgrown with brush.

"About twenty klicks away," Dresser continued. He felt the eyes of his subordinates burning on him; but he was in charge, and *SB 781* was going to carry out its mission. "We'll take the skimmers and set up an ambush."

"Take the boat," Thomson said through dry lips. "We'll want the firepower."

Dresser shook his head without taking his eyes off his display. "The boat'd get noticed," he said. "You guys'll be in hard suits with APOT weapons. That'll be as much firepower as we need."

"Lookit that!" Codrus cried, pointing across the cockpit to Dresser's display. "Lookit that!"

A family of Gersons bolted from the row of trees just ahead of the Ichton column. There were four adults, a pair of half-grown children, and a furry infant in the arms of the female struggling along behind the other adults.

The turret of the leading vehicle rotated to follow the refugees. . . .

"You okay, Sarge?" Rodriges asked worriedly.

Dresser crossed his arms and kneaded his biceps hard.

"Yeah," he said. "Sure." His voice was husky. "Seein' the thing there—"

He nodded toward the screen. The Ichton was sitting upright. The voice from the speaker said, "Don't try to use your conscious mind to control your muscles. You wouldn't with your own body, after all."

"You can't imagine how cruel they are, the Ichtons," Dresser said.

"Naw, it's not cruel," the technician explained. "You're only cruel to something you think about. The bugs, they treat the whole universe like we'd treat, you know, an outcrop of nickel ore."

"So cruel . . ." Dresser whispered.

The Ichton's tympanic membranes shrilled through the left speaker. The translation channel boomed, "Where the hell am I? Thomson? Codrus! What's happened to my boat!"

Sergeant Dresser closed his eyes.

"Where's *781*, you bastards?" demanded the Ichton through the machine voice.

2.

"The subbrain of your clone body will control the muscles, Sergeant Dresser," said the voice from a speaker in the wall. "You can't override the hardwired controls, so just relax and let them do their job."

The words were compressed and harshly mechanical; the room's lighting spiked chaotically on several wavelengths. Were they torturing him?

Who were *they*?

"Where's my crew?" Dresser shouted. He threw his feet over the edge of the couch on which he had awakened. His legs splayed though he tried to keep them steady. He collapsed on his chest. The floor was resilient.

"Your men are all right, Sergeant," the voice said. The speaker tried to be soothing, but the delivery rasped like a saw on bone. "So is your human self. Your memory will return in a few minutes."

Memory was returning already. Memory came in disorienting

sheets that didn't fit with the real world. Images that Dresser remembered were sharply defined but static. They lacked the texturing of incipient movement that wrapped everything Dresser saw through the faceted eyes of his present body.

But he remembered. . . .

The male Gerson—the tallest, though even he was less than a meter-fifty in height—turned and raised an antitank rocket launcher. The rest of the family blundered past him. The juveniles were hand in hand, and the female with the infant still brought up the rear.

"Where'd he get hardware like that?" Codrus muttered. "I'd've figured the teddy bears were down to sharp sticks, from the way things look."

The Ichton vehicles moved on air cushions; they didn't have the traction necessary to grind through obstacles the way tracked or even wheeled transport could. The leader's turret weapon spewed a stream of projectiles like a ripple of light. The hedgerow disintegrated in bright flashes.

"They sent a starship to the Alliance, after all," Dresser muttered. "The ones left behind still have some weapons, is all."

Brush and splintered wood began to burn sluggishly. The leading Ichton vehicle nosed into the gap.

"Much good it'll do them," said Thomson.

The Gerson fired. The rocket launcher's flaring yellow backblast enveloped twenty meters of brush and pulsed the hedge on the other side of the field. The hypervelocity projectile slammed into the Ichton vehicle.

Slammed, rather, into the faint blue glow of the defensive shield surrounding the Ichton vehicle. The impact roared across the electro-optical spectrum like multicolored petals unfolding from a white core.

The vehicle rocked backward on its bubble of supporting air. The projectile, flattened and a white blaze from frictional heating, dropped to the ground without having touched the body of its target.

The turret traversed. The male Gerson knew what was coming. He ran to the side in a desperate attempt to deflect

the stream of return fire from his family. His head and the
empty rocket launcher vanished into their constituent atoms as
the powerful turret weapon caught him at point-blank range. The
high-temperature residue of the sundered molecules recombined
an instant later in flashes and flame.

The Ichton gunner continued to fire. Projectiles scythed
across the field, ripping smoldering gaps in the vegetation.

The refugees threw themselves down when the shooting
started. As the gun traversed past, a juvenile leaped upright
and waved his remaining arm. Before the gunner could react,
the screaming victim collapsed again.

The turret weapon ceased firing.

The entire column entered the field. The leading and trailing
vehicles were obviously escorts, mounting powerful weapons in
their turrets. The second and third vehicles in the convoy were
hugely larger and must have weighed a hundred tonnes apiece.
They didn't appear to be armed, but their defensive shielding
was so dense that the vehicles' outlines wavered within globes
of blue translucence. The remaining vehicle, number four in
the column, was unarmed and of moderate size, though larger
than the escorts.

Dresser's mind catalogued the vehicles against the template
of his training and experience: a truck to supply the new colony
en route . . . and a pair of transporters, armored like battleships,
to carry the eggs and larvae that would populate that colony.

The Ichton convoy proceeded on a track as straight as the
line from a compass rose. For a moment, Dresser thought that
the Gerson survivors—if there were any—had been overlooked.
Then the supply truck and the rear escort swung out of the
column and halted.

A Gerson jumped to her feet and ran. She took only three
steps before her legs and the ground beneath her vanished in
a red flash. Heat made the air above the turret gun's muzzle
shimmer.

The supply truck's side panel slid open, and the defensive
screen adjacent to the door paled. A pair of Ichtons stepped
out of the vehicle. Heavy protective suits concealed the lines
of their bodies.

"Big suckers," said Thomson. Her hands hovered over the

console controls. Flight regime was up on the menu.

"Three of us're gonna take a whole army of *them*?" Codrus asked.

Dresser thought: It's not an army. It doesn't matter how big they are—we're not going to arm wrestle. You guys aren't any more scared than I am.

He said aloud, "You bet."

One of the Ichtons tossed the legless Gerson—the body had ceased to twitch—into the bag he, *it,* dragged along behind. The other Ichton spun abruptly and sprayed a ninety-degree arc of brush with his handweapon.

Though less powerful than the turret gun, the projectiles slashed through the vegetation. Branches and taller stems settled in a wave like the surface of a collapsing air mattress.

The Ichton with the bag patrolled the swath stolidly. He gathered up the bodies or body parts of three more victims.

"Don't . . ." Dresser whispered. Codrus and Thomson glanced sidelong, wondering what their commander meant.

The armed Ichton pointed his weapon. Before he could fire, the Gerson female with the infant in her arms stood up.

"Don't. . . ."

Instead of shooting, the Ichton stepped forward and reached out with its free hand. It seized the Gerson by the shoulder in a triaxial grip and led her back toward the vehicle. The remaining Ichton followed, slowed by the weight of the bag it was dragging.

Dresser let out the breath he had been holding longer than he realized.

"Now relax, Sergeant Dresser," said the mechanical voice. "Let the backbrain control your motions."

Dresser got to his feet, his four feet. His eyes stared at the ceiling. He wanted to close them, but they didn't close. A part of his mind was as amazed at the concept that eyes could close as it had been at the flat, adamantine images from Dresser's memory.

"You're doing very well, Sergeant," the voice cajoled. "Now, I'm going to open the door in the end of the compartment. Just follow the hallway out. Don't be in a hurry."

Dresser's right front leg bumped the table, but he didn't fall. He was terrified. His mind tried to focus on anything but what his legs were doing. The doorway lurched closer.

It was like being in free-fall. But he knew there was no landing possible from this mental vacuum.

3.

Rodriges manipulated his controls. The screen split. Its right half showed the back of the cloned Ichton shambling through the doorway, while a frontal shot of the creature approached down the hallway on the left.

"He's gonna get t' meet the brass," the technician muttered. "Horwarth and Dr. del Prato. Bet you never thought you'd be meeting an admiral and a top biochemist personallike, did you, Sarge?"

Dresser grunted.

Rodriges touched the controls again. The right image leapfrogged to the interior of a three-bed medical ward that included a well-appointed office. The admiral, seated behind a desk of what looked like real wood, was a stocky female. She wore a skull and crossbones ring in her left ear, and her right ear was missing. To her right sat a florid-faced civilian whose mustache flowed into his sideburns.

The door to the ward had been removed and a section of bulkhead cut from the top of the doorway. Even so, the Ichton lurching down the corridor would have to duck or bang its flat head.

"Why didn't they wake him up here?" Dresser asked. He made a tight, almost dismissive gesture toward the medical ward.

Rodriges looked sidelong at the scout. "Umm . . ." he said. "They didn't know quite how you'd—how he'd react when he woke up, y'know? They got me here for protection—"

The technician tapped carefully beside, not on, a separate keypad. It was a release for the weapons whose targeting was slaved to the screen controls.

"—but they don't want, you know, to lose the work. There's five more clones on ice, but still. . . ."

Dresser's face went hard. He didn't speak.

The Ichton paused in the doorway and tried to lower its head. Instead, the creature fell forward with its haunches high, like those of a horse that balked too close to the edge of a ditch.

"That's all right," said Admiral Horwarth brusquely. Her voice and the hypersonic translation of her voice echoed from the paired speakers of the observation room. "You'll soon have the hang of it."

"Part of the reason he's so clumsy," Rodriges said as he kept his invisible sight centered on the clone's chest, "is the body's straight out of the growth tank. It hasn't got any muscle tone."

His lips pursed as he and Dresser watched the ungainly creature struggle to rise again. "Of course," the technician added, "it could be the bugs're clumsy as hell anyhow."

"The ones I saw," said Dresser tightly, "moved pretty good."

The leading Ichton vehicle started to climb out of the dry wash; the nose of the last vehicle dipped to enter the end farthest from Dresser.

The scout boat's artificial intelligence planned the ambush with superhuman skill. It balanced the target, the terrain, distance factors, and the available force—the lack of available force—into a seventy percent probability that some or all of the scout team would survive the contact.

The AI thought their chance of capturing a live Ichton was less than one tenth of a percent; but that wasn't the first thing in any of the scouts' minds, not even Dresser's.

The convoy's inexorable progress led it to the badlands site within two minutes of the arrival time the AI had calculated. A wind-cut swale between two tilted sheets of hard sandstone had been gouged deeper by infrequent cloudbursts. The resulting gully was half a kilometer long. It was straight enough to give Dresser a clear shot along it from where he lay aboard his skimmer, on higher ground a hundred meters from the mouth.

The Ichtons could easily have gone around the gully, but there was no reason for them to do so. From what Dresser had seen already, the race had very little tendency to go around anything.

"Team," he said to his distant crewmen, "go!"

Codrus and Thomson fired from the sandstone ridges to either flank. Their weapons tapped energy from the Dirac Sea underlying the real-time universe, so the range—less than three hundred meters in any case—was no hindrance.

Sightlines *could* have been a problem. Since Dresser had only two flankers, it didn't matter that they had clear shots at only the first and last vehicles of the convoy. The tops of the huge egg transporters were visible from the crewmen's positions, but the supply truck had vanished beneath the sharp lips of the gully.

The beams from the A-Potential weapons were invisible, but at their touch the magnetic shielding of the escort vehicles flared into sparkling cataclysm. Dresser's helmet visor blocked the actinics and filtered the visual uproar. He continued to have a sharp view of the vehicles themselves—undamaged at the heart of the storm.

The APOT weapons could focus practically limitless amounts of power on the magnetic shields, canceling their effect—but the beams couldn't focus *through* the shields. The escort vehicles stopped dead. Their power supplies shunted energy to the shields—to be dumped harmlessly back into the Dirac Sea—but as soon as the APOT beams were redirected, the escorts would be back in the battle.

"Mines," Dresser said to the audio controller in his helmet, "*go!*"

The gossamer, high-explosive mesh the scouts had spread across the floor of the gully went off. There was a green flash, a quick shock through the bedrock that slapped Dresser ten centimeters in the air, and—a heartbeat later—the air-transmitted blast that would have deafened the sergeant without the protection of his helmet.

The explosive's propagation rate was a substantial fraction of light speed. The blast flattened the two escorts from the underside before it lifted them. Their wreckage spun into the air.

Though the supply truck's shields were unaffected, the shock wave bounced the lighter vehicle against the side of the gully. It caromed back and landed on one side. Its shields hissed furiously, trying to repel the washed stone. The generators didn't have enough power to levitate the truck, and the ground wasn't going to move.

Mass and magnetic shielding protected the egg transporters. The huge vehicles lurched, but neither showed signs of damage. The leading transporter plowed through the wreckage of the escort. The driver of the second transporter cut his controls to the right. Bow weapons, their existence unguessed until this moment, blasted an alternate route into the sandstone wall.

The mine's unexpected ground shock lifted Dresser, then dropped him back on the hard-padded couch of his skimmer. He tried to aim his weapon.

The bow of the leading egg transporter was pointed directly at him. A panel had recessed to clear the muzzle of an axial weapon like the one carving a ramp through kilotonnes of rock. Its bore looked big enough for a man to crawl down.

Codrus caught the Ichton vehicle with his APOT weapon. The beam held the huge transporter as rigid as a moth on a pin. The screens' watery glare vanished.

Dresser raked the undefended target lengthwise with his drum-fed rocket launcher.

The launcher cycled at the rate of two rounds per second. It was easy for an experienced gunner like Dresser to control the weapon during short bursts, despite the considerable recoil: though the barrel was open at both ends, highly accelerated exhaust gas gave a sharp backward jolt to the sides of the tube.

Dresser's first rocket exploded on the muzzle of the Ichton gun. The next two green flashes shredded the bow of the transporter as recoil shoved Dresser and lifted his point of aim.

He lowered his sights and fired again, probing deeper into the Ichton vehicle through the damage caused by his initial burst. His helmet dulled the slap*bang*! of the shots and protected his retinas from the bright explosions. The rocket backblast prickled like sunburn on the backs of his bare hands.

A sulfurous fireball mushroomed from the rear of the transporter, far deeper than Dresser had been able to probe with his rockets. The shield generators failed. Codrus's weapon now cut spherical collops from the vehicle.

Dresser shifted his aim to the remaining transporter. He thought he had half the twenty-round drum remaining, but he knew he was too pumped to be certain.

A pair of Ichtons jumped from a hatch in the side of the transporter stalled in the beam of Thomson's weapon. Codrus, bulky and rounded in the hard suit that was an integral part of the APOT system, stood up on his ridge to rip the vehicle while Thomson's beam grounded its shield.

Dresser punched three rockets into the transporter's broadside. Green flashes ate meter-diameter chunks from the plating. The individual Ichtons turned together and fired their hand weapons at Codrus.

The rock beneath the crewman blurred into high-temperature gas. The Ichton projectiles were near the range at which the flux expanded beyond coherence and the miniature generators failed. If Codrus hadn't been shooting, his APOT suit might have protected him against the attenuated forces—

But an aperture to fire through meant a gap in the opposite direction also. Circuits in the APOT suit crossed, then blew in a gout of sandstone so hot it fluoresced.

"Ship!" Dresser shouted into the audio controller. He slammed a pair of contact-fused rockets through a hole blown by the previous burst. "Go!"

Ten klicks away, *SB 781* was lifting from her camouflaged hide. The AI would execute the flight plan the AI had developed. Dresser could override the machine mind, but he wouldn't have time—

And anyway, he might not be alive in five minutes when the boat appeared to make the extraction.

Bright gray smoke rolled in sheets out of the two lower holes in the transporter's plating. Flames licked from the highest wound, sullenly red, and the smoke *they* trailed was sooty black.

The transporter began to slip back down the ramp its gun had carved. The forward half of the vehicle was shielded, but smoke and flame continued to billow beneath the blue glow.

Thomson shrieked uncontrollably on the team frequency as she lashed the two Ichtons with her weapon. The creatures' personal shields deflected the beam—to Dresser's surprise, but

ALBUQUERQUE ACADEMY
LIBRARY

if you couldn't *touch* the target, it didn't matter how much energy you poured into the wrong place.

Dresser kicked the bar behind his left boot to power up his skimmer. It induced a magnetic field in the rock with the same polarity as that in the little vehicle's own undersurface.

The skimmer lurched a centimeter upward, throwing off Dresser's aim. The last rocket in his magazine missed high. The transporter was beginning to sag in the center.

"Thomson!" Dresser shouted. "We want a prisoner!"

The rock beneath the Ichtons first went molten, then froze and shattered into dust finer than the sand that had once been compacted to make stone, and finally expanded into a white fireball that drank the Ichtons like thistle down in a gas flame. When transformed into a real-time analog, Thomson's A-Potential energy easily overwhelmed the Ichton defenses.

The skimmer wobbled downhill. Dresser steered with his feet on the tiller bar while he lay on his left side and fumbled a fresh magazine onto his rocket launcher. The Ichtons fired at movement. . . .

"Kill the fucking bastards!" Thomson screamed.

The front half of the damaged transporter began to crumple like overheated foil beneath its magnetic shielding. High-voltage arcs danced across the plates, scarring the metal like fungus on the skin of a poorly embalmed corpse.

"K—" said Thomson as her APOT beam drew a streak of cloudy red sky from another universe into the heart of the transporter. The back half of the vehicle blew up with a stunning crash even louder than that of the minefield that initiated the contact.

Because Dresser's skimmer was in motion, he was spared the ground shock. The airborne wave was a hot fist that punched fire into his lungs and threatened to spin his little vehicle like a flipped coin. The skimmer's automatic controls stabilized it as no human driver could have done, then shut down. Dresser kicked the starter again.

"Bastards!" shouted Thomson as she rode her own skimmer forward in search of fresh targets.

The explosion slammed the overturned supply truck into the gully wall again. The magnetic shielding failed; one side of the vehicle scraped off on the rock. A living Ichton, suited and armed, spilled out along with other of the truck's contents. Another of the creatures was within the gutted vehicle, transfixed despite its armor by a length of tubing from the perimeter frame.

Protein rations, bundled into transparent packets weighing a kilogram or so, littered the gully floor. The mother Gerson was only partway through processing. Her legs and the lower half of her furry torso stuck out the intake funnel in the truck body. The apparatus had stalled from battle damage.

The baby Gerson lay among the ration packets, feebly waving its chubby arms.

Thomson fired from her skimmer. She didn't have a direct sightline to the supply truck, but her suit sensors told her where the target was. The APOT beam ripped through the lip of stone like lightning in a wheat field.

Rock shattered, spewing chunks skyward. At the end of the ragged path, visible to Dresser though not Thomson, the damaged truck sucked inward and vanished like a smoke sculpture.

SB 781 drifted across Thomson, as silent as a cloud. The vessel was programmed to land at the center of the gully, since the team didn't have the transport to move an Ichton prisoner any distance from the capture site.

"Ship!" Dresser cried, overriding the plan. "Down! Now!"

The living Ichton got to its feet. Dresser, twenty meters away, grounded his skimmer in a shower of sparks and squeezed his trigger.

The rocket launcher didn't fire. He'd short-stroked the charging lever when the transporter blew up. There wasn't a round in the chamber.

The baby Gerson wailed. The Ichton spun like a dancer and vaporized the infant in a glowing dazzle.

SB 781 settled at the lip of the gully, between Thomson and the Ichton. She wouldn't shoot at their own ride home—and anyway, the vessel's A-Potential shielding should protect it if she did.

The team's *job* was to bring back a prisoner.

Dresser charged his launcher and fired. The warhead

detonated on the Ichton's magnetic shield. The green flash hurled the creature against the rock wall.

It bounced back. Dresser fired again, slapping the Ichton into the stone a second time. The creature's weapon flew out of its three-fingered hands.

At Dresser's third shot, a triangular bulge on the Ichton's chest melted and the shield's blue glow vanished.

The Ichton sprawled in an ungainly tangle of limbs. Dresser got off his skimmer and ran to the creature. He dropped his rocket launcher and drew the powered cutting bar from the boot sheath where it rode.

Dresser's vision pulsed with colors as though someone were flicking pastel filters over his eyes. He didn't have time to worry whether something was wrong with his helmet optics. Thomson's shouted curses faded in and out also, so the damage was probably within Dresser's skull. Fleet hardware could survive one hell of a hammering, but personnel were still constructed to an older standard. . . .

The Ichton twitched. Dresser ran the tip of his twenty-CM cutter along the back of the creature's suit. The armor was nonmetallic but tough enough to draw a shriek from the contra-rotating diamond saws in the bar's edge.

Dresser wasn't going to chance carrying the prisoner with inbuilt devices still functioning in its suit, not even in the stasis bay of *SB 781*. The tech mavens on the *Hawking* could deal with the network of shallow cuts the cutter was going to trace across the chitin and flesh. There wasn't time to be delicate, even if Dresser had wanted to be.

The air in the gully stank, but that wasn't why Dresser took breaths so shallow that his oxygen-starved lungs throbbed.

He couldn't help thinking about the baby Gerson vaporized a few meters away.

4.

There were two humans in the room with Dresser in his new body. The one behind the desk wore blue; the other wore white.

He wasn't sure what the sex of either of them was.

"As your mind reintegrates with the cloned body, Sergeant," said the mechanical voice, "you'll achieve normal mobility. Ah, normal for the new body, that is."

White's mouth parts were moving. Dresser knew—remembered—that meant the human was probably speaking, but the words came from the desk's front corner moldings. Ears alternated with the speech membranes along Dresser's lateral lines. He shifted position instinctively to triangulate on the speakers' precise location.

"I want to tell you right now, Sergeant, that the Alliance—that all intelligent life in the galaxy is in your debt. You're a very brave man."

The voice and the location were the same—the desk speakers—but it was the other mouth that was moving. A translation system in the desk piped the actual speech out in a form Dresser could understand.

Now that he concentrated, he could hear the words themselves: a faint rumble, like that of distant artillery. It was meaningless and scarcely audible. He would have to watch to determine which of the pair was speaking—

But watching anything was easy. Dresser could see the entire room without turning his head. He noticed every movement, no matter how slight—nostrils flaring for a breath, the quiver of eyelashes at the start of a blink. His new brain combined the images of over a hundred facet eyes and sorted for the differences in the views they presented.

"It was obvious before we started that the enemy's numbers are enormous," Blue continued. "We now realize that Ichton weapons are formidable as well. In some ways—"

The desk translated Blue's throat clearing as a burst of static.

"Well, anyway, they're quite formidable."

The difficulty was that almost all Dresser now saw *was* movement. The background vanished beyond ten meters or so. Even closer objects were undifferentiated blurs until they shifted position. Though Dresser knew—remembered—the physical differences between human males and females, he couldn't see details so fine, and he lacked the hormonal cues that would have sexed individuals of his own kind.

Ye Gods, his own kind!

"You'll be landed back near the site where your original was captured, Sergeant Dresser," Blue went on.

The machine translator rasped Dresser's nerve endings with its compression. Its words lacked the harmonics that made true speech a thrill to hear no matter what its content.

"You shouldn't have any difficulty infiltrating the Ichton forces," interjected White. "The natural recognition patterns of your body will appear—*are* real, are totally real."

Dresser suddenly remembered the last stage of the firefight in the gully. He perceived it now through the senses of his present body. The Ichton flung from the vehicle, under attack but uncertain from where—

Sound and movement close by, a threat.

Spinning and blasting before the enemy can strike home.

Reacting before the higher brain can determine that the target was merely a part of the food supply that hadn't been processed before the attack occurred.

Dresser screamed. Both humans flinched away from the high-frequency warble.

"I'm not a bug!" he cried. "I won't! I won't kill babies!"

"Sergeant," said White, "we realize the strain you're under—"

"Though, of course, you volunteered," Blue said.

"—but when your personality has fully integrated with the body into which it's been copied," White continued, "the—dichotomies—will not be quite so, ah, serious. I know—that is, I can imagine the strain you're experiencing. It will get better, I promise you."

"Sergeant . . ." said Blue, "I'll be blunt. We're hoping you can find a chink in the Ichtons' armor. If you can't, the mission of the *Stephen Hawking* is doomed to fail. And all life-forms in at least this galaxy are, quite simply, doomed."

"Except for the Ichtons themselves," White added.

The machine couldn't capture intonation; memory told Dresser that the bluster of a moment before had vanished.

Dresser's memory tumbled out a kaleidoscope of flat-focus images: a wrecked village; cancerous domes scores of kilometers in diameter, growing inexorably; an Ichton—

Dresser's body in every respect—blasting a wailing infant by mistake, a waste of food. . . .

"I can't l-l-live like this!" Dresser cried.

"It's only temporary," Blue said. "Isn't that right, Doctor? I'm not denying the risk, Sergeant Dresser, but as soon as the mission's been completed, you'll be returned to your own form."

"Ah," said White. "Yes, of course, Sergeant. But the main thing is just to let your mind and body integrate. You'll feel better shortly."

"I think the best thing now is for you to start right in on the program," said Blue. "I'll bring in your briefing officers immediately. You'll see that we've taken steps to minimize the risk to you."

Blue continued to speak. All Dresser could think of was that tiny Gerson, like a living teddy bear.

5.

The screen showed six personnel entering the ward where the Ichton clone hunched. One of the newcomers was a Gerson.

In the observation room, Dresser turned his back on the screen. "How much does he remember?" he asked Rodriges harshly.

The technician shrugged. "Up to maybe thirty-six hours before the transfer," he said. "There's some loss, but not a lot. You okay yourself?"

"Fine," said Dresser. "I'm great."

On the screen, a uniformed man without rank tabs outlined the physical training program. The clone's new muscles had to be brought up to standard before the creature was reinserted.

Dresser shuddered. Rodriges thumbed down the audio level, though the translation channel remained a distant piping.

"When I volunteered . . ." Dresser said carefully. "I didn't know how much it'd bug—bother me. To see myself as an Ichton."

"Naw, that's not you, Sarge," Rodriges said. "Personalities start to diverge at the moment the mind scan gets dumped in the new cortex—and in *that* cortex, the divergence is going to be real damn fast. None of the sensory stimuli are the same, you see."

Dresser grunted and looked back over his shoulder. "Yeah," he said. "Well. Bet he thinks he's me, though."

"Sarge, you did the right thing, volunteering," Rodriges soothed. "You heard the admiral. Using somebody who's seen the bugs in action, that improves the chances. And anyway— it's done, right?"

The clone was moving its forelimbs—arms—in response to the trainer's direction. The offside supporting legs twitched unexpectedly; the tall creature fell over. A civilian expert jumped reflexively behind a female colleague in Marine Reaction Unit fatigues.

"It's going to be just as hard for him when they switch him back, won't it?" Dresser said. He turned to the technician. "Getting used to a human body again, I mean."

"Huh?" Rodriges blurted. "Oh, you mean like the admiral said. Ah, Sarge. . . . A fast-growth clone—"

He gestured toward the screen. Dresser didn't look around.

"Look, it's a total-loss project. I mean, in the tank we got five more bodies like this one—but the original, what's left of that's just hamburger."

Dresser stared but said nothing.

Rodriges blinked in embarrassment. He plowed onward, saying, "Cost aside—and I'm *not* saying it's a cost decision, but it'd be cheaper to build six destroyers than a batch of fast-growth clones. Anyway, cost aside, there's no *way* that thing's gonna be back in a body like yours unless yours. . . . You know?"

The technician shrugged.

"I guess I was pretty naive," Dresser said slowly.

Rodriges reached over and gripped the scout's hand. "Hey," the technician said. "It's not you, you know? It's a thing. Just a thing."

Dresser disengaged his hand absently. He looked toward the screen again, but he didn't see the figures, human and alien, on it. Instead, his mind filled with the image of the baby Gerson, stretching out its chubby hands toward him—

Until it vanished in tears that diffracted light into a dazzle like that of the weapon in Dresser's three-fingered hands.

INDIES

ONE OF THE political peculiarities of the Alliance was the importance of the Indie (Independent) traders to its system of interstellar trade. At the end of the Family war, thousands of no longer needed ships were sold as surplus war material. Since the larger companies had already expanded their merchant fleets massively to fulfill the lucrative contracts the war produced, they had no need for ships that were not even designed to carry cargo. As a result these disarmed scouts and cruisers were sold to Independent traders, whose ranks were swelled by Fleet personnel released as the navy shrunk to a peacetime level of staffing.

As is their nature, the megacorps and their fleets of highly cost-effective merchant ships and liners monopolized the most lucrative trade routes. The Indies competed fiercely with one another for the marginal and frontier markets. They provided a vital service to thousands of worlds that otherwise would rarely merit a stop from the giant merchant carriers. When the three races arrived and made their public request for assistance, many Indie traders saw another opportunity as well. Here was a totally untapped market where there would be no competition from the megacorps. Once the star maps were released, many of the more adventurous stocked up on trade goods and began their long journey to Star Central two years before the battle station was completed. The presence of these Indies who had preceded them provided valuable information, and numerous complications, for the Fleet station when it did arrive.

TRADING
UP

by Mike Resnick
and Barbara Delaplace

"THEY'LL RUIN EVERYTHING!" Salimander Smith shouted at the group gathered at the bar. "Can't anyone but me see it?" He glared at his companions. "You call yourselves traders? Hah! You couldn't sell umbrellas in a rainstorm!" He picked up his mug of Arskellian beer—provided to him gratis by the management of The Lonesome Tavern, since he was the one who'd imported it for them—and drained it.

"You're out of your mind," said one woman. "The *Stephen Hawking* is one big enormous ripe market waiting for us Indies." She paused. "I hear it's got more than ten thousand personnel aboard. That's ten thousand reasons business is going to boom."

Smith looked at her with pity. "Delilah, my dear, you're as hopelessly ill-informed as you are beautiful." She glared at him, but made no reply. "I regret to inform you that a depressingly large proportion of that ten thousand consists of Independent traders like ourselves. This ain't exactly the virgin market you think it is."

"But even if there are a lot of Indies on board the *Hawking*, so what?" protested a tall man with a luxuriant beard and long, waxed mustaches. "We have the advantage of already knowing the territory. We've already got our contacts on the different worlds."

"If they're anything like your contacts, Davies," retorted Smith contemptuously, "I'd say the new competition hasn't got a thing to worry about. Made back your losses yet on that

27

deal for Zanther goldfish skins? I'll bet Manderxx the Nimble laughed all the way to what passes for a bank on his world." The bearded man looked uncomfortable as the others hooted with laughter.

"We can always act as middlemen and contacts ourselves to the new traders, though. There's enough business here for everyone," said another woman, who sported a massive ear broach inlaid with rare Sirel fire-rubies.

"Not with those damned insects ruining every planet they set foot on," said a third man. "They've wiped out two worlds that I had good trade deals with. I've lost markets worth millions. And don't tell me you can cut deals with Ichtons, Salimander old lizard. I tried, and just barely got out with my skin intact."

Smith surveyed the speaker with some distaste. "That's what I like about you, Harry. Your humanitarian attitude and deep concern for other living beings."

Harry eyed him truculently. "The bugs are bad for business. That's all I care about. Now that the *Hawking*'s arrived, the Fleet will wipe 'em out, and we can get back to trading for a decent profit margin."

"Not a chance," said the woman wearing the ear broach. "Those Ichtons are *tough* bastards. I think the Fleet's going to be around for a while."

"I agree," said Smith. "I've been checking with some of my contacts. It looks like we're in for a long war. Unfortunately."

" 'Unfortunately'?" repeated the woman. "Smith, you've been in space too long. The Fleet'll need raw materials. They'll need R and R. They'll need fresh air and the great outdoors. The on-board merchants will want to trade. We'll clean up."

There was a general nodding of heads along the bar.

Smith scanned the faces. "You *still* can't see it, can you? Now that the Fleet's in the Core, things aren't going to be like they were. The Fleet means law and order. No more unrestricted trade. *That's* what's bad for business." He paused. "I've been an Independent trader—"

"—all my life," the others finished for him.

Undaunted, Smith continued. "I've seen it happen before. The Fleet moves in, the Alliance starts breathing down everyone's necks, and next thing you know, you need a permit just to lift off. I've been working the Core for—"

"—fifteen years!" they cho`r`used.

Amid general laughter Davies said, "Oh, come off it! A few regulations won't get in our way."

"You think it'll stop at a few regulations?" demanded Smith. "You're a bigger fool than I thought! No organization stops after making just a *few* rules. And with the Fleet here, the Alliance is here. That means tariffs and duties and customs regulations. Do you really think they're going to let us keep trading rights to the worlds we've opened up when they're carrying five thousand traders of their own on that damned ship?" He stood up. "Well, I'm not going to just stand by and let it happen."

"What're you going to do—stop the *Hawking* single-handed?" sneered Delilah. The other traders laughed.

"Not stop it. But I sure as hell plan to make it swerve a bit." Smith picked up his vivid cloak and shrugged into it amid a general atmosphere of disbelief. "Good night, ladies and gentlemen. I've spent enough time with fools and losers."

He went out into the darkness.

Back on his ship, Smith propped his embroidered boots onto a hassock and settled back in an antique leather armchair (obtained in a complicated four-cornered deal involving a Hong Kong merchant anxious to clear her warehouse, a Fleet services-and-supplies officer with an unlawful addiction to an illicit liquor, and an alien species known as the Nest Makers). A freshly poured beer at his elbow, he contemplated the projected fire in the holographic fireplace.

The habitus of The Lonesome Tavern were fools. Well, he'd warned them; if they couldn't see the handwriting on the wall, it was hardly *his* problem. A trader always watched out for his own interests first.

And his interests were the trading deals he'd so painstakingly worked out with six alien worlds in the Core. It had taken years for him to build up his contacts and markets—fifteen years, just as they'd jeered in the bar. Well, perhaps he *did* have a habit of repeating himself; probably came as a result of spending so much time away from people, traveling his trading circuit.

After all that work, he'd be damned if he'd just stand by and let the diplomats and paper pushers and regulation makers move in and take over.

But how to stop it? The Fleet wouldn't step aside just for one man. . . . unless that man was somehow indispensable to them. *Indispensable.* To a trader, that meant supplying them something no one else could supply. Now the problem was couched in terms that he could deal with, deal-making terms. Stroking the old scar on his cheek, Salimander Smith stared into the cold flames of the hologram and pondered. . . .

Brad Omera, his face haggard, his back stiff and sore, glanced up from what was still known as "paperwork" even though paper had been out of use for centuries. I wonder if the ancient Egyptians called it papyrus-work? he thought. Whatever it was called, it seemed to follow administrators no matter what the era was.

"There's a Salimander Smith who wants to talk to you, sir," said his assistant, her face shimmering in the holotank at the corner of his desk. "He says it's vital."

"Don't they all?" muttered Omera.

"He claims to have detailed knowledge about several alien cultures we're unfamiliar with."

Omera became slightly more interested. "He does, eh? Well, I suppose he could be useful. Lord knows, we never seem to have enough alien specialists." He paused for a moment. Odds were that this was probably just another scam artist. On the other hand, they couldn't afford to overlook anyone who might enable them to establish contact with any of the races at the Core. They needed to unite against the Ichtons. "Set up an appointment," he said at last. "You never know who might turn out to be useful."

"Yes, sir. You never know."

"It's a pleasure to meet you, Mr. Omera, a real pleasure." Salimander Smith held out his hand, virtually forcing Omera to return the handshake. "I know what a busy man you are, and I appreciate the effort you made to find time to see me. I guarantee you won't regret it."

Omera surveyed Smith's gaudy clothes with distaste as he released the trader's hand and sat down again. Smith noted this—for a trader, missing the smallest detail might mean the difference between showing a profit or a loss for a year's worth of negotiating. Omera was obviously resolved not to let what he regarded as Smith's too-hearty manner and overdone clothing put him off. "My pleasure, Mr. Smith."

Bullshit. You don't like me and you didn't want to see me, but you don't want to ignore me in case I can be useful. "Let me tell you a little about myself. Can't expect a man to do business with someone he's never met before. I'm an Independent—"

"Mr. Smith, I'm a busy man, and I don't have a lot of time to spare. Let's get down to brass tacks. You're an Independent trader who's been working the Core for the past fifteen years. You've established trade relations with six alien races. Your contracts with them have been only moderately rapacious, and as a result you've made a very handsome living for yourself."

"I'm not sure I like the term 'rapacious,' Mr. Omera."

"I did qualify it, Mr. Smith. Compared to some of the Independent traders I've seen in action, you've been reasonably restrained."

Smith shrugged. "It's good for business. Alien races aren't stupid, and some of them have very unpleasant ways of dealing with traders they feel have cheated them." He paused. "I prefer a long-term, mutually beneficial trading arrangement with my alien partners. Then both sides prosper. In fact, that's why I'm here."

"To see if the two of us can come to a mutually beneficial trading agreement?" Omera's voice was cynical.

"Perhaps not a trading agreement, but some sort of under-standing."

"Mr. Smith, I've dealt with a lot of Indies. Usually when they start using words like 'understanding,' they want me to bend the rules. And they generally offer a sliding scale of incentives proportional to the amount of bending they want done."

Smith's expression spoke volumes. "Amateurs, every one of them," he said contemptuously. "I have no intention of offering you a bribe."

"Well, *that's* a novel approach," said Omera. "What exactly *are* you offering, then?"

"Mr. Omera, as you've already noted, I've spent a long time building up trade with those alien races. I've had a good deal of experience with their customs. I know their languages and their politics. I'm prepared to offer my expertise in those areas to you."

"In return for what, as if I couldn't guess?"

"In return for recognition of what already exists," answered Smith, unperturbed. "I want exclusive trading rights on those worlds."

Omera replied flatly, "Impossible."

"You disappoint me, Mr. Omera," replied Smith easily. "When dealing with the man at the top, there's no such word as 'impossible.' "

"We're in a state of war. I'm not empowered to, nor am I interested in, working out trade deals with any Indie who comes along."

"I'm not just 'any Indie,' " said Smith, radiating self-confidence. "No other trader has my knowledge of those worlds—you yourself admitted that I was the one who established relations with them." He stared into Omera's eyes. "I'd be a valuable addition to your staff of experts."

"Somehow I don't think you'd fit in very well on the *Stephen Hawking,* Mr. Smith, valuable though you might be. And as you point out, we do have experts already, experts who are experienced in dealing with newly contacted alien races."

"Of course you do. But as you say, you're in a state of war—and time is a valuable commodity in war. How long will it take those experts of yours to become familiar with the political situation on Meloth? Politics is a passion there, and they hold elections once a month. Make an alliance with the wrong splinter faction, and you could wind up alienating eighty percent of the power brokers on the planet. You'd lose a potential ally."

"If the situation is as delicate there as you say, we'd definitely want our own experts studying it firsthand."

"If they go there without me, they might be in for a hostile reception. Melothians prefer dealing with those they know."

"A threat, Mr. Smith?"

"Not at all, Mr. Omera. Simply a statement of fact. I myself nearly got killed when I first made contact. Of course," Smith added, studying the ceiling reflectively, "Meloth's not the only planet that's hostile to newcomers."

"It's certainly beginning to *sound* like a threat. A planet that hostile should probably be placed on the interdict list. We can't have a fellow citizen"—and here Omera paused meaningfully before continuing—"landing on such a dangerous world."

Smith studied the man on the other side of the desk carefully. The administrator's face was impassive. Yes, he probably was capable of doing just that, if he felt it was necessary to further the cause of the Alliance. Omera had countered every suggestion Smith made, and had just subtly pointed out that Smith was not playing from a position of strength. I must be losing my touch, he thought ruefully. Now there was only one option left.

"Not even if that citizen knew of an even more dangerous world? A world of strategic importance?" Smith watched Omera closely.

"What sort of strategic importance?" Omera's tone suggested he'd heard this sort of thing before, but Smith's years of practice in observation suddenly paid off. The administrator had a superb poker face, but the clenching of one hand gave him away. Gotcha, you cold sonofabitch!

Smith leaned back in his chair. "Of such importance that it might help bring victory to the Alliance."

"And just what might that be?"

"I know the location of an Ichton base."

Omera's eyes were suddenly intent. "Keep talking, Mr. Smith."

"There's nothing further to say," replied Smith. "I can pinpoint the world on any map you care to show me. For a price, of course."

"How much money do you want?"

"I don't want your money."

"Let me guess—trading rights to those half-dozen worlds, correct?"

"Correct," answered Smith. "But consider what you get in return: prisoners to interrogate, captives to study, a potential bargaining chip with the Ichtons. And it won't cost you a single credit." He paused. "I'd say you're getting a bargain."

Omera studied Smith for a long moment. Smith lounged easily in his chair. At last Omera said, "I have to consult with Commander Brand."

"Consult all you like," said Smith with a casual wave of his hand. "I have nothing but time."

"Excuse me." Omera stood up abruptly and left the room.

Five minutes later Omera returned. "Agreed. Tell me the name of the planet where the Ichton base is, and I guarantee you exclusive trading rights to the six worlds you opened up."

"I have your promise on record? Exclusive rights on Meloth, Sarn, Tellikan, Arskell, Merring, and Zel?" Smith's expression had turned calculating.

"Mr. Smith, let's not become coy, shall we? You spotted my holocorder the minute you sat down. Of course it's on record."

Salimander Smith always knew when it was time to give in gracefully, particularly when he'd gotten what he wanted. "You're absolutely right, Mr. Omera, I did. Please forgive my lack of manners."

"And the location of the Ichton base?"

"Looden III. That's a system about—"

"I know where it is. All right, Mr. Smith, you have your deal. Thank you for doing your patriotic duty. And now, if you don't mind, I have other matters pressing me. . . ." Omera's face was wearier than it had been a few minutes ago.

"Of course, Mr. Omera. A pleasure doing business with you." Smith stood up, thought the better of offering to shake hands again, and left the office.

There was a man waiting for him outside, a man wearing an air of command and the uniform of a senior officer of the Fleet. "Salimander Smith?"

"Yes."

"I'm Commander Brand."

"An honor to meet you, sir."

"I understand you know the location of an Ichton colony."

"Yes I do. As I just told Mr. Omera, it's on Looden III."

"Do you think you can pinpoint the colony's location? Lead a landing party directly to it?"

"Lead a landing party to it? Well now, you must understand that I'm not a military man," answered Smith. "Still, for the right price, and a hell of a big invasion force to protect me, I suppose we could work something out."

"The price is 173 credits a month," said Brand.

"I beg your pardon?"

"You've just been drafted as an alien contact expert. Welcome to the Fleet, Specialist Smith."

"What?"

"Oh, yes indeed, Mr. Smith." Brad Omera appeared in the office doorway. "As you've admitted yourself, you'd be a valuable addition to our staff. We've decided to take you up on that suggestion."

"But you said I wouldn't fit in very well on the *Hawking*! I'd be a disruptive influence!"

"Then how fortunate it is for us that you won't be aboard the *Hawking* for more than twelve hours before you are transferred to one of our gunboats bound for Looden III."

"I thought we had a deal!" shouted Smith furiously.

"We have every intention of honoring it," said Brand. "You have the sole right to establish trade with the worlds you named, and once the war is over and you are released from active duty, we wish you good luck in your enterprise. But until then, Mr. Smith," he concluded with a nasty smile, "your ass is ours."

Omera smiled to himself as he went back into his office. Somehow he just knew Salimander Smith would find a way to turn his time in the Fleet to good use. He sat down at his desk again and wondered for a moment if ancient Egyptian administrators had ever had to worry about traveling salesmen. Probably they did. *That* hadn't changed much down through the centuries.

He sighed and got back to work.

BATTLE STATION

ONE OF THE most important lessons the Fleet learned in its war against the Syndicate of Families was the near impossibility of supporting a fleet parsecs from its normal bases. The Fleet's first solution was to stockpile materials for up to a hundred major bases and repair centers, to be transported and set up behind the advancing Fleet units. This concept was discarded after one such modular base was assembled, when the cost was calculated. The immensity of the Alliance was so great that it was becoming impossibly expensive just to guard all of its borders, much less prepare for offensive operations beyond them. Yet it was inevitable that someday such a war would have to be fought.

This next solution was to create a mobile unit capable of supporting a large fleet. Fewer of these would be needed, and they could be kept secure within the heart of the Alliance serving a useful purpose from completion. Kilometers across, the station would contain the most massive warp drives ever attempted. Only recent breakthroughs resulting from the combination of Family and Alliance science even allowed for their construction. Unfortunately the cost of one of these mobile stations was immense. The construction of the first had been proposed over thirty years earlier, and similar proposals by the Fleet had been rejected by the Alliance Senate eleven times in the next twenty years. Eventually all the designs were filed away, but not forgotten. The necessity of sending a fleet halfway across the galaxy reopened the opportunity for the creation

36

of the mobile base. A series of seven were proposed by the Quartermasters Corps on Port, Tau Ceti. The funding for just one was approved by a very close vote.

To the dismay of the refugees, the mobile base would take almost three years to complete. Construction of this mobile base began around Tau Ceti when someone finally realized that the base would need to defend itself. It would be operating ahead of the Fleet lines, not behind them. This would add to its cost, but give it needed "survivability." The Senate balked at this added cost. The release to the Trivid stations raised enough public support that another compromise was finally reached. The station would be armed, but almost half its space would now be set aside for private interests. In return the corporations and a consortium of Indies would contribute a portion of the cost and provide a number of construction crews. Production continued and the mobile base became the first Fleet battle station.

GLOBIN'S
CHILDREN

by Christopher Stasheff

GLOBIN HAD BEEN the human leader of a band of Khalian pirates on Barataria, leading his Weasel crews against humans of any political stripe.

Globin had become the head of a vast trading combine and the architect of Khalian integration into the human-dominated Alliance—not because he wanted to, but because it was the only route to survival for the one-time outlaws who depended on him.

Now Globin was old and tired. Well, not really old, considering that he was only eighty, and humans of his day regularly lived to the age of 130, remaining in full vigor past their centennials—but he *felt* old. And weary. And, most especially, bored.

He was satisfied that he had established a stable government on Barataria that would continue to be viable and democratic without him, and he was certain that he was no longer necessary to anyone, least of all himself.

Then the voice of Plasma, his secretary, sounded from the desktop speaker. "Globin."

Globin gave the grille a jaundiced glance, then sighed as he felt the weight of his office settle again. "Yes, Plasma?"

"A new ship has appeared at the Galactic West frontier, Globin—a ship of a type that has never been seen before. To demands that it identify itself, it responds with unintelligible gibberish."

Globin frowned. "Interesting, but scarcely vital to the welfare of Barataria."

"True, Globin. I thought it might be of interest to you personally."

Globin smiled; Plasma had been his aide for most of his adult years, and knew that inside the statesman's hide lurked the scholar that had never quite been buried under the avalanche of bureaucracy. "You thought correctly. From which direction does it come?"

"From the interior of the galaxy, Globin."

"The interior! This *could* be interesting! Is there any video feed yet?"

"None for the public." Plasma's voice hid amusement.

It was well founded; so far as they knew, the Alliance was still blissfully unaware that the Baratarians had long since gained access to their sentry system's scramble code.

"Relay it to my screen." Globin swiveled about to the wall in which his viewscreen was embedded, a meter high and two wide.

The screen darkened, showing night pierced with the sparks that were stars. One glowed much brighter than all the rest, and Globin reached for his controls, keying in the code for expansion. The brightest spark loomed larger and larger until it filled the screen—a collection of cylinders bound together with a coil, looking like nothing so much as a collection of ancient tin cans tied together with baling wire. And they did seem ancient—scarred and pitted by collisions with countless meteorites, splotched by mysterious burns. That spaceship had come a long, long way—and at a guess, the aliens hadn't wanted to spend much energy on force-field screens.

Either that, or they didn't know how to make them.

Voices accompanied the picture, the voices of the sentry who had spotted the ship and his senior officer.

"You're getting *what*?"

"An outrageous radiation reading, Captain. I'd guess their shielding broke down."

Or, thought Globin, they hadn't had any to begin with— like the early torch-ships, which had shielding only between the engines and the ship itself. Why shield empty space from radiation?

"Could be they're using really raw fuel," a more mature voice answered.

Globin nodded slowly. If this species hadn't bothered developing more advanced engines, they might even be using U-235. Why go after higher elements, when the lower would do?

Had they even thought of fusion?

But surely they had to, if they had come so far.

Something else bothered him. Why five separate cylinders? Perhaps one for the engines, but why the other four?

A niggling suspicion joggled his brain. Could there be more than one life-form aboard? Could they need separate environments for separate species? Or perhaps . . .

He felt the compulsion seize him, the hunger for knowledge, and knew it wouldn't go away until it was fulfilled. He would study everything he could about these aliens, at every odd moment, until he was satiated. It was the old, old hunger that had driven him into scholarship, and was akin to the lust for revenge that had driven him to find the Merchant worlds. It was the same driving appetite that had led him to learn as much as he could about the commerce of the Alliance, and had allowed him to hew out a niche for Barataria.

He hoped this hunger would work for the good of his adopted people, too.

An hour later Plasma came in with some papers needing signatures and found Globin still staring at the screen, listening to the voices, ideas whirling in his head.

The conference was over; the delegation from Khalia filed out, their leader pausing to chat a little longer with Globin before they left. As soon as he was out the door, Plasma was in. "The aliens have docked at a western sentry station, Globin! I have been recording it for two hours! They are attempting to communicate!"

Globin stared, changing frames of reference in his mind. Then he frowned. "Alien! With so many races in the Alliance, how can you speak the word 'alien'?"

"*Truly* alien, Globin! Like no creatures we have ever seen before!" The secretary turned to the wall screen, keyed it in, and selected a channel.

Globin turned back to his desk. "Let us see it as it is now, Plasma! I will view the beginning later!"

He dropped into his chair to see the collection of cylinders, scarred and pitted. It was held to the dock by magnetic grapples only—of course; there was no guarantee that an oxygen atmosphere would not hurt its occupants, so there could be no boarding tube yet.

Behind him, Plasma said, "Fighters came out to inspect, and found an alien floating at the end of a tether with his arms up and hands spread open. They took that as the sign of peace, and towed the ship back to the station. I am sure there are a triad of blast cannon focused on it even now."

And a projectile rifle aimed at each alien, Globin guessed—for the top of one of the giant tin cans had opened downward, and four spacesuited figures stood on it. One was more or less anthropoid, standing on two limbs and having two others just below the sphere of the helmet—but it was broad and swollen, so much so that Globin had a fleeting notion that its suit was inflated, with nothing inside. Another stood on four legs with two more limbs extended for grasping, and a long extension behind that was probably a tail.

A tail? On a sentient being? How could its race not have evolved past the need for one?

Another alien stood on six, and one on none. All had extensions that looked like arms, though it was hard to tell in a spacesuit—but only the bearlike one had anything resembling shoulders. The one without legs was smallest, scarcely a meter long—and long it was, for its suit stretched out horizontally, floating in midair by some kind of field effect that was presumably built into the suit.

"Detail!" Globin pressed a ruby square on his desktop, and the picture enlarged. He maneuvered a joystick set next to the ruby square, and one single helmet filled the meter-wide screen. It was heavily frosted on the outside, but one square area was kept clear, presumably by heating. Reflection made the face within difficult to see, but Globin could make out a muzzle and large warm eyes. The face looked like that of a bear, but a very warmhearted bear. Globin knew it was completely illogical, but he felt himself warming to the alien.

He pushed the joystick to the right, and the bear-face slid out of the screen as the helmet of the centauroid slid in. Globin could make out sleek, streamlined jaws, and atop them eyes that were only dim glints, but enough to make Globin shiver—the creature might be sentient, but it was far from human.

He pushed the joystick once more, and shuddered again. The six-legged creature's helmet was in front of its body, not on top, and the face within bore clear convex lenses for eyes four inches across, fangs and hair shrouding everything else— at least, Globin thought it was hair; it was hard to tell through the frost.

All this time, he'd been absorbing the audio. A commentator, carefully neutral, was saying, "The ursine creature has presented a diagram of an oxygen atom; the centauroid and arachnid have presented similar diagrams of methane molecules. All have made sounds as they pointed to the diagrams, and the computer has associated those sounds with the names of the compounds. From this, we surmise that the ursine is an oxygen breather, though judging from the frost on its suit, it is accustomed to a much warmer median temperature than any Alliance species."

Globin pushed the joystick down and over—and received a shock. The horizontal alien had no helmet—only two clear bulbs, within which were antennas. They did not move; the creature might have been an inert lump. But one of the "arms" held a diagram of a molecule—no, two diagrams, Globin saw. He frowned and expanded the view, and recognized the second diagram—it was a silicon atom.

Globin stared.

"The meaning of the second diagram held by the fourth alien is unclear," the commentator said.

But it was very clear, to Globin. The creature lived in an oxygen atmosphere, but was made of silicon. He felt a prickling creep up across his back as he stared at it—a living, organic computer.

Then he remembered that that was what he himself was, that and considerably more, and the prickling went away. Still, how much he could learn from the study of such a creature!

The bearish alien touched its own chest and chuckled something that sounded, to human ears, like "Gerson. Gerson."

"The alien seems to be naming itself," murmured the commentator. "But is 'Gerson' its name, or the name of its species?"

The centauroid was touching its chest now, flutting "Silber." The six-legged alien gestured toward itself and said, in tones like metal scraping, "Itszxlksh." Then another voice, rich and resonant, thrummed, "Ekchartok."

Globin frowned, and peered more closely. The arm of the horizontal alien had begun to move toward itself—but slowly, very slowly. He wondered what means it had employed to generate the sound.

He was still watching its movement as the picture disappeared, and the commentator himself came onto the screen. "Since this scene was recorded, the aliens have been in constant contact with a growing team of Alliance scientists. They have established a very basic vocabulary . . ."

The picture dissolved back into the first.

" . . . by associating sounds with pictures of basic objects," said the commentator's voice, "then with sketches of simple action verbs. With a thousand such words entered, the translation computer has been able to enter into dialogue with the aliens, exchanging descriptions and explanations of more complex terms. With five thousand words learned by both teams, meaningful dialogue has begun to take place."

Globin nodded, so intent that he scarcely saw his secretary. The procedure was correct—in fact, it was classical. But what had they learned from their communication?

"The four aliens are representatives of four different species," the commentator explained, "and our computers have learned four different languages, plus a fifth that is apparently a lingua franca. According to the visitors' report, they are only four of a score or more of races that inhabit the stars near the galactic core."

Globin stared. Just how far had those visitors come, anyway?

Thirty thousand light-years. Of course. He knew that. Approximately. Give or take a thousand light-years.

A spacesuited human stepped into the picture, asking, "Why have you come here?" The translation computer issued a combination of growls and whistles that Globin presumed constituted the same idea in the aliens' lingua franca.

In answer, the bearish alien growled and barked. The computer translated, "We were attacked by alien beings." He pressed the top of his card, and the diagram of the oxygen atom disappeared. The card flickered and darkened into a picture of ships in space—a vast flotilla, without any apparent organization, though Globin felt instinctively that the pattern was there, if he could only take the time to seek it out. He keyed his controls to expand that picture on the "card" and found that the ships were of a design not even remotely familiar, with a strangeness about it that somehow grated, arousing apprehension and dread in equal measure.

"They came from the northwest spiral arm," the computer stated to the accompaniment of the bearish one's growls. "All efforts to communicate with them have failed; they make no response at all. We call them 'Ichtons'; in our communal language, it means 'the destroyers.' "

The picture faded away and returned—but now it showed the strange ships descending toward a tawny planet. "At first," said the computer, "they settled on several uninhabited worlds. They had tenuous oxygen atmospheres and some primitive plant life, but had never evolved sentient forms. Accordingly, we left them alone, but set probes to keep watch on them. Within a decade, we saw that their planets had become overcrowded with billions of Ichton workers. The soil had been torn away to bedrock, refuse had been piled high, and all forms of life had been exterminated.

"Then they left these used-up planets and attacked worlds inhabited by sentient races."

The picture dissolved into a scene of battle, showing a horde of insectoid creatures engulfing a band of desperate reptilian creatures who bore weapons that looked like muskets modified to fit an allosaur, but that fired blasts of light. The view narrowed, one single attacker swelling in the screen even as its image froze. Globin shuddered; the creature looked like the result of an unnatural coupling between a locust and an iguana. The trunk of the body was covered by a hard exoskeleton made up of sliding sheets. This carapace extended over the top of its head. It stood on four legs and used a third pair in front to hold a weapon that seemed to be little but a tube with a squeeze bulb on the end—but the chitinous claw rested on a button, not the bulb. There were three of those claws on each "hand." The head looked like a locust's, except for the eyes, which were much smaller than those of the terrestrial insect.

It was not so much that the creature looked fearsome, as that it was utterly, totally in contradiction of everything he had ever thought of as a sentient being—and from the silent ferocity with which it had attacked, it seemed completely soulless and mechanical.

The creature shrank back into the middle of its swarm; the tableau thawed, motion restored, and Globin watched the pocket of reptilians being engulfed by the horde. They streamed by, chitinous thoraxes and threshing legs and whipping tails, and when they had passed, there was not a trace of the reptilians.

"These are only a very few of a relatively small band of Ichtons," the Gerson explained, "but even so, they were enough to overwhelm the reptilian colony on what was once a lovely and fertile planet. The same has since happened to the home planet, and to those of three other species. On any world they conquer, the Ichtons exterminate all higher forms of life, especially sentient species, then begin exploiting the planet's resources."

The picture rose, looking out over miles and miles of barren sand.

"Where the horde has passed," the Gerson growled, "nothing remains; all life is erased."

The screen darkened; Globin moved his joystick to show him all four aliens again. The fluting voice of the Silber said, "We four races have joined together to protect our worlds. Together, we halted the Ichton advance, but only at grievous cost in lives and resources. We knew we could not hold them off for long without assistance—so we dispatched dozens of ships like this one, each with environments for representatives of each of our four species, to seek out aid for our home worlds and colonies. The Ichtons seem to have realized our goal, for they pounced on our ship as we fled our home planet. The battle was short and vicious, and our ship was damaged in the course of it, but we won free, and have come to you from the Core in only four months."

"Four months?" said Plasma. "Was their drive damaged, that they could not shift in weeks?"

"I think not," said Globin. "They seem almost to boast, as though they think four months to be excellent time. It is only conjecture, but I think their FTL drive is very primitive. After all, stars crowd densely at the Core; what need for a sophisticated FTL drive when you need never travel more than a few light-years?"

"We ask your aid," thrummed the Ekchartok, "not only for ourselves, but also for you. We believe that the Ichtons have conquered all the habitable planets of their spiral arm; if they conquer the worlds of the Core, they will begin to move out into other spiral arms. It may take a century or a millennium, but they will find your worlds, too—and then they will be virtually unbeatable; there will not be billions of them, but billions of billions. We appeal to you to fight this cancer and excise it now, while it is still far distant from you—and in the process, to aid four species who have been long blessed with peace, and have ceased to study the ways of war."

But the humans and Khalia had not succeeded in studying war no more, Globin reflected. Far from it.

He didn't bother following the debate that ensued in the Alliance Council; it had a foregone conclusion. So he was not at all surprised when Plasma burst into his office three days later, crying, "Globin! It is war!"

Globin stared, frozen for a moment. Then he snapped, "The screen! At once!"

"At once, Globin!" Plasma ducked back into the outer office, and the screen lit up with a view of the Alliance council chambers, with men in grim and very orderly debate.

"The Senate met in executive session as soon as the preliminary reports had been presented," the commentator said. "In view of the sufferings and peril of the Core races, they have decided to lend what aid they can against the Ichtons."

Globin smiled a small and cynical smile. "It is scarcely sheer altruism," he said.

"Truly," Plasma agreed. "Who does not know that the Fleet, idling in peacetime, is not always the best of neighbors? I certainly would not care to have a base on Barataria, with Fleet law virtually excluding our own government."

"Never," Globin agreed, "though we have more reason to dislike the notion than most. And there is a burden of support that accompanies a Fleet base—not to mention making your world a target for enemies, if war comes again."

"But what can they do?" Plasma wondered. "They cannot release millions of personnel into the labor force; that would cause a depression that would drain the Alliance's economy even more than the expense of maintaining the hundred thousand ships of the Fleet. They are allowing attrition to reduce the size of the burden, by refusing to replace ships that wear out, and refusing to replace personnel who retire or die—but they cannot forget that they came close, very close, to losing their war with us!"

Globin nodded. "It was almost impossible to supply so vast a force, so far from its base."

"What can they do, then?" Plasma wondered. "Create bases in the Core?"

But an admiral was standing before the Assembly, resplendent in battle ribbons and braid. "We propose to build a number of mobile bases. Each base would be capable of repairing, maintaining, and even constructing warships, on a limited basis. They would be moved by the most massive warp engines and gravitic drives ever built, and would be capable of accelerating at nearly half the speed of a destroyer. Their mass would allow them to pass through gravitic disruptions such as stars, while still in warp. Disruptions of this magnitude would tear apart a smaller field. Such battle stations would be so large as to form their own ecosystems, making them self-sufficient for food and water, and their closed environments would be capable of sustaining their inhabitants indefinitely."

"He speaks of artificial planets!" Plasma murmured in awe.

But a Senator was on his feet already, interrupting the Fleet spokesman. "That would be prohibitively expensive, Admiral! Just building such a battle station would be a horrible drag on our already sagging economy—and maintaining it would bankrupt the Alliance!"

"The station would be self-sustaining, as I've said, Honorable," the admiral answered, "not just in material resources, but economically. Raw materials would be obtained locally by merchant corporations. To accomplish this, sections of the stations would be leased to mercantile corporations, and even to independent traders."

"Globin!" Plasma cried, and Globin stiffened, feeling the thrill pass through him.

"We would construct only one battle station at this time," the admiral was saying. "It would be the prototype, and we would dispatch it to the Core, to aid these embattled species who ask our help. We would equip the station with a hundred ships and all their crews, plus the crew and support personnel necessary to operate the station itself. Existing, but aging, spacecraft could be cannibalized for the construction of the mobile base. Current Fleet holdings in the Alliance worlds would thereby be diminished by nearly ten thousand ships and twenty percent of total personnel."

A murmur passed through the hall, as politicians glanced at one another and calculated how much of the problems caused by the peacetime Fleet could be alleviated—and how many jobs the building of the station would supply.

"The enemy would be defeated far from home," the admiral concluded, "and an Alliance presence established among friendly species in the Core."

The Assembly chamber disappeared from the screen, replaced by the commentator. "The Privy Council continued in emergency session," he said, "and the president came forth today with an astounding conclusion."

A picture of the president of the Senate replaced that of the commentator. He was standing in front of the titanic surrealist sculpture that housed the Alliance's civilian government, its lighted windows refracted through the waterfall that covered the front of the building. It was an extremely dramatic background for announcements, as Globin suspected it had been intended to be.

"We have determined to respond to the Core's plea for help," the president said, "but in moderation—we will send only one mother ship."

Globin frowned. A token indeed.

"But that ship," said the president, "will be the size of a small moon, and will contain half of the current Fleet personnel. It will also house a substantial proportion of the Fleet's smaller vessels."

Globin's eyes fairly glowed.

"Such a vessel will of course have to be built," the president responded. "It will be named the *Stephen Hawking*. The cost will be as astronomical as its destination, but the Alliance government will pay only a fraction of it."

Globin noticed that he didn't say how large a fraction he had in mind.

"Many universities have already petitioned the Council to find room on the Fleet ships for their astronomers, physicists, and xenologists," the president went on. "They have indicated a willingness to assume the cost of their support."

Of course, most of those universities were supported at least partly by government funds, one way or another—but Globin nodded; the Alliance wouldn't have to contribute anything additional. The universities would take the money out of their research funds. They would ask the Alliance for more money, of course, but they were very unlikely to receive it.

"However, we anticipate that the major portion of the funding will come from mercantile companies," the president wound up. "The galaxy is huge, and may contain many new and valuable commodities; merchant companies will wish to explore and exploit. Several of the largest companies have already been in touch with the Alliance, asking for rights to exploit new goods the Fleet may discover. The Alliance has refused, of course, since we are committed to free trade—and therefore, no monopolies will be granted. But any merchant company that wishes to lease space on the new supership will be allowed to do so, though the rate will be very high—and from the proceeds, we anticipate being able to finance the greater portion of the cost of the expedition."

"Should we be interested, Globin?" Plasma asked. When there was no answer, he turned, demanding, "Should we show an interest?"

He saw Globin sitting frozen at his desk, eyes huge and glowing, lips slightly parted.

The Council of Barataria was in an uproar. Half of them were on their feet, gesticulating wildly. The other half were making more coherent demands, some of which Globin could actually hear from his seat at their head.

"What do you speak of, Globin? How can you resign completely from the Council?"

"How can the Council function without you, Globin?"

"How can Khalia endure without you?"

Globin sat still, trying to keep his face from showing how touched he was, reminding himself that the Council had become a prison to him. When they quieted, he began to speak, some inconsequential remarks at first, but they all quieted completely as he began to speak. Then, more loudly, he said, "It is not easy for me to leave you, my friends, but it is necessary. The glory of Khalia must be increased; the prosperity of Barataria must be continued. As you all know, our trade with Khalia has become a major element in their economy; without us, they would suffer economic disaster. But Barataria cannot merely continue as it is—it must grow or diminish, for all things change, and a people, like a single life-form, must build or decay. If other companies gain access to new resources and new markets, and Khalia does not, we will lose our share of the Alliance's commerce; our trade will eventually die."

"Surely, Globin! But does not this require that you continue to lead us?"

"Other leaders have grown up among you." Globin could see the gleam begin in the eyes of the party leaders. "The old must give place to the young—and it is for the old to lend their vision and experience to the beginning of new ventures. It is my place to lease factory and offices on the *Stephen Hawking,* and to organize and equip the exploration party that will travel aboard it, to walk new worlds and gaze into new skies—and discover new and precious substances."

The clamor began again.

When it quieted, they tried to talk him out of it, but Globin remained firm—and bit by bit, he caught them in his spell, communicated his zeal, his fascination to them. First one caught fire with the wonder and challenge of it, then another, then three more, then a dozen.

In the end, they voted unanimously to accept his resignation, call for elections, and invest in the *Stephen Hawking*.

"I don't like it, Anton!" Brad Omera, the civilian administrator of non-Fleet personnel, glowered at his military counterpart. "They can call themselves merchants if they want to, but if you scratch a Baratarian, you'll find a pirate!"

"That may be true, Brad," Commander Brand allowed, "but they pay good money, and they're hardy explorers. On a mission like this, I'd rather have a Baratarian pirate beside me than a squadron of Marines." He didn't mention that he'd far rather not have that pirate against him.

"But the Globin, Anton! The Globin himself! The arch-villain of the Alliance! The Pirate King!"

"He's a former head of state of a member planet." Brand put a little iron into his voice. "And he's a human."

"Human renegade, you mean! He's a traitor to his species, and he always will be!"

Brand didn't deny it; he only said, "He's a very skillful leader and an excellent strategist." But inside, he was fiercely determined to make sure Globin stayed in his own quarters.

It was two years between the vote in the Senate and the day the Baratarian liner matched velocities with the completed battle station, coming to rest relative to the huge maw of the south pole port. It drifted up into that vast cavern and over near a boarding tube. It stopped itself with a short blast from the forward attitude jets. The tugs answered with brief blasts of their own, bringing the mouth of the tube to fasten to the coupling around the liner's hatch.

Inside, Globin watched the process on the ship's screens,

and his lips quirked in amusement. "How fitting! The back door!"

"I see no 'back door,' Globin." Plasma frowned. "It is the southern pole of a huge sphere, nothing more."

"The huge port in the south pole, yes! The back door, for tradesmen!" Globin chuckled, aware that long ago, he would have been hurt and dismayed by the discourtesy. Now, though, it only gave him amusement, and aroused a bit of contempt for the Fleet officers who governed the ship. He knew his own worth—and had a notion of how quickly the Fleet's men would come to value their Khalian bedfellows.

The hull rang with the coupling of the huge boarding tube, and a voice from the *Stephen Hawking* advised them, in carefully neutral tones, that air was filling the lock at the end of the tube, which would soon be ready for their new passengers.

Globin rose and stretched, scarcely able to contain the excitement bubbling through him. He felt as though he were thirty again. "Tell the captains to prepare to disembark, Plasma. We've come to our new home."

With his hundreds of eager trader-warriors in their quarters, and their titanic stock of provisions, Baratarian gems, and electronic components stored, Globin was ready to face the necessary ritual of greeting the *Stephen Hawking*'s commander. Of course, many of those gems and electronic components could be fitted together to make devastatingly powerful weapons, and each Khalian had his own arsenal among his personal effects—but the *Stephen Hawking* did not need to know about that, and Globin felt no need to mention the issue in his upcoming conference with Commander Brand.

He was vastly amused at the size of the sign on the door that led to the lift tube that communicated to the world outside the decks leased to Barataria, Ltd. In Terran Standard and Khalian script, it warned "AUTHORIZED PERSONNEL ONLY."

Plasma frowned at the inscription. "Do they think we cannot read their words?"

"For myself, I have no trouble," Globin assured him. "Loosely translated, it means 'Pirates Stay Out.' "

The door irised open, keyed by his thumbprint—he was the

only Baratarian who *was* authorized—and he stepped in with Plasma only one step behind him. As they rode through the light show adorning the walls of the tube, Globin found time to wonder if the humans had already christened his decks "The Pirates' Nest," or if that was yet to come.

They stepped out into a reception that was so stiff and cold, Globin wondered how long it had been dead.

"Chief Desrick." Commander Brand bowed—or at least inclined his head. "I greet you in the name of the *Stephen Hawking*."

Behind him, his first officer glowered, simmering.

Globin blinked in surprise; it had been so long since he had used his human name that it took him a moment to realize the man was talking to him. He noted the Khalian idiom "I greet you," though, and chose to take it as a compliment, though he knew it was intended as an insult—he was pointedly not being told he was welcome. Slowly, he returned the bow, actually tilting his torso forward an inch—not enough to honor the admiral as his senior, only enough to show him how it was done properly. "I greet you, Commander Brand. We of Barataria are honored by our place in the *Stephen Hawking*."

Anton Brand understood the rebuke, and reddened. He looked as though he would have liked to refute what Globin had just said, but every word had been technically correct—the Baratarians did have a physical place in the *Stephen Hawking*, though not a metaphorical one. Instead, Brand only said, "I do not think we will have occasion to meet very often, Chief Merchant, barring incidents between personnel." His tone implied that Globin had damn well better make sure there were none. "So let us agree that you will work only within the framework of the *Stephen Hawking*'s mission, and will give advice only when it is asked."

"Indeed," Globin murmured. "Such were the terms of our contract, and we will of course abide by them."

"Then we need speak no further." Commander Brand gave him a curt bow. "May you fare well on the journey, Chief Desrick."

Globin returned the bow in millimeters, stifling a smile. He turned away, trying to catch Plasma's eye, but failing—the warrior was staring at the first officer, his lip twitching as though he were fighting the urge to smile.

"Plasma," Globin murmured, and the Khalian broke his stare reluctantly and turned to follow Globin to the drop shaft, every muscle stiff with the suppressed urge to fight.

The lift shaft doors closed behind them, and Globin began to chuckle. The light show gave an eerie cast to his features as they sank down, and the chuckling swelled into full, hearty laughter.

Plasma stared, scandalized. "How can you laugh, Globin? When he has virtually insulted you!"

"No, he has not quite," Globin gasped, letting the laughter ease away. "No, he meant to, I am sure—but he succeeded only in showing what a boor he was. Let it pass, Plasma—he has little understanding, and less true honor."

Plasma stared in bewilderment as Globin, smiling, shaking his head, chuckled again. He was thinking of the upcoming, and no doubt similar, meeting with Administrator Omera.

The days passed quickly, and the weeks. They might have dragged, but Globin saw to it that his lieutenants kept their men busy with fighting practice and lessons in business and accounting. He often stopped by the practice cavern to watch the training, and took his turn in the classroom, explaining the intricacies of finance to a group of youngsters who hung on his every word. Their excitement, their enthusiasm, their restlessness, made him feel years younger. He had recruited a force of young Baratarian Khalians who did not remember the Family war, except as stories their grandsires told them—but those tales had filled them with a burning desire for glory, and their youthful lust for females stirred them with ambition for reputation and wealth, that they might each attract the female he longed for, and have the right to mate. Globin watched them hone themselves in mind and body, and beamed with pride upon them.

They asked him to teach unarmed combat as well as commerce, but he declined on the grounds of age. Still, they did notice that he practiced, too, and they strove all the harder to emulate him in both book and boot.

"But how shall we need skill in combat as well as commerce, Globin?" Plasma asked him. "Must we fight even as we bargain?"

"We must be prepared to do so," Globin answered. "We must be prepared for anything, for there is no predicting the customs of truly alien species."

Privately, though, he doubted that they would encounter any completely incomprehensible behavior. He had a notion that the principles of commerce were as inherent and universal as those of physics. He was eager to find out if he was right.

The personnel of the *Stephen Hawking* were all subdued and angry at the horrors they had just seen, as the battle station accelerated and made the transition back into warp drive. They had expected to find a thriving planet, geared for war, perhaps even under attack by an Ichton horde—but they had not expected to find the barren cinder of a planet that had once been the Gerson home world. The Ichtons had come and gone, and where they had passed, only rubble remained.

In the caverns devoted to their own environment, the Gerson envoy moved in a daze, seeking to help the few dozen survivors the *Hawking*'s people had discovered. Elsewhere in the ship, all the other inhabitants of the battle station discussed what they had seen, in tones of outrage.

"How vile can they be, Globin! How insentient!" Plasma was beside himself, burning in agitation.

"It is thoroughly inhumane," Globin agreed, his face stony. "The planet completely bald! Scarcely a living being left!"

"And the Gerson emissary is a noble being," Plasma snapped, "good-hearted and valiant. How foul to exterminate so fine a race!"

"At least a few survived, and had the sense to activate their beacons when they saw our scouts." Privately, though, Globin wondered how many more survivors had not dared take the chance, and still hid on the remains of the Gerson planet, doomed to slow starvation. Certainly Brand had not taken any great amount of time to search for survivors; he had been too angry, too eager to go seek out the battle. "How are the men enduring?"

"In rage and ranting, Globin. They are young, they are warriors—and they are furious that they were not allowed to join the expedition down to the surface." He snorted with exasperation. "What did Brand think we would do—steal?" He turned to glare at Globin. "Could we not have invoked our contract, and insisted on our right to visit any planet at which the *Hawking* stops?"

"We could," Globin admitted, "but it did not seem politic, to seem to think of gain in the midst of such tragedy. That is, after all, the reason behind that contractual right—to search for marketable commodities."

"Commodities!" Plasma snapped, exasperated. "On a world milked dry, shorn clean, picked bare? What could we have found there?"

"Survivors," Globin muttered. He did not mention that he himself had been too stunned by the enormity of it, the scale of the inhumanity of the Ichtons.

But then, they *were* inhuman, were they not?

A new word was needed—"insentient." Any species capable of such unfeeling destruction could barely make claim to sentience itself. It was more like a natural force, a climactic disaster, unfeeling and uncaring for anything but its own goals. Globin began to wonder if "sentience" involved more than intellectual capacity.

Beside him, Plasma shuddered. "The tales those survivors tell! The vastness of the machines of destruction, the rolling mines and refineries, that gobbled up every trace of their civilization, all their antiquities, all their greatest works!"

"And the complete lack of feeling with which they treated the Gersons." Globin's mouth tightened. "To not even bury the dead! To do nothing but hurl them into those all-devouring machines! What do the young warriors say of this, Plasma?"

"What would you think they would say, Globin? They are unnerved, as are we; they are angered and appalled, as any feeling being might be! They speak already of revenge, Globin, though it is not their own race that has suffered!"

"Well, we can all see something of the best of us in the Gersons' emissary," Globin allowed, "and the fate of his home world has too many echoes of the defeat of Khalia; we cannot wonder if they feel the need for revenge as though it were their own."

The *Stephen Hawking* dropped out of warp drive, slowed over a period of days, and swung into orbit around the planet Sandworld (a very rough translation from the tongue of its dominant—nearly only—species, the Ekchartok). And they seemed to be not only the sole species of their world, but also the sole survivors of that species.

The alien emitted a high-pitched, keening sound as the screens of the *Hawking*'s briefing room showed them view after view of a barren, featureless plain.

"This is not as your world always was, then?" Captain Chavere, the chief of the Fleet xenologists, tried to word the question as gently as possible.

"No, never!" answered the flat, bland tones of the translator, though the sounds the Ekchartok were emitting were ragged as gravel, and its surface vibrated with contrasting wave patterns. "There were mountains at this latitude, with lakes and streams."

There was no water visible any longer, no mountains, and only vast raw gouges of valleys here and there, where titanic machines had chewed away bedrock to break out minerals. And nothing moved.

"The Ichtons have been and gone," the centauroid, amphibious Silber said. "Nothing survives in their wake; all life is eliminated, all growing things are eaten. They have scoured this world to draw from it every ounce of mineral they seek. Even their own body wastes have been processed to draw from them every molecule they can use; all that is left is the waste of their waste." It pointed, almost touching the screen where a flat, dark surface glimmered with sunlight.

"We must land and search," Chavere said, his face grim. "There may be an individual, perhaps a dozen, even a hundred, who have escaped the Ichtons' notice."

"There will be nothing, nothing!" the Ekchartok keened. "The Ichtons miss nothing; every gram, every grain, will they have sought out." Then suddenly it went rigid, totally quiescent.

The Silber stepped forward, reaching out a hand, then drew it back. "It is quiescent," said the translator. "Its suit will provide for it."

Captain Chavere hovered, almost frantic, at a loss. "What is the matter with it?"

"Shock," Globin answered. "It has gone into its equivalent of a coma, and the suit's life-support systems will sustain it."

Chavere favored him with a glare. "How would you know? This is not your field!"

"Personal experience," Globin returned. "I recognize the stimulus, and the symptoms."

Chavere reddened, but "It is logical," grated the arachnid alien, and the captain had to suppress his annoyance.

"We must search the planet! We must do that, at least!"

"Indeed," Globin murmured. "Indeed we must."

Chavere rounded on him. "You have no business in this affair, Chief Merchant! You will remain aboard ship!"

Globin had finally had enough. "I invoke the Landing Option clause in our contract, Captain. According to the terms of the agreement, when there is no condition of battle, we have the right to accompany every expedition to the surface of every planet visited by the *Hawking*'s personnel, for the purpose of investigating resources for trade."

Chavere's eyes narrowed. "Your contract? Why, what would you do on this planet?"

"Why, as our contract says," Globin murmured, "search for resources."

"But there are no resources left!"

"Nevertheless, we have the right to search," Globin reminded him.

Chavere locked gazes with him. Globin stared back, unperturbed. Finally, Chavere turned away with a snarl.

Globin permitted himself a small smile, gave a minuscule bow, and turned away to the drop shaft, Plasma behind him, showing the snarl that his chief suppressed.

As the door closed behind them, Globin said, "Select a landing party."

• • •

Chavere touched his helmet to Globin's; without a radio betraying him to eavesdroppers, he said, "There was no need for you to accompany the expedition."

"But there was," Globin returned. "I understand the need for vengeance."

Chavere scowled through his faceplate. "There is no one here on whom to revenge the Ekchartok, Chief Merchant."

"No," Globin agreed, "but there is information to be found that may show us the means of defeating the Ichtons when we find them."

Chavere's mouth flattened with disgust. "The contract only permits you to search for trade goods."

"Oh, we will," Globin assured him. "We will."

His helmet speaker demanded, "Globin? Is all well?"

Looking up, he saw Plasma with a dozen young Khalians behind him, devoid of weapons—except for the steel claw casings at the ends of the mittens of their spacesuits. Globin gave a fleeting smile to Chavere, and his smile was not pleasant. Then he turned back to his adopted children. "Nothing at all, Plasma—only myself and Captain Chavere, agreeing on disposition of personnel. Let us take our places on our sled."

"Behind us," Chavere's voice snapped through his headphones.

"Of course, the rear guard," Globin replied, amused. "Always the last."

A low growling filled Globin's helmet, coming on the private Baratarian communication channel. The young Khalians were experiencing the devastation of war for the first time, and were angered.

"But this was not war." Plasma shuddered. "This was a cold-blooded processing of life into death."

"They could not have defended themselves!" a young Khalian was saying to another. "With their cannon and ships gone, they are nothing, the slowest of the slow, small and weak!"

"But hard," his fellow demurred.

"Hard, and brittle," a third chimed in.

"But where are they all gone?" the first demanded. "To slavery? Or death?"

"If it was death," the second said, "where are the bodies?"

They were silent for a moment, considering the question. Then the first said, "Globin? Where are the bodies?"

Globin thought he knew, but he didn't want to say. "I can only conjecture."

"Then do, we beseech you!" said the second.

Reluctantly, Globin gestured toward the bare ground around them. "See how it glitters?"

There was an appalled silence. Then a young voice demanded, "Do you mean they ground them up and strewed their remains about?"

Globin was silent, not wishing to shock those he was beginning to think of as his children.

"Globin?" the first pressed. "Did they grind them to powder?"

"Worse," Globin said, as though the words were torn out of him. "They were silicate beings, after all, and pure silicon is the stuff of solid-state circuits."

This time the silence was the young's. At last one spoke, his tones filled with horror. "Do you mean they melted them down and strewed the ground with the parts of their bodies the Ichtons had no use for?"

"It is only conjecture," Globin reminded.

A low growling answered him, not of nervousness or apprehension but of mounting rage.

"What monsters can these Ichtons be, to place so little value on sentient life?" one demanded.

"Monsters indeed!" said another. "Pray we come to grips with them!"

"There is a whole planet here cries out for vengeance," a third agreed.

Globin reflected on what was not said, more sure than ever that the vision of a conquered species ground into dust awakened schoolbook memories of Khalia's defeat by the Fleet. He wasn't even sure his young warriors were even aware of this wellspring of their anger, but he was sure it was there.

An electronic tone sounded.

Amazed, Globin looked down.

"Globin!" Plasma cried. "There is a blip on the life detector!"

"I see it," Globin confirmed. "It is very faint, but it is unmistakable."

Plasma looked up and saw the other sleds speeding away. "They are going on by!" he shrilled. "Are they in so great a hurry that they cannot spare minutes to seek out a living being?"

Globin pressed down with his jaw, toggling the transmission switch inside his helmet. "Chief Merchant to Surveillance Captain. Our life detector shows a trace from the northwest."

"Too faint," Chavere answered. "We can dismiss it as background noise."

Globin glanced again at the trace. "It is a regular wave form, though it is of a much lower frequency than that belonging to any life-form we know. It should be verified."

"Look for it yourself!" the captain snapped. "We have a whole planet to cover! We can't go kiting off after every off-phase signal!"

Plasma snarled, his neck hairs lifting.

Globin glanced at him, his own face hardening. "As you bid us, Captain." He toggled his audio pickup closed and nodded to Plasma. "West-northwest."

Plasma pressed the stick, and the sled veered away from the expedition's line of travel. "Why is he so rude? By the stars, if he faced me now, I would . . ."

"Baratarians!" Captain Chavere's voice cracked like a whip. "What the hell do you think you're doing?"

Globin keyed the audio. "Just as you bade us, Captain— tracking the trace ourselves."

There was a pause, and Plasma hissed amusement.

"All right, go, and to blazes!" the captain snapped.

Globin hurried to close the pickup before it could send Plasma's snarl. "Such discourtesy should win him the death of five cuts!" the secretary snapped.

"It should," Globin agreed, "but in addition to his dislike of us, he is apprehensive—he and his crew grow nervous in the Valley of Death."

"Here is no valley, but an endless plain," Plasma growled.

"And endless death," Globin agreed.

"How shall we be revenged on them, Globin?"

"Why, by finding a survivor, of course." Globin leaned forward to peer more closely at the screen. "The trace is growing weaker, Plasma—we have passed it. Go back."

The sled swung about in a half circle.

"Holding constant." Globin frowned. "We must be at the circumference of a circle, of which it is the center."

"There is no pivot in sight but a slag heap," Plasma objected.

Globin looked up; the blue-black slag glinted in the sunlight. "It seems glassy," he said. "Perhaps it is silicon."

"Is there anything else on Sandworld?"

"It could hide a being made of silicon," Globin pointed out. "Surely it would not lack for food. Plasma, move toward that heap."

Frowning, Plasma turned the sled, then shouted with delight, for the trace was growing stronger.

It was quite strong as they settled to the ground beside the hill of glassy waste. As Globin climbed down, he glanced after the expedition's file of sleds, just in time to see the last slip over the horizon.

"How now, Globin?" Plasma asked. Behind him, the crewmen muttered.

"We take it apart, bit by bit," Globin answered. "Slowly, my children, and gently—do not dismember an ally as you seek to demolish its prison."

They whittled away at the huge hill with lasers, a slice at a time. After fifteen minutes, Globin called a halt, feeling apprehensive. "Plasma," he said, "take the sled to the crest, and tell me the reading."

Obediently, Plasma flowed back into the sled. It rose up, leveling off at the top of the hill. "The trace diminished as I rose, Globin!"

"Then it is beneath the heap," Globin interpreted. "We do not need to cut, but to tunnel. Take the portable detector, my children, and dig."

Three youngsters leaped forward faster than the rest, then hesitated. "What tools shall we use, Globin?"

"Those you were born with," Globin returned. "If you feel something hard, desist and bring the detector. Begin, now. To the center first."

The three spread out to the points of the compass as a fourth jumped around to the far side. Dirt flew; their remote ancestors had dug into burrows to follow their quarry, and the Khalian children tunneled for pleasure as human children climbed trees. A fifth followed with the portable detector that relayed its information back to the main screen in the sled.

They dug radii like the spokes of a wheel, first four tunnels, then triangulating from the circumference and two of the tunnels. The huge mass above them might have come grinding down if they had dug too many, but the detector showed them where to dig, and Plasma himself took the final tunnel directly to the spot. There, digging very delicately, he touched something hard with his claws. Carefully, ever so carefully, he dug it loose and bore it out.

It was oblong, it was flat on the bottom, it had antennas folded flat. It was unconscious, but the life detector showed it to be the source of the trace.

The Khalian warriors shouted with triumph, and Globin keyed for transmission. "Chief Merchant to Surveillance Captain."

"Of all the . . . What is it, pirate?" the captain exploded. "What mess do we have to dig you out of now?"

A score of snarls rose from the young Khalians.

Globin waved them back, smiling, but with a hard glitter to his eyes. "It is we who have been digging, beneath a mess the Ichtons left. We have found a live Ekchartok. It is dormant, but it emits brain waves."

The channel was silent for a few seconds. Then the captain snapped, "Homing on your signal. Keep the channel open."

"Give them our beacon, Plasma," Globin said. "After his rudeness, the captain deserves an unrelenting squeal."

Hisses of laughter answered him, though there was viciousness in their tone.

"How shall we repay his rudeness now, Globin?"

"Retract your claws, Plasma," Globin advised. "His embarrassment is punishment enough, but it is made worse because it is pirates of Barataria who were right, and who showed greater compassion than a human. Back aboard our sled, me hearties, with our prize."

They flowed back to their seats, Plasma asking, "What is a 'hearty,' Globin?"

"You are, Plasma—you all are. A 'hearty' is a bold and valiant fighter who delights in life, as we have this day."

Plasma sat, and turned back, frowning. "Will you not join us, Globin?"

"Yes, quite soon." Globin had taken out his pick, and was breaking loose a fist-sized sample of slag. He came back to the sled, sat down, and gazed at the glassy rock, frowning.

"Why do you bring such a piece of rubble, Globin?"

"Because," his chief answered, "I told them we would search for resources, so we must have something to bring back." But the intentness of his gaze went beyond a mere excuse.

Plasma noticed. "What troubles you, Globin?"

"Not 'troubles,' Plasma—'intrigues.' Why would an Ek-chartok hide beneath a slag heap?"

"Why—did they not dump it upon him, in lack of concern, and to slay him?"

"I think not, Plasma—I really do believe they used the dead bodies as a resource, horrible as it seems. No, this one hid, and from the shape of its body, I would conjecture that it is as skilled at burrowing as yourselves, though much slower." Globin pursed his lips, thinking. "Why would a silicate life-form hide beneath a slag heap? Food, of course, since there is silicon in it—but what else? Aorta, pass me the radiation detector."

"It is here, Globin." The young warrior held out the pickup. The detector fairly screamed.

"Transuranics," Globin explained, back aboard the *Hawking*. "Radioactive waste, to them—but potential fuel, to us. Their reactors and engines must be very primitive that they would throw away such treasure. It is well my warriors wore spacesuits, for it was only that shielding that saved them from exposure."

His chief physicist nodded, watching his men process the sample through a dozen different tests. "There are nodules of it embedded in the silicate slag."

"Will it generate power?"

"Oh, yes," the scientist said quietly. "Oh, yes—a great deal of power, Globin. If it were not for the quantity of slag holding the nodules apart, those heaps would blow up the whole planet. It is as though the Ichtons had operated a vast number of breeder reactors."

"Perhaps they did," Globin returned, "but their own technology is too primitive to make use of the product." He gave the scientist a smile. "We have learned as much about our enemy as about business."

"Business?" The scientist looked up, startled. "How is this 'business,' Globin?"

"Why," said his chief, "we are here to find marketable commodities, are we not? And what could be more marketable than Ichton slag?" He turned back to watch the tests, chuckling.

"Of course," the scientist breathed. "When will you tell Commander Brand, Globin?"

"When his fuel supplies begin to run low," Globin answered, "and he is more amenable to paying our price."

"You would not charge your own allies an extortionate rate!" the scientist protested.

"Of course I would," Globin answered. "He says we are pirates, does he not?"

"Surely you don't believe this claim that they are only looking for surviving Ekchartok, Anton!" Brad Omera was indignant.

"Surely not," Commander Brand agreed. "Why would such a search require them to set up a virtual refinery on the surface? And why would they have to ship quantities of slag back aboard in those huge canisters?"

"Oh, the Globin was very candid about that. He said that whenever they find a section that they suspect contains an Ekchartok, they bring it back up to the ship for careful handling."

"If you think you can trust what the Globin says." Brand turned to David bar Mentron, the battle station's chief technician. "Mr. bar Mentron, what sort of equipment was it they had you build?"

"Not much more than a cold chisel with a very fine edge, sir," Bar Mentron answered. "But it's in a standing frame that guarantees the chisel won't slip, and has a setting for calibrating the exact force of the blow, to the erg."

"That *is* the kind of equipment you'd need to chip away rock gradually," Omera said, frowning, "if you didn't want to take a chance on injuring a living being trapped inside it." He turned to Bar Mentron. "Tell the commander about that special room they had you build."

"Special room?" Brand frowned, alert for the slightest hint of treachery.

"Just a radiation chamber, sir—you know, a laboratory for handling radioactive materials. Nothing unusual about it, for what it is—just the shielding, the lead glass, the waldoes, the locks . . ."

"*Radiation* chamber?" Brand nearly leaped out of his chair. "What would they need *that* for? What are they doing—handling transuranics?"

"They told me the slag and the Ekchartok are radioactive." Bar Mentron shrugged.

Brand stilled. "Well, that's true enough. So would I be, if I'd spent a few months under a mountain of radioactive slag."

"Yes, but that's exactly why they've taken refuge in those slag heaps." Omera frowned. "Apparently the Ekchartok can use the radiation as a sort of emergency ration, absorb it and convert it to electricity—which is all they need to keep basic life systems going inside, while they're dormant."

"Love to find out what kind of evolution that species had," Brand muttered. "How's that first one doing? Can it talk yet?"

"Only a few syllables; it's still very weak." Omera shook his head in exasperation. "You really let those pirates steal a march on you, Commander."

"Yes, I know." Brand scowled. "I read Chavere the riot act about not having followed up that trace, so he has developed a tendency to track down anything that gives his detector the slightest hiccup. He's redeemed himself by finding six more Ekchartok—in heaps of quartz rubble the Ichtons apparently had no use for, and one of them was dormant under a brackish puddle the locusts seem to have overlooked. But the fact is that in Chavere's place, I probably would have done the same thing—gone on looking for something more obvious. The trace on his life detector was so small it could have been an earthworm."

"Or a dormant Ekchartok," Omera returned.

"Yes," said Bar Mentron, "but the Ekchartok emissary hadn't told us his people could go dormant."

"Understandable—the moment he saw this planet, he went into shock. But the fact remains that it was the pirates who found that live one under the slag heap, not the Fleet."

"Two more, now," Brand said, the taste of the words bitter on his tongue. "They found two others, and they're in the same condition the first was—dormant, probably in shock, but alive."

"They have?" Omera whirled about. "How come nobody told me about this?"

"Word just arrived, and the pair of them are on their way to the infirmary right now. The Globin claims they broke them out of a single slag lump in their workshop. Says they were nestled up against each other as though they were a Yin-Yang symbol."

"These slugs have sexes?" Omera asked.

"Ekchartok," Bar Mentron murmured. His voice was very soft, but Omera flushed. "Of course, Ekchartok. I'm sorry."

"Maybe the emissary will come out of shock, now that he has some company," Brand mused. "And I suppose we can't argue with what Globin's doing, if he found a couple more. But I really wonder if he needs to grind up all *that* much slag just to find Ekchartok."

"He can't be too careful, I suppose," Omera sighed, "though the pirates are certainly growing their own heap of recycled slag. And they've been bringing up an awful lot of canisters, for only two Ekchartok."

"They say the other slag lumps only had chunks of radioactive waste in them that fooled their detectors," Brand sighed.

"They say, they say!" Omera snapped. "I'd give a year's income to go in there and see for sure what they're doing."

"Then go." Bar Mentron shrugged. "The Globin's made it an open invitation."

"Of course he has," Omera snapped. "Who'd go into the Pirates' Nest if he didn't have to?"

• • •

Plasma clicked his timer and nodded. "Drill completed in sixteen seconds, Globin. If anyone who is not of Barataria should wish to come here, we will have the laboratory out of sight before he arrives."

"Not that there would be that much to see." Globin smiled. "We are doing no more than we have claimed—slicing apart suspicious lumps of slag, to see if there is a treasure therein."

"Certainly," Plasma agreed. "Of course, the treasure is far more often a lump of almost-pure transuranic than it is an Ekchartok—but who else could tell?" He turned to Globin. "Will not those who remain behind need equipment like this on the planet?"

"No—the dormant Ekchartok have survived till our coming, and they might not survive our rescue without the facilities of the hospital. They can wait in the slag until the *Hawking* returns."

Plasma nodded. "How soon will the battle station depart for the fray?"

"In two days, Brand said. He feels that Chavere and the other rescue commanders will by then have completed scouring the planet for survivors." Globin smiled. "But for some reason, they seem to be content to leave the slag heaps to us pirates."

"They who have volunteered to stay and process the slag will be in great danger," Plasma reminded him.

"Not so great as that—they have our fastest courier, and orders to board and flee at the first sign of an enemy."

But Plasma noticed his brooding frown. "What troubles you about them, then?"

"Will they obey orders?" Globin said simply. "Perhaps I should not have agreed to let them keep blast cannon and force-field generators."

"No Khalian would be parted from his weapons, Globin, you know that. And the work must continue—there may be more Ekchartoks in those slag heaps, as well as the transuranics."

"Yes, it must continue," Globin sighed, "and I will have to school myself to patience. The Ichtons have passed by, after all—they are not likely to return to a barren planet. No, certainly not."

But he did not like the word "likely."

• • •

The *Hawking* had been under way for two days when Brynn Te Mon's secretary notified him, somewhat hesitantly, of a request for an appointment.

"Send him to the science coordinator." The physicist didn't even look up from; his screen, with the three-dimensional model of a very complex molecule on it. "That's what top kicks are for—to keep the bored ones away from those of us who are doing the real work."

"He asked for you by name, sir."

"Tell him I referred him to Coordinator Cray, by name."

"Sir . . . it's Chief Desrick."

"The Globin?" Te Mon looked up, startled. "What would the Pirate King want with me?"

"He wouldn't say, sir—only that it had something to do with some artifacts he had discovered while he was looking for Ekchartok."

"More likely he discovered the Ekchartok while he was looking for something he could sell." But Te Mon pushed himself away from his desk. "I'll see him, now. I've always wondered what he was like." And he did mean "always"— Te Mon was only forty, and had grown up with tales of the Human Renegade.

Globin was waiting in a small, antiseptic reception chamber. He rose as Te Mon came in. "Scientist! So good of you to spare the time. . . ."

"And I don't have much of it." Te Mon cut him off, even as he looked Globin over with a microscopic gaze. "What can I do for you, Chief Merchant?"

Globin slowly drew a small pouch out of a pocket and spilled half a dozen gems out into his palm. Te Mon caught his breath at their scintillating beauty, and at the array of colors each one refracted. "Very . . . pretty," he said. "Of course, they weren't cut when you found them?"

"No—I had one of my technicians do that. I've been experimenting with them in my own laboratory, when I found a moment. They seem to have some strange properties."

"Other than swaying the head of any nubile young lady, I can't think what."

"They make light cohere," Globin said, "and with a slight energy input, they amplify that light by a factor of five."

Te Mon stared at the gems, then snatched one up. He held it up to the light, frowning. "You know what these are, if they do as you say?"

"Of course," Globin murmured. "The key element in a hand blaster that could be far more powerful than anything we have now."

"We'll run it through the tests right away." Te Mon looked back at Globin with a frown, weighing the gem in his hand. "They're for sale, of course?"

"Of course," Globin murmured.

"Success, Globin?" Plasma asked as the chief stepped out of the drop shaft.

"Success," Globin confirmed. "Contact the colony on Sandworld, Plasma. Tell them to pick up stones."

The *Hawking* dropped out of FTL mode to see the world of the Silbers floating like a blue gem in the void—a gem laced in by lines of fire and surrounded by twinkling motes.

"They're under attack!" a sentry cried.

"Battle stations!" Brand snapped, and the alarm howled through the *Hawking*. Pilots and gunners scrambled for their ships; artillerymen stood by the battle station's huge cannon.

In the Pirates' Nest, scores of young Khalians sat in the three-place cannon ships that were more weapon than vessel, fuming and chafing at the bit.

"Globin! Will they not permit us to fight?" Plasma pressed. "I swear that if they don't, our young bloods will blow up the locks themselves and be off to the battle!"

"Bid them bide in patience." Globin never took his eyes from the screens that showed the progress of the battle. "They do not trust us, Plasma, as we all know. They will call upon us only if they are desperate."

And surely they would not be; the screens showed a horde of silver sparks swerving about the planet, lancing at satellite defense stations with ruby beams, while much larger silver dragonflies stabbed at the planet itself with columns of fire.

But answering columns climbed up to meet them, and here and there, a dragonfly turned incandescent as its force-fields soaked up the energy of those gigantic planet-bound weapons, then turned into stars as the screens overloaded.

"They may be amphibians," Globin murmured, "but these Silbers can fight."

They were losing, though—there were simply too many Ichton guns against them.

"How many are there in that horde?" Plasma demanded.

"Thousands," Globin answered. "Listen!"

" . . . only a small force, our Gerson ally says," Brand's voice was saying from the screen. "A really big fleet would be more than a hundred thousand. They must have figured they didn't need more for such a small planet."

"They were right," Plasma hissed.

"But they could not know about the *Hawking*." Globin pointed. "See! The Fleet comes!"

Yellow lines stabbed down at the Ichton ships. They reeled, swerving apart in chaos; ship after ship exploded, bright in the eternal night.

In spite of themselves, the Khalians gave shouts of triumph.

But the Ichtons rallied quickly; half of their fighters peeled off to fight this new invader. Fleet ships began to glow and explode. Then the Ichtons went after them in groups of three, singling out one ship each. Quickly, separate Fleet ships peeled off to flank and pierce the enemy, reinforcing their outnumbered colleagues.

But it left a hole in their hemisphere—and through that hole stabbed a large Ichton ship with a score of smaller ones about it. Rear guns lashed out at them, but too late—only a few died in fire.

The view shifted—the Ichton column was heading straight for the *Hawking*!

"Batteries fire as soon as the enemy is in range," Brand's voice snapped. "Home Guard away!"

Mosquitoes boiled out, filling the screen, stabbing at enemy ships in twos and threes.

"We need more, Commander," a tense voice said.

"We can't commit the reserves already!" Brand snapped.

Globin leaned forward and toggled a key. "Chief Merchant here. I've fifty ships with pilots and gunners spoiling to get into the fight."

There was a long pause; then Brand snapped, "All right, pirates! But don't wait for ransom!"

Plasma's lips skinned back from his teeth, and, truth to tell, so did Globin's—but all he said was "Ships away."

A hundred voices shrilled a cheer. The huge hatch opened, and the Khalian ships began to lance out into the night.

They turned the tide; Baratarian cruisers swarmed out about the Ichton ships that were as yet unmolested. They had to slow and turn to fight—and their cruiser was suddenly alone, without its midget guard.

Golden fire enclosed it, from the *Hawking*'s batteries. The screens glowed, but held.

A dozen Khalian moths homed on that light.

Cannon beams stabbed out from the cruiser—and daring Khalians slid in under the beams and stabbed their own fire down next to the Ichton lances, piercing through the holes the locusts had opened in their screens to let their own fire out. Three of those valiant ships danced too close to the fire and burned brightly and briefly—but three more stabbed home, then sped away, just barely fast enough, as the battleship turned into a huge fireball behind them.

Brand's voice joined the shout of triumph. Then, directly, he said, "Damn fine men you've got there, Chief Merchant!"

"They are my pride," Globin rejoined—but mixed in with the joy was sorrow for the three who had burned.

The smaller ships had burst the last of the Ichton attackers. At the planet, a very few Ichton ships sheered away to flee; the rest were cinders.

Howls of triumph echoed through the vast bulk of the *Hawking*. Brand's voice overrode them. "Kill those ships! Don't let them take word of us back to their command!"

The bright gnats swarmed after the fleeing enemy, overhauling them easily—what the Ichton did, they did by merciless efficiency and great numbers, not by speed.

Globin stayed transfixed, watching until each ruby vessel had gone dark, and the surviving destroyers shot home to the

Hawking. His heart thrilled with victory even as it mourned the fine young pilots who would not come back.

Brand's voice sounded, closer, more intimate, and Globin knew it was a closed channel. "Your men shall have heroes' funerals, Chief Merchant. I am proud to have them aboard my ship."

Globin keyed transmission and answered, "Thank you, Commander." But he wondered how much of that pride would transmute into trust.

"But why would Brand summon you, Globin?" Plasma was beside him as they rode up the lift shaft.

Globin shrugged. "To congratulate us on our valor, perhaps, or our loyalty." But he had a notion the meeting would test that loyalty, not affirm it.

There were pleasantries and opening amenities this time, which Globin found agreeably surprising, though boring. Brand actually invited him to sit, and even served coffee. Finally the conversation turned to the recent battle, and the expenditure of energy—and Brand came to the point. "We used a great deal of fuel in that battle, Globin, and it was only a skirmish. We have enormous stockpiles left, you understand, we are in no danger of immediate depletion—but it does remind us that we will need to replenish our supplies continually."

"True," Globin agreed, "but we all knew that when we undertook the mission, did we not, Commander? In fact, the *Hawking* even has mining machinery."

"Quite so," Brand admitted, "but there is the matter of locating the raw resources. Now, gossip always moves, Chief Merchant, though I presume that, in this instance, it is based more on guesswork than knowledge . . ."

"Rumors are notoriously undependable, Commander," Globin said with a smile. "Still, what is the current rumor of interest?"

"That you and your pi . . . Baratarians have discovered a source, and are stockpiling fuel."

Globin's smile broadened. "The rumor is true."

"I am glad to hear it." Brand's eyes glowed. "And will you share those stocks with the *Hawking*?"

"Why, of course, Commander." Globin sat up a little straighter. "But you see, we are businessmen . . ."

When the drop-shaft doors had closed behind Globin and Plasma, Brand stood shaking his head, trying to recover from the price he had agreed to.

Omera was shaken, too, but he said, "Well, after all, Commander—they *are* pirates, you know."

"Chief Merchant!" The intercom in Globin's desk crackled. "Communications to Chief Merchant!"

Globin stiffened; for the communications watch to speak directly to his intercom meant they were using their emergency override. "Chief Merchant here."

"We have just received a squeezed message from the colony on Sandworld, Chief! They have detected an Ichton squadron moving toward them from the Core!"

Globin sat immobile for two seconds, long enough for Plasma to break in: "Is there any reason to think they are targeting our colony? How could they know of their existence?"

"From our communications with them," Globin answered. "We have been in contact several times a day. They had only to follow the beam. No doubt that is why our miners have sent the signal squeezed to less than a second."

"*But* why would the Ichtons pursue them? The planet is barren!"

"Revenge, perhaps," Globin answered. "It is a way to hurt us, where we are vulnerable. Perhaps to weaken the *Hawking*'s defenses. Or perhaps they have already deciphered enough of our language to know our people are refining fuel. In any event, we must aid them. All ship crews, prepare for battle!"

"But Commander Brand . . ."

" . . . knows which side of the battle line his fuel is on," Globin finished. "Leave him to me. Plasma?"

"Yes, Chief?"

"Commander Brand, if you please."

"Instantly."

It wasn't quite that fast, but it was only minutes. Brand's voice was guarded, though not overtly hostile. "Chief Merchant?"

"Yes, Commander."

"Your secretary indicates that you have a matter of importance to discuss."

"Yes, Commander. Our colony on Sandworld is under attack, or will be shortly."

"And our fuel supplies with them!" Brand saw the implications immediately. "But we can't leave the Silbers, or the Ichtons will be on them like the locusts they are!"

"Understood. Permission for all Baratarian ships to depart immediately for Sandworld."

"Permission granted," the commander said instantly. "I'll send a dreadnought to reinforce you."

"I . . . thank you," Globin said slowly.

"I'm surprised at your reluctance," Brand snapped. "Would you rather not have their support?"

"Not if we cannot agree on command, no."

There were a few seconds of silence. Then Brand said, "I'll tell the captain of the *Imperious* to follow your strategist's orders. That good enough for you?"

"More than good enough." Globin smiled, eyes glinting. "Thank you, Commander. We're off."

He snapped the key, and Plasma frowned. "What do you mean, 'we,' Globin? Surely you will stay on the *Hawking*!"

"When my warriors are all at risk?" Globin shook his head. "I have stood my share of watches in battle, Plasma. I will go on our own battle cruiser, the *Marco Polo*—but I will go!"

Sandworld loomed in their screens—but there were no silver mites circling about it.

"Where are the Ichtons, Globin?" Plasma asked.

A cold chill seized Globin's vitals. "I shudder to think." He keyed his audio pickup. "Globin to all captains! Descend at the colony's location—and descend ready to fire! The Ichtons may all be on the ground already!"

"It is true," Plasma moaned. "Our warriors had only the one blast cannon!"

"Have faith in them," Globin said grimly. "They may be unblooded, but they have been taught the ways of battle." Nonetheless, he was filled with apprehension.

"F.S. *Imperious* to Chief Merchant," a gravelly voice said

suddenly. "We have just dropped into normal drive, and are about one AU from Sandworld. In what way can we assist?"

Globin was surprised to feel a surge of relief. "Take up station around the planet, *Imperious,* to defend against Ichton reinforcements. I believe the first wave are all aground. We are descending. Thank you."

"Jump!" he heard the gravelly voice calling, just before the connection was broken.

"A warp jump of one AU?" Plasma stared. "So close to a planet? That is horrendously dangerous!"

"It is indeed," Globin said grimly, "but he knows we need him *now*—and is eager for battle. Have respect for our new allies, Plasma."

The secretary growled, but turned back to the screen. "I would we could descend!"

"As do I," Globin assured him, "but we had need of one mother ship among our fleet, and it is only fitting that we should . . ."

"Enemy!" a joyful yelp called from the communicator.

Plasma's claw jumped to a key, and an inset appeared in the screen, showing what the fighter's sensors saw—half a dozen cigar-shaped ships with faceted sides and ruby light spears stabbing toward the great slag heap on one side and what appeared to be barren stretches of sand on the other. Yellow beams answered them, and each ship had developed a glowing nimbus as its screens drank the energy of those shafts of light.

"There are Baratarians there, selling their lives dearly!" Globin called. "Ships One, Three, Five, and Seven, all on the enemy! Ships Two and Four, hover in reserve!" He waited a second for the howl of protest to pass, then snapped, "Ship Six, land behind the slag heap to rescue the warriors there!"

On the larger screen, the ships plunged like falcons stooping on their prey, and inside Globin a crazed voice was crying, *What am I doing, trying to direct a battle? I am a merchant and politician, not a general!*

Fortunately, his pilots couldn't hear. Their beams of light speared down, each striking a ship, and Six fired even as it sank toward the slag heap. Five Ichton ships glowed like candle flames—and Globin saw specks scuttling across the sand between the Ichton ships and the slag heap. They had landed ground troops!

Then a sentry shrilled, "Globin! Attack from space!"

"Fire!" Globin shouted automatically, even as Plasma put another inset on the screen, showing three double-convex hexagons swelling as they sped toward Globin's ship. The screen filled with a glare of light, then darkened as automatic sensors compensated for the glare of the force shield as it drank the energy of enemy fire; the screen flickered.

"Their beams pulse, they are not steady," Globin grated, gaze glued to the screen.

The ship shuddered, and a crewman cried out, "Screens overloaded! We are holed! Breach amidship, in cargo bay!"

They had no cargo, and one of the hexagonal ships glowed like a gem, first red, then orange, yellow, and on up through the spectrum until it suddenly flared white, and was gone.

But two more were battering Globin's ship with pulses of energy, and the deck shuddered under their feet as crewmen called out, "Holed amidships, in bay five! Holed astern in fighter deck! Holed in the bow—blast cannon three out!"

Globin felt a stab of sorrow for the gun crew that had just died, but his gaze stayed fixed on the screen, where his remaining cannon were pouring all their energy into the two remaining ships.

Suddenly, another beam lanced down from the corner of the screen, and one of the Ichton ships glowed like a ruby, then an emerald, a sapphire, a diamond—and flashed into an expanding cloud.

"Thank you, *Imperious*!" Globin shouted, his finger on the key, and his crew howled victory as the remaining ship swerved aside, turning to run—but the *Marco Polo*'s beams stayed with it, though a few made the view fuzzy as their focus shifted, trying to follow but not quite matching the enemy's changes of direction. Then the *Imperious* hove into view, its beams spearing the remaining Ichton like a specimen pinned to a board. Suddenly it flared through the entire spectrum and exploded.

"Glad to oblige," *Imperious* answered.

The crew howled with joy, and Globin with them. Then, as his crew quieted, he called out, "Remember your brothers aground, my children!"

The main screen showed what was happening on the planet's surface. One Baratarian ship was gone. Two more flew raggedly, but the beams from the six ships could not stay on them as they swerved and dipped, firing bursts at the enemy, whose screens were glowing more strongly. Ships Two and Four had dropped down to join the battle, ganging up on a single Ichton ship and avoiding the beams from the others. Six was shuttling back and forth and from side to side and up and down, playing peekaboo around the slag heap—and whenever it peeked, it spat fire. The Ichton bolts only flashed through the space where Six had just been—those that did not hit the slag heap. Many did; the slag had melted, and was flowing. The Ichton fighters were dancing away from it, still trying to shoot at something within it. Globin went cold at the thought of a gallant fighter half-buried in slag that he knew would kill him with radioactivity, firing burst after burst at the strange beings that strove to reach him.

A score of other fighters were tap-dancing around the beams that seemed to come from the ground itself. Their own beams lanced the sand, but weren't hitting whatever they were aiming at.

Then three of the remaining ships glowed blue-white.

"Chief Merchant," said *Imperious,* "I can reach the ground with two beams, and still stand watch."

"Can you be sure they will not hit our men?" Globin asked, and several Baratarian voices shrilled, "Yes!" even as *Imperious* answered, "Yes, if you tell your men to avoid being directly above any of the enemy's ships, for I am squarely above them."

As though it had heard him, an Ichton ship fired a beam straight up. Two Baratarian fighters took advantage of the opportunity to swoop in and snap solid projectiles at the Ichton—and it exploded as its overloaded screens tried to absorb the impact.

"Please, Globin!" a Baratarian voice pleaded.

"Very well. All ships avoid eight o'clock at seventy degrees."

On the screen, two of his own ships swerved aside.

"Fire!" Globin barked.

Two beams speared down from the corners of his screen to converge on an Ichton ship. It stood like a topaz for a moment, then flared and died—and, suddenly, all the Ichtons on the ground were running toward the remaining two ships. Globin reflected that if he could not hear their command channel, they could not hear his—then noticed that two Ichtons still stood near the slag heap.

"Magnify enemy at slag heap!" he snapped to Plasma, and an inset appeared with a close view of the two Ichtons. Globin looked, and thought again of the offspring of a lizard and an insect.

But these insects had sticky feet—they had become mired in the melted slag, that was apparently more akin to tar than lava.

Then, on the main screen, beams struck down from the *Imperious,* and the two remaining Ichton ships flared and were gone.

The sand was strewn with the ashes of dead Ichtons—and, outside the blast circumference, a few intact but very dead specimens.

"Well done, *Imperious*!" Globin shouted. "A thousand thanks! We have corpses and two prisoners for our scientists! Oh, bravely done!"

"Our pleasure," *Imperious* said gruffly. "Your men are valiant and intrepid, Chief Merchant. Now I know why you call your ship the *Marco Polo*."

Homeward bound, the Baratarians bound up their wounds and counted their casualties. Nine Baratarians had died, three of them miners, and they had lost two of the small fighter ships. But at least fifty Ichton foot warriors had died, along with six ships and all their crews—and the *Imperious* was bringing home a rich booty of four intact Ichton corpses and two captives.

Globin had guessed correctly—the Baratarian miners had not even tried to prevent the Ichtons from landing, but had bent their energies toward preparing a mammoth booby trap instead. They had rigged their single blast cannon for remote control and had hidden it in the slag heap with its power supply—it had come dangerously close to blowing up, but had held off the ships. The heap was of their own slag, of course, not the Ichtons'—no dormant Ekchartok had been destroyed in the battle. The miners themselves had gone to ground, quite literally, in dugouts walled with five feet of a kind of a cement they had improvised, at the first report of approaching ships that refused to give identity. By themselves, the colonists had killed a dozen Ichtons, and had bluffed the ships until help could arrive.

It had taken great courage, Globin reflected as he pinned medals to their bandoliers. Then he pinned new rank insignia on their commander, reflecting his excellent choice of tactics, as well as initiative, resourcefulness, and sheer ability to lead.

Now Globin was bound back to the *Hawking* in one of the small fliers with Plasma beside him. The *Marco Polo* remained in orbit around Sandworld with the rest of the fighters, a temporary guard for the invaluable transuranics, half of which reposed in the hold of the *Imperious*. Globin had taken a calculated risk on entrusting the fuel to the Fleet in advance of payment, but he did not think there was too great a chance of a bad debt.

And he was right—humans and Khalians alike thronged the staging chamber behind the *Hawking*'s landing bay, and a massed cheer went up as Globin stepped out of the airlock; the Baratarian home guard were only a thin line at the front, for behind them hundreds of humans cheered themselves hoarse.

Globin stood, blinking in amazement, then went rigid as a wave of emotion swept through him, a fierce, incredulous, exultant pride, as he realized that at last, and finally, he had become a hero to his own species.

THE *STEPHEN HAWKING*

UPON ITS COMPLETION the station was christened the *Stephen Hawking* after the First Age scientist whose theories were the basis for the development of the warp drive. The station itself was a globe over five kilometers in diameter. It left Alliance space with a mixed crew of over ten thousand Fleet and civilian personnel. Also on board were every member of the crews of the alien ship that had begun it all. Their own ship was long relegated to scrap.

The *Hawking* was so massive that before completion three construction workers became lost on its hundreds of decks and nearly died. To avoid this happening again, the walls of every deck were color-coded beginning at the top with red and descending through the spectrum to violet. Each color contained five major levels and up to three times that number of subdecks. Fleet activities were concentrated on the upper decks, red through yellow, and the civilians were concentrated on blue and indigo. Violet was almost completely taken with the warehouses packed with goods they expected to barter with the many races in Star Central. The central core of the *Hawking* was a three-hundred-meter tube running along the decks containing the massive warp drive and magnetic engines. Entrance ports were located all along the hull.

Along the hull were located 256 large aperture laser cannon. All were coordinated from a central battle bridge located in the center of red deck. Twenty-four were additionally fitted with experimental virtual reality targeting units. Backing these laser

cannon up were dozens of missile tubes and literally thousands
of missiles stored for station or ship use. The Fleet contingent
consisted of three hundred ships, with the preponderance being
scout and light attack craft. Replacement parts were sufficient
to almost totally replace this fleet. Keeping track of it all was
the full-time task of over a hundred quartermasters.

The journey to Star Central took over eight months. When the
Hawking arrived, they were too late to save the Gerson home
world. Most of those who remained behind had died two years
earlier in the futile defense of the world. The other remaining
Gersons may have been systematically exterminated by the
Ichtons. No sign of any survivors could be detected from orbit.
It was likely that the few dozen remaining on the battle station
were the last of the race. Feeling its way cautiously along behind
the swath of destruction left by the Ichtons, the specialists began
to draw conclusions from reports garnered from the intelligence
ships that had preceded them to Star Central.

THE EYES
OF TEXAS
by S. N. Lewitt

"I SURE WOULD like at least a chance to shower before I bring that up to the lady," Cowboy said, and grinned slowly. "Seeing as I smell like seven-year-old milk." He was covered in dust and his utilities were stained and rumpled. How it was possible to get filthy working in a clean environment on electronics he'd never figure out, but that seemed to be one of the immutable laws of nature. You open up the hull and you get dirty.

He'd been down in the bay calibrating the lasers on the *Glory*. She was a light cruiser, smaller than the *Imperious* that'd just put the bugs on the run at Sandworld. He'd heard the announcement over the loudspeaker while he was checking over the electron alignments in the controller.

Not that there was anything wrong with the *Glory*'s lasers. Far from it. But Senior Weapons Officer Logan Reyes lived by the motto that there was perfection and then there was everything else. He didn't bother with everything else. So the margin of error considered acceptable by bay crews and manufacturer's specs didn't cut it with him. Not when with a little tinkering he could eliminate at least twenty nanometers from the outer targeting range.

"I admit I have finished here for the moment, but I do need to put on a clean uniform before I go on duty. And I currently am not on duty in any case, not until sixteen hundred. Which isn't for another half hour yet," Cowboy repeated himself. "I was just doing a little tinkering on my own time."

But Vijay Deseka, the *Imperious*'s top Intel officer, was having none of it. "Those eyes will be useless in twelve hours, maybe less," he said firmly. "Dr. Blackwell needs them yesterday. And you are available now."

Cowboy wanted to argue. He was a gunny, not a messenger boy. If they wanted things hand-delivered up from the docking bay to Med Red, Mr. Analysis could just find himself some junior clerk and leave him alone. He never liked those Intel boys in the first place or the second. But the crew on the *Imperious* had just fought some fine battle and there wasn't anyone else available on the dock right at this second.

But the real reason he didn't protest anymore was that any excuse to see Doc Blackwell was fine by him. She wasn't even the kind of medic who grounded you, either, not at all. No, she was one of those xeno-types, specializing in alien anatomy. Add to that she was tall and pretty and had a smile that went kilowatts, and hell, even Med Red wasn't so bad.

So Cowboy shook his head and took the box. It wasn't a usual gift to bring a lady. The thick-sided box smoked a mist of supercoolant condensation, and even with all the insulation his hands were slightly chilled. And the idea of alien eyes rolling around in nutrient solution made his stomach pitch and roll like nothing had done since his first training runs.

Around him the mechanic crews were all over the *Imperious,* snaking fuel feeders and electrical lines already in place and pumping. Scrubs were working on the laser ports and the larger drones were maneuvering into position. It was beautiful.

Commander Deseka gave Cowboy a withering look. At least Med Red was only a deck away. That had been done on purpose, so emergency teams would have immediate backup where casualties were most likely to be admitted. Cowboy took one of the large service lifts up one and exited in a corridor of dark crimson, a color that in merely the past six months had become indelibly associated with Medical Services and sickbay for everyone on the *Hawking.*

There was a directory opposite the lift doors and Cowboy went to check out where the Xeno labs were. He'd seen Dr. Blackwell at a briefing on the Gersons and in the gym at Bright Orange 221. But like any member of any fighter crew, he ducked

Med Red like it was enemy barrage. The directory showed Xeno way in the back near the hull, and Avrama Blackwell headed the lab list.

He touched her name on the directory screen. The line remained dead for a moment, then he heard swearing in the background. A harried female voice answered. "Yes?"

"I have a little package you're looking for from the *Imperious*," Cowboy answered. "I'd sure be glad to hand it over to you."

"Oh. Right," the woman said. "I'm sorry, we're quite busy. Could you meet me in Ophthalmology lab six? It's right next to Psychiatric Services. I think you know where it is."

Cowboy knew where it was, all right. The eye clinic was washout city, requiring gunnys and hot shots to retest every four months. To be sure the laser range and the radiation hadn't done any damage, they said. Cowboy was convinced that it was to keep themselves in a job. After all, popping in new clone eyes wasn't enough to keep them busy. Not enough accidents of that nature aboard the *Hawking*. And to get there he'd have to pass Shrink Central, the worst of the worst.

"Sure, I know it," Cowboy said steadily. "You sure you don't want me to come down to Xeno for you? It would be no trouble at all."

"Ophthalmology," the woman said.

Cowboy shook his head. Well, he'd tried. "You got it," he answered with false cheer.

Actually, the halls weren't that crowded. And when people in med uniforms saw the box he carried they gave him a curious stare and then quickly glanced away.

Avrama Blackwell was waiting in the lab when he entered. She took the box from him immediately and set it in a tangle of equipment. "I'm sorry I was so brusque," she said softly. Her nose crinkled when she smiled and her large eyes glowed. "But we've got the Ekchartok survivors in Xeno now. And since they need radiation in the dormant state, the lab is lousy with it. And dealing with eyes, well . . ."

Cowboy knew what she was talking about. It was the first thing he'd learned as a weapons officer, before he knew how to play the circuits into nanometer precision. Radiation exposure was sure to damage human eyes, all the way back through the nerve. Khalian eyes, too, he remembered. And even with all the regrowns in the world they couldn't repair that level of injury. They could clone a body, but no one could replace the optic nerve. No matter how good the tech was, how minute the calibrations, nothing replaced a gunny's eyes.

"Why couldn't they clone eyes for you to work with?" Cowboy asked.

Dr. Blackwell laughed. Her laughter was musical and as warm as her eyes. "It would cost a fortune," she said. "And there are other priorities in the cloning tanks now. Priorities I can't even argue with." She shook her head.

She turned off the light and they were plunged into utter dark. Only a faint reddish glow illuminated the equipment on the lab table. Then she opened the box and took out one of the eyes with a long delicate field prong, the kind that was so low energy that it didn't glow at all, though it held the organ without touching it.

"If you want to help with the experiments that would be fine. But I've got work to do," she said.

Cowboy hesitated for a moment. To be quite honest, he was interested. But when she picked up a scalpel he decided that he wanted to know the results, not learn biotech at this late date. He'd managed to avoid it in school and saw no reason to start now.

"I'd love to be able to help you out, but I'm scheduled to go on duty at sixteen hundred," he said softly. "Would you mind telling me about what you find out? Over a beer, maybe, and a good-sized steak?"

Dr. Blackwell laughed again. "Don't leave until I give you the signal, I want to get this specimen shielded before you open the door."

He'd never been so disappointed to leave Med Red, though he had less than twenty minutes to shower and change into something respectable enough for roll call.

Combat was beautiful, Cowboy thought. Light danced around the board, red, yellow, green. It pierced the darkness and opened up the glints on the screen into explosive flowers. "Above," the green sphere of the watery Silber planet blossomed with colored blades that homed on the enemy emission traces and consumed the Ichton fighters. The small craft ignited and blew over kilometers of star-strewn space, their fragments invisible against the glare of the close-packed suns of the Core.

Cowboy sat strapped motionless at his screen, his mind as big as the battleground. He touched the screen gently, picking targets with the AI, directing fire. He was there, he was on top of it, he was cold as the AI plotting the fire patterns. Always been cold when the adrenaline hit, like time slowed down, and he could see into the patterns of movement, see the unexpected and preempt it.

There were others in the fire control station on the *Glory* in the dark. The only illumination under battle conditions was the boards themselves. But Cowboy didn't care if there was anyone else there. He didn't notice them at all. It was just him and the screens and the flashes of light, the hottest, fastest game in purblind creation.

Four bugs were zeroing down to a single ungainly Silber installation, the one targeting broad sweeps through the sky and disabling at least two bugs in every pass. Maybe killing them, Cowboy couldn't tell. Over the range he could only see that they were intact.

Don't forget Miss Ellie's old Maine coon cat lying out watching the squirrels looking deader than last week's lottery tickets all fluttering where the trash pickup had dumped them on the ground. That cat could even smell dead, for sure. Looked dead, smelled dead, lay there like carrion when the dog tried to wake it up in the sunshine. And it always got at least two good squirrels for the pot. Good eating, those squirrels were.

Now there were four coming down on the position, coming wide with shields glowing with energy burn, so that the pale wide-sweep of charged particles wouldn't touch them, swooping down like buzzards on a cold night. Hated buzzards.

And below them the Silber weapons station, hardworking, flaring desperately against the incoming enemy. They fired wide band again, but the bug attackers had spread and were dancing around the edges of the wave. They knew its range.

And it glowed less brightly against the million stars of the Core, losing energy, draining. Still the blasts came, acid green wavering down the energy spectrum to yellow, orange, red.

Cowboy could imagine the Silbers in this post, power running low and under attack, praying for reinforcements (if Silbers prayed, Cowboy rather thought under the circumstances they would) and knowing it was hopeless. And still firing, knowing they were dead and gone but draining every last erg and drop of blood to defend their homes and families.

He hadn't known more of the Silbers than he had seen in the same transmissions everyone else saw. Now he could imagine the defenders below, individuals, maybe a few young kids who'd never left their mothers before, who'd never done the Silber equivalent of a night on the town and who now would never get the chance. Maybe the commander was an older guy with a baby at home who only wanted to return to his family and eat some good cooking and play with the kid.

He touched the points of light on the screen.

"High error margin," the androgynous computer voice said without inflection.

"I got override and you better listen up or you are going to be one hunk of stinking burnt junk," Cowboy muttered as he studied the display. He touched the four specs again.

They were far away and moving, the trajectories on a max evasion curve. But he could see into it, the time slowdown and his own instinct coming together at that moment to see the pattern whole and complete. He did not touch the specs again. Instead he jabbed points a little beyond them in the hard fire-control order.

The AI obeyed but felt required to lodge its protest. Cowboy didn't even bother to listen. The streaks of light he had sent searing through vacuum touched four different bug fighters and took them all out together. All four flamed in unison creating a multihued spiral in the center of the screen.

And in the microsecond it took for the wreckage to clear Cowboy searched fruitlessly for another target. In range. In *his* range, a different range than anyone else in the whole Fleet.

No joy, no joy. Frustration welled up in him and he barked an order at the board to increase range spread. The AI refused to comply. Instead there was an announcement on the speaker that pierced his concentration. "The enemy is in retreat. Go after them. Do not, repeat, do not let any of them make it back."

Cowboy licked his lips. Easy pickings, too easy maybe for his liking. But he understood what had to be done. Couldn't let the damned bugs get word of the *Hawking,* no that wouldn't do at all.

The screens changed, flowing into each other like they were melting. The navigator and the helm were taking the *Glory* around and entering the pursuit, but from his strapped and bolted position in the gun station Cowboy knew only the stream of target screens as the enemy fighters before them turned Doppler blue.

And then something caught his eye and his intuition reacted with his hand. He touched a blue spot before them and then moved his finger back and to the side. "Area," he requested brusquely.

The screen immediately showed a detailed magnification of the subregion he had indicated. It was barren. The blue spec was to one side and not turning. Still, something rang like bells in his head and he knew.

"There," he said, jabbing his finger hard against the changing screens. There was nothing in the space he indicated, and it was behind and to the side of the running bug, not in his direction of travel at all.

"We are in pursuit mode," the AI informed him.

"I don't care if we're the Dallas Cowboys Cheerleaders, we're taking them," Cowboy insisted. And he felt the quiver of the firestrike through the bones of the substructure, although he knew that was impossible. Only imagination.

But what was happening on the board was not his imagination. The blue spec he had jabbed on a screaming hunch became less blue, slowing. And as they hit high definition he saw it wasn't fighter size. Larger. And at the far edge of his viewboard a bright orange friendly appeared alone.

Whatever he had shot at was much larger than a fighter, especially compared to the friendly at the far edge. It had to be a cruiser. And as he watched it began to slow and turn, attracted by the friendly coming on hard with guns blazing full. The cruiser avoided the blasts from the friendly fighter and came around hard horizontal. Just exactly to where he knew it had to be.

And then the blaze of *Glory*'s guns hit it full power. Its shields turned it bluer than running light and for a moment he worried that it was just going to cycle harmlessly forever, an APOT feedback loop. The Ichton cruiser sat there like a burning sapphire for what seemed like aeons. And then its systems went into overload and it exploded with such violence that the screen had to go to reduction eight to catch the whole show.

"So that's why they call you Cowboy," said Muller, who sat at the next board. But Cowboy wasn't listening. He was spread over a hundred klicks of vacuum as the enemy attack force was annihilated around him.

They were drinking down in civ country, in a place on Bright Green called the Emerald. Not real imaginative, though the smart money on the *Hawking* said it was named for the Emerald Isle and not the deck. This theory was borne out by the fact it was the only place on board that served Guinness Stout. Which was what Cowboy was drinking, courtesy of Sutter Washington the Third.

"Yeah, boy, you sure saved my ass," Washington said when he spotted Cowboy sitting with a couple of chief gunnies from the *Impaler* and *Kingdom Come*. "I don't know how you managed to nail that cruiser from your position, but I sure do owe you a drink and a favor. You ever in a tight spot, you know you got Sutter Washington the Third at your back, brother."

Cowboy just blinked. "I didn't know any of our people were out that far," he stammered.

Washington threw back his head and laughed. "Not many were. But I can push that baby so hard she don't know when to come. And chasing those bugs down the hole, well, they were sure pushing light. Though you know they don't have any kind of warp drive anyone'd care about. Lousy engineers, those bugs."

"Don't ever underestimate the enemy," said Chief Gunny Xia Ling. "That is the first and the second mistake. These

Ichtons are not going to roll over and die because we spray Raid."

"Like I said, those bugs are lousy engineers," Washington repeated and rolled his eyes. This time Ling got the joke and they all laughed too hard.

"Well, I was in what you would call hot pursuit," Washington went on. "I was ready to fire at anything. My granddaddy was an ace in the Fast Attack Wing in the last war. You might have heard of him, Sutter Washington. So I feel like I got to live up to the name, know what I mean? So I was going hot and heavy after them. Already got two in the battle here and wasn't near ready to stop. So there we were after them as they were trying to hightail it home, and I was way ahead of the pack. Luxury pickings, what you might call a seriously target-rich environment. And I had that cruiser baby in my sights and was ready to draw on him and he turns on me!

"Can you imagine? He slows to half-light and does a one-eighty and brings guns to bear. 'Course, that means when I fire I only got a little fellow, real disappointing." Washington stopped to wet his throat a little, telling the story was thirsty work.

Cowboy interrupted. "But it doesn't matter what size the thing is to make ace, right? The little fighter or the cruiser, either works in the rating. Or have I got it wrong?"

Sutter Washington smiled slowly. "Well, in technical terms it doesn't mean nothing, but truth to tell I really wanted to do my granddaddy one better. He was career Fleet, and so was my daddy and my momma and neither of them ever got to do more than push data around a screen. So I got a lot of making up to do.

"Anyhow, I don't know how you targeted the guy. He sure had me upside down and gravy. I only say, you ever need anything, you got a friend." Sutter Washington the Third solemnly lifted the remains of his Guinness and tapped glasses with everyone at the table.

"Intuition," Cowboy said seriously. "Just pure intuition." He didn't know what he meant by that, but somehow it seemed the only explanation he could find.

"You know, some researchers think that intuition is that the brain notices and processes data we don't consciously observe."

The voice was a woman's, low and familiar. Cowboy looked up, startled. Avrama Blackwell was standing over the group drinking, her clear blue eyes steady. She was looking directly at him. "Everybody here know Doc Blackwell?" Cowboy introduced her casually.

Sutter Washington's mahogany skin went mottled gray.

Avrama Blackwell actually giggled at the young fighter pilot. "I'm in Xeno, I don't do anything with humans," she said. "You're safe."

Washington's color returned slowly. "I would rather be surrounded by bug cruisers, would rather even be with one of those grunt reaction units on the ground, than spend ten minutes in Med Red," the pilot admitted. "Anything with a stethoscope gives me the tummy wobbles." He pointed to the pocket in the pale blue medical tunic Avrama Blackwell wore over her regulation utilities. The earpiece of a stethoscope was hanging out.

She stuffed it down hastily. "Take two aspirin and call me in the morning," she said, trying to make a joke of it. The others all forced some laughter and then found excuses to leave. Immediately. Which Cowboy didn't mind one bit.

"I didn't mean to make your friends uncomfortable," she told him.

Cowboy shrugged. "Their loss," he said. "Besides, I don't think they were so much uncomfortable as just giving me some space with a pretty lady. So, pretty lady, what are you drinking?"

Avrama Blackwell knit her fingers and looked down. "Actually, I'm not. I was just on my way down to Blue U to consult a little on the civilian side, and heard some scuttlebutt that a bunch of you heroes were in here. I thought you might be interested in coming along. I don't have all the answers yet, but you might find this informative."

Cowboy drained his glass and stood. Blue U was not his idea of a good time, and surely not where he had in mind going with a woman as winning as Dr. Blackwell, but it seemed like he had no choice. He was surprised to find that she even knew the slang term for the areas set aside for civilian research and scholarship. The term usually wasn't considered complimentary.

They crossed Bright Green to the far lift, which would be closer to scientist country when they arrived on Sky. The full science complement, including offices, labs, and lecture rooms, took a full quarter of both the Light Blue and Sky decks, one on top of the other, the two joined by the large amphitheater that doubled as the ship's main entertainment hall when it was not being used to display slides of alien viruses to fifteen lab assistants.

"Are we going to talk to Brynn Te Mon?" Cowboy asked. Te Mon was the only scientist Cowboy had heard of. Normally he never ventured below Dark Green. He didn't have the money to eat at any of the expensive restaurants in Violet and didn't need any of the luxuries sold at the civilian shops in the rest of the Blues. He could get the necessities from the commissary on Yellow with the military discount, and there were flea markets there on Sundays when some of the civ merchants came up.

Avrama Blackwell shook her head. "No. Brynn Te Mon is way too busy minding the existence of the universe to be interested in something as mundane as this. No, I sent my findings and the specimens down to Vladimir Tsorko as soon as I had my data. The eyes only live twelve hours, you know. But there are some experiments that can be done when they're less alive, and there's also a biochemical analysis. That isn't my specialty."

"There isn't anyone up on Med Red who could have done it?" Cowboy asked, interested. "You had to contract out?"

"We've got two full specimens to take apart, and five fast-grown clones lying in our one xeno cloning vat. And let me tell you, those cost way too much to let anyone just take them apart. Even in the interests of defense," Blackwell said matter-of-factly. "And Tsorko's specialty is radio astronomy. There were a couple of anomalies that I just didn't understand and Vladimir is, well, you'll see. A good friend. Anyway, he just came through with the results so he can explain the peculiarities I observed."

They stopped at a Sky Blue door covered with cartoons. In fact, Cowboy noticed, most of the doors down here were like that. It offended his sense of what was shipshape. Scientists were generally an unruly bunch. If they needed to put cartoons on their doors, the least they could do was use the inside.

Avrama didn't knock, she just touched the door panel. It was open. "We're expected," she explained before she went inside.

Vladimir Tsorko was a big man with a very big silvering mustache. He immediately jumped up and held Avrama by the shoulders. "Ah, my colleague, how very pleasant to greet you down here. I have looked at your specimens and run the tests as we discussed, and I have read your results. All I can do is confirm them. So I suppose I will be only a second or third author on your paper. However, I think that I have enough data to write one of my own, though it would be more in the nature of a note without further data. Of course, the more data I have the better. So if you come by any more specimens I would be so grateful. . . ."

Avrama flashed that warm, winning smile at him. "Of course, Vladimir, it would be my pleasure."

The older scientist seemed to notice Cowboy for the first time. "And who is this, your friend? Another optical specialist? If so we shall have to get the vodka and drink to all of us getting publications from this discovery! A very excellent thing, research."

Avrama Blackwell laughed again. "No, Vladimir, this is Cowboy, weapons officer on the light cruiser *Glory*. But he brought the specimens in and was interested in the tests, so I thought I'd bring him along."

"Ah, then, it is my honor to meet you," Tsorko said firmly. "And shall we get to business, then? Avrama, it is exactly as you suspected, only more so, if that is possible. I think the multiple structures you had questions about are suited to microwave reception. And the others, well, there is indeed an anomaly. However, I have a theory. . . ."

"Microwaves?" Cowboy asked.

Dr. Blackwell nodded. "Oh, yes. Maybe I should go back to the beginning and explain a little."

"That would be very helpful to me as well," Vladimir Tsorko agreed quickly. "I read your findings but you write so technically. And I have not studied any biology since I was an undergraduate, and then I threw up in the lab. I was excused from the practicums for the rest of the course. Ah, well, I had never planned on a career in surgery anyway."

Even Cowboy had to grin. There was something about the scientist that was so completely familiar. Texan, one might say, though it looked like Vladimir Tsorko had never heard of the planet called Texas or the Great Range system at all. But he had the expansiveness that made Cowboy suddenly, sharply, miss home.

Avrama Blackwell pushed the tea mug and a stack of papers to one side of the display monitor and put a stack of journal hard copies on the floor. Then she called up a series of pictures on the screen that meant nothing at all to Cowboy.

"These are photographs of the Ichton eyes," she stated, as if starting a lecture. "You will notice they are faceted, and that each individual facet is quite different. There are sections you will notice here with pupils and large sections that have no pupil structure at all. Of the facets with no pupils, there are two distinct types. One type has a strange structure that covers nearly the entire back of the retina, and the others are missing these structures. These were some of the anomalies that I consulted Dr. Tsorko about.

"However, as a first test, I placed electrodes in the cones of the retinas in all three kinds of facets, and shone light of different frequencies at them. The cones generate electrical current when they are stimulated by wavelengths they can detect." Then she paused. "How much do you know about waves?" she asked innocuously.

Cowboy shook his head. "I know that sound travels way slower than light and that some of them are no good for you. I guess I never thought about it."

"I don't know enough about waves, either," Blackwell admitted. "But sound waves and light waves are very different things. With sound you can hear ten different notes at once. If you aren't trained you might not realize what you're hearing, but a musician would. The wavelengths don't blend.

"Light is the opposite. Wavelengths blend, so you can't tell if, say, orange is the wavelength that produces true orange or a combination of wavelengths. What we see as colors are different wavelengths, and for us the visible range is from four hundred to seven hundred nanometers.

"Now, the longer the wave the lower the energy of the wave. The waves in our visible range are very small and X rays are smaller and higher energy than that. Infrared is larger, and microwaves at the long end can be a meter from peak to peak. Radio waves cover the largest range, from ten to the minus two meters all the way up to a million meters peak to peak. Which is why I wanted to talk to Vladimir, he knows all about radio waves."

"No, my dear, I wish I could know all about radio waves," the older man said sadly. "I know only a little bit about them." And then his eyes twinkled. "But what I do not know about them, nobody else knows it either. And I shall be the first to learn. But so far you are essentially correct."

Avrama smiled at him and then the picture on the screen changed to display a chart that Cowboy thought looked like a graph of his last poker winnings. It was a lot more pleasant than the alien eyeballs, though, and he was glad of the change.

"So I tried different wavelengths of light, first in our visual range. And until I hit red there was no response at all," Blackwell continued. "So I kept going lower. It seems that the facets with pupils responded to light from visible red through infrared."

"So these bugs see heat, basically," Cowboy said, thinking about it, wondering what it meant as far as *Glory*'s fighting capabilities were concerned.

"Well, yes," Dr. Blackwell agreed, "but that's not all. I ran the same experiments on the facet without pupils. Now some of the lower energy waves can pass through wood or paper or plastic. Microwaves, for example, and radio waves of course. So I tried them, and guess what?"

"The bugs see microwaves and radio waves," Cowboy guessed. "Must make cooking dinner a real experiment in living. But what does it change? I mean, it's all very interesting and that, but what use is it?"

"Well, it might help us find their home planet," Avrama Blackwell said. "Our eyes are adapted to our sun. Obviously theirs must have some advantage to wherever they're from."

Vladimir Tsorko nodded vigorously. "Indeed. But there is still more, very interesting about this species. Avrama asked me about the eyes with no pupils. Ah, I think, this is very strange, they react to very low energy waves. But how can they focus these waves? If you cannot focus, you cannot localize. It is like sound. We cannot focus sound waves."

"But you can tell where sound is coming from," Cowboy protested.

"Indeed," Dr. Tsorko agreed. "That is because you have two ears and you can triangulate. But sound waves travel so very slowly compared to electromagnetic waves. No, to focus these you need some antenna larger than the wave. If the wave is a meter long, then you need something bigger than a meter to focus it. We use dish antennas in great arrays to focus the long radio waves and we have only the two Trilimar observatories to focus those very long waves at the bottom of the scale. But the Trilimar observatory stations have dishes the size of a small solar system and it is so very difficult to maintain them. Even with all the graduate students one could want, and really they are more interested in doing theoretical work than going EVA and patching up dish plates two weeks away."

"So they can't see those waves," Cowboy said.

Dr. Tsorko beamed. "If you are interested in perhaps a small graduate stipend when we return it could be arranged. . . ."

But Cowboy shook his head. More school was not exactly on the immediate agenda, not at all. In fact, this long lecture about waves and eyes was starting to get a little dull and he still didn't see the point of it all. So maybe they could figure out from their vision what kind of star the home world of the Ichtons circled. Maybe there would be a strategic advantage there and it was important to the effort. Right now, though, he was more concerned with cleaning out this one little pocket of space.

Those Silbers down there, now, this wasn't one bit of use to them. They needed help, and fast. Cowboy silently wished the scientists would get on with it and maybe do something like make Ichton-free Raid. After what he'd heard about Sandworld and what was happening on the Gersons' home planet, this was one enemy he had no trouble using chems against.

"You are indeed right." Dr. Tsorko didn't notice Cowboy's lapse of attention. "They can see the smallest radio waves but they cannot focus them. The way we hear sound. But, and this is very interesting, the eyes with no pupils but with a strange structure before the retina, that structure is a type of organic dish antenna for the smaller microwaves."

"Like I said, dinner is a laugh a minute," Cowboy responded. His patience was just about used up. He'd known Blue U was not exactly his idea of a rec deck. Damn, the stupid things he'd do for a good-looking woman.

"So now you can write up your paper and I can write mine, and we can let the referees decide which of us will publish first," Vladimir Tsorko said gleefully.

Avrama led Cowboy to the door. "As always, it was a pleasure to have an excuse to visit, even if it was far too short," she said brightly.

"Indeed, we have to get together for some palmyari next week, of a certitude. My treat," the older scientist said firmly, then they stepped into the Sky Blue hallway and the door closed behind them.

"What are palmyari?" Cowboy asked with some trepidation.

"Dumplings," Avrama Blackwell answered firmly. "Delicate little dumplings in sour cream sauce."

"Speaking of which, I'm starving. Would you be willing to introduce me to these dumplings tonight?" Cowboy asked, his eyes twinkling. Maybe the lecture in Blue U was going to pay off after all.

Avrama's eyes lit up as well, with mischief as well as pleasure. "I think I'm more in the mood for Chinese, and it's dim sum night at the Golden Dragon."

"I know it well," he said solemnly and stepped aside formally as the doors to the lift opened.

He didn't sleep well that night and he couldn't understand why. Maybe it was the duck's feet; he usually didn't like duck's feet but Avrama chose two little plates of them. But when he left her after dinner and a stroll through the garden, without a single mention of bug eyes or any other educational topic, he couldn't get to sleep for hours.

And when he finally did manage to sack out the dreams came. Dismembered monsters were after him and he was small and afraid and in the boarding school in Sam's Town. And Jackson Byrne was there again, like all his nightmares, only now Jackson had faceted opaque eyes.

The dream followed the same structure. First Jackson erased every other line in his physics text, then the flash of the blind bomb that Jackson had thrown at him the day he moved into the Junior dorm and the headmaster's office, all reproak paneling and leather. The leather was real, butterscotch-colored even in his dream. Only the headmaster looked like Vladimir Tsorko and he was being sentenced to a life of auditing upper-level chemistry classes. Forever.

When he woke up he was soaked with perspiration and it was barely oh-dark-thirty. His two roommates were both snoring and Cowboy knew he should try to grab that last hour's sleep. What happened to the time in Weapons Command School when he could go to sleep anytime at all, when twenty minutes was enough for a good nap, and now he had trouble when the alarm went off at 0615 every morning?

Well, there was nothing he could do about it now. He knew he wasn't going to be able to drift back off, so he hauled himself out of the rack and spent the minimum in the recycle room. His utilities came out of the locker fresh enough to pass inspection. Dressed, he headed back to the bay where the *Glory* sat among all the light cruisers.

Cowboy loved the bay. He loved it when it seethed with activity, when men and women reported at a run when the enemy had been sighted, when the tech crews ran their refueling and prep after every mission. He loved it in silence when the lights were at half and the array of battle-weary light cruisers and scout boats waited in the semilights of the enormous bay. So large, so hushed, so like a church it made Cowboy want to pray.

But someone had violated the silence of the dark cycle of the ships. Crews worked round the clock, but there was no one else here now, no names on the door manifest, but a jangle of what passed for music somewhere out beyond Gremonsk still played on the wall plug. Made him think of Jackson Byrne playing that damned radio after lights out in the dorm, getting them all put on detention for a week.

Furious, Cowboy strode over and tore the offending box out of the jack. The only reason he didn't slam it against the composition bulkhead was that all hell broke loose.

A thousand watts of light came up on the registers in nanoseconds as orders boomed over the speaker. "All personnel report immediately to your assigned briefing room, bays six through nine, six through nine. All personnel report immediately to your assigned briefing room. Hot status, go, hot status."

Cowboy dropped the offending box without thought and ran top speed across the grate decking and into the hot status briefing room. The hot status team was assembled already, edgy, impatient to be gone. Cowboy recognized Sutter Washington the Third staring at the board with intense concentration and just the hint of a smile.

The briefing board glowed with bright red and tangerine displays, the data from which fed directly into the memories of every boat tasked. In enemy orange he saw a large ship surrounded by a host of fighters.

"This is what we want to get," the officer of the watch said. "It's an egg ship headed for the Gersons' world. They defend their egg ships more heavily than any other target, but these are the whole purpose of the Ichton conquest. Take out this baby and we hurt them where it matters."

There was only dead silence for a split second, and then the hot squad burst out of the briefing room and made for their craft double-time. They were out before the rotation crews arrived.

Cowboy stayed in place. His shipmates from *Glory* arrived, tousled and bleary-eyed, less than three minutes later. They didn't question him being there first. The briefing room locked cycle as the bay opened for the hot squad to launch.

This time the briefing was a little more involved. "We have sent the intercept team to attack the fighters and draw them off, if they can. We have various reports about how the Ichtons react to these tactics. It is Intel's opinion that they will not be drawn away from the egg ship, that they are instinctively pressured to protect it beyond any immediate danger to themselves."

Someone gave a raspberry cheer at the mention of Intel. Cowboy frowned. That was kiddie garbage; it had no place on the *Hawking*.

The watch officer didn't stop for a beat. "In any event, we want the light cruisers to back up the scout boats, play the heavies for them. Let the SBs take the fighters, we want the big guns on that egg ship. We have to destroy one. Not only will it be good for our effort and for our Gerson survivors, it will also demoralize the enemy. This is the crux of their mission. It doesn't matter how much territory they have taken if they can't move these babies in. Any questions?"

There were none. There was no time. The hot squad was already out there, the large schematic showed them closing fast. They were going to engage very soon now and they needed the backup of the heavier ships or they were in trouble. No questions.

They were dismissed as the bay doors went green, signaling that the bay was up to full pressure. *Glory* was ready. Cowboy ran to her with his shipmates, avoiding fueling lines and other crews without noticing them. Just one more distraction not to waste time.

The crew of the *Glory* had been together since before being assigned to the *Hawking*. They knew they were going to get the assignment, but even before they had never been the kind to let fifty years of peace make them lax. The *Glory* had won every readiness and shooting competition in her division for the past three years. And their rating aboard the *Hawking* was top ten percent. Which wasn't high enough at all for the skipper and the rest of the crew. Since they had emerged at the Core the skipper had been holding even more drills.

So that by the time the bay was ready for launch, the crew of the *Glory* was strapped in at battle stations, lights out and screens on, ready to come out shooting. They were hushed in the launch. This was not their maiden fight. They'd already been blooded once. Now there was only the task and the screens in front of them and the distance to cover before they engaged.

The screens were already reporting the hot squad closing on the enemy. Cowboy switched from schematic to actual view. The little scout boats seemed thick and not highly maneuverable compared to the sleek bug fighters. But as he looked closer he thought that perhaps the bugs didn't have the tech or weren't as concerned about it. He asked for mags on the screen and it complied. Yeah, no question, the bug fighters were old-style cockpit machines, helmeted figures sitting revealed under a transparent canopy. They fought visual, then, face-to-face because they either didn't have the instruments to keep themselves fully insulated from the field, or because they didn't trust the instruments they had.

Something about those canopies nagged at the back of Cowboy's brain as he touched the screen, commanding it back to schematic again. Easier to follow the patterns that way instead of being too involved in one particular fight. But of all the bluish blips on the screen, he wondered which one was Lieutenant Sutter Washington the Third, gunning for ace. Silently he wished the man luck, hoped that afterward they'd be able to drink another Guinness in the Emerald. That Sutter Washington's atoms would not be spread over a hundred klicks of vacuum. That his wouldn't be, either.

"Twelve minutes before reaching enemy position," the computer informed them all.

Twelve minutes. The entire universe could end in half that time.

On the screen before him, the hot squad executed a precise ninety-degree cartwheel and cut up the perpendicular vector, moving away from the egg ship pushing hard light. They executed a much more difficult fifty-degree wheel, neatly as the Fleet exhibition team, and cut back in at the egg ship from an angle that didn't give a clue as to where they had come from. Then they slowed as a single entity and regrouped formation so that instead of flying as a porcupine mass, they were strung out like an elongated arrow. And the arrow flew into place, tickling the edge of the Ichton defenses.

The shielding around the egg ship glowed like a star in the darkness. Even on the screen it quivered in the orange-colored wash that couldn't get a good enough fix to pinpoint it. Not that that mattered, Cowboy thought coldly. It was big enough that a few good hits in the general midsection should do some fairly useful damage.

But the fighters around it carried very little shielding, from the readout. Of course, they were the escort. They wouldn't be bringing this precious cargo into an embattled area.

The hot squad SBs were closing, teasing at the Ichton convoy. The lead boat of the arrow darted into the Ichton perimeter, looped and doubled back while the second SB followed in like mode.

The bugs didn't bite. They shot at the SBs when their defined perimeter was breached and Cowboy's screen erupted with red-yellow-green light. They were not anticipating the attack and were late. But they still didn't follow, weren't drawn off to pursue the enemy that must sorely tempt them.

The hot squad tried again, the SBs looking like stinging quick darts, teasing the Ichton fighters just at the edge of their formation. Ichton discipline held. They were not going to be drawn away this easily.

Cowboy watched as the blue blips of the SBs rallied and regrouped. Now they were in a double spiral. He's seen this maneuver once in a base show, one of those open-to-the-locals-let's-have-good-p.r. kind of things. It was the climax of the show, the SBs hurtling at each other, shooting down the spiral like a projectile in a barrel and crossing with only a breath between them. Then it looked like a piece of set bravado, though publicity for the show said that every maneuver and formation was part of the general battle training of all SB fighter squads.

Now Cowboy saw it in action. The spirals were good defense. The shooting lines and spirals would rotate enough that the enemy wouldn't know where the next SB would show. Using two of them should keep the Ichtons at least occupied.

Two SBs shot the spiral, laced through enemy territory, and scooped around to draw away. As they came around in position two more SBs loaded and released. These weren't so fortunate. The bugs were watching, wary, ready. They caught the first one in a green blast that bloomed and atomized. The second went evasive in the tail run, flipping and dodging and weaving. Two Ichtons pursued and looked like they were going to be drawn off, but no joy. They reached what had been defined as perimeter and turned back to their defensive position.

"Damn," Cowboy swore softly to himself. The word echoed in the silent dark of the gun station.

"Six minutes to interception range," the computer said.

"We're never going to get that egg ship if we can't get those fighters away," someone observed with frustration. Cowboy knew the voice, it was Maria Vargas, exec. And she was right.

Deep in the rush Cowboy knew perfect clarity, intuition. He could see into the patterns of combat like a crystal ball. But something hammered at the back of his mind, something fogged the sight. Everything clouded as he fought to bring it to his conscious mind. He *knew* it was there, teasing around like the SBs to the enemy. Taunting him, all the pieces jumbled like a dream. The music, Jackson's radio in the dorm, the eyes, the millions and millions of eyes. Avrama Blackwell, her crinkled nose when she laughed and her low, firm voice talking about waves and energy and eyes.

A dream, a nightmare, it swallowed him. Images overlapped, intertwined, merged with the readout on the screen.

"Two minutes to intercept," the computer said calmly.

Cowboy unbuckled his safety strap and made his way through the dark to the skipper. Captain Wurther Ali Archer stood behind the helm station, his eyes never moving from the complex-layered holo displays there. "Yes, Cowboy," he said evenly.

"Sir, I have it," Cowboy said, trying to keep the excitement out of his voice. "We have radio communication, all the light cruisers do. And the new data about the Ichtons say they can see radio waves."

"So we should cut off those communications?" the skipper asked, honestly concerned.

"No, sir, we need to turn them on. If we put our transmitters on full, all of us, and direct them at the Ichtons down there, it would read to them like a flash of light would to us."

The skipper never looked at him but a smile crossed that grim face. "Blind them, you think?"

"Can't hurt to try," Vargas said quickly. The skipper nodded and Vargas turned to the communications center. "Li, you heard that. Post it over to the rest of the flight, coordinate settings on radio. And then give it to them."

"You really think something as low energy as a radio blast is going to do anything?" Muller groused as Cowboy strapped back into his station. "If they've got any decent hull plating this is a total waste."

"But they don't," Cowboy said. "They've got a clear canopy. Look on your realmag, why don't you?"

Cowboy saw Muller's screens flicker in the change. "Damn," Muller said. "They are some kind of idiots."

"I don't think so, Mr. Muller," the skipper said softly. "If this works it's a one-shot deal. But it's worth a try, you copy?"

But Cowboy felt no victory in Muller's soft reply. The tension was growing in a way he had never experienced before. Always Cowboy had been ice-cold. Now his palms were covered with sweat.

"Coordinate transmission ready to go now," Li said.

On the screen nothing changed. For a moment everything remained perfectly static. "Blow them to hell, you guys," Cowboy whispered. "Blow them away."

The SBs and the light cruisers began firing at the same time. The hot squad mowed through the blinded Ichtons like a McCormick Combine.

The light cruisers left the immobilized fighters to the SBs and concentrated their fire on the egg ship. Its shields glowed blue, channeling the laser fire from the Fleet craft harmlessly into a power circuit. Harmlessly at first. The overloads could handle only so much power. The combined ordnance of three light cruisers stepped up the energy level exponentially.

On Cowboy's screen the shields went from orange to blue to violet to shrieking, shimmering wash. And when it finally exploded the massed shards took out nearly twenty Ichton fighters along with it, and two SBs. The screen looked like a Goanese abstract light-painting, a living flow of rich color that cycled through the spectrum, constantly revealing a new image.

Cowboy never had been much for abstract art. With the mission objective accomplished, he put his screens on passive sweep. No point in letting elation turn them into fools. There were a hell of a lot of Ichtons out there, and when they knew one of their egg ships had been blown they were going to be very angry. And it was still a good half hour back to the *Hawking*.

The Emerald was packed full that night. The whole hot squad and most of the crews of three light cruisers showed up, and the unlucky folk who hadn't been in on the kill were buying drinks for those who had. Cowboy's name was mentioned and toasted at least seven times. Maria Vargas and Li had to explain what had happened and how the radio transmissions had blinded the Ichtons in their fighters like a flash bomb until their voices gave out and someone else bought another round.

But Cowboy wasn't there to hear it. He was wearing his very best embroidered skintight and eating palmyari for the first time. They were very good, he thought. Very good indeed. But the company of one Dr. Avrama Blackwell was far better. Especially when no one was trying to get educated about science.

THE FIRST WEEKS

AFTER EIGHT MONTHS in warp, isolated within the *Hawking,* every member of the crew was anxious to return to normal space. During the journey there had been a number of violent incidents and even a few murders. Most of the problems were related to bad relations between the Fleet personnel, who knew it was *their* battle station, and the representatives of the commercial interests, who were equally determined to remind everyone that *they* had virtually paid for the place. By their standards the Fleet types were there as renters, not owners. Below this surface friction were the still-healing scars of the Family war. This old antagonism was complicated by the fact that there were a number of Khalians on the *Hawking,* serving as Marines. The more fanatic of the descendants of the families had never completely forgiven the Khalia for changing sides once it had become apparent they had been merely used by the Schlein Family and its allies to harass the Alliance while the families built up their strength. Most of the murders were, as would be expected, crimes of passion.

After arrival each member of the crew, civilian and Fleet, had to face their own mortality. By the third encounter with the Ichtons it had been decided that using the *Hawking* in combat was too great a risk. This battle had been over the world of the second race that appealed for help. They succeeded in driving off an Ichton force of several hundred smaller ships and two of the giants, but the *Hawking* was twice rammed and received considerable surface damage. This only increased the feeling of vulnerability and had a negative effect on the morale of all the races on board. Fortunately some provisions had been made to deal with the problem.

STARLIGHT

by Jody Lynn Nye

HE WAS THE most famous interpretive dramatist in the galaxy, renowned and beloved on every civilized planet in the Alliance and beyond.

She was the *Stephen Hawking*'s morale and entertainment officer.

Theirs should have been a love that shook the stars in their courses.

But it wasn't.

When she enlisted in the Fleet, Jill FarSeeker had promptly been assigned to the Morale corps. She was a cheerful woman of twenty-seven, unflappable, friendly, and comfortable with herself. Though a good listener, she was also capable of speaking tactfully to the point. Spacer rank had been only a brief stop for her, and ensign rank briefer. A mere three years in the service, she had risen to first lieutenant and had been recommended for an early captaincy. Blessed with straight black hair and large, round brown eyes, Jill thought of herself in a comfortable, kid-sisterish way.

When Kay McCaul was assembling her Space and Power Use staff for the *Hawking,* she requested Jill specifically by name as her second. There seemed to be nothing that would jeopardize the assignment. Jill was single and had no family. As soon as she gave her consent, she was added to the "Orphans Brigade," and put in charge of liaising with the civilian entertainment arm. McCaul gave her the power to make decisions at every level without having to refer back to Kay herself. Although Jill was only a lieutenant, she bullied, cajoled, pushed, and prodded the other Fleet staff, even those far above her in rank, until she had the entertainment division running like a hardwired computer chip. Jill was no less formidable than Kay, but was considered to be more approachable.

Sixty channels of music and trivid available three shifts 'round were created to amuse the ten thousand passengers anytime they wanted to tune in. The rec library featured centuries of printed works, and reruns of programming from every world in the Alliance. Community access video stations were provided on each level of the battle station, and Jill herself was the negotiating committee to whom small groups turned when they wanted to put their productions on line for general consumption. Her standards were clear—she would not stand for slander or hate shows—but within those parameters she was liberal as to what she would allow. She hated saccharine melodrama, so her roster of preference consisted mainly of meaty interviews and classics of literature and drama.

Jill's staunchest backers were the audio jocks, both civilian and military, for whom she championed nearly unlimited license. Her argument was that they were the voice of the people, into which the people could tune anytime, and that stifling them unreasonably was counterproductive. The shows became forums for arguments on philosophy and current events, and a shoulder for passengers to cry on when they could get no one else to listen to them. If there was something going wrong with the atmosphere controls, Jill was as likely to hear about it on an audio channel from one of her paladins, as she named them, as from someone who had complained to an engineer. She made Commander Brand and Administrator Omera admit that the complaints were handled much more quickly when they were aired publicly than if they remained private gripes. It didn't take a month before it was known all over the ship that Jill was the person to go to when the rest of the brass wasn't listening.

Arend McKechnie Lyseo was already in his fifties when the *Hawking* launched. He knew when they signed him to an open-ended contract that he would never return to the Alliance cluster, and considered it an adventure with which to crown his notable career. A coup for the largely unpopular battle cruiser program, the addition of the great Lyseo to its complement provided a cachet of respect, if not approval, from a larger segment of the population than it had previously enjoyed. His fan club spanned nearly the entire roster of Alliance worlds. There were other actors aboard, but none of them enjoyed the status of legend.

At first, Brand and Omera opposed letting McCaul sign Lyseo, and especially under the terms he demanded. Lyseo's contract allowed for periodic renegotiation, which they saw as a lever to extort privileges using the threat of nonappearance, but McCaul, who had had Lyseo investigated, knew there was nothing to worry about. Lyseo would never remain as a dead weight for any appreciable length of time. He was a workaholic. He might go off and sulk for a few days when he was on an ego trip, but then he would put on some marvelous heartrending or hilarious spectacle that would have everyone riveted to the trivid tanks. Throughout a forty-year career, he had a better attendance record than any aspiring performer, however motivated and half his age.

Publicly, he was magnificent. Whole audiences had been known to collapse into laughter at a single quirk of the dramatic black brows, such a contrast against his shock of prematurely white hair. A man of above average height, his frame sculpted into the long, thin lines appropriate to comedy or tragedy, he retained the suppleness of youth, both physically and mentally. Lyseo remained a current favorite when many of his contemporaries had fallen into the category of "classic" because he kept up with events, and was not shy about presenting his opinions of any of them.

"What an opportunity," he had announced at his final press conference before the *Hawking* blasted out of system, "to open up the rest of the galaxy to itself through the medium of my art."

The pronouncement pleased the top brass, who realized at last that having one of the preeminent human stars aboard and in favor of their cause meant that continuing interest in the battle cruiser would be maintained, even at the distance from the Alliance to the heart of the galaxy. That could prove vital to future funding of Fleet projects.

Every day, the slot on the entertainment network at sixteen hundred hours was set aside for Lyseo's daily performance. By written agreement it was guaranteed to last no less than a minute and no more than an hour, except by prearrangement with the Morale Office. His contract contained a clause that all of his performances would be recorded and sent back to the Alliance. No matter that it would take longer and longer for each message torp to reach its destination as the *Hawking* flew farther into the heart of the galaxy. It was meant, along with the factual news reports, to be a record of the journey, which would be of immense historical value. Lyseo vowed to reproduce through his art the feelings, hopes, aspirations, fears, losses, and discoveries of the warriors, merchants, and civilians aboard the *Stephen Hawking*. It was understood, though not officially condoned, that all activity stopped or slowed at 1600 so that everyone could see his newest work.

He had the best special effects holograms could produce, his own crew, and top-of-the-line production equipment, and a clothing synthesizer programmed with every garment worn by every being of any ethnicity, nationality, or planetary origin since the beginning of recorded memory. He was permitted to go where he wanted, whenever he wanted, within the ship, to gather impressions of everyday life. One further clause in his agreement that had nearly scuttled the whole arrangement was that he would be entitled to whatever quantity of power he needed, or claimed he did, to run his effects or synthesizers. His library of literature and music, when it was added to the *Hawking*'s complement, doubled the size of the memory needed to hold it.

"It is my legacy to the galaxy," Lyseo said. "Since I will not survive into the ages, my work and my philanthropy will have to speak for me to future generations."

Privately, he was nervous, easily depressed, and required constant reassurance that he was not wasting the universe's time. During these fits of insecurity, he called himself Hambone, and referred to his vast talent as a quirk.

After his first performance, Lyseo retired into his dressing room and locked the door, refusing to come out or answer communications signals.

The technicians on duty in the entertainment center sent for Jill. It was her job to handle her most famous passenger when he became difficult, a task that she did not find easy. From the time she was a teenager, she had admired Lyseo. She had watched every performance of his she could find on disk or cube. When she was informed by her boss that Lyseo was going to be coming on board, she was uncharacteristically nervous. At first, she was taken aback by the periodic snits and constant fretting exhibited by the artist whose public face she adored so much, but underneath the facade, she found a likable man. He was engaging and intelligent, and he genuinely cared for the people for whom he performed. Jill discovered that Lyseo would listen to criticism, truly listen, and apply it to himself if he found it honest. If not, it was as likely to send him into an explosive rage or an achingly pathetic depression. Lack of feedback had the potential to affect him the same way.

"It's just reaction," Kem Thoreson, Lyseo's manager, assured her as they waited at the door. "Come on, Ari, open up. You were fantastic! Everyone loved you." He kept up a steady rapping with his knuckles that Jill felt had to be as painful as it was irritating to listen to.

After a long pause, the door slid open, and Lyseo loomed over them. His eyes were mournful in the mottled mask of half-erased makeup.

"My greatest opportunity," the magnificent baritone voice intoned mournfully, "for the greatest audience a being ever had, and as you would so rightly say, I blew it."

Thoreson socked him playfully in the arm. "What are you talking about, Hammy? You were good! Wasn't he, Jill?"

Jill felt that instead of remembering, she was reliving his performance. Lyseo had enacted the chaotic arrival of the Core ship on the Alliance frontier, followed by the flurry of activity as the human and Khalian senates had decided what to do. With only changes in posture and gesture, he had gone from human to Nedge to Khalian, and back again, arguing the rightness of aiding the Core systems, while drawing the invisible sphere of the battle station within the heart of his stage space. At the height of dramatic tension, he had held his hands framed, and a hologram of the *Hawking* appeared between them, as if he had evoked it from the depths of his self.

"It was . . . indescribable," Jill said at last, feeling overwhelmed.

Lyseo regarded her. He dabbed at a bit of makeup on his cheek with the towel slung around his neck. "That bad, eh?"

"No! It was wonderful! I . . . how did you manage to be so many people at once?"

"We are all many people," he said, waving a dramatic arm. "Sometimes I can't sleep because of the crowd. It's all tricks. Do you see, if I turn my head this way, you follow the line of my head, and the dark stripe along my cheekbone suggests a Nedge beak?"

"Why, that's incredible," Jill said, looking more closely. "And the dark smudges there and there under your eyes look like a Khalian muzzle."

Lyseo nodded. "You see how simple?"

"But it isn't simple at all," Jill argued. "It's marvelous."

Thoreson, seeing that his client's ill mood was breaking, shepherded him back into the dressing room and sat him down on a couch, talking all the while he cleaned the makeup off Lyseo's face. The great man made no protest.

"There you go," Kem said, slapping him on the back. "Good as new. You get some rest, and you'll be all ready for your next show tomorrow."

The expressive eyes met Jill's in the mirror, and the brows raised sadly. "To think of pouring out my whole soul every day, to an uncomprehending mass," the magnificent voice rumbled. "Old Hambone reduced at last to the status of the evening news."

Lyseo's self-deprecation was for Jill and Kem only. Once he stepped outside the dressing-room door, he was once again the star. Over the course of the next six months, he alternated performances based on the exigencies of ship life with items from the classics. A sly sense of humor jibed at the constant warring between the factions on board. When one cruel and much quoted parody of the most prominent Nedge merchant executives provoked a demand for an apology, Lyseo laughed it off.

"The nature of my art allows no artificial defenses to stand in the way. More to the point, my contract allows for it. Sue and be damned."

He was unassailable from everywhere but within. McCaul sent Jill to talk the merchants back into a good humor. It took some time to smooth out literally ruffled feathers. Privately Jill agreed with Lyseo's assessment of the Nedge, but since they all had to live together for a long time, it was necessary to make peace.

"You should be honored, good sirs and madam," Jill explained during their meeting. "The great Lyseo doesn't immortalize just anyone."

The Nedge looked at one another, the round eyes bright on either side of the expressionless beaks. "Perhaps there is something in what you say," Braak Rokoru mused, turning back to Jill. "But he must not do it again. My hatchlings back on Eerrik III will see, when the broadcast reaches them, and be ashamed."

"Certainly they won't see it in that light," Jill suggested. "If my parent were so featured, I would be flattered, for myself and for my nest. You could message them about it. They might want to make a permanent recording."

The Nedge inclined his head slowly, openly considering Jill's enthusiasm. "Perhaps it is only that we do not understand the human sense of humor."

Inwardly, Jill let out a sigh of relief. "Perhaps not, honored sir. I can assure you that everyone else on the ship found it funny."

Solemnly, the Nedge bowed to her. "Then we will do what you suggest. We are most grateful for your explanation."

As soon as she could possibly excuse herself, Jill fled, and had a good laugh in her office with the intercoms turned off. Lyseo's imitation of the ponderous Nedge had captured them exactly. It had been tickling at her ribs throughout her meeting, and she could wait no longer to let it out. She longed to tell Lyseo about the meeting, but suspected that once he knew, the Nedge would appear again on a 1600 show, and she didn't think she could placate them again.

Lyseo continued to fascinate her as much as he had when

she was young. Whenever Jill had the time, she sat just outside of camera range in his studio and watched him work live. She regretted that it was impossible for everyone to see him this way. His personal magnetism enveloped her, drew her along in the fantasies he created, making her believe in them. A mere video of him seemed almost out of context.

Unexpectedly, the soaring audacity fell wing-clipped when the *Hawking* entered the system of the first Core world to beg for help. No planetary communication on Gerson answered any of their hails. Concerned, Commander Brand sent single-seat fighters in to do video reconnaissance. The data they sent back to base was horrific. Every population center, every domicile, every supply store, had been stripped or blasted. The carnage was evident even at a hundred fifty thousand meters. Sensors found no signs of life above animal intelligence. Word of the genocide and destruction below spread swiftly throughout the ship. The Gerson on board went crazy with grief and had to be put in restraints. After that, Jill had to put out a lot of emotional fires, and found she was counting on Lyseo's daily performance to cheer her up.

Apparently, so was everyone else. The ratings numbers showed that a record number of viewers tuned in to that day's broadcast. What they saw only deepened their feelings of hopelessness.

Lyseo, for once stripped of makeup and clever artifice, sat hunched in the middle of his stage on the floor, as the camera revolved around and around him. Arms gathering his knees protectively to his chest, Lyseo was the personification of despair. After what felt like an eternity, he lifted his head and stared hopelessly at the ceiling.

"Why did I ever leave the Alliance?" he moaned. "I was safe there. I had my friends, my family, all my comforts. I joined this fool's chase to the center of the galaxy, and for what? In aid of strangers, people who are already dead. Perhaps they are all dead, and we have come here for nothing. I will never see my birth world again. We are moving forward into the depths of the void!"

Jill, watching from a rec lounge on Orange level 2, felt her heart sink. She noted a shocked silence fall over her fellow viewers. Some of the humans sat with nervous grins on their faces, waiting for Lyseo to crack the joke. When he remained serious, they stared at him, uncomfortable and angry. After the screen faded, no one spoke for a long moment, then everyone burst out at once, most of them shouting to dispel their rage.

Jill stood up on a chair. "Now, simmer down, people," she called, signaling for attention. She tried several times to interrupt the furious chatter. No one listened. She climbed down and made her way smartly to the nearest control room. Something in the order of video sedatives was called for.

"Well, you've certainly got them talking," Jill said. Things looked bad. Lyseo was in a deep depression, and this time she couldn't use the lure of public acclaim to pull him out of it. He'd already been informed of complaints coming from the highest brass. Instead of provoking a roar of approval or a round of informed discussion, he had exposed primary fears that made most people curl up on themselves. The paladins reported no abatement in the number of frightened callers who just wanted to talk with a calm voice. She suspected that not all of them were civilian passengers.

Anticipating Kay McCaul's instructions, Jill had ordered a program of perky music, and the video terminals showed Fleet recruitment films and morale-boosting, mindless adventure sagas reaching back into a thousand years of mass entertainment. Then she went to visit the source of the trouble in his dressing room.

"I am fundamentally disappointed in the response of my audience," Lyseo said, mopping his face with his sodden tunic. "I re-create their very moods, and they turn on me. What do they want of me?"

"You frightened them," said Jill, squatting down beside his chair. "You reminded them how vulnerable they are out here."

"It was an honest assessment of the emotional sense on board this ship," Lyseo said. "I only told the truth."

"They're not prepared to deal with the truth," Jill said. "Everything that is happening is completely new to them. They are afraid of what's out there. The unknown scares them. You just reminded them of what they've been trying to suppress so they can deal with their day-to-day tasks. You're making that very difficult."

Arend Lyseo thought deeply for a moment, and sighed. "It was not my intention. I must have erred in my performance."

"Not at all," Jill assured him. "It was truly brilliant. But it wasn't what they needed to see. I'm scared, too, if you must know. I'm frightened rigid by whatever's out there!"

Lyseo stared down at her. "How miserably insensitive of me," he said. "What I do cannot make the slightest iota of difference in anyone's life if I am making it impossible for them to function. How presumptuous of me, a mere entertainer, to paralyze my viewers into immobility. I am an utter barbarian and a wretch and blind, blind, blind!" He pounded his hands on his dressing table.

Jill stood up and put her hands on her hips. "Well, at least you're not a hypochondriac," she said. "That's the one thing I just can't stand."

Lyseo gaped at her in open astonishment. Slowly, a smile crept across his lips, and he began to laugh. Jill relaxed, and grinned at him. He stood up and took her into his arms, and kissed her. Jill felt her bones melt. No matter how casually she tried to behave toward him, he was still her idol.

"You are the only thing that keeps me from despair, raven-winged maiden," he murmured into her hair. "It is your presence, your honesty, which allows me to believe that no matter what mistakes I make, it will all turn out right in the end." She raised her face to look into his eyes, needing assurance of the sincerity of his words. This man could imitate any emotion, create spun sugar out of air; it could be mere praise. She saw no artifice now, only affection and respect. He bent to kiss her again, and she responded with all her heart.

In a moment they were making love. Jill kept thinking that it was impossible, that this was one of the videos, not actual life, and certainly not hers.

"Okay, talk to me," Driscoll Strind said, picking up another comlink line. Strind, one of the most popular of Jill's paladins, had been fielding questions and frantic calls nonstop since 1615, when Lyseo's broadcast came to an end. Four hours had passed, but there were still people who needed to work out their anxiety.

"He was right!" the caller burst out shrilly, without identifying herself. "Lyseo was right. Everything he said—I felt that way. Are we going to die out here?"

"Suppose we could, citizen," Strind said calmly. "Space travel's uncertain even in this day and age."

"No! I mean could we be blown up, like those people down there? I never thought about it. I mean, when I went through the psychological tests, they asked me if I could live with never going back to my home system again. They never asked how I felt about being shredded by an alien enemy."

"You knew the job was dangerous when you took it, citizen. This is a warship. There's never been any secret about that. We're going to find the bad guys and shoot at them, and they will probably shoot back."

"But I'm a civilian! I don't want to die. Doesn't anyone care what happens to me?"

"We all do," Strind said. "It's the responsibility of the commanders to do their best to see that nothing happens to you. As for civilians getting caught in crossfire, what do you think happened to the people down there? They weren't all in the military."

"I wasn't frightened before," the caller admitted. "But I am now."

"Lyseo brought it home to you, didn't he?" Strind said, nodding into his headset as he disconnected that caller. "Well, we all want to talk about it. I asked Commander Brand to take a few minutes out to talk to us. He's here now." Strind nodded to the commander, who sat across the broadcast console from him in the semicircle of padded couch that served as Strind's studio. "You've been listening to the voice of the people, Commander. Can we have your feedback? Are we sacrificing ourselves needlessly?"

Brand cleared his throat. He hated being put on the spot, but accepted the necessity as Lt. FarSeeker explained it to him. "The way I see it, Strind, Lyseo pointed out that we could be destroyed, not that we will be. We could. You might think we were on a foolhardy errand, and wonder if we have done the right thing coming to the heart of the galaxy. And who hasn't felt that way? He told the truth. But the answer is that yes, we of the Alliance will go forth into the void to help those who come to ask for our assistance. If we did not, we would be abetting the enemy by our inaction. He made us talk about it, brought out our deepest fears. I suppose in a way we should thank him for it, but I have a difficult time feeling gratitude for a man who nearly precipitated a score of suicides. The psychotherapists report that they have been overwhelmed."

"I suppose it never occurred to anyone until now that we could die doing this hero stuff," the paladin said. "That's what I think. Now it's out in the open. We need to be kept up on the facts, Commander. The dangers. What you decide affects all of us, no matter whose department we're in."

"I acknowledge that, Mr. Strind. We'll try to keep you in the loop from now on—when it is not a breach of security to do so. That, too, is part of my responsibility in keeping the rest of you safe."

"You heard it here," Strind told his headset. "Me, I like Lyseo. He didn't get to be who he was by playing safe. He's not afraid to say what we're all thinking. Well, this situation is like any bogey in the closet: air it and we can deal with it, right? Can we have another question for the commander?"

The mood of the show improved slowly but significantly after that. The general consensus seemed to be that Lyseo had done the crew of the *Hawking* a service. The next day Jill brought a tape of the show to Lyseo and played it for him.

He paid half attention to it while putting on his makeup in the mirror and humming. The emotional storm had passed, and he was eager to go on again. He caught her eye in the glass and saluted her with the sponge.

"I don't know what I would do without you, raven-haired one." He smiled. "Will you be watching old Hambone today? I promise all will be strictly upbeat. Pure entertainment, no more. I'll save the lessons for another time. Will you?"

"Of course I will," Jill replied.

In spite of the devastation of Gerson only days behind them, and the possibility that in the days to come the battle station could be facing destruction, loss, and pain, Jill felt she had never been so happy. Humming, Lyseo went back to his pots and sticks, and Jill left him to it.

Kem took her to one side. "You're great, Lieutenant. Sometimes it takes me days to get him out of one of his snits. Can you stick around?"

"I've got other duties," Jill reminded him. "Don't get me wrong, I'd love to. I can't. But I'll be back, I promise."

Kem clutched her arm and glanced quickly at Lyseo. "What'll I tell him?"

"Whatever you told him before I came along," Jill said. "Tell him again. I've got 9,998 other people to look after beside the two of you. If you don't like it, take it up with McCaul."

Kem gulped visibly. "No, thanks. I still have some of my hide left over from last time. The rest is still growing back."

"Good," Jill said. "Bye." She waggled her fingers at Lyseo in the mirror, and slipped out of the door.

Outside of the dressing room, Jill leaned against the bulkhead and slowly drew in a few breaths of reality. She had to stop being the starry-eyed fan and go back to her job. At the end of the corridor, Lt. FarSeeker smiled blandly at a crowd of maintenance workers waiting for a lift, her hero worship tucked away into her private thoughts.

The representatives of the Core worlds aboard were growing more agitated as the *Hawking* neared the next system feared to be under attack. The mood of the Fleet personnel was grim. Lyseo's broadcast had aided in opening communications between the two groups, but it was an inescapable fact that the station was coming closer and closer to confrontation with an unknown enemy presence.

As they approached the second system, tension was high. The paladins mediated arguments on the air as to what they would find when they arrived.

The argument was settled early when, on their approach, long-distance telemetry picked up high-level energy readings dead ahead within the system, inconsistent with the normal bursts of radiation thrown off by a star system. There was a battle going on. The *Hawking* increased velocity, and prepared to intervene.

The unknown enemy had destroyed an entire civilization on Gerson, and had left little intact to give a clue as to its origin. No one aboard could guess whether the gigantic Alliance battle cruiser would be sufficient to defeat it.

As the *Hawking* swept into a close orbit around the second planet from the star, the combatants appeared on the bridge screens. Commander Brand ordered telemetry to track the various cruisers and fighters, and tried to make sense of the battle array.

"I can't tell which side is which! Get those two Silbers up here, so they can identify the power signature of their ships," he barked.

In a few moments, the two pale-faced natives appeared, followed unobserved by Lyseo. Brand swiftly requested the information he wanted and saw it entered into the battle computer.

"Thank you, gentle beings," he said, dismissing the two aliens briskly. "You may go now. I don't want any civilians on the bridge. You can watch the action on one of the trivid tanks." He flicked a hand toward one of his aides, who bustled the protesting Silbers toward the lift hatchway. Lyseo watched them go, taking in their agitation, and the impersonal efficiency of Brand's ADC. Lyseo leaned casually against a bulkhead, taking everything in. The action on the screen excited him. His bright, deep-set eyes flicked here and there, while his body remained still, almost slack.

Brand suddenly noticed him. "What's this man doing here?" he barked. "Didn't you hear what I just said? No civilians on my bridge." The aide leaped to take Lyseo's arm and show him to the door.

"But I am Lyseo," Lyseo said, shaking off the aide's hands. "I am permitted to be here."

"We're in the middle of a battle situation, mister. Get off my bridge!"

"I invoke the clause of my contract," Lyseo said haughtily. "It will reiterate for me that I may go anywhere on this vessel at any time I so choose."

The ADC was already bent over a keyboard before his commander threw a gesture at him. "It is correct, sir. It's in the records."

"I will not be in your way," Lyseo promised him. "I will stay over here."

"I don't care what your bloody contract said. It's against bloody regulations. Anyplace you stand will be a distraction. Haul it!"

"No, sir, I will stay right here."

"Commander!" the telemetry officer shouted. "Eight small, high-powered craft have disengaged from the battle and are heading toward us. They've noticed us, sir."

"Scramble fighters," Brand barked. "And get that man off my bridge!"

The ADC and a couple of the other officers moved in on Lyseo, who crouched warily, prepared to defend himself. One of them lunged at him, causing him to jump sideways, almost into the arms of the other two men. They were big and strong, but he was nimble and wiry, with thirty years experience on any of his opponents. He squirmed loose in a trice, and was standing beside the furious Brand's chair just as the eight small ships ranged into full view. Lyseo stopped. He had never seen anything like them in his life.

"Oh," he breathed, eyes fixed on the screen. While he was distracted, the guards went for him again, and carried him, shouting imprecations, off the bridge.

"The indignity of it," Lyseo raged. He had stormed out of the lift and directly toward Kay McCaul's office. The chief of Power Use was doing her best to reason with him.

"But I understand the commander's concern, Mr. Lyseo. Why didn't you stay away from the battle bridge with a potential conflict on hand?"

"I needed to be there," Lyseo insisted. "For my art. That was where things were happening. I am drawn to conflict."

Kay McCaul shook her head. "You could have been responsible for many deaths. What if the commander became distracted while you were gathering material for your . . . er, art, and misdirected a squadron of fighters?"

"I am not blind or stupid, Administrator," Lyseo said with

haughty dignity. "If he had not caused a fuss, I would have remained where I was, an immobile and noninterfering object. I am not to blame for his outburst."

Kay found his logic unassailable, but the primary purpose of the *Hawking* was military, for the defense of not only the Core planets, but also the thousands of beings aboard the cruiser. She smiled reasonably at the actor.

"Mr. Lyseo, I will ask you a great favor. I want you to stay off the battle bridge during combat. You can have any other seat in the house, but it would be better for everyone if you stay out of the commander's way. He hates an audience. Agreed?"

"Any other seat?" Lyseo asked, his black eyebrows quirking.

Kay nodded. "Anywhere."

"Where was he?" Jill asked, trying to translate her superior's furious squawk through the audio pickup in Lyseo's dressing room. The great man was in the shower, tidying up for his next performance. Jill could hear him singing loudly and cheerfully through the door, and he was drowning Kay out.

"The power center!" McCaul shouted.

"The power center?" Jill echoed. "But there's no room in there for an outsider."

"I stupidly told him he could go wherever he wanted so long as it wasn't the battle bridge. He told the technicians to check with me, and not one of them called to ask whether it was true. I would have chucked him out with my own hands if I had known. Stop him from going back there again. The techies were in a state of hysteria, having to crawl over him all the time."

Jill turned away from the pickup when she heard the singing stop and the bathroom door open and close. Clad in a toweling robe and an air of great good humor, Lyseo strolled into the room. He bent to give her an affectionate peck on the cheek. "Hello, my dear. I didn't expect to see you before today's show. What did you think of the battle our brave flyers put up? Fascinating! It has inspired me to the fullest."

"Ari, I just spoke to Kay McCaul. Were you really in the power center during the battle?"

"Why, yes," Lyseo said. "It was absolutely fascinating. In that small chamber, knowing that each new demand for power was focused to help secure a victory. Think of it!" he said, drawing an invisible panorama for her. "Discovering the sources of the demands for more energy as we rove through the battle, who needs more, and who requires less, almost as if we were seeing what was going through the lives of everyone on board for that single event, and all the time our fighters were out there in space around us, demolishing the evil Ichtons."

"There isn't a lot of room in the power center," Jill began, but her voice trailed off.

"It was a crux, a nexus," Lyseo crowed. "I could feel the tension as if I were experiencing it myself."

Jill knew that she would have to say something, but weighed her words carefully. He was so sensitive, anything that sounded too much like a criticism would make it impossible for him to function. "You . . . you won't be going back in there again, will you?"

"No, I have gathered all the impressions there that I think I will need," Lyseo said. "It's only worth one show. That kind of paraphrase can become old quickly. I don't want to bore my audience."

Jill heaved a sigh of relief. "Good. What's today's slice of life, then?"

"You'll enjoy it," Lyseo said proudly. "It'll be inspiring to all our young warriors, and the rest of us, who are young only in our hearts. It's an abstract piece, a light show, based on the grids in the power center. I intend to illumine, by starlight, if you'll forgive the joke, how it is we all contribute in our small ways to the war effort. I have dedicated it to Administrator McCaul, for her kindness in allowing me the freedom of her domain."

"I'm sure she'll appreciate that," Jill said.

Jill sat next to the light crew as Lyseo took the stage. At the left and right walls, the computer technicians who ran the lighting board and the special effects generator waited, fingers poised for Lyseo's cue. A prerecorded voice echoed through the chamber, announcing Lyseo's dedication to Administrator McCaul. The stage director counted down the seconds to sixteen hundred hours, and pointed a finger at the star. The light went on on the video camera directly before him, and Lyseo extended his arms over his head.

Throughout the chamber, tiny points of light appeared. Lyseo moved among them, gathering some of them in his hands, and balling them up to make larger ones, which he set back into the air. His skill with pantomime made it look as if the holographic projections of light were solid and malleable masses. Jill watched him with fascination, wondering what light would feel like. Lyseo accompanied his dancelike movements with a narration describing where the lights were coming from and where they were going over the course of a day. The little stars grew or shrank according to the needs Lyseo designated.

"No more to the galleys, the meals are served. Better to put more into the recreation centers. Botanics needs more, and engineering needs less."

With a trumpeting of martial music, the dance grew faster and faster. "What's this?" Lyseo demanded, staring at a little star that was pulsing with the beat of the drum. "Our ships require more. There is no more available. It will have to come from somewhere, or we will fail." He addressed the other twinkling lights. "Will you all give something of yourselves?"

The other lights sparkled eagerly, and he gathered part of each one's substance to add to the failing light. Under his hands, it became larger and stronger until it dwarfed all the rest. Lyseo sprang aside to avoid a dark red ball of flame that swept out of the darkness toward the small lights. The white globe swept between the red comet and its intended victims. The adversaries met in a crash of glaring light. Images of the Ichton fleet engulfed the red globe as it circled the white, now clad in a shell like that of the *Hawking*. Lyseo continued his declamation while the fight continued. It was thrilling and inspiring, guaranteed, Jill felt, to make everyone on the *Hawking* feel as if they were part of the battle, part of the great movement to liberate the Core planets. Lyseo whirled around the red globe, showing that it was weakening. The performance was working up to a grand and exciting climax when suddenly the lights dimmed, and the giant globes of light blinked out of existence. The special effects generator whined down to a dull hum, and shut off. The technicians sprang forward to see if they could restore power.

The interruption hit Lyseo like a blow to the solar plexus.

"No!" he shouted into the darkness, beating at the air with his fists. "Bring it back! I am not finished!"

"I'm sorry, Ari," the lighting director called, running an agitated hand through her short blond hair. "I was just on the horn to the power center, and they've cut us off. They need our juice for the weaponry. We're under attack!"

"I demand that they restore power," Lyseo shouted, drawing his fists down against his belly. It was a tight, fierce gesture that did nothing to salve the ache inside. "They can't simply interrupt me like that!"

"No can do, Ari," the young woman said, shaking her head. "We'll have to wait until it's all over."

"I have a contract that entitles me to whatever power my performance demands, and I demand that it be restored to me. Kem!"

"Right here, Hammy," the manager said, stepping into the low beam of the security lights.

Lyseo rounded on him. "Go down to the power center, since they ignore our summonses, and tell them to turn on the juice to my generator. I don't care what's going on topside." He flung a dramatic finger ceilingward, and stalked from center stage toward his dressing-room door.

Shocked, Jill rose from her chair and advanced on Lyseo, cutting off his dramatic exit.

"Hold it just one millisecond," she demanded, planting one hand on his chest. She glanced over her shoulder. "Kem, you stay right here. Ari, what do you think you're doing? Were you just blowing smoke, or do you really believe we should each work for the war effort?"

Lyseo stopped and regarded her with a bemused expression. "Of course I do, my dear. I mean it sincerely. I like to think I do my part."

"Then would you please stop invoking your precious contract and let the troops get on with their jobs up there? You sound like a spoiled brat, carrying on that way. If the power center cut you off, they knew damned well what they were doing. It wasn't to annoy you, it was to save lives. Possibly even your life."

"But to interrupt me in the middle of the flow—it was as if someone physically assaulted me," Lyseo pleaded, trying to make her understand. Jill opened her mouth to reply.

Suddenly the lights went out entirely, and Jill felt the floor drop a few inches under her feet. She staggered against Lyseo in the dark, and the two of them crouched onto the floor.

"We've been hit," someone whispered. "The station's been hit."

All around the black chamber there was a rising murmur of voices. Within moments the safety lights returned. Jill clambered to her feet, and headed for the door.

"Where are you going?" Lyseo called, hurrying after her.

"There are going to be ten thousand scared people out there, and I'm their morale officer. I have to find out what's happened and let them know."

Lyseo sounded almost desperate. "*I'm* scared, too. Please, please stay here with me, Jill. You have a shipwide frequency here. You can communicate with anyone you like without leaving. Stay with me."

"Ari, I can't. I've got a job to do."

The panicked look she knew had replaced the expression of arrogance on Lyseo's thin face. She remembered, with a pang, the sensitive, insecure side of him. Jill felt herself melting, and steeled her resolve. She was concerned for him, but couldn't afford to waste time in beginning damage control. The *Hawking* couldn't afford morale problems, not now.

Lyseo reached out for her hand. "I need you. Please stay."

Jill forced herself to draw back. "There are ten thousand people aboard this cruiser who also need me. What about them?"

"The needs of the many outweighing the needs of the few?" Lyseo threw at her bitterly. "And old Hambone is one of the few?"

He was going to have another temper tantrum, and Jill refused to coddle him through it. "If you like. If you didn't insist on being one of the few, I might be able to help you, too. I love you, but you are the most spoiled sentient being I have ever met in my life!" Jill looked around and saw that everyone was staring at them. She gasped. She had told off the great Lyseo, and right in front of a roomful of people! Jill felt color mount in her face, and turned to flee the room.

Lyseo grabbed her wrists before she could pull away. "Say that again."

"No," Jill cried, refusing to meet his eyes. "I can't believe I said it the first time. I'm so sorry. I shouldn't call you names."

"Please?" he coaxed her. "Before the line about the spoiled brat. I know I deserve that, but won't you?"

"I love you," Jill said, after a long moment staring at his feet. "I don't think I've ever said that to anyone but my parents."

"Then I am doubly honored." He turned her hands over one at a time and kissed her palms, a gesture that sent a tingle coursing through her. "My dear, with that to hold to my heart, you can go and help the multitudes, and I'll know that I'll have a part of you here that they can never touch. That small phrase alone gives me security I find nowhere else and with no one else. As soon as the lights come back up, I'll do my little part here to help out."

"I'll be back later," Jill promised.

"And I'll be waiting," Lyseo said. "Now then, people," he shouted, clapping his hands as Jill drew away, "let us try a technical rehearsal, shall we? I want to be absolutely perfect for our lads and lasses. From the top, if you please."

After the Ichtons were driven back, Commander Brand called back his forces to repair their vessels and heal their wounds. During the late shifts, Jill's paladins began to receive calls from viewers who had watched the most recent performance by Lyseo.

"It was terrific," a woman told Driscoll Strind. "I put it on disk so I can watch it over and over again. To think that when we put lights down during an attack, it actually helps the military to do their job."

"That's a simplistic explanation of it, citizen," Strind said, punching the cutoff button and switching to another call. "I think it has as much to do with moral support as electricity. Keep it up, folks. With your help, we're going to win this one."

Jill and Lyseo lay curled together on the couch in his dressing room listening to the audio channel.

"You made my job much easier today," Jill said, smiling lazily up at him. "I've never known morale so high. If pure optimism could stop the Ichtons, they'd be history."

"Ah, but without you, it would have been impossible for me to continue with my work," Lyseo said. "Audiences are fickle, but no matter what lies ahead, I will conquer the galaxy all by myself if I may count on one who will always care for me."

"I always will," Jill said, and shyly admitted, "I always have."

Theirs was a love that might have shaken the stars in their courses, but it wasn't. It was merely a comfortable, quiet center for both of them in an increasingly chaotic environment.

THE ICHTONS

**A Prelimary Briefing for *Hawking* Personnel
Unrestricted Release**

THE ICHTONS APPEAR to have evolved in a different spiral arm than the races of the Alliance. It is difficult to determine how long they have been ravaging their way across space, but the number of gutted planets discovered to date implies a very substantial period, perhaps even several millennia. We can assume they are experienced and adept at this practice.

Physically the Ichtons resemble both a terrestrial insect and mammal. The trunk of an Ichton's body is contained in an exoskeleton of considerable strength. Their multiple appendages are furred, contain an internal bone structure, and resemble the arms and legs of an earth gorilla or Altarian sermet. Their three-fingered hands are quite strong and capable of delicate work. They are believed to be egg laying, but nothing is known about their young.

As has been the case with all sentient races discovered to date, the Ichtons are individually aware. While it is convenient to attribute insect traits to the Ichtons, this is a fallacy based upon the similarity of their appearance to Terran insects. There appears to be no group awareness or similar connection between Ichton individuals, though they do tend to organize into groups and may be assumed to be highly social. Instinct may play a large role in the decision-making process of the Ichtons. Those few captured seemed almost unable to cope at first with the

131

radically different environment. This may be the main source of Ichton motivation on all levels. Intelligence of a level equal to the average human is merely another tool to fulfill their instinctive needs. A high level of instinctive motivation might explain why those Ichtons we have been able to communicate with are unable to understand the resentment of other races at being overrun and their planets pillaged. When asked why their race acts in this manner, all the prisoners taken to date simply could not comprehend what was being asked. Again, all those likely to directly engage any Ichton force should remember that this type of motivation does not make them any less dangerous as an opponent.

COMRADES
by S. M. Stirling

"OUT OF MY way, furcoat!"

Captain Alao ber Togren checked half a step as she came out of the adjutant's tiny office.

Shit, she thought, quickening her stride. Somebody—someone non-Fleet and human and *civilian*—was throwing species epithets around.

A high chittering sound echoed from the narrow corridors.

Someone was throwing insults at a *Khalian* who was also a *Fleet Marine*. The consequences were not likely to be pleasant, unless she got there soon.

The Marine officer walked with her right shoulder brushing the wall; the *Stephen Hawking* was the largest self-propelled object humans had ever built, with more than enough room to carry ten thousand crew from Alliance space to the Core of the galaxy—but it had been built by the Fleet, and Fleet Marine quarters shaved space as if this were an assault boat, not a battle station.

Stensini, she thought disgustedly as she turned the corner and saw who the human was. I might have known.

"Stensini, *back off*," she barked. "You, too, Senior Sergeant Yertiik. Carry on."

Like half her troops, Yertiik was Khalian—she made a long-accustomed mental effort and refused to even *think* "Weasel"—and quick-tempered even for that race. He let his fur drop flat under his coverall and moved his hands away from the hilts of the nonregulation knives at his belt, but the air stayed full of

133

the wet-dog smell of his anger and a low chirring sound. His eyes stayed fixed on Stensini as he stalked away, as stiff as the short legs and undulant spine allowed: staring was aggressive bad manners to his race.

"Ah, glad to see you, Captain," the human civilian said, then froze.

Anhelo Stensini was a big man, muscular and blond; the Marine officer was a stocky 160 centimeters, with bristle-cut black hair, a beak nose, and a complexion the color of teak.

"Wish it was mutual," Ber Togren said neutrally, after a moment.

She could smell her own sweat, under the neutral ozone and pine smell of recirculated air. *I could brig him,* she thought wistfully. The *Stephen Hawking* was technically on battle alert. The Gersons had been among the Core races who came looking for allies and found the Alliance, and the battle station had found their system under Ichton—enemy—control when it broke out of FTL drive. There had been a skirmish, nothing but an occasional shudder through the massive fabric of the battle station to her Marines or anyone else not in the Fleet's defensive units. But technically, they were under martial law and she could . . .

"Unfortunately, we're going to be seeing a lot of each other," she said with a slight sigh.

The blond eyebrows rose. "I was just coming by for the artifact boxes," he said.

"Turns out they want to take a look at Abanjul," Ber Togren said. According to their Core informants, that was one of the first planets the Ichtons had taken when they appeared in this neighborhood. Deserted by now, although many of the forces attacking Gerson had come from there. "Sending us on a corvette. Think there may be some bugs left. Deserters, stay behinds, whatever."

"Ichtons are not insects, Captain," Stensini corrected absently. Then the meaning of what she had said sank through, and he paled. His specialty would be needed.

"Whatever."

Krishna. The civilian was a sentiologist, a student of intelligent life; and, oddly enough, a xenophobe. Although only toward Khalia. Fifty years before, there had been a war; at first the Alliance Fleet had thought their enemies were the Khalia, muskeloid aliens, cannibalistic pirates. Then they had found the *real* backers behind the Khalia, the families, and the Weasel war had gotten serious. Toward the end the Khalia themselves had changed sides, with an eagerness that was only partly due to the Alliance dreadnoughts orbiting their home world. They just loved to kill, was all.

Stensini's father had been one of those human oligarchs of the Family Cluster; he hated the Khalia for what they represented, a lost heritage, betrayal.

Ber Togren hated them for a much simpler reason; Khalian raiders had hit the Fleet research outpost where her parents worked. What was left of her mother had been found in the raider's food locker after the pursuit caught it. Her father had spent the rest of the war in the 121st Marine Reaction Company, the Headhunters, collecting weasel tails; then he'd retired, paid for an orthowomb to hatch the frozen ova he and his wife had deposited, and raised her on war stories.

Naturally, she hated the Khalia. Almost as much as she loathed the Family rich kids who thought they'd *lost* the war, because they came out just obscenely wealthy instead of omnipotent. If Ber Togren had been in charge, they'd have really lost.

Have died. All of them.

"Get your kit together," she went on. "And don't even bother complaining to anyone, because this is Brand's idea." Anton Brand was Fleet commander on the *Hawking*. Not exactly God, or even the close approximation a Fleet ship captain was, but near enough. "You're the sentiologist they assigned me."

Shit.

Abanjul was dead. It *smelled* dead, a stink of acid and chemicals and raw earth and a little rotting organic matter. The area around the stealthed landing boat was chaotic, a wilderness of tumbled hills of some fine powdery material colored in sand red and scarlet and livid yellow. Cold wind blew it into the faceplates of the Marines and scientists, and several tonnes of it had made convenient cover for the prefab shelter; the new hill already looked as ancient as the others. The talclike substance was sahara-dry, too fine-textured to hold water, but there were pools of blue-tinted liquid running on the hard clay substrate beneath it. The sun was setting; Abanjul's star was a G4 like Sol, but from here it was a swollen red ball covering a quarter of the horizon, haloed by banners of color like nothing she had ever seen. The landing boat was gone, and the corvette would land only on receipt of the correct codes. That had been sensible, at least.

Ber Togren flicked up her mask. Dust settled on her lips, tasting of metal and rust. She spat.

"What *is* this stuff?" one of the troopers muttered.

"Mining by-products," a technician answered automatically. "Pure silica, traces of alumina and heavy-metal salts. Oxides of a number of things. Oxygen content in the atmosphere's dropping noticeably already. Couple of millennia and it'll be negligible, unless what's left of the oceans recover, which—"

A high, thin keening cut through the quiet whistle of the wind. Half a dozen Marines went into crouches, until they saw it was a friendly. One of the Gersons. The ursinoidlike aliens were wearing light environment suits and she could see the short-muzzled face quite clearly. The black button nose was dry and grainy-looking, a sign of ill health, and wet something ran from the eyes and nose and mouth. One of the technicians made a move toward the Gerson, stopped when the alien's own superior went over to it.

Thud. The senior Gerson had kicked the other one in the ribs—the teddy-bear-like aliens had skeletons quite close to the mammalian norm—and shouted something at it. Normally the Gersons' language sounded rather pleasant, like a combination of bees humming and choral song. *Thud.* More harsh shouting, and the prone Gerson picked itself up, still mewling, and staggered back to the ship.

"Uncharacteristic," Stensini murmured on their private channel. He was in charge of the civilian team. "Very uncharacteristic of Gersons. They're under considerable stress, of course."

Ber Togren ignored him. "All right, you people," she said on the unit push. "Let's get dug in and camouflaged. And remember, maximum priority is prisoners. Second priority is reasonably intact corpses." Command priorities, she left unspoken; grunts tended to put a higher value on their own ass than the brass did. They were Marines, though; mission first.

Stress, she thought, looking around. Ber Togren had been born—decanted—stationside, and had spent most of her life in space or hostile-environment habitats; what she saw around her was not too bad, in itself. The Core holos of this part of Abanjul had been taken before the Ichtons arrived, an anthropology mission to study the primitive natives, and showed rolling hills covered with silvery-green trees.

"Yeah, fairly considerable stress," she muttered.

Gerson was occupied by the Ichtons now, and in a generation or two it would look just like this.

"It is good to see you back," Chief Worker hummed.

He had an individual name, compounded of his smell and markings on his exoskeleton and some of the tones the tympani along his thorax made when they vibrated, but there was no need to use them here.

Fighter sounded a *recognition* and pushed past into the warren, his patrol with him. The worker waved his unit out to unload the trucks; those were big vehicles slung low between five-meter balloon wheels, but shabby, patched. Like everything else in the improvised warren.

"Fuel," Fighter hummed. "Seventy-seven kilos liquid hydrocarbon; three tonnes of protocarbon foodstuffs, supplemented; assorted machine parts, some electronics."

"Excellent!" Chief Worker replied. "Our reserve was running low and the hydroponics facility is behind schedule."

He turned and limped away; the right limb of his forward pair of legs was missing halfway down. Ichtons had little curative medicine and no artificial limbs. There had never been any need for such, replacements for injured individuals were in plentiful supply and much more efficient than feeding the wounded.

Fighter turned to one of the technicians. "Any more activity?" he hummed.

"None since the last indication, Fighter," the technician hummed. "Definitely a fusion-impulse engine of some sort.

Apart from that—" The operator's forelimbs moved in a fluid gesture of resignation, the three-fingered hands clenching. The equipment was cobbled together, here in an off corridor of the abandoned mine. Everything had been second-rate to begin with, and nothing useful had been left in the evacuation.

Including us, Fighter thought bitterly. Including us.

"Do you wish to make contact?"

"Negative!" The ultrasonic whine of the Ichton's tympani keened upward until the technician winced and turned his faceted eyes away.

"Then how shall we arrange for evacuation?" The technician must be desperate to question a military order.

"We are not even certain it is an Ichton vessel," Fighter hummed. "Carry on. Passive sensors only."

"We are to avoid contact?" said one of his patrol, newly promoted to warrior status and fingering his converted mining laser uneasily.

"On the contrary," Fighter replied. "We will mobilize all trained"—half-trained, his mind filled in mordantly— "personnel and investigate at the end of this diurnal period."

The others of the patrol split off, each speeding up a little as they headed toward their dens and their mates; none of them had been allowed breeding privileges before the evacuation. They would have been evacuated, if they had.

Fighter stepped wearily through into the main brood chamber. Half a dozen incubators lay grouped around the infrared lanterns, each holding two eggs. None of the clutch of females had laid more than two, not on the minimal rations available, but they would all be hatching in a month. The creche mother was estivating in the far corner; her exoskeleton was mottled with age, and her mind wandered—this world had been polluted enough to reduce the life span well under thirty years, Fighter himself was twenty-eight—but she was the best they had. At the vibrations of his entry she stirred and unfolded her limbs.

"You!" she hummed in the female tongue. It had less vocabulary than the male, but its intonations carried power. Deep within himself Fighter felt needs stirring, to protect and guard, a flash of guilt. "You! Facilities *inadequate*. Conditions *bad*. Hatchlings endangered!"

"They will improve," he soothed. They stood and groomed each other's carapaces, until the old female sulked back to her corner.

Fighter's mandibles ground together as he wearily sought his niche and ate, longing for the digestive torpor that would let him forget his worries.

We are breeding, he thought. Of course; they were Ichtons. This world is no longer fit to support us. Equally obvious; the people would not have abandoned it, if it was. Abandoned Fighter, in a recuperative coma from a training accident . . . Few had been left behind, but the absolute numbers had been quite large. Fifty billion of the people had inhabited Abanjul in its prime, a few generations after the native sapients had been exterminated. Most of those judged not worthy of evacuation—in coma sleep, packed into the transports like cargo—had suicided when they found themselves left, or starved. Ichtons had had a technological civilization for a *very* long time, and they were not good at surviving on their own with no reason to live.

Fighter had not. Fighter had found others, built this little base, scrounged and improvised. Now they were breeding, and that had solved most of the morale problems. Any male of the people knew there was work worth doing when eggs and hatchlings were about. The others were content, but the data tormented him. In only twenty generations the atmosphere would be incapable of supporting life. Their descendants would be thousands by then, and they would have to establish a self-sufficient sealed environment. Could they? And their numbers would be growing exponentially, doubling every decade, on a planet stripped bare. Impossible to construct ships and escape . . .

He let his nictitating membranes dim his vision, the warm incubators blurring into a heat-source glimmer. Several of the eggs had been sired by him.

If the ship is not Ichton, we will take it, he decided. We will not follow the people. The thought was heretical enough to make him stir in the sleeping niche, the hard chitinous surfaces of his body scraping at the padding. Why? They have already judged us unfit. We will take the non-Ichton ship—

some of the crew, if necessary—and we will find a habitable planet.

A wild dream. Stumbling across an ecology that would not kill them would be difficult, the more so as they would not dare seek one pretamed by a sapient race. They would have to take an uninhabited planet, or one with pretechnological sapients that could be exterminated piecemeal. Ichtons did not need energy weapons to fight, and they bred very fast.

Fighter glanced back at the eggs. Anything necessary, he would do.

"Nothing. Absofuckolutelydamly *nada*," the sensor operator said.

Ber Togren rocked back on her heels and looked around. They were on the roof of a complex of buildings; Stensini and the others said they had been electronics-heavy administrative headquarters of some sort. Now they tumbled in ruin almost to the horizon, except where they ran along the edge of a green-acid sea. The . . . buildings, she supposed . . . had been made of concrete. Concrete with single-crystal silica fibers and silica fumes added, which gave it roughly the consistency and tensile strength of medium carbon steel. The Alliance hadn't used either for a very long time, but she supposed it was cheap and effective and the Ichtons didn't waste resources on fancywork. Evidently they hadn't wasted time getting the machinery out of it, either; from the looks, they'd just used a plasma gun wherever the walls were inconvenient.

Despite herself, Ber Togren was starting to *like* the Ichtons a little.

"There were heavy-duty superconductors in the structure," the tech went on. "Cermet stuff. And dick-all I can get below, but it all goes down *deep*."

"No more of the—" Ber Togren stopped herself; if there had been any more of the modulated discharges, the technician would have told her. He was a Marine, she didn't have to draw a picture for him.

Sodding hell, she thought, going to as close to the beveled edge of the rooftop as she could and flipping up her visor so that she could pop a hard candy into her mouth. They had spent two months looking at traces that turned out to be bits of equipment giving up the ghost, and seen a *lot* of ruins.

This was a waste of time and personnel. The corvette was off looking at the rest of the system; the Ichtons had used the other planets and asteroid belt rather intensively. But for Abanjul, just the landing party. There were a lot of people on the *Stephen Hawking* but not all that many Marines. Not nearly enough to look for a couple of dozen bugs who didn't want to be found, on an entire *world*.

"Either Anton Brand is a complete fuckup, in which case we're all doomed, or—"

The technician swore mildly. "Now, that *was* a surge," he said. Then he frowned. "Captain, I can't tell you right off, but either it faded in and out, or it got closer and then farther."

"I—"

Anhelo Stensini looked at the odd angular script on the tunnel wall and swept the reader's pickup over it; the light of the jury-rigged lantern was dim and red but more than enough for light-enhancement equipment. The acid smell of the Abanjul-now atmosphere was a little less down here, but the readouts said there was a worrying concentration of heavy metals, particularly mercury. They would all need a course of chelating drugs before lift-off.

Fascinating, he thought. There had been plenty of bodies, and from the tissue samples, the Ichtons had had time to adapt to large-scale industrial pollution, plus radiation levels that would fry a rat's genes. Not engineered, it was too messy for that. Just good old-fashioned Darwin.

The reader beeped. *All broodcare technicians will assemble evacuees at the third landing below,* it said.

Behind him the two Weasel hired killers were chittering to each other. The Alliance gunsel with them was fiddling with her communicator. He ignored the noise, continuing a slow, careful scan of the corridor. It was twenty meters in diameter, a pure cylinder with walls of fused rock, slanting down almost imperceptibly to the west, under the dead sea. Armored doors spotted the walls at patterned intervals, flush with the surface.

"Hey, Yerti, we're out of touch," the human Marine called.

The chittering stopped. Stensini felt a tug at his elbow, and turned to see a Weasel face peering up at him from shoulder height. It was encased in the long-snouted helmet, with the muzzle-protection wings folded back, and the teeth showed wet and pink as the thin carnivore lips curled back. Academically he knew it was the equivalent of a nervous frown, but he jerked his arm back. He might have pushed, if the Weasel had not been carrying a long curved knife in one paw and a short bulky-looking slug thrower in the other. His stomach lurched and spat acid into the back of his throat; it had been *behind* him with that, all the time. Usually he could make himself forget, but it had had to remind him, the treacherous little vermin were always looking for an opportunity to—

"Gum dis wey, nu, nu, nu," it chittered and barked at him. "Toksiik, Anna, gover me me me." Then it thrust past him, glancing down at a display woven into the soft armor. "Zummmthing is—"

A door swung open down the corridor with noiseless speed. Stensini only saw the beginning of it, because something struck him very hard in the stomach and he fell down, just in time for something else to hit him on the back.

The first blow had been Yertiik's, kicking back and using him as a jump-off point in his leap. The second had been the other Weasel bouncing off his shoulder blades because they were under his feet. A *thing* was in the doorway, whipping at Yertiik with a long bar held in its forward pair of limbs. The Weasel twisted in midair and landed where the upright part of the— the *Ichton's*—body met the horizontal portion, and his hand was stabbing with the knife so rapidly that the arm blurred and there were the crisp *pockpockpock* sounds of density-enhanced steel crunching through exoskeleton. That was lost in the long *crakkks* as Yertiik fired his machine pistol in bursts through the open door and the rounds exploded off whatever lay behind. Toksiik sommersaulted past the fight, flinging in a stick of bouncer grenades as he did. More doors were opening, flooding low-level light into the corridor, and a dry rustling sound.

Anna Steenkap's hand fastened on his collar and dragged him ruthlessly backward. She was firing bursts from her assault rifle one-handed over his head, the muzzle blasts slapping at his head, and shouting into her pickups. Anhelo Stensini was looking over her shoulder when the door *behind* them began to open. Steenkap could not possibly have been able to hear it, but she still managed to drop the civilian and turn herself and the muzzle of her rifle three quarters of the distance before the Ichton in the doorway fired his weapon. Most of her upper torso disappeared into a blood mist with a quiet chuffing sound. Something thin and very cold sliced into his legs.

Captain ber Togren threw herself down and to the side without breaking stride, landing on her shoulder blades and firing. Half a dozen assault rifles tore into the Ichton before it was halfway through the ceiling hatch; bits of body and gobbets of body fluid dropped down on the Marines.

"Report, Beta Platoon," she said, backflipping herself onto her feet.

"Found Toksiik," the voice said. "And what's left of Anna. No sight of Yertiik or the civvie. *Shiva, watch it*—" A blast of static, most likely from the aura of a plasma discharge. "Shiva and *Vishnu,* Captain, we can't hold this. It's like a fuckin' cheese."

She nodded bleakly. The Ichtons didn't seem to have much weaponry; half of them didn't have real weapons at all, just tools like welding lasers and the equivalent of staple guns. Most of them weren't very quick on the uptake, either. On the other hand, they were completely willing to die, and they knew this heap of tunnel-spaghetti like it was home. Which it was. There seemed to be a fair number of them, too.

"Pull back," she said. Pushing farther was just going to lose more of her people. Too bad about Steenkap, and Toksiik had been efficient for a . . . Khalian. Losing Stensini was going to put her in very bad odor with the brass, but she would worry about that when the time came.

"Captain." The home-base push. "We gotta anomaly here."

She froze, motioning her escort to guard positions.

"Exactly what."

"Sonic reading. Sort of like frying bacon—"

She blinked. "That's . . . *Get out! Get out* now, *get out of there!*"

"Captain, we—"

Silence.

"Ma'am?" One of the platoon leaders. "What *happened?*"

"I think we all died," Ber Togren said. Then her voice snapped out: "All right, consolidate on the roof. Move it!"

Anhelo Stensini cringed against the cold stone at the whistling shriek from the nearby . . . cell? Compartment?

"Die, die, please die and stop doing that," he mumbled. The Weasel had lasted . . . there was no way to tell how long. It was completely dark here, and there was usually little noise. He was very hungry and thirsty when the dry rustling of the Ichtons came for the feeding. Water that tasted like poison and was, rations from the Fleet stocks. Very occasionally one came with a light, dim and ruddy, and chalk. Then it sketched and he gave it words, and it never forgot and never made a mistake twice. When it went away the darkness closed in again. How long? Days, many days; weeks, maybe months . . . sensory deprivation destroyed your sense of duration first of all.

Another long whistling scream. "Die!" Stensini screamed. "Die and shut up. Die!"

A long bubbling moan. The worst of it was he thought the Weasel probably would die, if only he could.

"I am uncertain as to my interpretation," the bioanalyst hummed uncertainly.

Of course you are, Fighter thought. You were not worthy of evacuation with the people. He felt his forelimbs quivering with long-held tension, his membranes were slow and sticky as they wetted his eyes. The muscles at the base of his forelimbs ached sharply where they spread over the thickened area of exoskeleton. Several of the trainee fighters with him had folded into limb-wrapped lumps of exhaustion in the corners, estivating.

Aloud he hummed confidently: "Your logic train seems sound. The small, more heavily furred species is utilized by the taller?"

"Yes." They both flexed fingers and nictitated in puzzlement. The Ichtons sometimes utilized sapients prior to their extermination; as sources for biocircuits, for research, sometimes for casual labor in their own disposal. Utilizing such a species for high-risk functions such as warfare seemed inefficient. . . . A scritching sound brought Fighter and several of his aides around, manipulators darting for their bladecasters, but it was only a pair of hatchlings playing tag up the walls and over the ceiling. Fighter scooped them down and handed them to the brood mother, who carried them away with a sharp chirr of reproach.

"Perhaps the smaller are biological constructs?" Fighter hummed, returning to the business at hand. There had been theoretical studies on developing such from wild sapients, but in the end it had always seemed non-cost-effective to waste habitat on constructs that could rarely perform more efficiently than Ichtons.

Bioanalyst ground his mandibles. "They seem entirely wild— unless a methodology unfamiliar to our concepts was used in their construction."

"Yet they show equal geneloyalty!" Fighter hummed, with a *tock-tock-tock click* of his mandibles to indicate extreme puzzlement. All Ichtons were of the same genotype, and had been since the time of legends. Ichton loyalty was faultless; that of other races dubious, accordingly. Here there were bonds without any sharing of genes at all, which was madness and chaos.

Think, think, Fighter told himself. This was not his training. He was an instructor of surface troops, no more. You will do this because you must.

"First, we must determine the balance of power," he said. "There are time constraints. We do not know when the alien vessel will return."

"Here the poor bastards come again," the technician said.

Ber Togren nodded soundlessly. They were all wearing improvised sound-boots cut out of the insulation and scanty padding of the two transports left. Not much fuel left for either; not much food or ammunition, much of anything. They had enough water but a declining supply of filters. . . .

The area they were on looked fairly good, solid red sandstone cut into gullies hundreds of meters deep. There were cirrus clouds high above, and a cold wind flicked grit into their faces. Here and there a patch of lichen—something like lichen— struggled to grow. They had a good triangulation on the spot now, although whatever the Ichtons used to cut rock was incredibly quiet.

You have to avoid the cities, she thought. It had cost them, to learn that. Not easy, most of this continent had been built over. But in the cities there was too much cover, and the tunnels were too numerous and close to the surface, the Ickies could come up under you with virtually no warning. It looked like the Ickies spent a lot of their time underground anyway; they'd found bits and pieces of hydroponic tunnel farms that must have been thousands of kilometers long when Abanjul was a going concern. Yeah, the cities are bad. Out in the open country all you had to worry about were the deep transport tunnels that laced the whole planet. They'd been sealed and vacuum evacuated originally, but the Ickie holdouts could still use them and still burrow up. You could hear them, though.

Unless there was a maintenance shaft near. That was pretty bad, too.

"*Ready,*" a radio voice whispered in her ear. Lying pressed to the gritty pink surface of the rock slab she felt a vibration, then for an instant she could actually hear the Ickies boring up.

"Wait for it," she said softly. "Nobody jump the gun."

Nobody did. The circle of rock in the center of the mesa began to tremble; it was a feeling like fear through the soft armor between her stomach and the stone, shaking gut against bone.

"Now," she whispered.

Pdamp. The explosion wasn't very loud. The string of cord around the Ickies' drillhead was thinner than thread, but the explosive propagated at near light speed. You were safe enough a few meters away in open air. Closer, rock shattered into powder and burned white because it didn't have time to move away fast enough. A flash of white light ran around a circle, and within it sandstone collapsed downward in chunks and blocks. Rock hit her again, an angry blow this time, then trembled beneath her like a lover. Something huge and metallic swayed through the air in the maelstrom of churning blocks. Then a plasma lance cut across it like a bar of orange-red light, and it blew up. *That* was loud. Her face shield and earphones cut it to protect her senses, as the center of the drill zone collapsed downward.

Figures dashed forward, and the satchel charges dropped into the hole. More explosions, and the technician relayed the sound of things falling far down in the rock. Everyone else stayed ready, and when the lone Ickie crawled out someone put a neat four-round burst of prefrags through its central exoskeleton. They had learned. You didn't waste ammunition when no more was coming, and apart from a risky head shot the central body mass was the best place to get them. There was an internal skeleton—sort of an extension of the exoskeleton and an internal frame for the limbs—but the Ickies were still squishy inside and *real* vulnerable to hydrostatic shock. The problem was that the Ickies showed plenty of ability to learn as well; faster than humans or Khalia in some ways, slower in others.

Pordiik came up beside her, pushing back the wings of his muzzle guard. "Gat was haff haff herd," he barked; her ear translated automatically. His pelt was looking a little mangy; patches of her own hair were loose. Too many trace elements in the air and water, no drugs. They were all tired most of the time, too, and nothing healed quite right.

"Yeah, pretty half-hard," she replied.

"Why tey bodder wittt us us us?"

That was a difficult question. The Ickies held more than half the expedition, captured when the base camp was overrun—*assuming they haven't just eaten them or whatever*—and more than half its equipment. Including the main transponders, which meant that nobody here could communicate with the corvette until it went into low orbit, if then. Properly handled the main transponder could be used to jam the weaker signals from the transports and helmet coms; nobody had thought to bring along a tightbeam light sender.

"I think I've figured that out," Ber Togren said. "Look, these Ickies are the rejects, right? The ones the others couldn't be bothered taking off."

Pordiik laughed, snapping several times, his tusked jaws clumping. "Not good good to be here before tey leff leff."

For a moment Ber Togren blanched at the thought of trying to fight a ground action on this planet when there were fifty billion Ickies and a functioning civilization.

"Yeah, so, they're not fools. They know Abanjul's going down the shithole—couple of generations, you won't be able to breathe."

Pordiik made the Wea—she corrected herself again—Khalian equivalent of a shrug. "Couppple of gen-gen-genrations, ev'rone dead."

"Ickies don't think that way. One of the few good things that bastard Stensini figured out from the records. So . . . what have we got that the Ickies here want really, *really* bad?"

"Urrk." Pordiik raised his nose skyward, in symbolic surrender. "Bud tey tey haff te transponder."

"And Stensini knew the codes. He's probably dead." She sighed. "You know, for a while I thought Anton Brand was an idiot for sending us to find a few thousand Ickies on a whole planet. How could we find them if they hid? Now I know *I'm* the idiot. He knew the Ickies would come looking for us—he just didn't figure I'd fuck it up so bad." She grimaced. "Live and learn."

"Learn otter ting ting," Pordiik said, pushing himself up with the extended stock of his machine pistol. It was time to police up and move out. "Learn not to look at my tail tail with knife and trophee in mind," he concluded.

Ber Togren stood thinking for a moment. True enough, she conceded. Brotherhood of the about-to-die, that's us.

Stensini's face looked hollow and gaunt and mad-eyed on the screen. Better than mine, Ber Togren thought bleakly. Much better than Yertiik's, which was naked and eyeless. Not much was left of the rest of him, although he wasn't quite dying, since the wounds had been inflicted carefully under antiseptic conditions. Saliva worked around the thin sagging carnivore lips, and a trickle of sound.

"—so *tell* them, you stupid bitch, *tell them I'm telling them the truth!*"

Stensini was screaming, and she cut the gain down on him. It was understandable, of course. From what he said they didn't bother with lights, much. The Marine officer swallowed slightly: complete darkness, and the Ickies moving in it. . . .

"Why don't you believe Stensini's code?" she said to the Ickie that had called itself Fighter Leader; his image held center screen. The interior of the transport was dark otherwise, the air blessedly clear. She needed to be able to think, and they had to spare the fuel to filter and compress.

"Because the subordinate species has also given us a code, and several crucial symbols are different," it said. There was a high whistling background; it was using a modulator to bring the vibrations of its tympani down to the level humans could hear. "This code was supplied only after extreme coercion," Fighter was saying.

They learn fast. This one speaks better Standard'n I do. But then, it had learned from Stensini and his techs. Ber Togren was a promoted ranker from a long line of grunts. Dad had had better things to teach her than upper-class diction. For a moment Yertiik's face reminded her of the picture of Mom. Mom's gnawed bones, at least. Quite possibly chewed on by Yertiik's grandparent . . .

" . . . since the specimen put up such resistance, there are grounds to believe that it is speaking correct information. It is also evident that the human Stensini is a status rival of Ber Togren. We know status rivalry. Perhaps this status-conferring information is not shared within the genotype, but only with a noncompetitor subordinate species?"

"The Weasel is just trying to save itself," Stensini barked.

"This is possible," Fighter agreed.

"Why should I confirm or deny?" Ber Togren said softly.

"You and your genesharers will die soon, without reproduction," the Ichton said seriously. "We have that which you need for survival. If you can survive for some time, your Fleet will send rescuers. If we have your ship, we will depart. The people have no use for us, but we will go elsewhere to expand the realm of the people; we have proven our fitness. Thus all benefit from a temporary truce." The Ichton was leaning forward; Ber Togren had an eerie feeling it was desperately trying to convey sincerity.

She sighed, looking at Yertiik. Beyond help. "Yes, there's only one sensible answer," she said.

Fighter looked up. The humans and their subordinates were grouped nearby, and the thundercrack across the sky bespoke a hypersonic transit. He signaled to the technician, and mentally inventoried the huge piles of supplies; they must take all that was practicable, for a primitive world. The hatchlings whistled through the lattice of their traveling cages, already becoming torpid with traveling-estivation.

"You shall awake to a boundless feast," he murmured, and watched the tech's manipulators touch the keyboard.

"Kali damn you, Yertiik," Ber Togren said, looking down at the limbless body, still barely breathing. Khalia were *tough*. She was glad he was unconscious, though; they felt pain, too. "You didn't leave me any fucking choice at all."

Across the shallow valley from her, the Ichton was ordering the code transmitted. Yertiik's, and quite genuine.

Fighter looked up. It had been worth the effort, worth resisting the temptation to curl up and dream away the effort and grief and pain. He had won, for his people—his own people.

For a moment there was sunlight.

GUNG HO
by Judith R. Conly

Grandmother's children cut their teeth on Fleet medals,
on glory tales of conquest and heroic sacrifice,
of battle companionship grown to life bond
and heart's partner exploding in tragic loss
along the mine-studded course to stable alliance.

Father's comrades gleamed with the reflected glow of legend,
and smugly accepted inherited tranquillity
with eyes averted from parents' unsightly scars.
Their patrols wore tracks in the space between the stars,
and their shift-end dinners appeared on schedule.

We, the restless heirs of memory and routine,
trained to revere past generations' rites of valor,
retrace history-blessed patterns of combat
with no adversaries but our ancestors' shades
and the boredom-born hazards of careless assumptions.

With erstwhile enemies who have echoed our yawns,
now we congregate in decades-suppressed anticipation.
Through the battered lens of new neighbors' desolation
we gain grief-focused perception beyond united borders
and rediscover our uniforms' peace-deferred promise.

Together we gather, admiral-shriven of guilt in our joy,
excitement-fueled, to transport our sphere of protection
in defense of disparate strangers' kindred cause.
To repel the ravenous avalanche of devastation,
we launch our laser-bright ranks toward victory.

CIVILIANS

ONE OF THE greatest assets of the *Hawking* was also the source of the greatest complications to its performance. This was the large number of civilian specialists and merchants that comprised nearly half of the battle station's inhabitants. While technically under martial law when in a war zone such as Star Central, these were still civilians who were unused and unwilling to become very military.

Among the most difficult types of civilians for the Fleet to deal with were the dozens of top scientists who had joined the mission for a wide range of reasons. Often eccentric and aware that they were terribly vital, some of these civilian experts often had to act as the sole resource for their specialty for the entire station. With the round-trip from Star Central to the nearest Alliance world taking nearly a full year, the analysis of vital information often had to depend on the insights of a single individual.

BLIND
SPOT

by Steve Perry

GIL WAS INSERTING a smokestack on the model of the *Toya Maru* when the woman walked into his shop. The model was of a Japanese ferry that had sunk in the Tsugaru Strait on Earth in 1954, killing over eleven hundred people. He held the tiny stack in place long enough for the bond to set before he put the miniature vessel down on his bench and ordered the work light to dim. The voxlume obediently dialed itself down by half and the pix he was using for reference faded from the tabletop.

The woman was tall, wearing green skintights that showcased a sthenic and most attractive figure, and he guessed she was about his age, thirty. Her jet hair was chopped short, worn very curly, and her features were not quite balanced enough to be called classically beautiful. Her nose was a tad too long, her lips a bit too full, her green eyes large and on the edge of *sanpaku*, the tiniest bit of white showing under the irises. No, not classically beautiful, but the combination of features was synergistic and quite striking. Amazing that the *Hawking* was large enough so that he had never seen her before. And surely he would remember if he had.

"Yes?"

"I'm looking for M. Gil Sivart."

"You've found him."

The woman glanced around, and if she was impressed with what she saw, it didn't show. Gil's model shop was deep in the Dark Blue small-biz section, halfway to the hull. The place was not much bigger than the main room of a personal residence

153

cube, jammed between the much larger cloned spidersilk shop and the kung fu school, but it suited Gil's needs. It didn't require a lot of room to build ZZZ-scale models—a couple of magnifying cams, a few microsurgery tools, and a moldmaker table would just about do it. Of course, there were some exhibits set up, but a two-centimeter-long version of the *Titanic* or the *Hsin Yu* under a magnifier hardly needed a landing bay for display.

"Were you looking for a model?" he prompted.

She sighed. The words tumbled out, all in a rush: "No. I need your help. Somebody murdered my lover and I want you to find out who."

Gil opaqued the front window, the plastic going indigo to match the level color, and had his security computer lock the door. "Have a seat," he said.

The woman sat.

"You are . . . ?"

"Linju Vemeer. I work in sensor construction on Bright Green, that's J1."

"Well, M. Vemeer, I watch newsproj. I don't recall hearing anything about a murder."

"It was a week ago," she said. "A robot on Orange 5 pinned Hask to a hatch and . . . crushed him." Her emotions welled, but did not spill into tears. Gil could feel her pain almost as a tangible thing in the air.

"I do remember something about that," he said quietly. "A terrible accident. Near the hull."

"It wasn't an accident, M. Sivart. Hask was too careful a man to let a drone just roll up and kill him!"

"Have you said so to ISU?"

"Yes, loud and repeatedly. Internal Security thinks I'm a grieving mate whose brains have been short-circuited by my loss, though they didn't put it quite like that."

"Why should I think otherwise?"

She looked at him. "You're a pretty large man and you work out, right?"

"I have an arrangement with the kung fu school next door, yes."

"You would go maybe a hundred eighty-five centimeters tall and about ninety, ninety-one kilos?"

"Pretty close to that."

"Could you stop a C-class drone, a sweeper, say, from pushing you off a walkway?"

"I expect so."

"Well, Hask is—was—ten centimeters taller and fifteen kilograms heavier than you, M. Sivart. He was a weight lifter, he could benchpress almost three hundred and twenty kilos. He could have torn that drone apart if he had seen it coming, certainly he could have pushed it away or flipped it over."

"If he had seen it coming," Gil said.

"His *back* was pinned against the hatch," she said. "He was looking right at the thing that killed him. He couldn't have missed it."

Gil thought about that for a second. Yes, that seemed on the face of it odd. Still, this was out of his area of expertise. "I'm afraid I couldn't be of much help to you. I sometimes do favors for people, to facilitate the, ah, return of certain things that have . . . gone missing, when nobody wants ISU to get involved, but I don't have any official standing. Station authorities might take a dim view of somebody meddling in an ISU investigation."

"There is no investigation," she said. Her voice was bitter. "How could you interfere with something that isn't happening?"

"I'm sorry—"

"I can pay you whatever you ask," she said. "Hask left me his insurance. DOJ—death on the job—pays a quarter of a million stads. I'm rich—but he's *gone*."

"It's not the money—" he began.

"Look, I don't have anybody else! Please!"

Gil looked at her. She was in pain. She was going to start crying in a second and this was obviously something she needed to do to get past this tragedy. A vital man, her lover, had been cut down unexpectedly. She had to deal with that and make some sense of it, only she couldn't accept the explanation. So here she was, asking him for his help. That was usually his problem, he couldn't turn away from somebody who really needed him. Especially women who were not-quite-classically-beautiful. A character flaw, no doubt, but one he had learned to live with, being that he didn't have any choice. So what would it hurt if he asked a few questions? He could talk to the cools and the medics, likely confirm what they thought, and make Linju Vemeer feel as if she had done all she could to put her dead lover to rest. It was little enough. Besides, he was a puzzle addict, and there was a little piece here that didn't seem to fit. He would worry about that until he found out where it went.

He looked at her and nodded. "All right. I'll check into it."

Now she did start to cry. "Thank you," she said. "Oh, thank you."

Accident reports were generally unclassified, and Gil had no trouble downloading the file and storing it in his personal flatscreen. He scanned the text, scrolling through it rapidly. It seemed straightforward enough. Burton Haskell, aged thirty-one T. S., had been found by a coworker in the induction space between the third and fourth hulls on Red 2 one week past. He was apparently dead upon discovery—here was the medical report, cause of death a crushing chest injury that ruptured the heart. M. Haskell had been an inspector/supervisor for two years, a sensor installer for a military hitch for four years before that, and had worked in other aspects of electronic construction since graduation from secondary ed, having been with the *Hawking* since construction began. No brothers or sisters, parents both deceased in a shuttle accident ten years back. Not officially married, but an SO of record, Linju Vemeer, listed as beneficiary on his insurance policy.

Gil smiled, his mind working. The classic triangle of any crime was constructed of three sides: means, motive, and opportunity. A quarter of a million HS standards was certainly motive. But Gil didn't think Linju had killed her lover, not if the cools had signed off on it as an accident. She would have to be incredibly stupid to stir up an investigation if she were the killer and already cleared of any crime. She didn't seem that stupid.

He went through the rest of the information. ISU had sent a man as a matter of form, there was the name of the officer. Here was the medic's name and that of the worker who had found the body. He would start there. Assembling a puzzle was not all that difficult if you had a knack for it. Like constructing a tiny model, it was simply a matter of basic logic. First, you gathered pieces, then you put them together. If they didn't fit, you went out and found some others that would.

Gil glanced at his chronometer. A couple of hours before midshift change. He could take a lift up to Dark Green and enjoy a nice stroll to the medical center. Or he could go all the way up to Orange, to the ISU substation and locate the investigating cool and see what he had to say. Or walk to the hull and catch the slant tube to Bright Green and the coworker. In truth, he could visit all these people via the com; he could link and find out what he wanted without ever leaving his shop. But there was no substitute for personal contact, he had found. Pheromones didn't traverse the com, neither did subtle body language, and sometimes these things told you more than words.

All right. He would go and gather a few pieces of this puzzle and see what they looked like.

The air in the induction hull felt stale, it smelled faintly metallic, something like the injection mold Gil used to form model parts did when it was cooking permaplast. The supervisor had cleared him to talk to the man who'd found Hask.

"M. Rawlins?"

The man's head was depilated and he had a mandella tattoo in shades of true red and blue inscribed on his bare scalp, making it hard to focus upon. He was thin, medium height, and wore installer's recycled gray-paper coveralls and biogel slippers. According to his public information file, Rawlins had been working here for six months; before that, he had been employed by Kuralti Brothers, one of the larger commercial merchants in the galaxy, at various of their six branch outlets on the station, transferred in from one of their planetoid-class stores in the Tado System. He was a sensor installer, one of the dozen who had worked under the late Haskins.

Without making it obvious, Gil tapped at his right breast pocket, activating the tiny ball recorder he carried there. True, it was a violation of civil privacy, but he was gathering information, not legal evidence; he'd never present the little steel marble recording to any official scrutiny, it was only for his personal use.

"Yeah?"

"I'm Gil Sivart. I wonder if I might ask you a couple of questions about M. Haskins? I cleared it with your supe."

"You a cool?"

"A friend of M. Vemeer's."

Rawlins shook his head. "I feel sorry for her, you know, but Linju's got a bug up her twat about this. Talking about somebody killing Hask."

"I understand you found him?"

"Yeah, I was the first one to see him dead. I was scheduled EVA, to the outer hull to do security scanners, you know, dopplers. The drone had squashed him against the V-wall lock."

"How would that drone have done that?"

"Well, it's a garbage ram, it shoves stuff into the recycle chute to the hoppers on five. Normally there's a canister there, when it gets to a certain weight, the drone dumps it into the lock."

"Why would M. Haskins have been there?"

"It looked like he was trying to fix the lock. It was jammed, something out of the last canister that got dumped, that happens. He was big enough to make the drone think it had another load waiting, so it went to dump him."

"Isn't there a safety of some kind?"

"It was turned off. It's usual to run a bypass when you work on a lock, the door won't open with the safety off."

"And the drone doesn't have a human recognition circuit?"

"Most of 'em do, but this was an old one, a Brooks bug brain, it hadn't been upgraded yet."

"Strange set of coincidences, isn't it?"

Rawlins shrugged. "Accidents happen. Last year a hatch tech got spat into vac without her suit and there's five different safeguards that missed her. Karma."

"Haskins was a pretty big and strong man," Gil said. "He was looking right at the drone when he died. Any ideas as to why he didn't just shove it away?"

Rawlins shook his head, irritated. "Look, f'l'owman, I'm supposed to be an installer, I didn't design the station, okay? It was bad juju and I'm sorry he's got to be dead, but don't ask me."

"His SO is in pain and she's looking for reasons."

"Tell Linju I said I'm sorry. You can tell her I said I think she's off the track here, too."

"Thanks for your time, M. Rawlins. I expect you're right."

The cool shook his head. "Officially, it's an accident," he said.

Gil had offered to buy the man lunch in exchange for his time, and the pair of them sat at the little café a lot of the military noncoms liked, F3, where orange shaded into yellow. The cool drank splash, a mild form of beer, and Gil sipped at coffee. The cool's name was Millet. Once again, Gil's recorder was running.

"Unofficially?"

"Well, my opinion is suicide."

Gil blinked. "What makes you say that?"

"Hell, he was looking at the drone when it got him. He had to have let it happen. Guy like that could have picked the damn thing up and thrown it one-handed, he wanted, he was a big sucker, muscular as a gorilla. I think he wanted to get around the suicide clause in his insurance, so he made it look like an accident. Only thing that makes any sense."

"He didn't have any enemies who might want to see him dead?"

Millet shrugged. "Maybe, but not any we could find. He spent a lot of time in the gym, he was well liked, nobody with any grudges. Nice guy, minded his own biz, didn't step on anybody's toes. We did a shallow scan on everybody who could have been in there with him. That's not a high security area or anything until you get outside, but the doors are wired to record anybody who comes or goes. There were a couple dozen workers in and out of there that day and we checked 'em all. Nobody made the scanner squeal. So it had to be an accident or suicide."

Gil nodded. "Thanks for the help."

"No problem."

At the medical center, the shrugging continued.

"What is your interest in this, M. Sivart?"

"Haskin's significant other has some questions about the death."

The medic, a portly woman of fifty, shook her head. "No question about it. He got squashed like a fly."

"Any drugs in his system?"

"No, he was clean."

"I see. Any history of depression?"

"Not in my records, no."

"Could something have happened to him before he was crushed? Some illness or trauma hidden by the injury?"

"Yes, of course. We would have found an infarct so it wasn't an MI, but a nodal malfunction is possible, though I don't think this was the case. Not a CVA—a stroke, we'd have seen that. The man was very well developed, he had an excellent cardiovascular system."

"Thank you, Doctor."

After he finished with the medic, Gil walked to the tube that would take him back to his shop. So far, it had played out about as he had expected. The one anomaly was the dead man's physical position when he died. It nagged at Gil, but by itself wasn't enough to indicate homicide. Murder was rare on the station; there had been a couple during the out voyage, but both of those had been easily solved, crimes of passion. A man had been stabbed by his lover when she caught him in bed with her mother; the other was a fight in a bar that had escalated, the killer waiting outside for the victim and bashing him over the head with—of all things—a bicycle. No mystery either time.

On the way to the tube, a beeper signaled the start of a military drill. Gil stopped walking. The tubes would be closed for the duration of the drill, could be two minutes, could be ten, depending on the computer scenario. Already all decks above Yellow would be buttoned up, and Military Command Center would be issuing orders to affected personnel. Sometimes the civilian population was included in the drills, having to rig for combat, but those were fairly rare. If it was military only, then the commercial comchans would still be working. Since he wasn't going anywhere, he put in a com to Linju Vemeer.

"Yes?"

"Gil Sivart, M. Vemeer. I'm checking some things. Was M. Haskins depressed about anything?"

"Depressed?"

"Unhappy. Distressed in any way."

"No. Why do you ask?"

"The possibility of suicide has been raised."

"Suicide? That's crazy! Hask would never do that!"

"You sound very certain."

"Listen, the night before he died, he and I were together. We had a wonderful time. We were talking about getting a formal cohab contract. He wanted to have children. So did I."

"And you say the evening was pleasant?"

"We drank wine, had a meal that he cooked, and then made love five times. That pleasant enough?"

Gil stared at the com unit. Well. A man who had made love five times in a single evening certainly didn't seem to be a candidate for suicide, unless fucking himself to death was the way he wanted to go. And considering fathering children argued against it, too.

"Thank you," Gil said. "I'll get back to you."

Hmm. Just for the sake of the puzzle, assume that it was murder. The means was evident. What would the motive be? Who had the opportunity? If you knew one, you could get the other, but which would be easier to determine?

The all-clear chime sounded. The drill was over.

Gil headed toward the tubes.

The kung fu class lasted an hour and a half, after which Gil usually did a short meditation alone in his cube. Because he was sitting quietly on a floor cushion trying to clear stray thoughts from his mind, he heard the sound he probably would have missed had he been watching the trivid or listening to music. A tiny *click* in the hallway outside his cube.

He thought about the sound. His cube was the last one in a feeder hall cul-de-sac two hundred meters or so away from his shop. He had chosen the unit because it was at the end of the hall and thus apt to be quieter than most. There wouldn't be any foot or cart traffic going past, just the residents of the two cubes slightly uphall from him, neither of whom had much company. The old man to Gil's left was retired from his former job as a food service tech and was generally asleep by 2100. The cube to Gil's right belonged to a woman having a liaison with two other women a level down, and she spent most of her time in the larger cubical belonging to one of them. So— who's there?

Came another *click*. It was right outside his door.

He sat there for another two minutes, but his meditation was shot, he might as well satisfy his curiosity. He unwound his legs, stood, and moved toward the door.

The door slid open and Gil stepped out into the hall. Nope. Nobody home. The question was, what would have made that clicking sound? It was familiar, though he couldn't place it at the moment. Still, the hall was empty and there was nothing to indicate anybody had been there. He turned to go back into his cube. Another mysterious noise in the night, probably some kind of plastic or metal stress—

Wait a second. The circuit breaker.

The plastic cover to his cube's circuit breaker had a latch on it, so when you opened or shut the little plate, the latch made a small noise. And the breaker was immediately next to the door, where they were for nearly all the cubes on the station. They could be locked, to keep bored children from playing their little switch-off-all-the-lights games, but hardly anybody ever actually used the locks, certainly Gil didn't. The lights hadn't gone off, there hadn't been any interruption of power in his cube, so why would anybody have opened and closed the panel?

Gil reached for the circuit breaker's cover and opened it. There was the *click,* sure enough.

Whoops. Hello?

A black plastic nodule about the size of his thumb was stuck to the board, just over the cube's shower circuit.

A cold finger jammed itself into his bowels. Gil recognized the device. There was a similar, smaller unit augmenting the battery of his molding table. Damn! A power pusher!

Since all water had to be recycled on the station, there were shunt circuits built into showers, fountains, sinks, toilets, and whatnot for proper recovery of gray and stink water. And since water and electricity were a dangerous combination, special care was taken to be certain that amperages and even voltages were kept very low in those systems that came into contact with people.

The device stuck to his circuit breaker was a specialized piece of hardware, used to amplify and focus electrical current. A kind of superconducting capacitor with microcomputers and a Henley's Loop, a pusher could take regular power, store and step it up on the order of fifty to a hundred thousand times, then discharge it as needed, over a programmed period—or all at once. Thus it could allow a small battery to operate even a very heavy machine for a time, inducing the needed current by focused broadcast.

Gil stared at the pusher. He felt cold. If this thing were operative, and if it were set as he suspected, then the next time he stepped into his shower, he would have been in real trouble. The five or six volts of operating current in the thin wires of his shower, the head and floor and wall recovery systems, would suddenly have become maybe six hundred thousand volts, with a big rise in amperage, too. The wiring would surely have overloaded and spewed much of the excess juice into the water showering down upon him and puddled at his feet. And a wet body grounded in more water has little electrical resistance.

He would have fried like soypro in boiling oil.

And if he hadn't heard that small sound in the hall, it was likely they would have succeeded. He could have died in the shower and not have been missed for a few days, giving the murderer plenty of time to come and remove the pusher. An unfortunate accident, it would seem, some freak induction thing with the shower, and wasn't that too bad?

If somebody wanted him dead, then they had to have a reason. Unless they were unhappy with a model he'd sold them, then that reason must be connected to his other activities. He got along with the kung fu class and he didn't have any major enemies he knew about due to his personal history, not on the station, anyway. The thieves he had brokered with various organizations were usually grateful to him that they weren't going to do locktime or brainscramble. That left the investigation he was pursuing. And if somebody was willing to kill him to keep him from continuing it, then Haskin's death surely hadn't been an accident or suicide, because who would care?

Despite his brush against death, Gil smiled. Seems as if he had gathered more parts to this puzzle than he had figured. Things were getting interesting.

In the morning Gil called Linju Vemeer. They arranged to meet for breakfast. "This won't cause you a problem with work?" he asked.

"I don't need to work any longer, M. Sivart. Hask saw to that."

"Call me Gil."

"All right. Gil. Might as well call me Linju."

The restaurant on Green 3 was an "outdoor" cafe, with tables outside of the place where it opened into the deck park. The small trees and open space had been carefully created to give the illusion of a much a larger area, and it was pleasant to sit sipping coffee with a handsome woman, watching children play under the artificial sun on the live grass in the park.

"You were right," Gil said. "Hask was murdered."

Her face tightened, then relaxed a little. "How do you know?"

He told her about the incident at his cube. She was disturbed by it and said so.

"Have you called the cools?"

"No. Not yet. I would rather have something more to give them when I do."

"It could be dangerous for you to continue. I would understand if you stopped."

He smiled. "I'll be careful. I put a lock on my breaker."

"This doesn't make any sense, you know. Why anybody would want to kill Hask."

Gil said, "Well, if we believe that he was killed and we know how, all we need to do now is figure out who or why. Either of those will eventually give us the other."

"What will you do?"

"I'll have another talk with ISU. Maybe I can narrow things some. Oh, and one other thing. If the killer tried for me, he or she might also feel disposed to try for you."

She looked startled. "Me?"

"If you were gone, they might assume the investigation would stop. It wouldn't, but they might not know that."

She looked at him. "What would you advise?"

"Simple caution. Don't walk down any deserted corridors alone. Keep your doors locked. Take care when you shower. Call me immediately if you see or hear anything suspicious."

"I will."

After she left, Gil walked toward the tube station and entered a lift to take him to see Millet. He didn't really think Linju was in danger, but it didn't hurt to be careful. As the tube, only half filled with passengers, lifted, the newsproj lit and began to rattle on about what was happening on the station and in the galaxy beyond. A group of visiting Gersons, those teddy-bear-like aliens, were enjoying their tour of the *Hawking*. The amphibian race of Silbers were engaged in battle with the Ichtons, the latter's fleet having laid siege to, and nearly having sacked, the Silbers' planet. In the financial news, a number of major businesses had recently suffered reversals, including among them the Luna Industrial Complex, the Milview Starfreight Lines, and the Kuralti Brothers chain of stores.

Gil listened idly to the news. Sometimes he forgot that the *Hawking* was an instrument of war, sailing the vacuum of deep space to fight against the Ickies who would, if not stopped, wipe out every other race they met. A single murder didn't seem like much compared to planetcide; still, he couldn't do much to affect a war but he might be able to help here. Life, after all, was lived in the details.

Indeed, it was the small details that added up to make the whole. For instance, he knew that whoever had meant to kill him was technically adept. It required a certain amount of knowledge to know how to use an electrical pusher, and to come by one without it being missed or accounted for. Gil had done a search of pubinfo files and had discovered that there had not been any sales of this particular model and brand of pusher to private citizens recorded in the last month. Likely it had been stolen. If he could find out where the pusher had come from, it would help the search for whoever had taken it. He had an idea about who that might be, but he needed more.

Gil met Millet. They stood in the back of the big rec room on Dark Yellow watching the skaters slide in their smooth boots across the low-fric surface.

"I checked you out," the cool said. "You have some friends in high places."

Gil shrugged. "I've done some favors for people."

"Yeah. I heard."

"Do you suppose I could get a copy of the names of those people who came and went to Haskins's location on the day he died?"

Millet shook his head. "That wouldn't be likely, no. The privacy rules wouldn't allow us to reveal that outside official channels. Why do you want it?"

"Because I'm sure he was murdered."

Millet sharpened, his eagerness apparent. "You have proof?"

"Not yet. The list of names might help me get it. As would the results of the scans."

Millet shook his head. "I can't reveal them. It would be my ass if anybody found out. Talking invasion of privacy, civil torts, like that."

A skater fell in front of them and laughed as she slid spinning across the floor. Other skaters leaped over her or veered to the sides to keep from tripping.

"You're a patrol officer," Gil said. "Senior grade?"

"That's right."

"So you could get to be a subcommander if a slot came open?"

"Yeah, me and ten other seniors. Lot of competition for the nonmilitary openings."

"A nice rise in status and pay, though, right?"

"Yeah. What are you shooting at here, Sivart?"

"Well, let's suppose here that you uncovered a murder and another attempted murder and caught the perpetrator. Would that give you an edge for promotion?"

"An edge? Yeah. Sharp enough to cut anybody else out of the way."

"Suppose that I could give you that? I figure out who it is *and* give you the reason and enough evidence to justify a deep scan. You get all the credit."

Millet watched the skaters circle past. He was silent for maybe thirty seconds. Then, "What do you get out of it?"

"I get to solve the puzzle. And you owe me a favor."

Millet looked at him. "That's it?"

"That, and the gratitude of a not-quite-beautiful woman."

"Ah."

"Well?"

"Let's go someplace private," Millet said.

Gil had in his flatscreen a no-print-no-transfer copy of the lists he wanted, courtesy of the ambitious Millet. The names were simple enough, there were thirty-four of them. And although he wasn't a tech, the results of the truthscans were easy enough to follow. They were only shallow scans, verifications of questions asked, as opposed to deep scans that could dig into the memory and unconscious mind of a subject, were he willing to speak or not. Still, shallow scans worked better than basic lie detectors. When asked about the death of M. Haskins, none of the thirty-four people questioned registered any direct knowledge of the cause.

Gil sat in his shop, waiting for the molds of several hair-fine extrusions to finish producing the tiny model parts. Something was definitely wrong with this picture.

If, as he had good reason to believe, Haskins was murdered, then either the door scanners had missed somebody or the truth scanners had erred. Occam's razor said that it was the latter: the door cams were difficult to rascal, they were hardwired and fed into a central recorder, whereas the the truth scanners required human operators. Assume the killer was one of the thirty-four. Then he or she had lied about it and the shallow scan had missed it—or been altered.

Gil plugged into the library and downloaded several files on the history of electroencephaloprojic readers. It took nearly two hours for him to finish reading, and it wasn't until the final section that he found what he was looking for. He smiled.

Gil put in a com to Millet.

"Did you know that a shallow scan can be beaten?"

Millet said, "I've heard that it is possible. Some hypnotic drugs supposedly'll fuzz the test. But we do drug scans on everybody to check for that."

"There's another way," Gil said. "By telling the exact truth."

"Huh?"

"Suppose you ask me if my name is M. Gil Sivart. Is there any way I can truthfully answer that no?"

Millet rolled that one around. "I don't see how, that's your name, isn't it?"

"Not precisely. I have a middle name, too, it's Meyer. Technically speaking my name is Gil Meyer Sivart, so I could say no to your question and be telling the truth."

Millet considered this. "Yeah, I can see that. But you'd have to be real clever to get through a whole session without slipping up," he said. "And it wouldn't fool a deep scan."

Gil went on. "But if you had an idea of what they were going to ask you and you had time to set up your replies, the machine would never blip because you would be telling the literal truth, right?"

"You're reaching."

"Oh? Assume you're the killer. The tech asks, 'Do you know how M. Haskins died?' And you take his question to the limits of knowledge—you don't know the precise cause of death, yes, he was crushed by a robot, but what *exactly* killed him? Unless you had access to the autopsy report, you couldn't say for certain, could you?"

"Come on. What if I asked you point-blank, did you kill Haskins?"

"Nobody asked that question. I have the list right here. And even if they had, the killer could have safely answered no and have been telling the truth. *He* didn't kill Haskins. The *robot* killed him. Yes, he *caused* the robot to do it, but he could have touched a control and turned away, say, not looking at the actual event, and would have been able to deny that he had seen Haskins die."

"This is real iffy stuff here, Sivart."

"I know. But it opens up an otherwise dead end."

"You won't get a legal order for deep scans on thirty-four people, not unless we are talking about espionage, station security. You'd have to bring the military in on it. Even so, they'll hear screams way out in the spiral."

"I think we might be talking about just that," Gil said. "But maybe I can narrow it down. I'll get back to you."

Gil went to see Linju at her cube. Partially this was to ask her some questions, partially it was to see where she lived. She was on Basic Green, a quarter of the way from the hub, in a neighborhood that was much like Gil's own. With her new credit line she could easily move to one of the luxury places, on Dark Yellow, or even down in the Violet, where a lot of the commercial rich folk lived. Double- or even triple-sized places with all the perks that money brought. A lot of his sculptures occupied display tables down in Violet, given that he didn't give them away. Truth was, Gil could probably afford one of those places if he wanted, the going price of one of his models being as high as it was. He didn't need the room, though, and his ego wasn't so fat it needed an expensive address to drop into polite conversation. That was too easy, to get snared in the mine-cost-more-than-yours trap.

Linju met him at the door. She wore a long robe of pale green silk that was belted at the waist. The robe covered her, save for a flash of leg when she sat, but it was thin enough to cling in interesting curves and hollows. After appreciating those interesting places, he remembered to look around. The cube was clean, furnished in basic extruded furniture, a lot of cushions on the floor. A couple of paintings were hung, acrylics, one of two nude people embracing, the other of a group of children playing in a water fountain. There was a small statue of a dancer in a ballet pose on a table near the door, bronze or resin cast to look like bronze. There was a rack with infoballs slotted, books, and holovids. Here was a place where you could feel comfortable, and he did.

"Chair or a cushion on the floor," she said.

He chose the floor. So did she.

"What have you found out?"

"Not as much as I need for legal reasoning," he said. "I want to know more about Hask's work. What exactly did he do?"

She thought about it for a few seconds. "You know that the military subcontracts out a lot of things. Hask worked for Sensor Systems. They do a lot of different projects, but their biggest contract was to install and maintain the external hull pickups. Doppler, radar, light-spectrum visuals, magnetics, like that. It's an ongoing process. FTL screws some of them up, microdust and stray hydrogen atoms knock them out of tune or even off-line."

"Go on."

"Hask checked on the installations, making sure they were working and encoded properly. He had about a dozen people on the team; he was responsible for making sure what they did came up to milstan specs."

"I would have thought the military did that themselves."

"They're supposed to, technically, but they're stretched thin. The officer in charge might suit up and go EVA for form's sake, but basically he signs off on the subcontractor's inspection—if he knows him. Hask spent most of the trip out doing this, plus he was ex-military himself, so the military guys knew his work was clean. Once a year there's a major systems check and if everything passes they figure they can trust you. Hask's sections always passed. He had the fewest glitches on the station last test. He was proud of that. Hask would laugh and screw around with the best of them, but when it came to his work, he was tight, he didn't goof off."

Gil considered that.

"Any help?"

"Yes. We know he was murdered and we know how. I think maybe I've got part of a reason why, and that gives me some possibilities as to who."

"One more question. Do you know when the last major system check was?"

"Couple months ago. No problems."

"So there wouldn't be another such test for maybe ten months?"

"That's right."

"In which time the station would be likely to see more action against the Ichtons."

She shrugged. "Military hasn't said for sure and of course they wouldn't, but that's the scat."

He nodded. "I'll call you soon. I think we're getting close."

At the door, she touched his shoulder. "Gil?"

"Yes?"

"It means a lot to me to put this to rest."

"I know."

"I appreciate all you've done, even if you don't figure it out."

The weight of her fingers through his tunic was small but much of his attention was gathered on the spot; suddenly it had grown warm almost to the point of heat. There were a lot of things he could have said, but he only managed a somewhat flustered thanks.

As he walked away from her cube, Gil grinned wryly at himself. Careful there, Sivart, your professional judgment is about to fall off a high-gee mountain. And it would be all too easy to take advantage of her grief. Not something a decent man should do.

Hell of a thing, ethics. Tended to get in your way all the time. Damn.

Back in his own cube, Gil listened to the recordings he had made with his sub-rosa device. Rawlins, the man who'd found the body; Millet the cool; the medic; Linju. There was a piece missing, one crucial part. He felt it tapping at the perimeter of his mind, a small thought he could not quite catch. It was a key, if he could only slip a net over it and grab it, it would somehow open the hidden door.

He went through the flatscreen's material for the fifth time. Nope, it wasn't there, whatever it was he wanted.

He accessed the library computer and began searching and researching material he had read before. Along the edge of the computer's image, the on-line charges blinked and grew. This was going to cost him a nice piece of change, all this blind skipping hither and yon. He almost had it, he was sure of it, he had a reason, though it was iffy, it didn't quite make enough sense to nail down and call it that, but it was *almost* right, he knew it. Damn!

He was watching the on-line charges get bigger when it suddenly came to him. Of course! There it was, right in front of him, crap, how could he have missed it?

Gil grinned. Had it been a micrometeor it would have taken his head off because he'd been too stupid to duck.

He ran through his recordings and nodded to himself. With a specific idea in mind, the library obediently gave him the correlations he needed. There it was, plain as white bread.

Time to go and talk to the murderer.

Rawlins's skull tattoo was beaded with sweat as he stacked honeycombed plastic crates of sensor components on a lift. He was alone in the storage room when Gil arrived.

Rawlins looked up. "Sivart? What do you want?"

"A confession would be nice," Gil said.

"Confession? What are you talking about?"

"Killing Haskins. Trying to kill me. Espionage. Anything else you'd like to unburden yourself of."

"What, are you crazy?"

"I don't think so. It took me a while to put it together, but anybody who looks carefully can see it."

Rawlins stepped away from the stack of crates and stood facing Gil from five meters away. His hands were empty. "See what?"

"Why you did it. It went past me at first, the motive, because I was too close in, I couldn't see the larger picture."

"What is this larger picture?"

"Oh, you know that. I'd guess you are in for a full wipe at the very least. Me, I'd shove you out a lock if capital punishment were still legal."

"You are crazy," Rawlins said. He put one hand behind his back.

"Nope. And I have enough to get a judge to go for a deep scan to prove it."

Sweat ran down Rawlins's face. He blinked it away, appeared to consider things, then pulled something from under his back coverall flap and pointed it at Gil.

"Well, well," Gil said. "What have we here?"

"It's a heartstopper," Rawlins said. "Induces cardiac fibrillation out to about twenty meters, in the hands of an expert. I'm an expert."

"So that's how you managed to get Haskins set up in front of the drone. I expected it was something like that."

"No, you didn't, or you wouldn't be here. Who have you told?"

"Nobody, yet. I wanted to get your confession recorded first." He pointed at his breast pocket.

Rawlins laughed, a nasty sound. "You don't think I'll get to play with that recorder after you, if I want? You *are* crazy."

"You'd be surprised," Gil said. "I scored very well on my last psych test."

"All right. Let's cut the scat. How much?"

"How much are you offering?"

"Don't play cute, pal. If you aren't greedy, you can retire in comfort. Half a mil."

"What I'd really like is to see you swing from a yardarm," Gil said. "That's an old nautical term. They'd tie a rope around your neck and hang you by it. Death by choking, or, if you were lucky, a broken neck."

"You're not in any position to be threatening anybody." Rawlins waved the weapon.

"Another accident will be hard to explain."

"There won't be an accident. You'll just disappear."

"I might have told somebody where I was going and why," Gil said.

Another laugh. "No, I don't think so. I think you're one of those guys who thinks he can handle anything. All that kung fu stuff you play with, the kind of work you do for the corporations to keep the cools out of it. Yeah, I checked up on you, pal. You're gonna make the carp in the recycle ponds real happy when they find you chopped up in their food. This is a discom, sucker."

Rawlins aimed the heartstopper and pressed the firing stud.

There was a high-pitched burble from the device.

Rawlins's grin faded as Gil's grew.

"Can't trust technology, can you?" Gil said. He pulled the crow strip on his tunic open and revealed a thin and glittery gold mesh vest concealed under the clothing.

Rawlins threw the heartstopper and tried to rush past, but Gil ducked, then slid over and snapped a fast counter sidekick up. The fleeing man more or less impaled himself on Gil's heel, whacked himself smack on the solar plexus, and stopped cold, unable to breathe.

Gil stepped in and swung a backhanded hammerfist to Rawlins's temple. It was a solid strike, he felt it all the way into the middle of his back, and it stretched Rawlins out full length, unconscious before he hit the floor. It was unnecessary, the hammerfist, but it made Gil feel a lot better. His hand would be sore, but it was worth it. He touched his personal com.

"Officer Millet? I have a present for you."

Once again in Linju's cube, Gil sat sipping at tea.

"Very good," he said, nodding at the cup.

"Yes, sure, it's wonderful. Come on, Gil."

He smiled. "Okay. Once we were pretty sure that Hask was murdered, the first question that has to come up is why? Since nobody seemed to have any personal grievances against him worth homicide, then that left his work. The killing was carefully planned and executed, so that argued against a crime of passion."

Linju nodded.

"What he did was inspect sensors, equipment essential to the battleworthiness of the station. So I figured that it was either something he had discovered or was about to discover that somebody didn't want found out. That narrowed it down to the people who worked for him."

"But they all had passed a scan," she said.

"Right. So I dug around and found a way that you can rascal a shallow scan. That opened it back up again. Hask had a dozen people working for him, but some of them worked pairs, some of them were off-duty, and some of them were EVA when he was killed. That left me with two possibles, one of whom was Rawlins.

"I went over the scans, and I went over the tape I made of my first conversation with Rawlins. When I listened to it enough times, I realized he had evaded some of my questions, but very skillfully. When I asked if he knew how Hask had come to be where he'd been found, he sidestepped it. I didn't realize it at the time. Very sharp."

"So you suspected Rawlins all along?"

"He got better as a prospect after I found the pusher on my circuit breaker. He was a tech, he knew how to work such stuff."

"Then why didn't you turn him in?"

"Before I could point the cools at him, I needed a reason. Why would Rawlins in particular want Hask dead? What did he want to hide that bad?

"Rawlins was an installer. He put sensors onto the outer hull itself, the first line of defense against any incoming threat." He paused, waiting to let that sink in.

It only took a second. "He was sabotaging the sensors," she said.

It pleased him that it didn't get past her. "Yes. And according to what Millet found out from the military, they wouldn't have found out about it until the next full-scale test of the system. Until then, they would work well enough, unless triggered by an esoteric combination of radio and radar pulse. Once activated, there was a computer rigged to reroute the feed from fully functional gear so they would still *seem* to be working, but in fact would leave a rather large blind spot in the system.

"The military is reluctant to say just how big this gap would have been, or if it would have constituted a real danger, but I suspect that the hole created would be enough for an attacker to slip an antimatter spike or maybe a ceepee beam through it. It's classified information, where the hole was, but depending on where it was, it could cause major damage. Maybe even destroy the station entirely."

"Christo," she said.

"Exactly."

"So Rawlins was a spy? An agent of the Ichtons?"

"Well, yes and no. That was my problem. There's no record of Rawlins leaving the station since he arrived, no indication of how he would have been contacted by them. There are ways, of course, but it's not as easy as the trivid dreadfuls make it out to be.

"My problem was that I was looking at the motive wrong. Little versus big. On the near end, we had Hask discovering the tampering, and that was a problem for Rawlins that had to be corrected. Probably he called Rawlins on it and Rawlins stalled him long enough to set up the murder. We'll find out for sure when they do the deep scan. But there didn't seem to be anything in Rawlins's background to show him as a traitor in the employ of enemy aliens. It was when I was watching how much my library charges were going to cost me when I remembered one of the oldest rules in investigation, something I should have been looking at all along."

"Which is . . . ?"

" 'Follow the money.'

"You see, the Ichtons don't try to communicate with men, at least they haven't so far. They squat on a planet, kill everything that moves, and take over. While they might have a lot to gain by taking out the *Hawking*, they probably wouldn't have any idea whatsoever of how to go about hiring a human agent."

"So, who . . . ?"

"I was in the tube, on my way to see Millet when I heard the news," he said. "There was an item about galactic companies that weren't doing too well. One of them was the Kuralti Brothers."

"The big stores?"

"Yep. And I found out from Rawlins's records that he had worked for them for several years. They have half a dozen outlets here on the station."

He waited to see if she would put it together. After a moment she did. "My God. Rawlins was going to help destroy the station and kill ten thousand people and friendly aliens for the *insurance*?"

He nodded. "War insurance is very, very expensive. And it pays off very, very big—but only if the loss is in actual combat. If this station went *boom!* under the guns of an enemy alien, there would be sufficient documented records of it transmitted to require that the insurance company pay off policy holders. I would bet that the Kuralti Brothers have unusually large policies for the six stores on *Hawking*. And that they found some way to let the Ickies know just where to shoot."

She shook her head. "My God."

"I expect Rawlins bribed somebody to allow him access to some kind of escape ship. When the shooting started, he would have slipped away. Risky, but he was being well paid."

"Hask died so somebody could make a profit," she said.

"Yes. People have been killed for a few coins in their pocket. We are talking about billions. Big money blinds some people to everything else."

"You took a big risk facing Rawlins alone."

"Not really. He worked with electronics. I figured he must have used some kind of cardiac stunner on Hask, a neural tangler would have shown up on the autopsy, but the fibrillation damage was covered by the drone. That's why Hask was facing the thing, so his heart would be crushed. He was probably almost dead when it hit him. I wore a faraday vest I borrowed from Millet, so I wasn't in any real danger."

"He could have used a needler or a zester," she said.

"Nah. Too risky. No chance of calling that an accident."

He stood. "I need to be be getting along. Officer Millet wants to buy me lunch. To celebrate his recent promotion to subcommander."

She walked him to the door. "Listen," she said, "I'm still grieving over Hask. I expect I will be for a long time."

He looked at her and nodded, not speaking.

"Maybe," she said, "maybe you might feel like calling me in a month or six weeks?"

"I would very much like to do that," he said.

She raised herself up on her toes and kissed him lightly on the lips, the softest of touches, then pulled back. "Thank you for all you did," she said. "And what you probably could have done—but didn't. Call me."

When the door closed quietly behind him, Gil let out a long sigh. Well. Maybe ethics were useful things after all. Lunch with Millet would be good, but a month from now, things could be a whole lot better, couldn't they?

Oh, yes, indeed.

THE EDGE

OUTNUMBERED BY A factor of thousands to one, the crew of the *Hawking* had a few advantages that they had to make full use of. One of these was their more efficient warp drive. The warp drives used by the Ichtons, and most of the races inhabiting Star Central, were incredibly inefficient by Alliance standards. It took any Ichton ship almost a week to cover the same distance as could be traveled by the slowest Indie tradeship in a day. The most modern Fleet scouts were as much as ten times faster when under warp than their equivalent Ichton vessel.

The Ichtons did not use scoutships as such. Perhaps their communal instincts mitigated against the smaller vessels and isolated duties. More likely their greater numbers simply allowed them the luxury of making every reconnaissance one made in force. As the swarm of hundreds of mother ships and their escorts moved from system to system, the Ichtons would invariably send ahead smaller fleets comprised of several cruisers.

Counterbalancing the Alliance edge in technology to the dismay of the Fleet representatives, was the almost complete unwillingness of most races to even acknowledge the Ichton threat. Even when a race did recognize the danger, which might not directly affect them for generations, they often chose to fortify their own worlds and send only token forces to support the *Hawking*. The *Hawking* was, after all, crewed by outsiders. Their explicit intention to organize all the planets of Star Central under their coordination often appeared a greater threat to the local leaders than the distant Ichtons.

THE STAND
ON LUMINOS
by Robert Sheckley

FRANK LIVERMORE WAS on his way to the blue briefing room, where the assignments for his section were being given out. Frank was more than ready, too. He was tired of waiting around while the high brass sat in their plush conference rooms on the *Hawking*'s upper levels and decided the fate of middle-level officers like Frank. He might be assigned to outpost duty on some lonely, deserted little world where he'd be expected to watch for the arrival of the Ichton fleet, and then try to get out at the last minute. Or he could be assigned to one of the task forces that civilization had set up in various locales as part of their great effort to contain the Ichtons before they reached the home worlds.

"Hey, Frank, wait up!"

Frank turned, recognizing the voice of Owen Staging, the trader, who had made his acquaintance early in the trip. Staging was a big, barrel-chested man with a boxer's pug nose and the forward-thrust shoulders of a belligerent bull. He was a tough man, cynical and profane, who managed to stay popular with everyone aboard the *Hawking*. Frank liked him, too, though he neither entirely trusted Owen nor subscribed to his ethics.

"Where you off to in such a hurry?" Owen asked.

"They've called a briefing session," Frank said.

"About time," Owen said.

"These things take time," Frank said.

Owen shrugged. "Where do you think they'll send you?" the trader asked.

"You know as much about it as I do," Livermore said.

"I just might know *more* about it than you do," Staging said.

"I don't get you," said Frank.

Owen smiled and laid a forefinger alongside his nose. "I got a kind of idea about where they'll send you."

"Where?"

"Hell, no sense talking about it yet, it's only a hunch," Owen said lazily. "Tell you what, though. Come have a drink with me after you get your assignment, Frank. In the Rotifer Room, OK? I've something to tell you I think you'll like to hear."

Frank looked at Owen with mild exasperation. He knew how the trader loved to pretend to inside information. And perhaps the man *did* have such knowledge. Some people always seemed to know what was going on behind the closed doors in the upper-level boardrooms where senior officers conducted the day-to-day business of fighting the war against the Ichtons.

"All right, I'll see you there," Frank said, then hurried off onto the express walkway that led to Blue Briefing B.

The small auditorium had seating for about five hundred people. Frank noted that it was about half full. It was a circular functional room with no pretense to grace. There was mellow indirect lighting, as in many places on the *Stephen Hawking*. The place looked somber, shadowy, and official. Frank found a seat in one of the front rows between a bearded gunnery officer and a uniformed woman from Ship's Stores. Frank couldn't remember seeing either of them before. It was strange, how long you could live on the *Hawking* without meeting any appreciable number of its ten thousand mixed personnel. At the end of a five-year tour of duty you rarely knew anyone beyond the core group of ten or twenty people with whom you had immediate business. Although most of the *Hawking*'s great expanse of space and its array of stores, shops, buildings, and structures of all sorts were pretty much open to everyone, people tended to live pretty much in their own section and to limit their friendships to people with similar job descriptions.

The gunnery officer sitting beside him unexpectedly said, "You're Frank Rushmore, aren't you?"

Frank looked at the man. The gunnery officer was in his late sixties, like Frank. He had that tired, somewhat cynical look that some officers got when they stuck too closely to their specialty for too long. Officers are not encouraged to sound off about matters outside their own competence, of course. Phlegmatic and incurious, that was the desideratum; but some measure of the simian quality was needed if a man was to stay mentally alive.

"Hello," the gunnery officer said. "I'm Sweyn Dorrin." He was broad-faced and clean-cut except for the tufts of hair on the points of his jaw that proclaimed him a follower of Daghout, a mystery cult that had made some inroads into the loyalties of Fleet personnel in recent years. Dorrin did not look the religious type, however. He had a dull and incurious look about him, as if hardly anything was worth his while to consider, or even to wonder at.

Yet he was wondering something now, perhaps just for the sake of the conversation, for he asked Frank, "Do you know where they're posting you?"

"My superior hasn't discussed it with me," Frank said, not particularly wanting to talk with the man but unsure how to extricate himself without seeming rude. "Do you know?"

"Of course," the gunnery officer said. "My CO said to me, Dorrin, you're the best man we've got on Class C Projectile Spotting Systems. No combat zone assignment for you. We need you to train new troops. They'll be moving you back to the secondary services depot at Star Green Charley."

"Good for you," Frank said.

"Thanks," the gunnery officer said, ignoring Frank's irony. "What about you, Frank?"

"How do you know my name?" Frank asked.

"I used to see you at the Academy outpost at Deneb XI. They said you were a square shooter."

Frank knew he had been a good officer, conscientious, thorough, but never flashy, never seriously considered for higher ranks. They'd never put his name forward for promotions above and beyond what fell to him through seniority. He was twenty-nine years in the service, and what had it gotten him? A lot of traveling, a lot of staring at the insides of spaceships, a lot of leave in strange places, a lot of women he didn't remember the next day, and who didn't remember him the next minute. That was about all the years in the Fleet had brought him, and he wondered now why it had all gone by so fast. Retirement time was coming up and he wasn't sure what he was going to do, retire with thirty years or take another hitch. There was a war on, of course, and some would say that now was not a time to be leaving the Fleet. But there was always a war on somewhere and a man had to think of himself sometime, didn't he? It seemed to him that a man owed something to himself, though Frank wasn't sure what that something was.

The gunnery officer wanted to talk about old times, but the assignments officer had entered the auditorium and obviously wanted to get on with it. This officer's name was James Gilroy and he had been doing this for a long time, reading out the assignments as they came down to him from the Fleet Planning Offices.

Frank's speculations were stopped when he heard the assignments officer call his name.

James Gilroy's dry voice said, "Mr. Rushmore? You have been given a special assignment in sector forty-three. Lieutenant Membrino will meet you in Room 1K and give you the requisite information and documentation."

Frank groaned inwardly. He had just come back from a three-month mission in his single-man scoutship. He could have used some time off, a chance to have a little fun in the honky-tonk bars on the Green-Green level of the *Hawking*. But he made no protest, saluted, and left the conference hall.

Lieutenant Membrino was quite young, no more than his early twenties. He had a small mustache and a serious case of acne.

"You are Mr. Rushmore? I have all the data right here for you." He handed Frank a small black plastic satchel and motioned for him to open it. Within were star charts, a stack of printouts, and an assignment list. In a separate envelope were his orders.

Frank read that he was to go to the planet Luminos, and there present his credentials as a messenger from the *Stephen Hawking* Battle Station. Once he had established his bona fides, he was to inform the inhabitants of the planet of their situation apropos of the Ichtons. A position paper on Luminos followed. The gist of it was that Luminos was in the path of the oncoming Ichton space fleet.

"I don't understand," Frank said. "Why does someone have to go there and tell them? Why not just send a voice torpedo?"

"They might not pay attention," Membrino said. "Luminos is a new world, and the Saurians are not very sophisticated in the ways of interstellar politics. Their electrical technology is scarcely a generation old. They're still pre-atomic. They have only recently encountered the idea that other intelligent races exist in the galaxy other than themselves. If we sent a message, it would simply confuse them. They have had so little experience of other races that a lot of them still believe some of their own people might be trying to pull off a hoax. Whereas if you appear in a scoutship that employs a technology a thousand years beyond anything they've got, and deliver your message . . ."

"I get the idea," Frank said. "In how much danger are they?"

"That's the sad part. According to our best calculations, Luminos is directly in the Ichton invasion path."

"How much time do I have before they show up?"

"It looks like three weeks, maybe a month. Enough time. But you'll have to move lively, Mr. Rushmore, to get in and out of there without getting into trouble."

The Rotifer Room was an expensive eating spot and nightside hangout much frequented by the better-heeled members of the *Hawking*'s personnel. This tended to limit it to upper ratings and wealthy or at least affluent traders. Frank had often passed by its discreet entrance on Green-Green with the plastic palm tree copied from the logo of the ancient Stork Club of Earth. He had never gone in, not because he couldn't afford it— anybody could buy a drink at the Rotifer—but because his tastes tended toward the egalitarian and he was more than a little uncomfortable in close proximity to wealth and position of a sort he had never attained.

Owen Staging was waiting for him inside, seated at a table near the small, highly polished dance floor. This was not an hour when people were dancing, however. Not even the orchestra was present. The place was empty except for Staging and Frank and one or two couples in dark corners, and a discreet waiter in black tuxedo who moved around noiselessly, making sure everyone had drinks.

"Take a seat, Frank," Owen Staging said. His voice was vibrant, with strong chest tones. The big trader was wearing a shirt of some iridescent material decorated with many bits of cloth and metal sewn on to it. The fashion was a little too young for him to carry off successfully. His wristwatch was a genuine Abbott; aside from keeping time it also regulated his body's autonomic systems, checking and smoothing out any disparities when they deviated from Owen's previously established norm. The Abbott also had an automatic yearly adjustment for aging, and in most ways took the place of a personal physician, with advantage, some would say. The big trader looked the picture of health. He was in his late fifties, the prime of life, a big man, on the corpulent side, with large fleshy features and lank blond hair cut in a short brushcut. The smile on his face came easily and seemed genuine. This is a pleasant man, you would have said to yourself. Then, a moment or two later, you would have thought, But there is something about him . . . You'd mean something unpleasant, but you wouldn't know just what it was. Perhaps it was the flat, appraising way Staging looked at you, sizing you up and deciding what use you could be to him. That might have been it. At the present moment, however, the trader was all affability as he pushed a chair out for Frank and clicked his fingers for the waiter.

When the waiter came with the wine list, Owen pushed it aside. "Try some of the Vivot Clique '94, Frank. The sommelier didn't even know he had it until he was looking for something else in his Violet deck storage bay and found this. Pricey, but worth every credit of it."

"Just a beer," Frank said to the waiter.

He was uncomfortable around the trader, but had come to think of him as his friend. They had done a lot of drinking and talking together on the long trip out to Star Central. The trader had been affable and had shown interest in Frank.

"So what assignment did you get?"

"I'm dispatched to a planet called Luminos," Frank said.

"Luminos?" The trader's yellow eyes closed as he thought for a moment. Then they snapped open. "Luminos! Right on the edge of the war zone, isn't it?"

"I'm not supposed to talk about my assignment," Frank said.

"Come on, Frank! What am I, an Ichton spy?"

"Of course not," Frank said. "It's just that some things are best kept private."

"I already know," Staging said. "So they're sending you to Luminos? It's a useless assignment."

"Well, someone's got to warn them," Frank said.

"But why you? It's a rotten assignment, Frank. You just got back from a long one-man run. You'll be weeks getting to Luminos in a scouter, and once you get there there'll be nothing for you to do. The Saurians of Luminos won't want to talk to you; not after the news you bring them. And there'll be no traders there to talk to because the whole thing's in a war zone. And while you're being bored to death on this provincial little planet, there's a good chance you'll be rather messily killed if the Ichtons come through earlier than expected."

"Somebody has to do this sort of work," Frank said. "That's what the Fleet's out here for. We have to warn all intelligent races who are in the path of the Ichtons."

"I know that, Frank, but it's more than a little futile, isn't it? What good will a warning do them?"

"At least it gives them a chance."

"But what can they *do*? They can't move their planet out of the Ichtons' way."

"I know," Frank said, feeling defeated but stubborn. "But we have to give them the chance anyway."

Owen Staging leaned back and sipped his tall, dew-beaded drink. Ice cubes tinkled as he raised his glass in a humorous gesture. "What I don't understand, Frank, is what's in all this for you?"

"Why should there be anything in it for me?"

"Don't give me the humble crap, Frank. I guess humanity owes something to the men and women who are fighting to keep them alive and free. Twenty-nine years in the service putting out your all for humanity and what do you have to show for it? Just another crappy assignment that won't make any difference anyhow."

"Now look," Frank said, "that's enough. You can make a case against anything. Service in the Fleet is honorable work and the Fleet has been good to me."

"I'm not saying otherwise," Owen said, "but it *is* a little ironic, isn't it, that this assignment that is going to be a dangerous bore to you could be a source of considerable wealth to me?"

"What are you talking about?" Frank asked.

"If I could go in to Luminos," Owen said, "I could follow up on a very fine business opportunity that has just come my way."

"I'm not going to take you into area forty-three with me," Frank said. "I go into Luminos alone. Anyhow, you know the rules; no traders are allowed in war zones."

"I had no intention of going," Frank said. "Luminos is very soon going to be a dangerous place to be in. I don't get my jollies off by taking risks. War is your business, profit is mine. I'd like to make a profit with you, Frank. A profit for us both."

Frank looked steadily at the trader's tough face for a moment. He'd been expecting something like this. Ever since the trader had begun to curry favor with him back at the beginning of the trip, Frank had had the feeling that the man wanted something. And, in a way, Frank didn't mind. He liked the trader, liked his rough jokes and easy manner. And if the trader *did* want to win his favor, what was so bad about that? No one else cared that much for Frank's opinion on anything. It was flattering that the trader, a bold and successful businessman, did, whatever the reason.

Frank's face was expressionless when he said, "Profit? I don't know what you're talking about, Owen."

The trader dug two stubby fingers into the breast pocket of his twill jacket and fished out a brown chamois bag. The neck was held shut by a cunning knot. Tugging at the knot, Owen collapsed it and opened the neck of the pouch. He turned it upside down and teased it gently. Out of the sack rolled what looked like a pebble. But no pebble had ever possessed that fiery pulsating rose color. Looking at the gem Frank felt a brief touch of vertigo, and a feeling that he was entering a strange blue twilight zone where he was suddenly very far away from himself and very close to something he couldn't put a name to.

"What is that thing?" Frank asked Owen.

Owen put the stone down on the table between them. He gently poked it with a forefinger. "That's a Gray's fire stone," Owen said. "It's one of the rarest things in the universe—a psychomimetic mineral that can amplify and alter the mood of whoever holds it. Notice how it changes colors as my hand gets close to it. It responds to each holder with a unique array of colors. The scientists still don't know what that means."

Frank said, "I've never seen or heard of anything like this."

"That's because you don't read the fashion news," Owen said. "Gray's fire rings have made a great splash on the fashion scene in recent years. In fact, they've become the most important accessory of the year according to *Universal Humanoid Stylings* magazine."

Frank lifted the gem and felt it pulse in his hand. "Are these very rare?"

"Only a few hundred of them appear on the market every year. You can imagine what price the top designers pay for them."

"Where do they come from?" Frank asked.

"That has been a mystery for a very long time. It was definitely confirmed only last year, Frank. These stones are from Luminos."

"The place I'm going to?" Frank asked.

"The very same," Owen said. "You see, Frank, if I were going there, I could trade for these stones. I have a dozen outlets back in civilization that are ready to bid against each other once I have them."

"Well, you'd better forget about it," Frank said. "You know very well that no traders are allowed in a war zone."

"No," Owen said, "but there *is* something you can do for me, Frank."

Frank thought for a long moment. "Why would I want to do something for you, Owen?"

Owen grinned and said, "In order to do an old friend a favor. And to earn a considerable sum of money for your retirement fund, partner."

"Partner?"

"I want to go into business with you, Frank."

"You want me to get Gray's fire stones for you?"

"That's it, Frank. And we'd split the proceeds fifty-fifty."

"But what would I trade for the stones?" Frank asked.

"I've got something the Saurians are going to want," Owen said.

"Are you talking about whiskey?" Frank asked.

"No," Owen said, "though they could probably use that, too, with the situation they're in. But I'm talking about something they really need, given the present circumstances."

"Well, what is it?"

"I'm talking spaceship engines, my friend. That's what the Saurians are going to need, since all hell is going to break loose in their neck of the woods pretty soon now."

"Where did you get the spaceship engines?" Frank asked.

"I've got a cousin works in General Offices Surplus and he has a friend in job-lot disposals. They're just starting to dispose of the L5 components."

Frank knew that the L5 had been the heart of the drive shield mechanism in recent years, and of the cold fusion warp generator that made FTL travel possible. It was a unit of considerable antiquity as such things go, nearly ten years in steady production. Frank was not surprised to find that the old model was superceded by a new one. What did surprise him was that Owen had gotten his hands on some of them so quickly. He must have acquired them hours after they were decommissioned, before the big planetary dealers got a chance to bid. Or had the situation been rigged to give him sole bid?

"What are you going to do with the L5s?" he asked Owen.

"I already told you," Owen said. "I am going to give them to you on consignment. Then I am going to stay here on the *Hawking* and wait. You are going to put those engine components in your hold. There's plenty of room for them; there's only thirty-one of them and they just weigh a couple hundred pounds apiece. You will take them to Luminos where they'll be hot items once you tell the Saurians what's in store for them. Once that's established, you trade engines for gems at the best rate you can get, bring back the stones, and we both make a nice profit."

"It's a pretty smart deal," Frank said a little sadly.

"What's more important, it's an open and aboveboard deal between you and me."

"You forget that I'm an active officer in the Fleet and you're a civilian."

"There's no law that prevents an officer from trading on his own account."

"As a matter of fact, there is such a law."

"Oh, *that*," Owen said. "No one pays any attention to that old statute anymore."

"I do," Frank said.

"That's what I like about you, Frank," Owen said. "You're honest and that means I can trust you. That's why I'm going to put thirty-one L5 engine components into the hold of your scoutship and not even ask you to sign a piece of paper. I know you, Frank, and I know you'll be honest with me on this matter."

"I'm not taking your engines," Frank said, "and that's that."

"Are you so afraid of doing a humanitarian deed?"

"Since when is selling engines for you a humanitarian deed?"

"It's selling engines for *us* and it's humanitarian because those poor Saurians need all the help they can get."

"Why not just give them the engines, then?"

"Because I had to pay for them," Owen said. "I won't be able to keep up my good deeds unless I get paid for them."

Frank saw nothing strange in this proposition. The self-serving nature of it disturbed him, however. "I don't like the idea of making a profit on people's misery," Frank said.

"Then give your percentage to charity," Owen said. "Just make sure I get mine. Seriously, Frank, you'll be helping the Saurians in the only really tangible way you can. You'll be giving them a chance to defend themselves and a way to strike back at the Ichtons."

Frank didn't much like it, but he found the logic inescapable. Thinking it over, it seemed to him that by selling the engine parts to the Saurians he would be doing something for them. And it was perfectly in line with his orders to warn the Saurians of their imminent danger of attack. So he could follow Frank's scheme, do his duty, and also provide for himself in his old age. What was wrong with making a profit? Everybody else did it! Why should he hold out? And as for becoming a partner with Owen Staging, well, what was wrong with that? He could do a lot worse. He had done a lot worse most of his adult life, serving in the Fleet.

"All right," Frank said. "I'll do it."

Owen Staging stuck out a meaty red hand. "Put her there, pardner."

Luminos was a small planet in the region of the galactic center. Although close to its neighbors, it was far enough from the next planet bearing intelligent life to require a full-fledged space era technology for trading and cultural exchange. This technology the Saurians of Luminos had not yet achieved, though they were right on the verge of it when the Alliance contacted them.

On Luminos, even electrical generators were still fairly recent developments. The Saurians were only one or two generations away from gas lighting.

After a long boring trip in space, the planet became visible on Frank's viewscreen as a blue and green globe, laced with stringy veils of white cloud. Frank began radioing while still well out to space. He got no response. He turned toward the planet's surface, moving in a shallow deceleration curve. Soon he could pick out cities and roadways, the usual indicators of civilization. The Saurians still weren't making any attempt to communicate with him, nor had they responded to his own broadcasts.

As Frank piloted his scoutship down low through the atmosphere, his radio finally crackled into life. A voice demanded in the Southhoe dialect used by many races of the Star Central region, "Who is that?"

Frank identified himself as an officer of the Fleet, detached from the *Hawking* and sent to the planet Luminos as a special messenger bearing important news.

There was a stunned silence at the other end. A Saurian said, "Just a minute . . ." There was a delay of several minutes. Frank continued to decelerate. It was a bit of a bore, having to go through all this confusion, but that was how it often was with races that had little experience with others not of their kind. Every race that came to spacefaring went through the shock of discovering other forms of intelligent life where before they had thought they were alone. This was bad enough. What was worse was discovering that these other forms of intelligent life often brought with them problems nobody was ready for. This seemed to be the case with the Saurians.

The Saurian came back on the air. "Just a minute, I'm getting my orders . . ." There was another delay, then the Saurian said, "We're putting aside a special landing area for you. We are calling officials from all over the planet to be present for your arrival."

"No need for all that," Frank said. "I come with news of an urgent situation that I need to bring to the attention of any responsible official."

"Don't tell *me* about it," the voice said. "I'm just an aircraft landing officer."

Down on the ground, huge crowds had gathered. They were overflowing all the runways except the one assigned to Frank, where a cordon of uniformed police kept a semblance of order. After landing and closing down his engines, Frank allowed small tracked vehicles to approach his craft. They maneuvered the scoutship to a section of the field where a reviewing stand had been placed and grandstands hastily erected. The crowd was already in place when Frank finally emerged. A covering of royal velvet led from his spaceship to the most elaborately decorated spot on the reviewing stand. Frank walked down this and was greeted by a small, splendidly dressed group of Saurians.

At first Frank and the Saurians just looked at each other, because they were physically quite unlike. Frank looked like a typical man. The Saurians looked like typical dogs of the Airedale variety, with a bit of hyena thrown in for good measure, and with opposable thumbs on a fingered hand rather than the claws more common among the canine species. Frank was not prejudiced toward creatures of shapes other than his. Multiplicity had long been the rule in the great assembly of star-roving peoples. The Saurians, however, were new to the situation, and they gawked at Frank and passed comments among themselves in lowered voices, which, nonetheless, Frank heard and understood.

"Looks like he's descended from a monkey, don't you think?"

"Yes, or possibly a baboon."

"I wonder what color his ass is?"

"Jethro, not so loud, he'll hear you!"

These Saurians and their boorish comments were about what you'd expect from an unsophisticated new race first encountering one of the high galactic civilizations.

Meanwhile, the opening ceremony looked like it was becoming a flop. The Saurians stood around in their splendid uniforms and looked uncomfortable and unsure what to do next. Frank had been trained for these situations. He took two steps forward, raised his right hand with the fingers opened in a universal gesture of peace, and said in a clear voice, "Hello, I am a friendly messenger from a place beyond your sky. You do know about other races in the galaxy, don't you?"

"We've heard," the eldest of the Saurians said. "But we still do not entirely believe."

"Better believe it," Frank said. "There are many worlds out there, and many different kinds of people, and not all of them are friendly. In fact—"

He stopped. The eldest Saurian had raised a hand in a universal gesture that asked for a pause or break or change of venue.

"Yes," Frank said. "What's the matter?"

"It sounds," the Saurian said, "as if you have a serious matter to discuss."

"Yes, if you consider an approaching race of venomous insects a serious matter."

"I must ask you," the Saurian said, "not to say anything about that at this time."

"Why ever not?" Frank asked.

"What we have here is a stranger-welcoming ceremony. That must be completed. Then we can turn to the information-disseminating phase of our relationship. Also, you can't tell the information because there is no one present to tell it to."

"There's you," Frank pointed out.

"I am what we call in our own language a hectator second class. That means I take trash in and out of buildings. You simply do not give official messages to someone like me."

"Suppose I tell one of these fellows," Frank said, indicating the other two Saurians.

"No," the hectator said. "They are my assistants, which is to say, even less than nothing."

"Surely I can tell someone! What about all these people here?" Frank indicated the big crowd of alert hyena-headed Airedales in the reviewing stand, watching the proceedings with the greatest sign of interest.

"Audiences always turn up when something happens," the hectator said. "They come for the show. But they aren't going to listen to you. It's not their job."

"Look," Frank said, "I've got to give my information to someone and get out of here."

"It's a problem," the hectator said. He thought for a minute. "You could always write it out, and I'll see that it gets to someone who knows what to do with it."

Frank was tempted. This assignment didn't seem to be getting anywhere. But it was his duty to make sure that the Saurians really understood about the Ichton danger. Besides, there were the spaceship engines he'd taken aboard for Owen. Now that he had overcome his qualms about selling them, he was suddenly interested in doing so. He could really use some money for his retirement. Selling the L5s presented a fairly honorable way of earning it. He just needed to be patient.

"I'm going back to my ship now," Frank said. "I want to tell my information to someone quick. Otherwise I'll broadcast it to your capital city through my loudspeakers."

Hectator said, "That would never do. No one would listen. The officials always interpret and explain matters of any importance for the people."

"But this is urgent!"

"Oh. In that case, wait right here. I'll go find out what they want to do."

The hectator went away and whispered with a small group

of Saurians at one side of the reception platform. After a while the hectator came back.

"They said they'd send someone to talk to you tomorrow."

"But didn't you tell them this is urgent?"

"They said that they're not prepared to accept your unsupported word on that this early in the game."

The next morning an official came to call on him. Before Frank could speak, the official raised one pink-fingered paw.

"You must understand," the official said, "we officials don't really run anything. Luminos is an anarchy with no one really in charge. But people like to have rulers they can follow when that seems the best way to go, and blame when the officials turn out to be wrong. So we appoint people. It makes things easier."

"Your local arrangements are no concern of mine. I've brought news of the utmost urgency."

"So I gather. But I'm not the one to tell it to."

"That's what the hectator said."

"And very correctly, too. What would we do with mere hectators running the government?"

"Why can't I tell it to you?"

"Because I'm not supposed to be told anything important."

"Who is?"

"I think you'd better speak with Rahula."

Over the next few days Frank learned that the Saurians had many ceremonies of an extremely boring nature and he was supposed to be the centerpiece of all of them. They mainly involved a lot of bowing and posturing, all of it performed with fixed smiles on everyone's faces. The Saurians were extremely cautious, though perhaps "suspicious" would be a better word. It was obvious that they were not a sophisticated people. They kept sneaking looks at Frank, like they couldn't quite believe he was there. Their newspapers had front-page stories about him, getting all the details wrong and pointing out in tedious detail how Frank was a sample of man from the future and going into endless specious detail on how the Saurians stacked up against him. All in all, it looked like the Saurians were having a bad case of culture shock.

From the first minute of his arrival Frank was trying to get the Saurians to discuss the Ichton situation with him. But they didn't want to talk official business or to get down to anything important. "Look," they told him, "don't get us wrong, it's a very great pleasure to have you here with us. We're really honored, if you know what we mean, but before we can discuss interstellar matters we need to finish the new interstellar conference hall. Then we'll have a place worthy of receiving an ambassador like yourself. Believe me, we want to consider your important tidings just as soon as we are set up for it."

"Look," Frank tells them, "this matter of the Ichtons, it won't wait . . . ."

But they wouldn't listen. They would just smile and back away from his presence, leaving him finally talking to himself. Othnar Rahula was the only one who would even pretend to listen to him.

Othnar Rahula was a member of the Saurian aristocracy and was in every way a being to be reckoned with. He was handsome as Saurians go. His ears were always cocked attentively, a sign of good breeding in man and beast alike.

Rahula was affable but there was a mystery about him. Frank couldn't figure out what sort of job he held or what his position was in the Saurian scheme of things. He seemed to be important, and other Saurians were in awe of him, but he never seemed to do anything. It was not polite to ask directly, so Frank decided to put some questions to the Saurian servant who brought his dinner.

"What government post does Rahula hold?" he asked Dramhood, the servant.

"Government post?" Dramhood was puzzled.

"All the government officials seem to defer to Rahula's opinion. Yet he doesn't seem to have an official function."

"I understand what you mean," Dramhood said. "Rahula has a function, but it's a natural one, not an official one."

"What is it?"

"Rahula is this year's official Exemplifier for the Saurian race."

Upon further questioning, Frank learned that the Saurians

worked on a role-model system. Every year the high priests of the culture, duly elected by newspaper vote, went to an ancient monastery high in the mountains, there to confer and decide who would become this year's role model for the inhabitants of Luminos. Rahula was that year's standard-bearer of cultural self-identity, the one the other Saurians wanted to model themselves on.

This custom, Frank learned, had some interesting consequences. What the role model did was what everyone wanted to do. What he believed quickly became what everyone believed. What he thought was what was on everyone's mind, and what he considered unimportant hardly counted at all.

After a week on Luminos, Frank had been unable to get any response to his threats and warnings about the Ichtons. His mention of the spaceship engines he wanted to sell had met with polite disinterest. This led Frank to conjecture that the Saurians had by no means reached their full intellectual potential yet. In fact, as Othnar Rahula remarked one afternoon, sitting in the cabin of Frank's scoutship, where Frank had asked him for afternoon tea, "We've just entered into the idea of even having a potential. We've just discovered intellect and all of its pleasures. It's like we've just woken up onto the stage of galactic history and here you come telling us we're in danger."

Frank said, "I'm sorry if your intellect is taking a beating by discovering you're not the only kids on the block."

"I understand your metaphor," Rahula said. "I think it does not apply in our case. Or, perhaps, it does. I don't know. I just know that it's pretty shoddy when you come here from a superior civilization and tell us that we are about to be wiped out by a race of large carnivorous insects."

"So you *were* paying attention to what I've been talking about all week!" Frank said.

"Yes, of course. But frankly, Frank, your news is too important to take seriously. Besides, I mean, if it's so important to do something, why don't you sentient beings with battle fleets do something about it?"

"Maybe I haven't somehow made myself clear," Frank said. "We, the allied forces, are doing everything about it that we can do. The war has been going on for years. Either we destroy the Ichtons or they wipe us out."

"Well, it may be as you say," Rahula said in a tone that left no doubt as to his uncertainties.

"You simply are not acting in a realistic manner," Frank said.

"Is that what you asked me here for?"

Frank shook his head. "The real reason I've invited you to my ship is to try to convince you of the emergency one last time."

"It's easier for us to believe you're mistaken in your facts about the Ichtons," Rahula said, "or that you are drunken or drugged or a crazy person. It is very difficult for us to think that our entire race may be going down the tubes in a couple of weeks due to an alien invasion we can't do anything about. If the Ichtons come, we will bargain with them. We are a clever people. We will come out all right."

"Your strategy of bargaining," Frank said, "is based upon a delusion. I have something to show you." Frank touched a button on the scoutship's switchboard. Well-oiled motors sprang into instant hum. Rahula sat up, startled. The great tuft of silky blond hair that depended from a knob in the center of his forehead rustled with the sound almost that of a snake shedding a skin.

"You have started the ship's engines!" he said.

"I'm taking you for a little ride," Frank told him.

The spacecraft doors clanged shut. Machinery hummed into life. Red and green lights flashed, then steadied.

"I don't want to go for a ride!"

The generators kicked in, and a low throbbing replaced the sudden, high-pitched whine of servos. Lights flashed on the banks of dials above the instrument panel. There was a soft chittering sound as circuits opened and closed.

Rahula said, "You must let me out of this ship at once. I have a luncheon appointment in fifteen minutes."

"You're going to see what I want to show you," Frank said. "Think you can bargain with those guys? I'm going to give you an idea what it means for a planet to come up against the Ichton horde."

"But I really don't want to see this," Rahula was saying pettishly as the scoutship moved through Luminos's upper atmosphere and then into the darkness of space.

It took Frank only one FTL jump to get to the location he wanted. It was a system of one planet and three moons circling around a red dwarf.

As they came within visual range, Rahula could see that the place had an oxygen atmosphere and possessed the deep green-blue colors of living matter. But as they came closer though, he saw that most life had almost been expunged from the surface of this place. Sweeping low over the planet, Rahula saw that no birds flew in the sky. They passed over dry ocean bottoms; the very water had been sucked away and put into tanks for Ichton use in other places. The land had become mainly desert, and there were miles-deep scrapes where the surface had been strip-mined, ruthless machinery tearing apart the fundamental rocks to get at the valuable minerals and rare earths. A vast cloud of smoke lay over the land, hugging the mountain contours in great, greasy coils. Here and there were shallow ponds that had not been entirely sucked up by the Ichton salvaging and reclamation operations. Higher magnification revealed that these ponds were pustulant with noisome lower life-forms.

They swept over the land at what would have been treetop level, had there been any trees left standing. Beneath them, miles and miles of rocky devastation sped hypnotically past their eyes. And this scene, monotonous and horrifying, repeated itself endlessly as they traversed the planet, until Rahula finally cried, "Enough, Frank, you have made your point. What is this place?"

"This planet is called Gervaise. It is a sister planet to the Gerson world that received similar treatment at the hands of the Ichtons."

Rahula was silent during most of the flight back to Luminos. His soft, shiny brown eyes seemed turned inward. His blink rate was up; he seemed to be thinking very rapidly indeed. When they came down on the landing field at Delphinium, capital city of Luminos, Rahula turned to Frank and said, "How many of those ship's engines do you have to sell?"

"Thirty-one," Frank said.

"And what do you want for them?"

Frank took a deep breath. "My partner and I want to get ten fire gems per engine."

"So many? But it would take us years to find a quantity like that."

"Well, make it five per engine, then. If you all worked together, your people could probably get that together in a matter of weeks."

"Perhaps we could," Rahula said. "But meantime, we can't kid ourselves any longer, the Ichtons are coming toward us and there's no time to waste."

"Nor any need to waste it. I will let you have the engines now, if you give me your promise to pay the agreed-upon price of five stones per engine."

"Yes," Rahula said, "I agree to that. Now bring us back to Delphinium. I must arrange transport for the engines."

"Are you sure you can speak for your people?" Frank asked. "Will they agree with you about the engines?"

"I believe what I'm doing is correct," Rahula said. "Therefore the others will also think it correct. They will do what I do. It is our system."

Frank had to admit that having all the people believe what you believed was a political advantage few races ever possessed. Overnight, and as though by magic, all of the Saurians were aware of the menace that confronted them from space, and, rather than being blasé and evasive about it as before, were, like Rahula, suddenly and deeply concerned. Within minutes after Frank's talk with Rahula, through a sort of racial telepathy, which was immediately reinforced by unprecedented coverage in the newspapers and television, the Saurians all knew they were about to be attacked by the Ichtons, a six-limbed insect species of unparalleled ferocity. Everyone also knew and approved of trading fire gems for spaceship engines.

The Saurians sent several heavy trucks to carry off the thirty-one L5 engine components. The trucks brought them to an industrial complex in a park not far from the capital city. On radio and TV, Frank heard about the organizing of the search for fire gems. Expeditions were quickly organized and sent out to the little-visited regions of the planet near the polar caps, where fire stones had been discovered in the past. Great numbers of Saurians were enlisted into this search, which was supported by all the considerable resources of the planet. Soon the first fire gems began to arrive. Rahula made himself personally responsible for ensuring that Frank got what had been promised him. That meant that all the Saurians considered themselves responsible. It was one of the best-secured debts in the history of loaning.

For a few days Frank could take some time off from the concerns of war. He visited the best-known wonders of the Saurian world. These included the upside-down waterfall at Forest Closet, the Twisted Volcano at Point Hugo, and the Glass Dance Floor at Angelthighs. These were not the spectacular sights for which some of the worlds in the region were known. But they were very special, and carried a load of sentiment. Frank especially liked Forest Closet with its ranks of whispering willows. It was disagreeable to realize that the Ichtons were about to cancel all possibilities, good or bad.

It took the Saurians eight days to collect all of the promised fire stones. There were 155 stones in all, and the presence of so much concentrated mood essence in crystalline form was more than a little overwhelming. There was a special ceremony in which Frank accepted the fire stones on behalf of himself and Owen Staging.

Next day, Rahula took Frank out in one of the surface cars and brought him to the main factory where the engine components were being built into fighter bodies. Frank was a little surprised to find that the Saurians were planning an active defense of their planet. He had somehow assumed that a government group would try to save their own lives, escaping to another world in the ships they could build before the onslaught of the Ichtons. He had seen this happen before. It was typical behavior.

But not for the Saurians. With rapidity and efficiency, they were putting their planet into the best state of defense possible. Under the goad of this emergency, they produced great quantities of jet fighters and equipped them with improved models of the basic jet fighter engine. These were for defense in the atmosphere. To fight between the worlds they had constructed separate bodies to house the thirty-one spaceship engine components purchased from Frank. Their ship designs had been purchased from reliable off-planet sources. Looking these plans over when he was taken for a tour of the factory, Frank could spot some mistakes. Luckily, they were matters he could correct on the spot.

A voice tube torpedo arrived for him. Captain Charles Mardake, head of his section, wanted to know when Frank would be back. Frank sent back a reply in which he explained that the situation on Luminos was still fluid, and that although the Saurians were now working actively in their own defense, they still had a ways to go and therefore Frank could still be useful here. The Ichton attack was still not imminent and so he was exercising his discretion and staying on a while longer.

That morning another message rocket was recovered and brought to Frank in his ship. It was from the office of the Fleet observation corps. They reported that the Ichton fleet had diverted slightly because the big insects had to take care of a larger planet that lay close to their invasion path. It was a planet where high gravity beam installations had been causing problems to some of the outlying Ichton ships. "So the main horde is going to miss you," the report went on, "and that's the good news."

However, the message went on, the bad news was, some Ichton squadrons were being sent to check the flanks for overlooked worlds that could be usefully stripped. One such squadron was coming directly toward Luminos. It consisted of between five and ten cruisers and would be there in about a month or three weeks. They appeared to be Stone-class cruisers and were judged very dangerous.

The message was a blow to Frank's hopes. He had begun to believe that the world of Luminos might be overlooked, but this news dashed that possibility. A group of even five Ichton battle cruisers was potentially as devastating to Luminos as the arrival of the entire battle fleet. The Ichton ships were of a technology far superior to anything the Saurians had been able to put together. Not only that, there was also the matter of battle savvy. The Saurians had never fought a modern space war. Their own wars against each other would have to be considered the equivalent of the bow and arrow struggles of primitives.

But the Saurians were prepared to fight, and the raw youngsters piloting the thirty-one ships built around Owen's L5 units had a lot of esprit de corps. They had memorized some of the fighting tactics as taught by the standard training manuals. But they were a long way from being prepared to face up to the reality of a murderous opponent. They needed more training.

Frank decided abruptly that he would take the situation in hand himself. He announced through Othnar Rahula that starting that very day he was giving classes in spaceship tactics as they pertained to planetary defense. There was no lack of enlistees for his crash course. The Saurians picked up the main concepts with great rapidity. Soon Frank was able to lead the thirty-one new ships in simulated battles in Luminos's troposphere. By rapid shuffling of personnel, and keeping the ships occupied all of the time, Frank was able to train a good number of Saurians in spaceship tactics. The civilian population, meanwhile, made its own preparations, working day and night to get guns of appropriate mass and shocking power on-line in an attempt to defend the cities against the onslaught that now might be no more than days away.

Another voice torpedo arrived. It was a message from the trader Owen Staging. "Frank," it said, "I don't know what you're staying around there for, but please get out. Now! You've done all you can. Maybe a lot more than you should have. It's time you got out of there. Remember, you owe me something, too, like half the stones. That's a joke. But seriously. C'mon back, partner. We've got a great future ahead of us!"

Frank was resting in his bunk aboard his own spaceship when the trader's message came. Soon thereafter there was a warning signal from a long-distance satellite warning station: first elements of an Ichton battle group had been detected at the fringe of radar receptivity.

Frank stood up, and with a heavy heart activated the switches that closed the main airlock. Yes, like it or not, it really was time to get out. He had almost cut it too fine. He'd gone right down to the wire with these Saurians. He would have liked to take station with them and have it out against the Ichtons here and now, but he knew that he couldn't do that. His loyalty was to the Fleet and it was to the Fleet that he had to return.

Losing no time getting aloft, Frank directed his ship to an asteroid belt that formed a maze of rocky moonlets in space near Luminos. He knew he should be kicking back up again into FTL drive, but he couldn't resist waiting long enough to see how his protégés did against the Ichton battle group.

Long-distance radar reported the progress of Ichton spacecraft into the Luminos system. Five cruisers were identified. They were some new class, smaller than Stone class, less well shielded, a sign, perhaps, that some of the Ichton manufacturing units were having to cut back to simpler models. Although they were not Stones, they were still formidable.

For Frank, it was getting very late indeed. But still he delayed in the asteroid belt, waiting for news of the engagement.

Five Ichton ships in line-ahead formation suddenly clashed with the thirty-one Saurian ships in three half-moon formations. Beams flared, shields ran up through the spectrum as they staggered under the energy of multiple strikes. In the first five seconds of combat, seventeen Saurian ships were disabled or vaporized entirely. But two of the Ichton ships were out of the fight, and a third looked like it wouldn't last much longer. The matter seemed to have been decided in that first instant of colliding energies. The Saurians were still hanging in there.

The surviving Saurian commanders learned fast. There were some things about space combat that had to be learned on the spot. No amount of theoretical reading, and not even well-designed simulation equipment, would do. Learning was greatly stimulated by surviving that first engagement.

Now the third Ichton ship was down, dissolving into the raging maw of its own wild-running main engine. Two to go! A group of Saurian ships led by Othnar Rahula surrounded the fourth Ichton cruiser. The smaller ships buzzed around the cruiser like maddened flies. Electrical potentials danced off the edges of ships' shields in wild coruscations of curling force as more energy weapons came to bear. In that confined area space itself heated significantly for a moment. The beleaguered Ichton ship blew out its rearmost shield, tried to rig a temporary one, and was caught without adequate defense when Othnar Rahula swung his ship around and slammed a volley of torpedoes into the stricken cruiser. Brilliant explosions shuddered out into the blackness of space. The Ichton cruiser was still trying to reply with her guns when her FTL equipment vaporized and she was gone as though she'd never been.

Meanwhile, Frank had been dawdling in the asteroid belt, not wanting to turn on his FTL just yet because he wanted to know what was happening.

Then the remaining Ichton ship suddenly began to lose power. The blast from its drive jets faltered, the color of its propulsive flame lances changed from golden yellow to cherry-red. It wobbled, yet somehow remained in precarious control, and began to descend into the atmosphere of Luminos. The land masses of the planet rushed up to meet it, and so did a full squadron of Saurian jet fighters. Colored a metallic liquid black, except for the white markings on their wingtips and tails, these fragile machines clawed up into the stratosphere, higher and higher, until their engines began to flicker and die out through lack of oxygen. They fell back to denser atmospheric levels. The Ichton spaceship now had descended to meet them, still fighting for control, less agile than before, but still moving at a speed no jet ship could match. The fighters replotted their trajectories and flung themselves in for the kill. The high, thin air of Luminos was alive with explosive projectiles from the jets' wing guns, hammering at the Ichton cruiser's screens. The projectiles bounced harmlessly off, as did the rocket torpedoes and small guided missiles. The Ichton ship seemed to be recovering its poise and getting more maneuverable by the second. And it seemed that its commander was realizing that the Saurian aircraft could do little or nothing against his screened spaceship.

The Ichton commander ignored the fighter attack and turned his attention to the planet below him. Explosive rays lanced out from the cruiser's underbelly. Big chunks were torn from the heart of the large city beneath him. A pall of oily black smoke rose into the air. The Ichton spaceship slowed to a deliberate pace. It seemed determined to do a really good job, destroy anything that crawled or swam or flew, strip out the minerals and other valuable things and take them off to the Ichton fleet.

The fighters seemed useless against the well-shielded Ichton cruiser. Seeing this, Frank realized he was going to have to do something. He activated the controls, and somewhere inside of himself it occurred to him that he didn't have to do this, not really, he'd just been sent here to warn these guys, he wasn't supposed to be getting into the fight, he wasn't supposed to be dying for them. But that thought had no time to take hold, because Frank was filled with the simple need to take action and preserve a situation that was threatening to go very badly for the side he had decided to fight for. It didn't occur to him that he had returned somehow to one of his original intentions, formed back when he first joined the Fleet, concerning what to do with his life, how to spend it, what it was for. He knew it was not for making a profit like Owen the trader, but for some other reason, something that had to do with serving humanity in the broadest sense, against its enemies like the Ichtons.

Frank found the Ichton ship in range and fired. As he had feared, his rockets bounced harmlessly off the ship's shields. The Ichton ship fired back. Frank managed to elude the missiles, not trusting his shields to take too heavy a load. When matters quieted down for a moment he saw the Ichton ship coming after him again. He countered. It was stalemate.

There was nothing Frank could do. He and the Ichton canceled each other out. He was going to have to try something different if he was to have a hope of putting the Ichton ship out of action before it destroyed the planet Luminos.

There was one thing still left to try. It was a very old tactic, and it dated back to the days when ships were made of wood and sailed on water. He could ram. It was an almost unheard-of maneuver in the modern world of space combat, but circumstances made it possible now.

Frank put the controls on manual and aimed his scoutship

directly at the Ichton cruiser. He watched, fascinated, as the image of the enemy ship grew in his viewplate from a tiny dot to a vast metal war machine of incredible and still growing proportions. Frank felt himself tense as the moment of impact grew closer and closer. And then ...

Before his eyes, he saw what looked like a meteor arc in from the side and impact with the cruiser. To Frank it looked like an act of God. It took his tired brain a moment to figure out that it must have been one of the Saurians in a fighter craft, ramming the Ichton from the side. The Ichton cruiser exploded in a silent blossom of light and energy, a light that bounded up and down the visible spectrum and seemed to light all of space before it died.

"Nice job, Frank," Owen Staging said. It was a week later. Frank had returned to the *Hawking,* filed his report, and was awaiting further orders. He had also taken it on himself to issue urgent requests to Star Central.

He had told the examining board, "Gentlemen, the Saurians need to be supported in their efforts against the Ichtons. I respectfully request that we send them considerable more military assistance than we have done before."

"They're not a very big power," one of the admirals on the examining board said.

"No, sir, they're not," Frank said. "But they won't quit on us. And that's worth quite a lot in this day and age."

A temporary aid package was approved on the spot. Frank found himself quite a hero back at the *Hawking.* He'd taken a chance, exposing himself for so long in Ichton-dominated space. He'd helped a friendly planet pull off a victory. It was a small one, but it was nice to have any sort of success among the many defeats that had been inflicted by the Ichtons.

Frank didn't particularly want to discuss these matters with Owen Staging when he met him, this time at the Wahoo, a common sort of tavern on Green 2 that was a favorite with Frank.

"Here's what your engines sold for," he said to Owen, taking out of his backpack the hefty chamois bag that contained the gems.

"You did well, partner," Owen said, bouncing them up and down in his hand. "Although you did leave your departure until very late."

Frank shrugged. "I want an advance on my share in folding money."

"Of course, partner, of course! I've got it right here for you." He took a cashier's check out of his pocket. "It's unusual to use paper anymore for transactions, but I thought you'd like it. I know you're an old-fashioned man at heart. There'll be more after the sales."

Frank glanced at the check, folded it, put it in his pocket. "This will do for a beginning. But I'm afraid it's going to cost you more than that, Owen."

"What are you talking about? Half was our agreement, and it was very generous on my part if I do say so myself."

"It's going to cost you three-quarters."

"I'll see you in hell first!" Owen snapped. The trader got to his feet. The expression on his face was not pleasant. His fingers slipped around a hardened glass tumbler as he turned to face Frank.

"You won't need that, either," Frank said. "You're not crazy enough to attack an officer of the Fleet."

"Your commission expired yesterday," the trader snarled.

"Correct. And on the day before that, I reenlisted."

"But our agreement! You were going to resign from the service and be my partner!"

"Sometimes people lie," Frank said. "You told me that yourself, Owen. And you told me it was all right, that was the way human beings were."

"What are you trying to prove, Frank? What do you want with so much money?"

"Guns and ships cost plenty. While the Fleet brass tries to decide how much to help the Saurians, I'm going to send them what they need."

"You're using my money to buy those people weapons?"

"Yes, yours and mine, too."

"Frank, I don't think I understand you."

"I understand you, though," Frank said. "There are a lot around like you, Owen."

"A lot of what?"

"Civilians. You people just don't know what the score is, really."

"Maybe not," Owen said. "I don't understand you at all. But maybe we can do another deal one of these days." He held out his hand. "No hard feelings?"

Frank shook his hand. "None at all, Owen."

He watched the man walk away. He'd never understand men like the trader. But he didn't have long to ponder about him. He had to start the flow of weapons flowing. Weapons to the Saurians.

ORIGIN OF THE SPECIES

THE PRELIMINARY ANALYSIS of the data obtained by deep exploration of the Ichtons' arm of the galaxy was hardly reassuring to those commanding the *Hawking*. It appeared likely that the Ichtons had been methodically pillaging their way down their arm of the galaxy for tens of thousands of years, not just one or two millennia. Some civilian specialists even brought up the possibility that the Ichtons weren't moving toward resources, but like the barbarians that caused Rome to fall were actually running away from something even nastier. *Hawking*'s officers decided to refit one of the Fleet's few brainships for an extended probe up that arm in the hope of finding the edge of the Ichton infestation. This would give them some idea of the scope of the resources controlled by their adversaries. It would also serve a number of additional purposes that even those making the mission were not aware of.

KILLER
CURE
by Diane Duane

SHE DISLIKED HIM from the first moment she saw him . . .which was not a good state of affairs, since he was her new brawn.

Maura was MX-24993 now. She had just begun growing used to it. It wasn't that she hadn't liked her last brawn. She was an intelligent enough woman, and kind; but she brooded, and Maura had never been the brooding type. All her young life working with Fleet she had leaped into missions without a shade of concern for herself. She knew life was short, but hesitation and caution were not going to prolong it. Cecile, her brawn, had been an expert on the Ichtons, as much as anyone was; and she brooded. Maura had never understood why she wasted her time. Now Cecile was gone, and Maura had been called into *Hawking* to have the new engines installed. Also the new brawn.

He was very young, by her standards, at least; surely no more than twenty-six or twenty-seven years old. His records were still being uplinked to her computers, and she would have exact data later. But at the moment, she looked, and saw the young, handsome (almost too handsome), slender form, in Fleet fatigues, come striding into her control room as if he already owned it. Well, perhaps he was part owner, but it was not an auspicious beginning.

His name was Ran Nordstrom, and he was out, apparently, from Helsinki—the city, not the planet. He was very fair, very blond, even to the eyebrows and eyelashes. The eyes were a surprise: they were very green where you expected blue, and they were frighteningly enthusiastic. That worried her. Maura had seen enthusiasm. It tended to create dead brawns. But also, at the ripe old age of two hundred, she had long since put excitement and enthusiasm behind her.

"It's just a training run," he was saying. Maura looked at him out of her introspection. "Oh, really," she said. "What makes you think that?"

"Well, I mean, look at the brief." He cocked his head. "Twelve pages of dithering that boils down to 'Go find somewhere where the Ichtons haven't been.' That'll take us about a day, especially with the new engines. . . ." He grinned at her. Or in her general direction, the way a blind person looks more or less toward the source of a sound.

Maura put aside her annoyance. They could teach you to look at a brain's column while at school, but some brawns never quite got it, preferring to treat the brain as a whole ship, rather than someone located.

"The question is," Ran said, "where will they send us after that?"

Maura chuckled at that. "Son, in this business, and these days especially, you learn not to look too far ahead. Just when did you graduate?"

"Four months ago, on the *Hawking*."

Maura sighed, but kept the sound to herself. A virgin brawn. What had she done to deserve this? But she was going to have to make the best of it. And if as he said, this mission was going to take less than no time, all the better. For longer-term problems . . . well, there was always divorce if things didn't work out. Or the Ichtons, who sometimes provided much more permanent separations.

She would not let them anesthetize her when they put the engines in. Maura had heard all the stories about the trauma of seeing yourself operated on, but she was not convinced. She took a nerve block, yes; she shut down the neural and bioneural transmissions to the parts of her that were involved, and then watched them open up the panels and slide the black boxes in.

They weren't really black boxes. They were shiny silver—shells, like hers, modules; everything installed in the drive compartments and sealed away, under ultra-clean conditions.

"There's someone here to see you, Maura," one of the engineers said during the installation.

She was reading just then, and didn't actually hear him. "Who is he? What does he want?" And how did she know it was a he?

"Says it's your brawn. Says he wants to see the engines go in."

Maura could think of several reactions to this, but suppressed most of them. "Tell him his security clearance isn't high enough," she said.

The technicians guffawed. "A bit sensitive about showing him our private parts, are we?"

Maura didn't reply. Maybe she was. Or maybe—She didn't know what she thought, really. This was one of the newest technologies of Fleet, these jumper engines. Only the fastest scouts had them, and she was going to be one of the fastest, now. She was being seriously overengined for her size. They plainly meant for her to go a long, long way. How far? she wondered. And where? There was an awful lot to the galaxy. The thought of having Ran with her for who knew how many years—It was ironic to be the fastest thing on jets, and not be able to run away from your problems, because you were carrying them around inside you. . . .

They finished with her, and she watched them finish sealing her up—making the neoneural connections. Very gingerly she felt the new engines. They felt hard and shiny and cold yet. Very slowly the fingers of her probing slipped inside them, like a stiff glove. She worked the logic probes around, touching the engines' intricacies. The new cesium arsenide/cold helium circuitry was in now, that allowed the fast shunt of the Olympus engines to work the way they did. Where the usual neural-current paths in the average engine felt like water running, this felt much different. Most peculiar. It had weight; it slipped in globules, like mercury, but moved faster than it should—squirted, almost—like something under pressure, at the molecular or subatomic level rather than any higher one. It was all very strange. A new feeling. . . . One was in serious danger of becoming enthusiastic about it. She set herself to doing system checks, and waited for Ran.

He started moving his things in the next morning. It was a very small collection, for weight's sake, as it always was—but very eclectic. He had hard books and solids and vids, and a couple of paintings, rather well done in the Neoimpressionist style; though small, as they needed to be for approval for on-ship transit.

"I can't wait to leave," he said. She knew, and it made her head hurt.

"Listen, Ran," she said. "Have you ever seen an Ichton?"

"The reconstruction? Yeah." He shook his head. "Nasty buggers, but we'll beat them."

"Yes, well," she said. "I just want you to be clear about something. If we run into any, we're not going to hang around."

This time he looked right at her column, with an expression of such shock that Maura almost laughed out loud. But she managed to restrain herself.

"What do you mean?" he said. "I saw the weapons they were installing in you!"

"They're mostly defensive," she said. "Haven't you read the briefings? Don't you know the kind of armaments the Ichton ships carry? We've got just enough to singe their tails with, and then we run away. So don't get any cute ideas."

"Wouldn't help me much if I did," Ran said. "You've got control of all the weaponry anyway."

At least he knew that much. "Your business is to stay alive," she said. "So is mine. We have more important things to do than fight. If we run, we run. That's life."

He didn't actively look sulky, but there was still an air of vague disappointment about him. He opened his mouth, then closed it again as if thinking better of something he had been about to say. "There anything I can bring you from stores?" he said. "Not that we'll be out there that long anyway. Just something to while the time away."

Maura had to chuckle. He had no idea how short this mission was going to be if he kept on in this vein. "I'm fine," she said, "but thank you for asking."

He went out and fetched another small carton with his

spare uniforms in it, and a few other pieces of bric-a-brac. They genuinely were bric-a-brac; one of them was a small Staffordshire china dog, its paint well worn off it. "Where'd you find that?" she said, interested in spite of herself.

Ran laughed. "It was my mother's. She had it from her father . . . it's been passed down, oh, four or five generations now, I guess. The member of the family who's going farthest away always gets it. It's well traveled, this critter."

It looked it. Its paint was faded, and it had a faintly cross-eyed expression, like someone who's taken too many jumps too fast. "Amazing it hasn't been broken," Maura said.

"Most of us tend to keep it under our beds," said Ran.

"What? You don't put it out on a shelf and let it take its chances?"

Ran raised his eyebrows. "Crockery shouldn't take chances," he said. "People, though . . . that's another story." And he glanced at the column and walked away.

Maura swore softly to herself. Brawns! What was she going to have to do to this one to calm him down?

They left the next morning. Maura had been cautioned to put a lot of distance between herself and the *Hawking* before she jumped the first time. For my good, she had thought, or for theirs? It was well known what happened if a jump engine happened to malfunction . . . and the first time a brain used one, there had been accidents and miscalculations. . . . It was easy enough to understand. What happened when you suddenly had a new part of your brain installed that worked forty percent better and faster than the rest of it? There were sometimes mishmashes, problems with coordination. For a human being to move an arm or leg fifty percent faster might not make any difference, but when the motor control involved was running a matter-antimatter conversion engine, and the mix suddenly went south . . . well.

Ran was sitting in the chair in the control room, drumming his fingers on the arms of the chair, trying to control his excitement and nervousness, and doing very badly. "Have you had time to look over the navigation plan?" Maura said.

"I saw it three days ago. It's fairly straightforward. A hop-skip-and-jump setup: hop to the system, skip any planets not populated or showing signs of interference. Survey what's there, then move on to the next star."

"It's a fairly extensive list, wouldn't you say?" she said. "Forty star systems, with an option for forty more?"

"Piece of cake," he said. Somehow Maura had known he was going to say that.

"There's some in the galley," she murmured. "First jump. Five minutes, counting from—now. Do you have trouble with fast jumps?" she said.

He blinked. "I've only done it once. Didn't bother me much. It felt—" He shrugged. "Like going up in an elevator, actually. That pit-of-the-stomach feeling."

Maura had never been in an elevator, but she knew that pit-of-the-stomach feeling. The sudden, bizarre pressure all over the hull, where there couldn't be any pressure; the sense of not discontinuity, but of wrongness. That was the strangest thing about it. It was more a pang of conscience than anything else; there was a sense that it was morally wrong to be jumping. As if the laws of the universe were for the first time speaking and telling you directly that they were being violated, and they didn't like it. Maybe that was just a side effect of being in a shell— the tendency to perceive physics directly, instead of through the film of less-sensitive senses. "Well," she said, "then you won't mind this one. It's only forty light-years or so."

He gulped. Maura found it briefly satisfying . . . and then was ashamed of herself. There was no point in deriving enjoyment from the discomfort of her brawn, even if he was a total prat.

The engines built power. There was no sound of it. They were quite silent; no moving parts, not even any moving plasmas, remained in the engines. The antimatter mix was coming up to the correct richness. That was the secret of making these engines move smoothly, Maura had been told; not just dumping the masses together, but keeping the mix slow and low at first, then enriching it as you went along. George, of GB-33871, had told her that it was very similar to making a cream sauce. Add the active ingredient slowly, taste as you go along, heat gradually, not too fast so that it doesn't curdle. Slow and easy. . . . It'll be worth waiting for when it's done. George was a little strange, being about four hundred years old now; he would make jokes about being near the end of his service life. But he had survived a lot, and strange or not, his advice was worth listening to. . . . even if he couldn't eat his own cooking.

Maura didn't say anything further, but sat there and watched Ran sweat, and counted the minutes down. *If only he knew that I hate this as much as he does.* . . .

They jumped, and found the first star, a little K0 with no name but a string of numbers and letters out of the catalog. There were three planets: two gas giants, and a third of Earth type.

Maura said nothing for a while, letting Ran get himself up and stalk around the cabin with the air of a man just released from prison. Trainees were only taken on the shorter jumps. Maura wondered if this one had finally gotten further into him than the pit of his stomach, after all. He looked haunted. "What news?" she said. She could easily have found out by using her own sensors, but you had to let a brawn do something.

He was leaning over the computer, looking at the readouts. "Infested," he said.

"How much?" They had been using percentages to talk about how much of the planet was domed-under. The Ichtons did not waste much. The strip-mining of old Earth was positively environmentally kind compared to the way the Ichtons used the planets that became theirs. Anything that could be termed a natural resource, however rare or common, was used. Everything was taken; mined, drilled, dug up, scalped off, and the proceeds shipped off to those domes to make . . . heaven knew what. The materials for more domes, Maura thought. This planet would have showed, to the human naked eye, a handsome blue-green ball; nothing strange about it. Unless you looked down to its southern hemisphere, and saw the blot that was not the color of earth or sea; the blot that under higher magnification could be shown to glitter balefully, like a many-faceted eye. A thousand domes, ten thousand, a million, packed together and expanding. The eye glittered at them.

Maura breathed out. "What percent?" she said again.

Ran was still looking at the readout screen. "About ten," he said. "There's a lot more undermining going on than shows at the moment. They're under all the seas contiguous to that continent, and spreading. Maybe they're trying not to attract too much attention here."

"Too late for that, then," Maura said. "Anything noticeable in or near the other planets? Orbital facilities?"

"Nothing."

"All right. Then we move on."

Ran went back to the couch and strapped himself down again, with an unhappy look. "That last jump—" Maura said.

"It was all right," said Ran, and finished his strapping. "Let's go."

"As you say," Maura said, and took the next jump without even bothering to count it down—fifty light-years, this time.

And she did it again, and four more times after that, and barely let him have long enough to stretch his legs in between. Each time they found the same infestation; sometimes lesser, sometimes greater. Ran was beginning to frown, and to look frazzled. After the twelfth, she said, "Are you sure you want to keep going?"

"Oh, yeah," he said. "Let's get this done."

For her own part, she was finding it very hard to be cool. She could see, as if it were with her own eyes, what he couldn't; the detail on those domes. There was always a sort of no-man's-land around the domed zones, protected by force-field from intrusion; a wide barrier, just dirt or rock. Very often, on the far side, there would be large or small groups of the indigenous species—just looking. Sometimes they were trying to attack—futilely, of course; sometimes doing nothing, just gazing in horror at the sudden inoperable cancer growing on their world. She wondered whether the numbers, the figures and statistics, called up anything in Ran's mind—any image of something real. She was familiar enough with his train of thought, anyway. Even if relatively young as brainships went, Maura knew what to expect. "Honeymoon syndrome," as it was somewhat derisively called in the corps, the actual opposite of a honeymoon—when two people who didn't know each other were thrown together to do highly dangerous and professional work, in a relationship that one way or another wound up being more intimate than many marriages.

She kept offering him chances to stop, but he wouldn't. Rolling up to the twentieth planet, she said to him, "Look. That's enough for one week."

"I want to keep at it," he said.

"I'm sure you do. But I for one want some rest, and I am not going any farther. You can get out and walk if you like."

"I just want to get this job done," he said.

Maura looked at him. Sensors picked up the elevated heartbeat. The sound of his EEG rattled against another sensor like pebbles shaken in a can. Agitated. Mustn't let him get into this state again. "Look," she said, "I'm sure you want to keep going. But we have more work to do."

He turned away from her, the color rising in his face. "It can't all be done in a week," she said, trying to be gentle.

"It can!" he said, wheeling on her. "It's only the tools that are ineffective. Not the mission. Not the goal." And he strode off toward his cabin.

She looked after him from another camera. I could lock his door, until we settle this. I could lock him out, as well as in. . . . But she let him go in and shut the door unhindered, and lie on his bed.

Maura didn't bother waiting for him to come out. She had her own business to take care of on this mission. She idly pulled a copy of his records, and ran her optical scanners over it.

The picture was much the same as the man she saw now. A picture of the parents: one dark-haired, one fair. The fair hair came down through his mother's side. One brother, also in the Fleet; lost, some time ago, at Balaclava. Several postmortem commendations—he apparently had been leader of a fighter squadron that had managed to take out several Ichton ships, before being destroyed. That was the pity of it; no speed or cunning mattered, when you were dealing with odds of fifty or a hundred to one. The Fleet might be more maneuverable than the Ichton ships, but there were always more of them, no matter how many of you went down fighting valiantly.

The lost brother . . . who knew what effect that would have on Ran? She thought of Loni. It had been a while since she had thought of her. They weren't sisters, really, but they had come into the brain facility at the same time; they had worked together and trained together, and played the games shell kids play together—chasing each other around the center at high speed and putting the lives of many at slight risk. They had had a good time together. Then they had both been commissioned as brainships. Loni had gone on in Fleet service after her payoff, and was last seen near the Rift. Her last communications were untroubled. But there had been reports of Ichton fleets out that way. No news ever came back, no wreckage. Nothing but silence where Loni had been.

Maura considered this bit of her history in conjunction with Ran's, and snorted to herself. Was some amateur shrink out there trying to do a good deed? The Med Psych people out at *Hawking* had been known to pull such stunts every now and then. Well, Maura was having none of it. There was nothing wrong with her.

Nothing that seeing Loni again wouldn't cure. . . .

There was of course no chance of that. Maura laughed hollowly at herself, not caring whether Ran heard her or not, and went back to her hobby.

She had been dabbling in code holography for a long time. It was very enjoyable to encode holograms of places that didn't really exist, or ones that did. That was a challenge, too—to engrave pictures of places she had seen pictures of, and compare them to the originals. Image processing without the image, that was all it was. A very basic sort of pastime for a brainship, but it pleased her.

She was doing an unabashed pastoral that had so far cost her several weeks labor; a not-very-subtle takeoff on some paintings she had seen dating back to Earth's seventeenth century. Rolling hillsides, green fields, hedgerows, various stock animals wandering about; nattily dressed young men and young women in long dresses and carrying frilly parasols, standing under trees and admiring the view. But the view was clearly not on Earth—it was the upcurving interior surface of a Dyson sphere, with the "afternoon" sun hanging up in the midst of it all.

She was working on the clouds in that sky, some hours later, when Ran woke up with a start. For amusement's sake, she put a copy of what she was working on up on the screen in the control room, so that he could see it. He didn't come into the control room for a long time. He made his breakfast first, and took a long while over it, before finally wandering in. There he stood, and looked at the picture. "Nice," he said.

Maura chuckled at him. "Thank you. How did you sleep?"

"Badly," he said. "Can we get started?"

"In a little while. I'm still running some system checks." This was not strictly true. There was one check she had left running all night—engine status—but she let it stop now.

"And how are the engines doing?"

He might be an annoyance, but he was an observant one. "Greenline optimum."

"But you weren't expecting them to be doing that."

"Young man," she said, "you will have the courtesy to ask me what I think, not tell me." When he merely raised his eyebrows at her, Maura said, "No, I didn't expect that. I expected—some slight hiccup, some change in the wave form. It's not as if these are standard components . . . or, rather, not as if you're hooking these components into a standardized system. There is one very idiosyncratic component." He nodded. "These engines tend to react one way with one brainship, another way with another."

"And you were expecting them to malfunction?"

"No, but to produce some idiosyncratic—" She sighed. "I don't know what. Are you about ready?"

"I have been for a while," he said.

They started out again. This time it was a longer series even than the last. They were almost halfway through the list by the time they were done, and nothing was working out the way Maura had planned. He was supposed to be weary and frazzled at this point; she was supposed to be cool and collected, and in control. But he got cooler as the days went by, and the planets—the ravaged shells. The percentages got higher and higher. She was getting frazzled. The sight of the species of many worlds, standing, staring across the no-man's-land; the sight of ocean creatures scrambling out of water and dying in the air, unable to deal with the alien presence that was changing their seas, polluting the water or drinking it dry. Fourteen planets, all complexed—all infected, from ten to thirty percent, sometimes more. Icecaps being mined off for their water, atmospheres being pumped away, pressurized, shipped out in cans; planetary crusts being mined straight down through the discontinuity layers for the liquid metal inside them.

They paused long over one planet. So much of its core had been mined out that there was now no sign of the robust magnetic fields that should have been there. Its rotation had slowed. Half of it was baking, half freezing, and a slow nutation was dragging the frozen side around for its turn, ice giving way to fire.

"We're all going to die," Maura heard herself say.

Ran's head snapped around. "What?"

"They're all going to die."

He looked at the viewscreen. This world was a watery one, better to look at than most; the damage wasn't visible. But the sensors clearly showed, under those oceans, the terrible changes in the temperature of the ocean floor, where Ichton drilling through the crust was exposing magma to the sea bottom, and the seas were slowly coming to a boil. Only the changing color at two or three points of the world, from a dark blue to a lighter one, betrayed that anything was happening at all. It was a very gradual change—you almost might not notice it, unless you were far enough out in space and could see the spots. Ominous, like the spots on Jupiter.

"Die?" Ran said. "Yes. Eventually, so we will."

Maura gulped and tried to turn her attention elsewhere, for the little time while Ran was completing his readings. There was really nowhere else to look. The dead black of space, or this dying blue. She peered around the ship here and there, glanced into his cabin . . . saw that the crockery dog was sitting on a shelf, on a pile of books. "Came out from under the bed, did he?" she said, trying desperately for levity.

"What?"

"The dog."

"I suppose we all have to come out sometime," Ran said.

They went on, through the weary day, and through another. On the morning of the fourth day in this series Maura could barely stand the sight of Ran; but he got up more energetic than ever, somberly eager to get about their work. They were almost through their list of star systems, anyway—there was that small consolation. No more than ten left to get through. . . . But Maura found herself dreading the next jump, even as Ran strapped himself in and waited for her to report herself ready.

I could plead engine trouble, she thought. *Except that I have this feeling he'd know there wasn't any. And I wouldn't give him the satisfaction of knowing I was having trouble carrying out this mission.* . . . Besides, wasn't she a good member of the Fleet, always doing her duty without stint or shirk? What kind of chance would humanity and its allied species have against the Ichtons if everyone just quit working whenever they wanted to?

"All set," she said.

They jumped. The jumps had been bothering Maura more and more over the past couple of days, while Ran sat there as unmoved as if he were watching an entertainment. It was not so much the physical sensation of the jump anymore, but the sure knowledge of what they would find on the other end of it. Maura prayed for uninhabited planets, for mistakes in the list— there had been a couple of these, and they had come out to find no planets around a star at all—but these were unmercifully few . . .

"Here we are," Ran said. She looked around, got a glimpse of the star, a ravening-hot blue B2, and scanned for its planets. Found three of them, gas giants, and the fourth, a barren rock swinging in close orbit: and the fifth—

Baleful, a single huge, gibbous eye, faceted, it glittered at her. There was no land to it, no sea, no icecap, no air. Nothing but the hard outline of glass and plex against naked space: a million million domes, overlaid on the corpse of a world, dry, empty, dead. . . .

She began to weep.

Ran was staring at her.

Maura didn't care. She moaned, and sobbed, and cried, and the inside of her hull rang with it. System alarms went off as her blood chemistry and EEG went askew; she ignored them. Ran sat and watched her column, and Maura spared only a second to wonder why he looked so horrified, yet still so calm—then lost herself in her grief again. Death, nothing but death, that's all we'll find from here to the Core. We've watched this problem get worse and worse as we've come farther and farther up this arm of the galaxy. The Ichtons have left nothing but corpses from here to the heart of things. If we had hopes of settling anyone out this way, they're dead now. And what will happen when they finally come upon the Alliance worlds, and Earth?

That was when more alarms started going off, and there was abruptly something to look at besides the poor husk of a planet that hung below them. Maura wished there weren't. She had to fight with her grief now, try to force it down. She thought she had had enough practice at that, but it was harder work than she thought. "What is it?" Ran was saying, up out of his seat now and looking really upset for the first time. "Maura, listen to me! What's happening?"

"Trouble," she said, and gulped, still looking for control. "Far perimeter."

"What is it?" Ran headed back for the control seat.

"Ichton fleet. What else, out here where there's nothing but us?" She paused, gulped again, straining her "eyes" out into the darkness. The traces were faint as yet.

"How many?" Ran said.

"Hard to tell. They're out at the far fringe. Could be a hundred—could be two." She reached a finger of probe back into the engines, feeling for their readiness. They were ready enough—She poked them again. There was a slight sluggishness about them—"Not now," she muttered. "Oh, not now, when you didn't show anything all the rest of the time!"

Ran watched her, then looked over at the small screen by the command chair. "Do they usually move that fast?" he said.

She glanced back at the Ichton fleet. "No, they don't!" she said. They were coming up much faster than usual, faster than she had ever seen in many engagements. "This is no time to act this way," she said to her engines, poking them again, more sharply, trying to jar that abnormal wave form out of existence. "Wake up!"

They came on-line, but not at the level of response she would have liked. "Shall I take gunnery?" Ran said.

Maura burst out laughing. "Against them? Here," she said, patching the controls for gunnery through to his console. "Do what you like. I'm leaving!"

And she ran. There was nothing decorous about it; she just ran. The problem was, the Ichton ships were running right up behind her. Second by second they slipped away from the fringes of her sensor perimeter, into prime-detail sensing range. There were a hundred fifty-four of them. They had been massed, originally, in their usual free-flight "pack" formation. They were spreading now, the first of three steps toward an englobement. Then after they englobed, they turned their weapons onto any unfortunate ship in the middle, and blew it away. Was this how Loni went? Maura thought. Likely enough. Caught all by herself, out in the rear end of nowhere—

Maura had no desire to stay around for such a party. But it began increasingly to look as if she was not going to be offered a choice. She went on standard evasive for a few minutes, changing course four, five times. Distantly, from Ran's cabin, came a muffled crash; she looked for a fraction of a second and saw the crockery dog lying on the floor in pieces. Too bad. . . . She had other worries. She was trying hard to give the Ichtons the impression of a ship running panicked and with no plan in force. The second wasn't difficult, since, distraught as she was, she had no plan. This situation had been in many a mission simulation, but the results had always been so hopeless that Maura had long since decided the best solution to an englobement was to be several parsecs to one side of it, and accelerating outward. She was in no position to do that; the Ichton left flank of the englobement group was reaching out toward her. Now she ran, just ran, channeling power to the engines, pushing them as hard as she could. And triggered the jump—

—and nothing happened—

She was so shocked, she couldn't even swear. Maura looked at Ran, but there was no help there: he was busy at the gunnery console, programming her few bombs for what looked like an optimum spread, a pitifully ineffective stroke against the force that was chasing them. The beam weapons wouldn't be much help, either. She flipped desperately into diagnostic mode, and her world filled up with numbers and figures. That suspicious wave form was missing now, missing completely—but at the same time, she couldn't jump. *Don't tell me the thing was necessary to the engines' functions, there was nothing about that in the docs—!* Maura began stepping down power to the jump engines, taking pressure off the systems she had been poking before, while at the same time pushing herself along at conventional boost, as fast as she could. *Even without the new equipment I should be faster than any Ichton—*

No one seemed to have told them that, however. They were gaining, and the righthand side of the englobement was catching up to her now. *Another lobe coming in at twelve o'clock—* Dimly she could sense Ran firing several of the beam weapons in chord: there was a strike on one of the Ichton ships "above" and behind them. Then another, and two ships of the hundred fifty-four puffed into vapor and vanished.

As if it's going to be much help—the globe was tightening around them. The beams lanced out again, and another ship vanished: one of the "coordinator" ships, Maura suspected, for the lobe of Ichton ships "above" them began to fall back slightly from the others, and lost some of its coherence. "There!" Ran shouted.

It was the only chance she would get. Maura turned all her attention inward, ignored Ran and space and the Ichtons and their billions of dead; looked for that wave form, and when she couldn't find it, picked another and coaxed it, willed it, pulled it into the right shape. Down in the engines, something felt as if it turned over and started to wake up—

"Now! Maura, for God's sake, now!"

She ignored him. *Not ready yet—not ready—almost out of reset—*

"*MAURA!*"

Her engines opened their eyes and looked back at her.

Reset—

As the righthand and lefthand arms of the restored englobement locked around her, Maura jumped, hard and high. The wrong feeling twisted her gut, harder than she had ever felt it.

They came out in clean space, empty of stars, or planets, or Ichtons.

For a few minutes Maura just drifted, and made no sound. Ran was looking at her in concern; she let him. Her navigational systems spent the time finding several Cepheid variables they recognized, and determining position from them. They were a long way from the Core.

"Maura?" Ran said at last.

She was almost too tired to answer him. And too frightened, and too sad, and too upset.

"What, Ran?" she said finally. It came out sounding more like a moan than anything else. And then, to her utter surprise, a joke occurred to her. "You're going to tell me we should get back to work on the rest of the list, huh?"

"No," Ran said. "We can go home now." He got up from the control chair, went over to the main console, and tapped at the console keyboard, just a few characters. "The mission's over."

The knowledge came on in the back of Maura's head, like a light. She gazed at it in horror and growing anger.

"You are from Psych," she whispered.

Ran nodded. "Personal Intervention," he said.

"A fardling shrink! So the whole new-kid act was just that. The tantrums, the nerves . . . and the engine malfunctions were your fault, then. . . ."

"Judiciously applied stress," Ran said, "is one of the best ways to produce a result. Striking at the heart of someone's strength. In your case, the engines . . . and your perceived ability to get out of any problem that came after you, or just generally 'rise above it.' Impair that, and all kinds of interesting issues come up to be handled. Like your detachment from your work, which has been increasing noticeably over the past few years."

"You could have gotten us both killed!" she yelled.

"Of course," Ran said. "I was willing to take that chance, for both of us. Me, I'm expendable. But a dysfunctional brainship is worse than a dead one, in Fleet's opinion."

He got up from the console and walked back to his cabin. She stared at him as he went, shocked speechless for a moment. But only a moment. "Well, isn't that just fine!" she shouted after him, making her voice follow him down the hall by the speakers set there. "And what goddamned sonofabitch sent you here to do me over? What gives you the right—"

"No one sent me," Ran said. "You can't be 'sent' on a kill-or-cure. You volunteer."

She stared at him. Ran stood in his room and gave her camera pickup a crooked sort of smile. "You wouldn't make it easy for me, either," he said. "I could have done all this in virtual experience, if you'd let them knock you out to put the engines in. But no, you had to play it stoic. Typical of you, actually."

She fumed, but helplessly. That was the worst part of it. He was right. "Too much detachment," Ran said, "is a bad thing for brain or brawn. You get callous, you get uncaring, your reaction speed goes down, you get one or both of you killed. Why do you think Cecile left you? She saw what was coming, and didn't feel like getting killed. Fleet Psych noticed the problem. Decided to do something about it. The only question was what."

"So they sent you to freud me over," Maura said.

"Don't talk dirty. Who has time to freud people anymore? We need cures, not progress. For too much detachment, the cure is reattachment to the realities of the world, by the most violent means possible. The Ichtons seemed like a fair bet. Not combat with the enemy, by preference—that's only made you more detached, in the past. But rather, contact with their victims. Intensive contact, the worst that could be found. And when *Hawking* Defense let it be known that they had this mission waiting, well, you were the obvious choice."

"Two birds with one stone," Maura said sourly.

"Two birds," Ran said, "yes." He bent down to pick up one of the shards of the china dog, and turned it over in his hands. "As I said, we would have preferred to do this in virtual reality, controlling the circumstances more carefully."

" 'Virtual,' " Maura scoffed. "Not much danger in that."

"Cures work there," Ran said. "But so does death. If you had died, so would I have. Just as if it were real."

He kept smiling that annoying smile at her. She wished she could say something that would wipe it off his face, that would let him know how upset she was, how she hurt. But then again. . . . how long had it been since she hurt, since anything hurt? There had to be something wrong with that. . . . "I suppose I should thank you," she said, "for risking your life for me."

"Don't bother practicing manners on me, Maura," Ran said. "You're much too angry to care about being polite at the moment. I would say rather that you're more concerned about seeming sane to other people, when you're none too sure yourself that you are. As for me, I was doing my job. So were you, both while we were out there, and all the times before I met you . . . while what you experienced was crippling you slowly. The Fleet takes care of its own, dead and alive. Even if sometimes the caretaking does annoy the shit out of them. So jump for *Hawking,* now, and get this information back where it will do someone some good. And then, after you've dropped me off, you go back out again and do what you have to do— taking care of yourself, now, as well as of your brawns. That'll be thanks enough for me. And now, with your permission, I'll start clearing my things out."

He had never asked her for permission for anything before. It was a little strange. Maura watched him start putting things away. I'll be glad to see the back of him, she thought.

All the same . . . I wonder what the next brawn will be like?

NO WIN

THE MEETING WAS short and the conclusion clear. They had fought over twenty Fleet actions, won almost every one of them, and saved over a dozen worlds, temporarily. They were also losing the war. There was no way that the *Hawking* and any number of Star Central allies would be able to stop the Ichtons using just military intervention. There certainly had been limited successes, thousands of Ichton ships destroyed at the cost of only a few dozen Fleet vessels lost. That wasn't enough. There were tens of thousands more and the Ichtons had infested so many worlds it was likely they were building warships faster than the Fleet and all their allies were destroying them.

Another solution had to be found. To do this a lot more had to be learned about the Ichtons. And they had to find these things out quickly, while there were still worlds in Star Central left unmolested, no matter what the cost or sacrifice necessary.

A TRANSMIGRATION OF SOUL

by Janet Morris

ONE MINUTE, SERGEANT Dresser missed his human body. The next, he didn't. Loss. Relief. Pain. Pleasure. Awkwardness. Dexterity. Confusion. Command.

Command. He must take command of his body. Of his mission. Of his emotions. Of his life.

But he couldn't. He was lost, twice lost, and deep in an alien jungle that fouled his feet and arms and dragged nearly invisible tendrils across his face, trying to scratch him and catch him.

Dresser was lost and alone. So alone. Barefoot and nearly naked. Exposed.

His breathing was too loud. His heartbeat was out of sync. His stride was uneven.

Where was everybody?

He thrashed before him with his arms, trying to beat back the jungle. He mustn't get caught here. Caught in a web of sticky stuff that would hold him forever. . . . Caught, and prey to the hairy carnivores of this stinking, rotting world.

If he could have managed it without falling, he would have run. But he couldn't run without falling, not in this weak light of an alien sun; not in this jungle so hungry to eat him. If he fell, something in the murk might jump out and wind him up in its arms or its leg or cocoon him in some viscous mass and he would be trapped.

Trapped until eaten. Trapped and struggling.

He was whistling in fear. He could hear the pathetic sound

231

of it. The keening of his heart came up through his body and
made an awful sound that was not the sound of a soldier.

Take command. Take control. The hairs on his head itched.
He rubbed them against each other. . . .

He stopped short and stood there, as still as he could manage,
wavering on his feet. Sergeant Dresser stood there, counting his
arms. Two too many. His head itched.

Remember who you are. What you are.

Take command. Take control.

Dresser was a volunteer for a mission too terrible to be
contemplated, not that there was any way out but to go on
with it.

Remember what you aren't: a human being. Not anymore.

Breathing hard and listening to his own pulse that pounded
so wrongly, he wanted to retch. But his head itched too much.
And the sound of fearful whistling wouldn't stop.

Then he remembered that the hairs that itched weren't on
his head: they were on his antennas. It was the itch of terror
and it was nearly overwhelming. And the terrible squeak of
fear, so paralyzing, a sound that might give him away, came
from rubbing those antennas together.

He had to stop it. The sound of so much fear made him
ashamed. The sound of it could give him away.

He was still a soldier, even if he was a bug soldier. He
reached up with his combat knife and began hacking at his
own antenna, sawing away at the base of his skull. The pain
took a long time to run down into his brain, and . . .

. . . He had to stop the sound, before it brought all his
enemies down on him. . . .

The pain finally stopped him. Blood rushed into his eyes
and made everything twice as dim and ominous.

His gut churned. He was bleeding. He could hardly see.
He could barely smell. He couldn't hear the keening sound
anymore, though.

That was something.

He dropped to his knees and hung there, on fours, staring at
the knife in his hand. There was flesh on the knife. His flesh.

He had to get hold of himself. He needed his antenna; he
needed every sensory clue he could get to help him maneuver

this alien body through a twice-alien landscape not its own. He needed every edge he could get.

The knife edge glittered in his gray hand. Ugly hand. Alien hand. Bug hand. But a knife was a knife, all over the galaxy— maybe all over the universe. He needed the knife and he was willing to see it through faceted eyes as long as he could take comfort from having it in his hand.

And he needed the strong gray hand holding the knife. He needed to remember that he was a soldier. And he needed to smell his way home, if he still could.

Feel his way home. Stumble. Crawl if he had to. Wriggle through the loamy dirt with all its hidden threats and sweet/salty delicious smells. Find the group. Find himself.

Take control. Take command. He was a soldier. He was still that.

He had to remember who he was. What he was. He was Dresser, but he couldn't say that. Couldn't form the words. Couldn't really hear that way anymore. Couldn't make that sound. Not that sound.

So then, what did you do, when you were a bug and you had to find your way home?

Get up, that was what you did.

He was still a soldier. Take command. Take control.

He had to get up, before something dashed from the shadowy jungle and caught him in its jaws. He had to find the others. He had to get on with his mission.

He had a mission. One hell of a mission. The most important one of his life. Maybe the most important one of anybody's life.

It had cost enough in lives, to put him here.

He remembered a bit of combat, an exploding globe of force; a blue glow that both attracted and repelled him: home; the enemy. Home sign. Enemy spoor. Both and neither.

Jesus God, what had he let himself in for?

He was in the body of the enemy, shoehorned in here like a wrecked pilot punching out of a derelict vehicle in an escape pod.

But worse. There was no place to go home to, when you were a man in a bug suit.

Or a bug with a man in your head.

He shook his, and the antenna he'd hacked at twinged warningly.

He raised his head to the sky that must be up there somewhere and screamed his name as loud as he could.

Dresser! he wanted to shout. *Now you've done it, Sergeant Asshole. See where your macho bullshit got you this time?*

But nothing came out.

He tried again, as hard as he could, to bellow at the sky. Somewhere up there, his guys were waiting for his report. He had to take control. Take command.

Or was it the other way around?

He heard his own voice, screeching: *Greel.*

He screamed it three times and then had to drop his head to shake the blood from his eyes. Green blood. Green. Greel. Greel. Greel.

What the hell did it mean when you wanted to say your name and it came out sounding like that.

Greel.

Not even close. If his head didn't hurt so much, and if the blood wasn't still streaming over his face, he'd have banged his forehead on the ground.

Stupid fool. Why'd you volunteer? Huh, Dresser? Why?

Dresser couldn't remember why. He didn't care why. He wanted to check in with his controller. Hear his name. Have somebody validate him.

Maybe he was a bug with delusions of humanity.

But he knew better.

He was Sergeant Dresser. If he played his cards right, he'd come out of this war a hero. Somebody had said to him, a world away when he awoke in this body, "Your men are all right, Sergeant. So is your human self. Your memory will return in a few minutes."

Maybe he was still waiting for those minutes to pass. Maybe he was still in the experimental station.

No way. No such luck.

His mind wanted to hear him say that he was Sergeant Dresser, but he couldn't say that. He didn't have the lips for it.

What was in a name if you couldn't say it?

He was Greel, anyhow. He knew it. His body knew it. The name felt good along his entire length. It made his thorax warm and he felt, for the first time in this nightmare shadowscape, safe. Greel. Greel. Greel.

Mama come and get me. Brothers, gather 'round. Greel is here.

Alive. Safe. With stories to tell and a dark spot inside full of wisdom. Knowledge such as none have ever had. Feast with me, feast of my knowledge, and learn all of my stories if you can.

Dresser pushed himself to his feet and didn't realize he was licking his own blood from the knife until he began to chew a severed chunk of his antenna. Chew your own flesh.

Dresser's heart shriveled.

But the antenna was in his mouth.

It tasted good. It tasted of home and hearth and salts so precious that they'd heal any hurt.

He sucked at the knife until the blade was shiny because every drop of precious blood was in his happy mouth again. He examined the knife with his eyes and with his antenna, making sure it was spotless, perfectly clean.

Then he put the knife in its sheath on his belt and trudged on, feeling stronger. He held his head up, so that the blood didn't run into his eyes.

He knew he was leaving a trail for the carnivores that had overrun this place and destroyed the balance of nature here.

But he couldn't stop to worry about it. He had to find his unit. Take control. Take command.

He was a soldier. Lost or not, alone or not, he was still that. Both of his souls knew it. Both of his hearts were sick at the way he'd broadcast fear all around him.

He was disoriented, but that was no excuse for hacking himself up like that. You didn't try to kill yourself. You didn't maim yourself. You didn't weaken yourself or make yourself a target. Especially now, when the enemy was everywhere, lurking in a jungle of alien spirit on a planet only a fool would die to save.

All around. In the jungle, full of shadowy, creeping, choking growth and hiding vermin. In the huts of the carnivores that ate all the other food here. In their skies. And beyond. Even beyond the sky, enemies were hiding—stinking things with obscene desires and infectious ways.

Coming to get him.

He bolted. He ran unseeingly through the thick growth until his heart nearly burst.

When he stopped, bent nearly double in pain, he had no idea where he was in relation to the original bearing he'd taken.

He was doubly lost. Doubly afraid. And mortally alone.

Dresser didn't know how to stop the fear in his heart, but at least this time his new body wasn't broadcasting that fear by rubbing its antennas together.

One antenna was swollen, stiff and short and caked with blood.

So he'd stopped his new body from broadcasting that telltale fear. He'd win this war yet. Take control. Of his flesh, at least. Take command of his exoskeletal, six-limbed, horror-story self.

Do his mission. Get home. Get out of this despicable body and eat out on the war stories for years to come.

Sure he would. Tell Codrus how he'd been so freaked when they'd dropped him in the jungle that he'd hacked off one of his cloned antennas before he realized what he was doing.

And ate it. Funny how that made you feel better, when you were an Ichton on an alien world.

He was getting the hang of it. Sure he was. This place gave both of his minds the willies and was wrong to both sets of his senses, the remembered ones and the actual ones.

He'd give anything to see this world through human eyes. See the trees he knew were there. See the grass, so green, underfoot. See the local teddy-bear inhabitants for what they were, not as enemies. See the sky, blue with fleecy clouds, not gray and grainy and muzzy and dark.

So he missed being human. So what? If this had been an easy job, anybody could have done it. He had to find the nest, or whatever it was.

Find his target. Do the infiltration.

Find the group. Report to group leader. Section Leader Greel, reporting. . . .

Oh, man. This was harder than he'd thought it was going to be. He turned in place and his good antenna waved violently. The wounded one only twitched.

But he caught a directional telltale, a sound, a waft of homelike scent, of female musk and warm metal.

This was so damn bizarre, being down here this way. Harder than anybody'd thought it was going to be. Harder than anybody'd warned him it would be.

Being human was a piece of cake, next to being a three-meter tall soldier bug who'd lost his unit.

He reached up to brush the sweat out of his eyes and saw the ugly bug hand just as it swiped bug blood from his bug eyes.

This was one creepy-crawly mission, that was for sure.

But somehow he felt better, having sensed a new direction. Finally, his limbs seemed to know how to behave. His head still hurt, so he carried it to one side, favoring the hacked-up antenna. Well, he had a war wound. Close contact with the enemy, he'd tell them when they asked. Lost his helmet that way, too. And his battle suit, along with most of his weapons, in life-and-death combat with one of the sluglike monster soldiers of the enemy. Escaping with his life had been a near thing.

Ha. That was the truth, in a way. Only he had to make sure they didn't realize that he'd brought the enemy back with him—that the enemy was within him, inside him, a part of him?

No, that wasn't quite right. Take command. Take control.

Whose bright idea was it to make an infiltration agent wear a cloned bug body, anyhow?

He couldn't imagine how he'd had so much trouble moving through the growth before. Now he was on the right track. His path was clearly marked.

Olfactory clues nearly sparkled before him. His four legs churned with a professional efficiency. He knew where he was going. He found a clear place without even thinking about it.

His antenna hurt. Some enemy had jumped him, after the battle. He'd been out picking up chunks of dead carnivore—as bad as the hairy things tasted, food could not be wasted.

He remembered. One of those slugs had come out of nowhere, shooting.

He touched his chest, remembering the pain, the blast overpressure his suit couldn't absorb or deflect.

One of those slugs had overpowered him. They were so slow-moving, they were hard to see when at rest. But this one hadn't been at rest. Greel had struggled, but it had nearly hacked him apart.

He remembered the terror. When it got him out of his suit it was going to eat him alive. It was peeling him as if he were a Meal, Ready to Eat.

He wanted to wipe the alien memories away. But they wouldn't go away.

And at the end of all the alien memories waited Dresser—the unpronounceable name, the alien identity—and the key to resolving all this confusion.

Dresser understood everything important. Take command, take control. Do the mission. Report back.

Almost everything important. He couldn't fathom how to find his way home, through the growth, to his cloned body's unit. . . .

Dresser felt as if he were coming up for air, breaking the surface of a dark deep pool.

For a moment intent sparkled like sunlight, mission overcame misery, and Dresser was fully in control of everything—except his limbs, his senses, and his body. Even the pain receded. It belonged to somebody else.

Then he sank back, inexorably, as if an undertow were pulling him down. But he had no choice. He was drowning in unresolvable stimuli, in knowledge that wasn't his and impulses he couldn't sort.

This body had once belonged to someone named Greel who'd known how to use it—who *still* knew how to use it. Greel knew everything necessary for Dresser to survive. How come they hadn't warned Dresser about this, when he'd been briefed?

You couldn't be yourself *and* somebody else—especially when that somebody was as alien as this bug, whose body had its memories of personality genetically imprinted in its every fiber. You couldn't try to be a human in a bug suit and succeed well enough to survive.

But Dresser had to do it. Somehow. Or he'd die here.

And he didn't know what to do next. But Greel did.

Dresser couldn't see right. Greel saw just fine.

Why the hell hadn't somebody warned him that this was a suicide mission?

Darkness full of memories that Dresser couldn't sort lapped at him, threatening to close over his head like oily water. Dresser panicked.

Panic shut down every reasoned impulse, even doubt. It nearly shut down thought.

Take command. Take control.

Take . . . a step.

Move! Blindly, he rushed forward at hellish speed. He crashed onward, away from confusion, toward certainty.

Away from the alien presence in his head. Away from the ghost of madness.

Toward home. Toward help. Toward his own kind.

He kept his wounded head to one side, to ease the pain that was driving him home.

Greel knew the road back. He'd helped build it. The road was broad and clear of the mold that grew over this world so thickly.

He could nearly make out the encampment's identifying signature.

It was going to be good to be home—or, at least, among soldiers, among the force, among his own in their home away from home—among the people.

How did you lose your weapons, brother?

Say again the story of escaping from the slugs.

Tell the tale of capture, of being stripped of your suit, and of your triumph and escape.

Now, all together: Sing of valor; sing escape; sing return, brothers and sisters.

Mama, our valiant Greel is back with us!

Sister ReScree, your beloved section leader is full of wisdom, back again.

Under a canopy of blue, the people sat to feast the dead and sing. Around them were ranged the fierce-armed cars of their battle and the deep-dug engines of their home and hearth. And these space-going sons and daughters of a race of voyagers sang sweet songs: all who'd found a home here, on a distant shore, sang of where they'd been, and what they'd left behind. And brave songs, too, they sang: songs of a new home here to fight for and to win. All together, they raised their voices to praise their hundred heroes newly fallen, and one more.

In the place of honor, Greel sat, saying long songs of strife and woe, his mutilated antenna waving stiffly, his voice soft as a soldier's song always is when loss and death make victory partial and life so sweet.

He was witness to the battle, sole survivor. He had braved the clutches of an awful enemy and survived.

Sweet was the feast they gave him, of dead brothers and lost songs, sitting all around the sacrificial ground where a festival for heroes was laid.

Drink was there, and meat of long acquaintance. Everyone tasted the souls of dead friends and lost comrades, of lovers who could only be redeemed through ceremony.

Immortality was close, for the dead. It hung over the festival site and it sweetened the meat of the departed. It made every mouthful of lost heroes' flesh a sacrament to be savored before swallowing.

And in all the remembering of all the dead and gone, Greel took part with his lies and his split soul crying out for redemption. But Greel could not redeem his sins before the family, before the ancestors, before eternity.

The enemy was within him, looking out through his eyes. The enemy didn't understand how beautiful were the songs of dead heroes.

The enemy was repelled at the most sacred ritual. But the enemy dared not move or speak or do any obscene thing at all.

This was Greel's place, Greel's world, Greel's seat at the heroes' table.

All spread before them, on a long cloth of gold, were the hearts and eyes and heads and hands of a hundred departed heroes. On plates and dishes of copper lay the brains and tongues of the dead.

And as the extended family of the Four Hundredth Unit of Mother Sree feted its dead and ate their wise flesh, Dresser was only an obscene dream that had overcome Greel in his terrible ordeal.

There was no enemy within him. There was only the new life ahead, and the new struggles to come. There was only this moment to revere the dead and take them into every living soul.

The bodies of their heroes, whatever had been salvaged, were ready to eat. Lying in state.

Greel had come home just in time. Woe if he had not, and missed a chance to eat the flesh of his beloved group leader, of whose eye and of whose brain he was privileged to taste.

The stories of his beloved group leader took a long time to tell. Each who ate must stand and say his part. And when those tales had all been heard, then the heroes who'd died while Greel had lived must be eaten, too, and learned by all.

Learned by heart. Learned by hearth. Never forgotten, but becoming one with every other soul.

And Greel was honored, strengthened, and filled with wisdom he hadn't had before.

Singing and dancing and night-long prayers left every soul among them better. Even Greel's uncertain tale and the lies he told went into every heart with reverence.

But though he was ashamed, Greel could do no different. He had eaten of his group leader's eye, and now all eyes were on him.

His sister ReScree, who led the unit for Mama Sree, was watching him with soft and inviting looks.

He had survived a test of soul. He was group leader now.

Before him was the greater portion of his former group leader's brain, to prove it.

Such a gift was more than he deserved, and he tried to tell the true story of unworthiness, but Dresser stopped his story, froze him with fear.

Take command. Take control.

The threat was clear. The struggle inside him made him shiver with its onslaught. And he understood the warning for what it was. Let loose this evil phantom from inside him and he would die. Should he be found out, the thing within would die as well. Then what?

All the smells and sights, all these memories and gifts from brothers and sisters—all will be lost if you say wrong things. No one will eat of you. You will be desolate and forgotten, a rotting carcass left behind to become nothing forever.

No one could imagine the horror inside Greel. The worst horror anyone could comprehend was being Missing In Action, lost to the group, lost to the people, lost to history, to time itself.

And Greel would suffer all those punishments, if Dresser were a real presence in him, not just a figment of stress and sadness.

But Dresser was a figment. Must be. Would be. Around Greel were all his comrades. In his heart was a battle song. And in his veins ran the blood of heroes stretching back a million years.

Grief in Greel came pouring out in a long song. He ate all of the group leader that was left, and as he became one with his predecessor, he faced death.

Memory so clear that life was circumscribed by it. Fighting on, against terrible weapons. Facing heartless enemies and giving back no ground. Standing firm as melting armor and screaming troops assigned an agonizing doom.

And soft sweet breath of peace.

Death ran through him, as it must, and made him stronger. He faced it and faced it down, and sang a new song of rebirth on its far side while all his family sang harmony.

Too many fools had been less than they could, group leader used to say. So Greel said it now, and delight came among the gathered throng, laced with melancholy.

Everyone who missed their dead embraced, and the honored Sister ReScree eyed him, then got up on her four feet and keened.

He did, too.

Such an invitation was not to be denied. Such an honor was granted few soldiers. He would breed tonight, in the honor of the dead—of all the dead, but especially in honor of his beloved group leader, whose soul was now inside him.

He would be honored by the womb of ReScree, and all their eggs would be heroes of the blood.

He couldn't cry enough for joy, or sing enough for vengeance upon the slugs. The day would come when all his offspring would go forth from this sad ball of bloodied home, into the black universe, hunting the terrible, soulless slugs who'd put a memory in Greel's heart worse than a glittering blade.

The memory of Dresser would be among those memories that the children carried. Greel's get would have his every memory of violation more terrible than death.

If he had eaten an enemy honestly, and then found so awful a taint remaining in him, he might have found some way to refuse ReScree, despite the honor.

But this thing in his head had not come to him through hungry victory, or by way of the jaws of strife. And refusing would dishonor his dear departed group leader, and make an end to Group Leader Greel, whom he'd just become.

He wanted life too much. He wanted ReScree too much. So only the children would know what had truly happened to him, what was real and what was not.

And if the mighty Sister chose, then ReScree would eat his head when the breeding deed was done.

If she ate him, then the guilt inside him would be hers to bear.

If he pleased her, and she let him live as the previous group leader had lived, then he would be twice honored among the people. At least until the children hatched. And then?

Only time would tell.

History was only truth, and truth would come with time. When the children hatched, they would seek out slugs with all the hatred that Greel had in his heart for the phantom in his soul. They would make a crusade against this most hideous enemy that lodged within a hero's heart and hung there like a ghost.

If ghost this were, this Dresser in his mind, haunting him, then that ghost would beget ghost upon ghost in the minds of all the children of the people, for millennia.

He knew this truth to be unshakable, when ReScree's four legs brushed his own. He knew ecstasy such as only one in a thousand soldiers ever knows.

And he knew risk beyond reason, the helpless risk of passion, when only his mighty sister's forbearance would say if he would live to fight another day.

In such an embrace, even life was less than the chance to give the gift of life.

As his body grew great and strong, and then exploded in upon his nerves, and then spent itself within her, he understood all of life's mysteries.

It was a gift beyond all other gifts, an honor beyond comprehension, that Greel had come to this moment, where an open womb invited him to true immortality.

He closed one last time on his destiny, and waited, unable to move even an antenna, barely breathing.

If she chose to destroy him, now, to take his flesh and use his sustenance to nurture her brood with him, nature had decreed that he could not resist, even if he wished to try.

But Greel didn't wish to try. He was a soldier, but now he was a father of a generation. And he knew that there was no honor as great as this, which had come to him partly because of all he'd suffered.

So maybe the ghost of Dresser, the slug, would go into the children's souls and wreak havoc, and maybe not.

ReScree got up heavily, all his juice dripping out of her, and turned to face him. Her eyes were as bright as suns. Greel could see himself, his chin propped upon the ground, reflected back from the facets of those eyes: tiny Greels, as many as her womb would spawn, spent, helpless, a thousand husks of a thousand heroes waiting to live or die.

ReScree raised herself up on her hind legs. She pawed the air above him.

And she began to sing.

While ReScree was telling him all her stories, life was fuller than a great, round abdomen of promise, and he had no shame that he begged for his life and took it when she offered the favor.

After all, he had bred her, but now there were within him

all the former group leaders who thought that they, too, could do as much. Each wanted their turn. Each promised life for memory of life, as long as Greel's strength held out.

Later, when the dawn was nearly come, the mighty Sister left him. Exhausted, shriveled, and nearly dead of ecstasy, Greel lay by himself out under the blue canopy of the encampment and stared at the sky beyond.

Had he done a dreadful thing? Was he dishonored? Was his taint a disease that would spread and make heroes into cowards?

Was he himself a coward?

Had he accepted honors under false pretenses? Had he begged for his life because life was full in him, yet, or because the alien thing in him had not the grace or the wisdom to know how to die?

Not even ReScree's passion had killed him. Was this a great moment in history, or the worst? Had he sown seeds of rebirth, or of his own people's destruction?

He'd soon find out. He was group leader, now. He'd found the strength of his predecessor and the strength of a hundred predecessors in the sacrificial meal. He'd survived through all, despite all. Despite even the ghost within him.

ReScree had looked upon his virile heroism and found him good. She had taken him to her, and granted him another season. So he was in some way worthy of the favors granted.

History is only what it is, never what it isn't. And Greel was now a father of history.

A father.

So few ever became one.

He wanted to sing, but he was spent and sad and full of doubts and fears once again. There was this creature in his head again. In his heart again. In his soul again.

Sergeant Dresser of the slugs.

And the creature wanted to destroy all his children.

This Dresser, this slug whose blood he could not remember sucking, whose flesh he could not remember eating, was all inside him like a fever.

This Dresser, this thing inside him, was more powerful even than his just-departed group leader, insistent and demanding, wanting him to get up and go out into the night, beyond the blue perimeter, where it could begin its evil work.

Unthinkably evil was that work. The thing called Dresser wanted to keep Group Leader Greel's children from being born. Even more horridly, it wanted to keep this planet from being cleaned, from being food, from being home.

It wanted everything that Greel did not want. It wanted slugs everywhere, triumphant slugs with the blood of the people on their shoes. It wanted a universe where only slugs lived.

Dresser wanted to exterminate the people altogether. Dresser was appalled and repelled by the most tender rituals of antiquity. Dresser didn't believe in immortality. Dresser only believed in death.

And the thing called Dresser that was lodged within Greel's heart and soul was strong. It wanted to use him for its perverse desires. It had been lying in wait for him, all this time.

Now it was clawing at him. Now he was weak. And it knew his every thought. It knew he was weak. It was chanting to itself, deep inside him.

Take command. Take control.

No.

Take command. Take control.

Greel had done that. He was group leader now. He had become a father.

Take command. Take control. Report, quick. Get out of here. Get up. Reconnoiter. Get into the transport. Into the power station. Into the ships. Check out the hardware. Find the weak spots. Warn the guys.

No.

Sleep.

No.

You're dead, you damned bug.

No. I am reborn.

You're dead. We grew you in a tank.

No. No. No.

Greel almost screeched in fear, then. But suddenly he couldn't move. He was imprisoned within himself.

His body was not his own.

Fear came up from his belly and tried to swallow him

whole. He nearly lost his battle with Dresser, with the evil within him.

And he called for help, silently, within his heart and within his soul.

Help.

He couldn't give up. He couldn't find the strength to resist. He couldn't bring death home with him, he who had so recently brought life to his mighty sister.

He wanted, suddenly, to die. He wanted Dresser to die with him, then and there. He held his breath. He tried to stop his heart.

He would die before he destroyed his own children. He wished that ReScree would come back and find him. He could convince her to kill him, if he could not find the strength to stop his heart.

He slowed it. He counted its beats. Heart, stop. Body, die.

Die and take the evil with you.

Die, die . . . die . . . die . . .

Once more, he called for help.

And his group leader heard him, as group leader had always done. The group leader whose brain he had so recently eaten had been through many trials, including death. He did not want to die again, so soon. And before his time, another had fought on distant shores and eaten many alien minds and hearts, and died and died again. He, too, wanted to live, to fight this enemy and destroy this threat.

So all the ancients within Greel's stomach now rallied and, making their desires known, began to fight against this devil spirit.

The survival of all their children was at stake.

Life as the people knew it hung in the balance.

A society can do no greater good than provide for its children. Food for the children was here. Life for the children was here. This planet was a womb in the making.

They could not let it go. They could not pick up and leave. They could not do anything but fight for all their children and their children's children who would be born here and go from here among the stars.

Take command. Take control.

Help.

All the spirits of his ancestors spoke in Greel's heart. They harangued his weakened soul. Greel must fight the invader.

Take command. Take control.

Help.

He had special wisdom. He had the black wisdom of the enemy within him. ReScree had spared him to lead the fight.

And fight he would. Take command. Take control. Death was an earned reward, to be achieved in glory and heroic deeds.

Death was no refuge from the truth.

If Greel had not been possessed by the ghost of his enemy, he would have remembered that.

So Greel could not die now, in shame, fear, and anguish.

He must fight through to the end of the battle against this most horrid of enemies.

And when the fighting was done, and the worlds made safe for the children of the people, when every threat was countered and all the food was eaten—then the children would all remember the nature of the slug enemy that, by luck and fate, had become a story known to Greel.

Group Leader Greel had wisdom enough inside him, now, from feasting upon his kind, to understand that the spirit of Dresser was a gift, not a curse.

And though only his own heart and his own souls knew what special truth he had discovered, that truth would make the people strong enough to destroy this enemy forever. The children were at risk.

Therefore, Greel had no choice.

Despite his labors of the night, despite his captivity, despite his honors and his feasting, he pushed himself to his feet. Time to go inside. Get new armor. Appoint a new section leader in his place. Choose new weapons.

Time to plan a sortie against this enemy. As soon as the mourning time was done, they must strike.

Before the slugs struck them.

On his four feet, Greel wavered. A strange hesitation overtook him.

He managed three steps, then four, toward the open door of the unit home. Then he collapsed, exhausted.

His antenna ached beyond measure. His heart was sore. He had given his all in ReScree's embrace.

No matter how urgent, he could not begin his offensive now.

He had to sleep. He had to wait. He had to digest. To recover, if he could.

Sleep. Sleep.

But sleep was a shiny place of peace, and between him and it was all his guilt.

He wanted to go back to the ceremonial ground, but he couldn't move. He wanted to sort out the confusion in his head, but he couldn't sing. He wanted to find ReScree and warn her that perhaps the children might not be . . . as other children.

But he couldn't even do that.

He was too tired. He was too weak. He was too guilty that he had coupled with a sister when he knew he was infected with . . .

With what?

He wasn't sure. He was too tired to be sure of anything. Not even all the wisdom of the former group leaders within him could help him, now. His trials were beyond even their experience, and their souls were already merging with his.

Greel was too tired to do any more.

He was safe, back with his people. He needed to sleep, pass away the memories and let wisdom absorb itself into him. Sleep. This was the way of it after feasting the dead, and breeding the living. He couldn't put off his body's needs much longer.

He should have realized that he was too tired to do anything more.

When he was rested, this phantom would be nothing but a false memory.

There would be no doubt, when he was rested, that he was a group leader and greater than any group leader before him.

Had he not triumphed over the slug enemy? Escaped the hideous doom of a death without ceremony, without rebirth in the bodies of his peers?

Was he not, now, Group Leader Greel, consort of ReScree,

and forgiven for risking himself to a nameless enemy grave?

He lay there, helpless and torn within himself, on the ground, until ReScree sent orderlies to help him inside.

He pretended to the sleep of heroes. It was due him. He'd forgotten, somehow, that eating the family brought a great lassitude.

The ceremony always made the great ones weak. That was why children were born from the frenzy, why breeding was ritualized at the time of death.

Otherwise, how would there be more people?

Otherwise, how would the best survive?

And if there was truly an evil within him, then that evil would be absorbed by the wisdom of time itself, as evil was always absorbed.

He didn't need to be afraid for his children.

Only for himself.

Dresser was so goddam happy to be out of the bug encampment that if he'd had lips, he'd have been whistling. The whole mission was a real screwup. A gut-twister. Enough to make you forget you'd volunteered.

He was angry at everything. He flailed at the thick jungle with his armor-plated arms and blasted helpless trees with his bug weapons as he drove his one-bug recon vehicle through the jungle at breakneck speed.

Whenever he depressed the firing stud on his bug-style armored jeep's control panel, little globes of force spat out of the muzzles of the two forward guns. The globes coming out of the barrels looked like bubble stuff fired from a giant air gun—until they began to do their lethal tricks.

He was carving a few new paths to nowhere, but the bugs wouldn't ask any questions he couldn't answer. And he had to get a handle on the capabilities of these bug weapons, if not an understanding of the science behind them. He couldn't make a damn thing out of bug science.

It wasn't easy to get at technical intel here. There were bug science types who were born with hardware affinities, and all sorts of inherited information from bug techs who'd come before them. But Greel wasn't one of them.

His body was a shooter's body. It thought like a soldier, not like a scientist or like an engineer. When something didn't work, it got a replacement unit from supply. At best, it could cannibalize pieces of fried equipment. . . .

Wrong word.

The bug orgy, complete with other bug friends as the main course of the dinner, still made him queasy when he thought about it.

Anyway, when he thought about stuff like that, this bug body got all excited and the bug personality started to give him trouble.

Greel, stay asleep. You need the rest. You fucked your little bug heart out, and now you've got to do a bit of on-site perimeter recon. After all, you're the specialist in slug—in human behavior.

You bet he was.

Greel's close encounter with the slugs—with the humans—had helped him get one mother of a promotion.

Dresser geared the jeep up into its fastest mode, and then had to back off before he crashed himself into a tree. These jeeps were wheelless, and they had two sets of clutches: four pedals in all.

He tried not to think about the details. When he didn't think about that extra pair of feet, they seemed to know what to do just fine. Muscle memory, he'd been told by the techs, would help him out at times like these.

And it did. His guys had done lots of homework. He wasn't blaming them. He was doing pretty good.

He steered the jeep toward the bug "road," and onto it.

He hoped to hell he knew where he was going. He was almost sure he did.

You had to give credit to the DR&E guys who thought up this mission. Directorate of Research and Engineering had really topped out on this one. All you had to do, to handle the normally delicate stuff of infiltration bug style, was sort of curl up in the back of your head and let the bug body do its thing.

This bug body came complete with an autopilot that did bug stuff whenever bug stuff was appropriate.

But how the hell was he going to report to his human handler about the bug fucking and what it mean to humanity, if those eggs hatched knowing as much about slugs—about humans—as Greel now knew?

Shit, what a mess.

Well, never mind. You can't explain what you can't explain. Nobody up on the ships was going to want to think about what would happen if the next generation of bugs hatched. The mission was to make certain that the next generation didn't hatch.

And never mind the bit about bug dinner parties with bug officers as the main course.

Well, promotions were always hard-won, in any man's army.

You had to do the best you could.

When Dresser got back to his human body he was going to parlay this mission into a couple pay-grades worth of special expertise.

Especially since the next generation of bug babies all had him as a father. Sort of.

No matter how hard he tried, he couldn't imagine how the hell he was going to get any of what had happened to him into a cogent report.

Luckily, his new status as Top Bug for this installation made him the last word in security for the area.

So he could probably make sure personally that none of those bug babies of his ever grew up to eat any of the teddy-bear natives of this planet. It was a nice planet once, before the bug infestation.

It could be a nice planet again. Would be a nice planet again.

Thanks to his bug girlfriend's decision not to eat him alive.

Jesus, how had he gotten into this?

And, more to the point, what kind of report could he give that would get him extracted, soonest?

Maybe he could say that ReScree might change her mind and eat him. If he got eaten, whoever chowed down on him would know everything he knew.

Talk about ways to blow a mission.

But nobody would believe him when he told them they'd better get him out of here because his very death could give him away—and every secret human capability and plan as well. They'd think he was making it up, grasping at straws, manufacturing excuses.

They'd think Dresser had lost his nerve.

Death was real different for slugs—for humans.

Maybe he was taking the wrong approach.

Maybe the new equipment he had with him would help. Command would want to examine all this stuff: the jeep, the weapons, the command and control hardware.

You couldn't really make much of it without his bug sensibilities.

Maybe he'd give a technical report, along with a request that he and this gear be extracted together so he could show them how it worked, back home.

On that ship. Not home. "Home" was bug-think. The bugs couldn't go home, once they'd left a place. They made one interspatial journey, one landfall, and that was it. They had to make a home wherever they ended up. Must be a lot of bug colonization ships that never found a landfall as good as this one. When that happened, they just ate each other and fucked their brains out until they all died of lack of life support.

So was the history of the people. So was the fortune of the Hundredth Mother and her Unit, to have found such a fertile, food-bearing home.

Here they'd stay until a new generation could be launched to the stars from this home. . . .

Dresser shook his head so hard in his helmet that his wounded antenna twinged.

Shit, this bug-think had to be controlled. He had to find a way to control it. Otherwise, Greel would come awake and then there'd be trouble.

Let the bugger sleep.

Ha.

But it wasn't funny. He couldn't do this mission without the bug expertise that came with this body. Had they known, back on the *Stephen Hawking,* that the body would come with an inboard intelligence as well as with operating instructions? Known and not bothered to tell him?

Or was Dresser just the luckiest sonofabitch this side of
Scout Boat 781, his old command?

Whatever the truth, Dresser wanted to be extracted, and fast.
He could give them more relevant data than they'd ever dreamed
he'd find out.

Troop strength. Site reports. Logistics. Battle plans. Long-
term strategy. Doctrine. Order of battle.

You name it, Greel knew it.

And there was no use wasting all this critical intel dithering
around on a standard infiltration mission. . . .

Jesus, they hadn't known squat, shipboard.

The realization broke over Dresser so suddenly he almost
veered off the road and hit a tree. If they'd known what he
knew, up there, they'd never have sent him down here in the
first place.

They'd have kept this Greel body up there and interrogated
it until it died of stress or its own will.

But they didn't know anything about the people. They hadn't
known anything about Greel.

They couldn't have known. Dresser started the jeep again:
rest right rear foot on pedal. Push down on button with right
front foot. Stomp bar's left side with left front foot. Pump with
left rear foot until angle relative to ground is achieved. . . .
Piece of cake.

They couldn't have known, up on the ship, what kind of
bug body they had. They didn't know a section leader from
an orderly. They still didn't know what it meant to have your
infiltrator become an agent of influence.

Shit, if they knew, maybe they wouldn't let him come in,
after all.

Maybe they'd keep him down here, hardware or no hardware.
He could read the compass directions of the bug world, now, and
translate them into his own with hardly a second thought. He'd
better figure this out, fast. He was almost at the coordinates
where the communicator was secreted, and he didn't want to
draw attention to the site by spending too long there.

*If the real advantage in this war is understanding the enemy
power source and technology, so that we can counter the
enemy's weapons, then they'll let me come in.*

If they decide the advantage is in understanding enemy psychology and having an ear in the planning meetings, then I'm stuck here for the duration.

Dresser really wanted to be able to make a case for the former. It was human-think to expect to learn about bug tactics and throw a monkey wrench into enemy strategy by infiltrating the bugs' planning sessions.

The enemy's senior war planners were mostly dead and living in the backbrains of their descendants, anyhow.

You couldn't really skew the family's thinking. The people had no choice but to stay here, to live here and die here. They couldn't retreat. They had no way off the planet once they'd made landfall. They'd cannibalized their interstellar vehicles to make the systems they used to chew up these planets.

They'd stay here until their were enough young bugs to do the work, and then they'd start rebuilding a spacefaring capability, using up the planetary resources to fuel the expansion.

When they were done, the new generation would be starborne, thousands upon thousands of them. But the cycle was nowhere near that stage.

They were digging in, still in colonization stage. And so you had to eradicate them. . . .

Dresser started to feel sick. The dreaded psychic undertow began tugging at him. He could barely see. Barely control his limbs.

Don't be scared, Greel. Go back to sleep. Everything's fine.

He let memories wash over him of vast clouds of colony ships leaving a used-up world. He stopped the jeep as the memories overwhelmed real-time stimuli. He put his head on his arm and concentrated on maintaining control.

Take command. Take control.

When the memories subsided, he resumed driving toward his contact coordinates.

Ol' Greel had the clout to come out here, alone, with all the newest bug hardware. It was a lot easier to control the bug body when it wasn't afraid. Originally, it had been naked, afraid that some snake or anteater or teddy bear would come out of the jungle and eat it.

The bugs were real picky about how they died.

Now that he had to frame his report, he needed to be very careful not to make Greel afraid that he'd eradicate Greel's offspring—their offspring. Dresser began trying to feel paternal about the eggs.

It wasn't easy. He wasn't the guy for this part of the mission. They should have used a psychologist. Or a xenobiologist. He was just a soldier. A shooter.

But maybe that was what he and the bug had in common. This bug, no matter how high he'd come in his hierarchy, was still a soldier.

And the trouble with cohabiting a body with another soldier was that soldiers were tough, disciplined, and resourceful.

They knew that some things were worth the ultimate sacrifice.

Dresser had one advantage over the bug body and its innate intelligence: he didn't give a damn how he died. He didn't care about the disposition of this carcass, or any carcass he might end up inhabiting, including his own.

Dead was dead, to Dresser.

So when he got to the contact point, he didn't flap because he couldn't find the APOT transceiver right away. He wanted to give his report, you bet.

But if he couldn't, he was willing to wait and try again. Or kill himself and his bug body if he thought that was the only way to protect what he'd already gained on this mission.

And he'd gained plenty, he thought, rummaging around in the undergrowth for the transceiver. But maybe not enough to die for. He just needed to keep the bug body under control by letting it know that he'd kill it where nobody would ever find it, if it gave him any shit while he was trying to make his report. Kill it where nobody'd ever find it to eat it. Kill it where everything it knew would die with it. Forever.

It didn't want to die alone.

He sympathized with it, but not enough to be afraid to crawl around on the ground. The bug body was having its equivalent of the heebie-jeebies, down on all sixes in the bush: it had a hereditary fear of spiders, snakes, and most furred mammals.

Even in its suit, it was beginning to drool a brown fluid from its anus: when it was this tired, it couldn't control its bowels if it was afraid.

You had to ignore the stuff you couldn't control.

You just kept your mission in your mind. You just kept doing the job.

Eventually, you were supposed to win that way.

Only sometimes, you didn't.

Where was the damned communicator, anyhow?

When he found it, he was nearly weak with relief.

It had an inboard autotranslator, thank God.

He sat there in the grass and burst out the first identifying transmission.

It seemed to take forever to get a response from the *Hawking*.

When he got it, it made him want to cry.

Nobody was buying his story.

"But I'm telling you, you ought to extract me and this bug buggy I got here. I got weapons. I got intel. I got everything you need."

"No way," came the response. "Not if what you say about your infiltration is true."

What had he said? He didn't remember saying anything.

"What do you mean," he chattered in bug speak, and the machine translated.

Had he blanked out? What the hell had he said?

"Confirm," said the voice from his ship, "that you're group leader of the Hundredth Unit, that you're in the planning sessions, that you're able to call strikes and plan incursions and determine force mix."

"Confirmed," he admitted. He hadn't meant to tell them so much. He remembered now what he'd said. But he'd been light-headed when he'd said it, giddy with contact, trying to make them see reason. . . . He'd just been trying to explain why they ought to bring him in. Bring him back aboard ship.

Bring him. . . .

"You just get next to that big female and stay there," the voice told him. "We don't want to rock the boat. Keep up the good work. *Hawking,* out."

All he could hear was static.

He wanted to cry, but these eyes couldn't. He wanted to laugh, but he had no lips.

The alien body was already up off the ground, heading back toward the safety of its jeep.

He was hopping up into it before he realized that he was singing a soft, happy song of parenthood, of home, and hearth, and children.

"Fast-paced...realistic detail and subtle humor. It will be good news if Shatner decides to go on writing."—*Chicago Sun-Times*

__WILLIAM SHATNER__

TEKWAR

Ex-cop Jake Cardigan was framed for dealing the addictive brain stimulant Tek. But now he's been mysteriously released from his prison module and launched back to Los Angeles of 2120. There, a detective agency hires him to find the anti-Tek device carried off by a prominent scientist. But Jake's not the only one crazy enough to risk his life to possess it.

__0-441-80010-6/$4.50

TEKLORDS

Jake Cardigan is back when a synthetic plague is sweeping the city. A top drug-control agent is brutally murdered by a reprogrammed human "zombie," deadlier than an android assassin. For Jake, all roads lead to one fatal circle—the heart of a vast computerized drug ring.

__0-441-80010-6/$4.99

For Visa, MasterCard and American Express orders ($10 minimum) call: 1-800-631-8571

FOR MAIL ORDERS: CHECK BOOK(S). FILL OUT COUPON. SEND TO:

BERKLEY PUBLISHING GROUP
390 Murray Hill Pkwy., Dept. B
East Rutherford, NJ 07073

NAME_____

ADDRESS_____

CITY_____

STATE_____ZIP_____

PLEASE ALLOW 6 WEEKS FOR DELIVERY.
PRICES ARE SUBJECT TO CHANGE WITHOUT NOTICE.

POSTAGE AND HANDLING:
$1.50 for one book, 50¢ for each additional. Do not exceed $4.50.

BOOK TOTAL	$ _____
POSTAGE & HANDLING	$ _____
APPLICABLE SALES TAX (CA, NJ, NY, PA)	$ _____
TOTAL AMOUNT DUE	$ _____

PAYABLE IN US FUNDS.
(No cash orders accepted.)

394

DAVID DRAKE

__NORTHWORLD 0-441-84830-3/$3.95

The consensus ruled twelve hundred worlds—but not Northworld. Three fleets had been dispatched to probe the enigma of Northworld. None returned. Now, Commissioner Nils Hansen must face the challenge of the distant planet. There he will confront a world at war, a world of androids...all unique, all lethal.

__SURFACE ACTION 0-441-36375-X/$4.50

Venus has been transformed into a world of underwater habitats for Earth's survivors. Battles on Venus must be fought on the ocean's exotic surface. Johnnie Gordon trained his entire life for battle, and now his time has come to live a warrior's life on the high seas.

THE FLEET Edited by David Drake and Bill Fawcett

The soldiers of the Human/Alien Alliance come from different worlds and different cultures. But they share a common mission: to reclaim occupied space from the savage Khalian invaders.

__BREAKTHROUGH   0-441-24105-0/$3.95
__COUNTERATTACK   0-441-24104-2/$3.95
__SWORN ALLIES   0-441-24090-9/$3.95

For Visa , MasterCard and American Express orders ($10 minimum) call: 1-800-631-8571

FOR MAIL ORDERS: CHECK BOOK(S). FILL OUT COUPON. SEND TO:	POSTAGE AND HANDLING: $1.50 for one book, 50¢ for each additional. Do not exceed $4.50.
BERKLEY PUBLISHING GROUP 390 Murray Hill Pkwy., Dept. B East Rutherford, NJ 07073	
	BOOK TOTAL $ _____
	POSTAGE & HANDLING $ _____
NAME_____	APPLICABLE SALES TAX $ _____ (CA, NJ, NY, PA)
ADDRESS _____	
CITY_____	TOTAL AMOUNT DUE $ _____
STATE_____ZIP_____	PAYABLE IN US FUNDS.
PLEASE ALLOW 6 WEEKS FOR DELIVERY. PRICES ARE SUBJECT TO CHANGE WITHOUT NOTICE.	(No cash orders accepted.)

317

**From the writer of Marvel Comics'
bestselling *X-Men* series.**

CHRIS
CLAREMONT

The explosive sequel to *FirstFlight*

GROUNDED!

Lt. Nicole Shea was a top space pilot—until a
Wolfpack attack left her badly battered. Air
Force brass say she's not ready to return to
space, so they reassign her to a "safe" post
on Earth. But when someone begins making
attempts on her life, she must travel back into
the stars, where memories and threats linger.
It's the only way Shea can conquer her
fears—and win back her wings.

_____0-441-30416-8/$4.95

For Visa, MasterCard and American Express orders ($10 minimum) call: 1-800-631-8571

FOR MAIL ORDERS: CHECK BOOK(S). FILL
OUT COUPON. SEND TO:

BERKLEY PUBLISHING GROUP
390 Murray Hill Pkwy., Dept. B
East Rutherford, NJ 07073

NAME_____

ADDRESS_____

CITY_____

STATE_____ZIP_____

PLEASE ALLOW 6 WEEKS FOR DELIVERY.
PRICES ARE SUBJECT TO CHANGE WITHOUT NOTICE.

POSTAGE AND HANDLING:
$1.50 for one book, 50¢ for each ad-
ditional. Do not exceed $4.50.

BOOK TOTAL $ _____

POSTAGE & HANDLING $ _____

APPLICABLE SALES TAX $ _____
(CA, NJ, NY, PA)

TOTAL AMOUNT DUE $ _____

PAYABLE IN US FUNDS.
(No cash orders accepted.)

383

CYBERPUNK

__Islands in the Net__ Bruce Sterling 0-441-37423-9/$4.50
Laura Webster is operating successfully in an age
where information is power--until she's plunged into a
netherworld of black-market pirates, new-age
mercenaries, high-tech voodoo...and murder.

__Neuromancer__ William Gibson 0-441-56959-5/$4.99
The novel of the year! Case was the best interface
cowboy who ever ran in Earth's computer matrix. Then
he double-crossed the wrong people...

__Mirrorshades__ Bruce Sterling, editor
0-441-53382-5/$4.99
The definitive cyberpunk short fiction collection,
including stories by William Gibson, Greg Bear, Pat
Cadigan, Rudy Rucker, Lewis Shiner, and more.

__Blood Music__ Greg Bear 0-441-06797-2/$4.50
Vergil Ulam had an idea to stop human entropy—
"intelligent" cells—but they had a few ideas of their
own.

__Count Zero__ William Gibson 0-441-11773-2/$4.50
Enter a world where daring keyboard cowboys break
into systems brain-first for mega-heists and brilliant
aristocrats need an army of high-tech mercs to make
a career move.

For Visa, MasterCard and American Express orders ($10 minimum) call: 1-800-631-8571

FOR MAIL ORDERS: CHECK BOOK(S). FILL
OUT COUPON. SEND TO:

BERKLEY PUBLISHING GROUP
390 Murray Hill Pkwy., Dept. B
East Rutherford, NJ 07073

NAME_____

ADDRESS _____

CITY_____

STATE_____ZIP_____

PLEASE ALLOW 6 WEEKS FOR DELIVERY.
PRICES ARE SUBJECT TO CHANGE WITHOUT NOTICE.

POSTAGE AND HANDLING:
$1.50 for one book, 50¢ for each ad-
ditional. Do not exceed $4.50.

BOOK TOTAL $ _____

POSTAGE & HANDLING $ _____

APPLICABLE SALES TAX $ _____
(CA, NJ, NY, PA)

TOTAL AMOUNT DUE $ _____

PAYABLE IN US FUNDS.
(No cash orders accepted.)

264